THE GATE OF DAWN

THE GATE OF DAWN

BY

MARINA J. NEARY

www.penmorepress.com

The Gate of Dawn by Marina J. Neary
Copyright © 2016 Marina J. Neary

ISBN-13: 978-1-942756-74-3(Paperback)
ISBN :-978-1-942756-75-0 (e-book)

BISAC Subject Headings:

FIC052000FICTION / Satire
HIS032000HISTORY / Europe / Russia & the Former Soviet Union
FIC014000   FICTION / Historical

James Thomas, photographer and studio provider,
Logan Devlin as the model,
Walt Neary as the "hand" model.
Cover by Christine Horner

Address all correspondence to:

Penmore Press LLC
920 N Javelina Pl
Tucson AZ 85748

Reviews

In *The Gate of Dawn*, Neary hits the trifecta of great historical fiction: a descriptive mastery of time and place; late 19th Century Vilnius, Lithuania, with all its eastern European trans-class intrigue; plus authentic, memorable personages, in particular two strong women, and an engrossing multi-plotted narrative. It's a journey to the past well worth taking.
 —Lou Aguilar, author of *Jake the Mayor*

Neary brings her passion for history and her storyteller's gift to this dark and richly detailed novel set in Lithuania under imperial Russian rule. Exhaustively researched, the story is a blend of Baltic folklore and unflinching historical realism. It makes for a compelling—and sometimes unsettling—read.
 —Eileen Kernaghan, author of *Sophie, in Shadow*

Neary's latest novel *The Gate of Dawn* is nothing less than a breathtaking saga of real people caught in one of the greatest popular upheavals in world history. The author's knowledge of Northern European history and lore is extensive, yet shared effortlessly with western readers.
 —Douglas Hearle, author of *Outsource*

In *The Gate of Dawn* Neary has given us what is perhaps her finest work of fiction to date. The plot is complex, with well-developed characters whose connections are gradually revealed to the reader, culminating in a satisfying conclusion that is a *tour de force* tying all of the narrative threads together.
 The setting—a time in history that showcases Lithuanian culture and its clashes with Russia and Germany in the 1880s—is both unique and rich in detail presented so naturally that the reader learns much without feeling as if the details are there merely for the sake of context. And as

part of this distinctive setting, the novel's exploration of the relationship between Jews and Gentiles in Vilnius reifies a vanished world that will be of particular interest to scholars of the history of Jewish Lithuania.

Of special note, *The Gate of Dawn* is informed throughout by Neary's characteristic sly and wry sense of ironic humor, which lightens the tone of what might otherwise be perceived as a dark and pessimistic vision of history and human nature.

—Shifra Hochberg, author of *The Lost Catacomb*

Once again Neary has demonstrated her mastery of historical fiction. She brings late nineteenth century Vilnius, Lithuania to life, peoples it with engaging characters, and weaves a complex plot in which cultural and religious traditions compete with human emotions. As the descendant of Eastern European Jews, I felt that Neary's outstanding book introduced me to my ancestors and helped me to appreciate the world in which they lived.

—Kenneth Weene, author of *Widow's Walk*
co-host of *It Matters Radio*

Neary once again throws us into her fast moving universe. This time she describes the Baltic town of Vilnius in the 1880s, a world forgotten and unknown to most of us. Renate, a 16 year old strong willed girl with artistic talents, is made to marry too early when her father dies. Being a woman, she is not trusted to take care of her own fortune and future. But Renate is a resourceful girl and finds her own way of protesting against this cruel treatment. She seeks out her Jewish friend Benjamin and continues her relationship with him behind the back of her new husband. With her colorful language Neary catches our attention and describes the interesting mixture of different nationalities and religious background, and above all she gives us insight into the way the world worked at this time in Eastern Europe. A book to be recommended.

—Gry Finsnes, author of *Vanished in Berlin*

A Gothic tale so unabashedly spicy, you may forget it takes place over a century ago. *The Gate of Dawn* dishes up the palpably foreign atmosphere of a Baltic capital, with pagan peasant traditions, nationalist and ethnic strife, and eternal themes of love and lust. The many storylines linking eccentric characters bring to mind *Great Expectations*, and with story-telling worthy of Dickens, you won't want to put it down.
—M.J. Daspit, author of *Lucy Lied*

The Gate of Dawn is historically educational and accurate for the time period it is set in. Renate, one of the main characters is a hard, stone-hearted girl who has the personality of a middle-aged woman. Her arranged marriage to a man twice her age sets the scene and you are hooked from then on. All of the characters have a part of play and each of them have their own circumstances to deal with. Marriage, debauchery, and murder.
—Carol Sharma, author of *Julie & Kishore*

In this gripping tale of passion and betrayal, Neary's unflinching picture of clashing cultures and deadly rivalries will hook you from the start. Driven by the author's unmistakable voice and biting wit, *The Gate of Dawn* delivers an emotionally charged journey packed with drama and intrigue that will leave you breathless and begging for more.
—Ginger Myrick, author of *The Welsh Healer*

The Gates of Dawn is a story of epic portions, epic characters, and epic theme, set in Poland during a dark period in history. Neary plays conflicting relationships to the hilt as outside forces apply undo pressure to her characters. A great read all the way through.
—Lynda Lippman-Lockhart, author of *The Laundry Room*

Dedication:

To my Polish birth father and my German-Hungarian stepfather. Gentlemen, thank you for your ultra-masculine camaraderie. Truly, there is nothing more pernicious for a female than being treated like a princess by her father figures. Thanks to your wholesome Central European sausage-and-beer influences, I have grown up to be the "man" I am now.

CHAPTER 1

An Iron Fist Wrapped in Cotton

Vilnius, North-West province
of the Russian Empire—June, 1884

Hermann Lichtner, a former textile oligarch, knew his lungs were failing—his mind was lucid enough to register the direness of his condition. The best physician in Vilnius declared that a patient with such severe burns would not last more than two days. Dehydration and sepsis would set in. Not that Hermann was pursuing survival at that point. He only wanted to use the remaining time efficiently, for there were a few last-minute business transactions to be completed. Knowing that he would not have any peace at the elite hospital in the center city, where he would be harassed by gendarmes and reporters, he requested a transfer to a small infirmary by the train tracks that mainly serviced railroad workers.

Pauline, a mousy orderly assigned to him upon admission, had built a protective tent around his cot using three wooden rods and a large sheet to keep the flies out—the room was not particularly clean or well-ventilated. Judging from the tremor in the girl's hands and the way she kept averting her eyes, she was still green and unaccustomed to such gruesome sights. Pauline had seen crushed bones and open wounds, but not the expanse of foul-smelling blisters. Gasping and retching were not allowed in her trade. If she was ever to secure a higher position in an upscale medical establishment, she would have to learn to freeze both her face and her stomach. Every time her leg brushed the side of the cot, causing it to wobble, she would wince and mumble apologies in Polish. The German patient understood her language and responded with groans of reassurance. In her brief tenure she had already learned that most patients were not quite as tolerant of her blunders—gratitude was not dispensed liberally at that infirmary.

Pauline repeatedly offered Herr Lichtner an additional dose of morphine, but he kept refusing, as he needed to stay alert for the upcoming meeting with his lawyer. The pain itself was surprisingly bearable. Hermann had once heard from a medical student that deep burns did not hurt due to the extensive nerve damage. The period of searing agony was brief, like a wave that receded as quickly as it engulfed him. The lower part of Hermann's body had already died. One of the fallen beams from the ceiling had crashed his spine, severing all sensation from the waist down, though he still felt some sticky tingling around his trunk. He had no desire to lift the blanket and look at his scorched limbs. He had even less desire to prosecute his murderers, though he had a fairly good idea who they were. The fire that had destroyed his textile factory was no accident, but rather a collaborative effort of expert arsonists.

***

Hermann Lichtner had arrived in Vilnius twenty years earlier, in the winter of 1864, at the height of the January Uprising. He and his eighteen-year old wife Katherine drove their buggy through the Gate of Dawn, the only city gate of the original nine that had not been destroyed by the steadfastly encroaching Russian imperial forces. After seven decades of the Czarist regime, the Gate of Dawn served as a symbolic monument of the dismantled Polish-Lithuanian Commonwealth. The specter of the Baltic metropolis in turmoil stole the young man's breath. The blood of Polish insurgents glazed the cobblestone sidewalks. Hostilities, public executions and deportations to Siberia were in full swing.

"I feel like we're inside a Bruegel painting," Hermann murmured as the wheel of his buggy ploughed through a puddle of bloodied rainwater.

Katherine squeezed his elbow with an air of menace. "You better not be thinking of turning back."

No, Hermann was not thinking of turning back, not after having jumped through hoops to obtain a commercial permit enabling him to set up a business in what was now Russian territory. He knew next to nothing about the conflict unfolding before his eyes. Katherine, who was better versed in interethnic politics, explained to him that after losing the Crimean War, Mother Russia was trying to tighten her grip on her Baltic territories. The insurrection had started with a few Polish and Lithuanian nobles refusing to serve in the Russian army. The Lichtners were riding straight into the heart of the storm. They were entering the city not as insurgents, law-enforcers or even peace-makers, but as merchants, waving their business permit as a white flag. Anyone can appreciate a piece of high quality fabric, Balts, Germans, Russians, Poles and Jews alike. Even the poorest homes needed curtains, tablecloths and bed covers.

Hermann surveyed the slimy sidewalks with an entrepreneur's eye. As he inhaled the frigid air tainted with the smell of gun powder, his breast swelled with healthy greed. Through the gun volleys, he could hear the jingling of coins. With serfdom officially abolished, peasants were moving to the city in search of work, and he would have his pick of the most skilled.

The Lichtners' first purchase was an abandoned warehouse by the rail tracks, which they ended up gutting and filling with top notch equipment imported from their native Brandenburg. Hermann had completed an apprenticeship in textile processing and handled the technical aspect of the enterprise, while Katherine handled the finances and legalities. She also designed exquisite prints. Some of the quilts she had patterned were luxurious enough for the Czar's bed.

Within the next few years the Lichtners had mastered Polish, Russian and even rudimentary Yiddish. The only language they never bothered to learn was Lithuanian, which was dying out anyway thanks to the press ban imposed by the Russian government. From a purely esthetic point of view, the Baltic tongue was not without a certain sing-song charm. Every sentence sounded like some pagan incantation. While suitable for reciting fairy-tales, Lithuanian was not for conducting business.

Over time, Hermann had grown to admire the agents of Czar Alexander II, and they returned the sentiment. He was welcomed in the homes of most prominent imperial officials. His linens graced their drawing parlors. Among his early sponsors was Konstantin von Kaufmann, the Governor General of Vilnius, whose family hailed from Austria but had been in the service of the Czars for over a century.

The last step Hermann would not take to finalize his alliance with Russia was to convert to Orthodoxy, even though Von Kaufmann had proposed it as a clever political move. To leave the comfort of lukewarm Lutheranism would mean alienating the German community where he still had valued business partners. With all his respect for the Czar and the Empire and the two-headed eagle, he still considered himself German, a sentiment he hoped to pass on to his offspring.

Then early in 1880 Katherine died, leaving behind a row of hanging jaws and raised eyebrows. Such a rude and unceremonious exit! She could not have chosen a less opportune moment, two weeks before an imperial trade show in Riga. One evening, while entertaining the governor's family, she suddenly felt faint and feverish. Before retreating into her bedroom, she gave the servants copious instructions to ensure that the apricot-stuffed duck would be served on the right platter. *I'll only be a minute.* Those were Katherine's last words. The sturdy Aryan matriarch, who had never as much as complained of a sniffle in her life, she was carried out in a coffin made of highest quality wood, feet first. Complications from acute influenza, Dr. Klein concluded in the post mortem statement. The fumes from the fabric dyes had corroded the lining of her lungs, making them more vulnerable to disease. Her reproductive organs probably did not look much better. No wonder Katherine had been able to bear only one child, a taciturn girl named Renate who never played with dolls or sought the company of other children.

Hermann had never fully accepted the finality of Katherine's departure, discarding the bottle of opium-based sedative the physician had discretely slipped into his coat pocket after the service. That concoction would only make him drowsy, whereas he needed to stay awake. The ill-fated dinner party was just an absurd dream. Eventually Hermann convinced himself that Katherine was away on a business trip. To nourish the fantasy, he would send her letters and telegrams.

"What would you like Mutti to bring you from St. Petersburg?" he asked his daughter periodically. "I'm about to seal the envelope. Your birthday is coming up."

"A microscope, just like the one we saw in Warsaw."

Unlike Hermann, the girl was not in denial but thought it her duty to play along, if only to keep her father from becoming ineffectual. Vati had a factory to run. Taking a sabbatical would mean inevitable loss of revenue and more room for his competitors to wedge in. Besides, Renate had assets to protect. If Hermann accepted Katherine's death, he would eventually remarry. The girl had read enough fairy-tales by the Grimm brothers to know what an avaricious stepmother was a distinct possibility, as well as half-siblings to tap into the inheritance. *Danke schön!* What if Vati's new wife gave him a son? Renate could not allow for that to happen. She liked being the only heiress, even if it meant perpetuating her father's delusion.

During the sporadic moments of lucidity Hermann realized his limitations as a parent. He could not give Renate the multidisciplinary upbringing befitting a lady from the merchant class. When the girl turned thirteen, he sent her to boarding school run by Frau Elsa Jung, a noted watercolorist whose paintings graced private galleries and the homes of German families in Vilnius.

Renate did not relish the idea of being immersed into the world of other adolescent German girls, whose company she had been fortunate to evade for the first thirteen years of her life. She would just have to tolerate their high-pitched shrieks and secretive whispers as she would any other unpleasant stimulus, like being tickled or forced to chew on garlic during the winter months to ward off infections. Vati in his wisdom would not subject her to this ordeal without seeing some long-term benefit. The experience would strengthen her willpower as well as sharpen her sense of humor. Ah, the plight of being a magnate's only child! Renate knew she was lacking in the diplomacy department, a little too quick to use her index finger against stupidity, incompetence and deceit. Vati needed a suave politician for a partner, not a barking foreman in a petticoat. So she packed her trunk and moved into the dormitory on Main Street. With a flippant "Guten Tag" that sounded more like "bugger off", she zipped past her gaping roommates to claim the solitary bed in the corner.

"That Lichtner girl has a metal rod in her neck," her school mates would whisper. "She always looks ahead, never over her shoulder."

Renate would spend her weekends with her father, shadowing him through the noisy workrooms where, with the exception of Sunday mornings, activity never ceased. It pleased Hermann to see that his daughter had not adopted any of her peers' feline antics. She possessed the rudiments of an astute businesswoman who would rule with an iron fist wrapped in cotton. Hermann would not hesitate to compare her to Catherine the Great, another icon of enlightened Teutonic despotism. Germans were put on this earth to organize, fortify, reform and redeem. One day the textile empire would belong to Renate. In another ten years he could contemplate stepping down and buying that idyllic coastal cottage in Palanga.

But a leisurely retirement was not in the cards for Hermann.

Rotting away in his infirmary tent, he strained his memory to replay the final moments of his reign. He was sitting in his office on the third floor, pulling together some receipts to be reviewed by his accountant the next morning.

It was fairly late, about nine o'clock in the evening, maybe ten, and all workers had left for the day. They had no reason to linger past the closing whistle—or so he thought. It was not the smell of smoke or the heat that caught his attention but a shriek coming from the bleaching room at the other end of the hallway. *Vati, hilf mir!* The voice belonged to Frieda, a sixteen-year old weaving apprentice and notorious flirt. Hermann knew she was carrying on with one of the draw boys, but looked the other way. The girl was a studious worker and had enough decency not to flaunt her affair. She would dutifully wait until the main gate was closed and the lights were off to offer her plump pink breasts to her equally youthful *Liebling* on a heap of greasy wool. Who was he, Hermann Lichtner, to interfere with a torrid summer fling? He believed that carnal gratification increased productivity. The bleaching room was a convenient rendezvous spot. It also was a fire trap with all the flammable chemicals stored on the shelves against the wall. The only window was about ten feet from the ground and covered with metal bars. Perhaps, the lovers in the throes of passion knocked down a kerosene lamp. Hermann could only hear Frieda's voice, which sounded very much like Renate's.

He grabbed the key chain from the wall, rushed down the hallway and saw black smoke pouring from under the door of the bleaching room. The door itself was locked from the outside. The foreman must have locked it on his way out, trapping the lovers inside. It took Hermann about ten seconds to find the right key. In those ten seconds the shrieking had turned to faint whimpering and finally faded into silence.

The moment he entered the room, he doubled over with vertigo and nausea. "Frieda!" he called out hoarsely, straining his tearing eyes to detect the girl's form through the wall of smoke.

For an instant he thought he saw some movement in the corner, an outline of a bare leg, a sharp bend of an elbow. He darted forward and felt a blow to the back of his head, an unmistakably deliberate, thoroughly calculated blow that could only be administered by a male hand. He heard voices and pitter-patter of feet against the floor. The door behind him slammed. It was done. The rescuer had traded places with the victims.

The technical conundrum would not let Hermann rest. The building was regularly inspected and fortified against ignitions. The fire must have been instigated by one of the insiders, someone who was familiar with every square meter of the factory and knew how to disable the intricate safety mechanisms that had been put in place. Having invested all his trust in the superior German engineering, Hermann had discounted the element of human malice. After such a steady and smooth climb upward, he was due for a fall. He had prospered long enough. Thankfully, his injuries were deadly. He would not have to live out his remaining days as a disfigured cripple.

CHAPTER 2

Patriarchy Restored

The attorney arrived after dusk, a lanky, fidgety young man with a sharp nose and a glossy mustache the color of hazelnut cream. His name was Sebastian Messer. Two years earlier he had graduated from St. Petersburg Imperial University. Unable to secure employment in Russia's northern capital—the city was eager to educate outsiders but not necessarily employ them—he had moved back to his native Vilnius to service the German community. Hermann Lichtner was one of his most prominent clients, and Sebastian was visibly distressed by the idea of losing him.

Bending under the pressure to remain stoic and professional under such grisly circumstance, the young lawyer took a seat on a bench outside the fabric tent, instinctively trying to put sufficient distance between himself and the dying client. One of Sebastian's compulsive habits dating back to his days as a schoolboy was tattering paper to soothe his nerves. All his notebooks had torn edges. His teachers would smack the otherwise exemplary student on the knuckles. Sitting two meters away from his scorched client, Sebastian felt the old demons stir inside him. As he opened his folder with legal forms, the sight of smooth ivory paper made his heart beat a little faster. Those clean sheets were calling his name, begging to be rolled, torn and chewed.

"I'm ready when you are, Herr Lichtner."

Without further ado, the dying German started dictating the terms of his will.

"I, Hermann Franz Lichtner of Brandenburg, the sole proprietor of the Lichtner Textiles, do hereby bequeath all my liquid assets to my past business associate, Thaddeus Dombrowski of the Raven's Bog, who had on several occasions supplied raw flax for my business. This transaction is contingent upon Master Dombrowski's marriage to my daughter, Renate."

The lawyer cleared his throat.

"What's wrong?" Hermann asked. "Is the smell bothering you? Feel free to open the window."

"I just wanted to make sure I heard you correctly. Did you just name Thaddeus Dombrowski your beneficiary?"

"That's right. You should have my old contract with him on file somewhere."

"But you haven't made any purchases from him in two years. You said you were not going to use him anymore, because his flax was of poor quality."

"Most terrible quality! Moist and rotting. The man doesn't know first thing about cultivating and harvesting flax. Half of his merchandise was unusable."

Sebastian shuffled the papers for the umpteenth time. "And you want this man to be your beneficiary?"

"I'm not choosing him based on his business acumen but rather on his character."

"What do you know about his character?"

"I know enough. When I look in his eyes, I see something I don't see when I look in the mirror. He's a better human being who hasn't lost his soul yet."

Mein Gott... Sebastian's wisdom teeth started throbbing. A hardened businessman lapsing into that mystical bosh? Herr Lichtner's brain must have been damaged by the smoke.

"It's not my custom to argue with my clients or question their judgment," the lawyer endeavored, "but perhaps you should wait for the morphine to wear off to finalize your will."

"I'm not delusional or delirious. My head is perfectly clear."

"I just think that these metaphysical musings should be shared with a minister, not a lawyer."

"Herr Messer, try to see the situation through my eyes. I cannot leave my fifteen-year old daughter with money on her hands, even if I restrict her access to it until she reaches adulthood. Imagine the disaster. An orphan girl with a hefty fortune will become a magnet for scoundrels. I'd hate to see her inheritance squandered by some libertine."

"In other words, you're adding your daughter as a bonus in a business transaction?" Disgust made Sebastian's voice thin and shallow, like a pan flute. "So much for your progressive banter on the equality of sexes...."

"Renate will grow to like her new husband. I'm certain of that."

"He's a peasant, that Dombrowski fellow!"

"A clean and well-mannered one."

"Does he have any education? Have you seen his diploma?"

"Not everyone can be a graduate of St. Petersburg Imperial University. I'm sure Dombrowski had tutors growing up. We used Russian to discuss business matters, but Polish is his native language. He also understands Lithuanian. Most of his servants are Balts. He's deeply

Catholic. Not a bad-looking fellow, neither fat nor bald, and only thirty years old."

"Which would only make him... twice Renate's age? Splendid!"

"And in a few years the gap won't be noticeable. Renate is an old soul. I simply cannot envision her with a pimply youth who gropes and slobbers. There're many benefits to marrying a man with some... prior experience. I was a much better husband and lover at thirty than I was at twenty. Poor Katherine had suffered through my juvenile clumsiness. I didn't know any better. It took me a while to learn the intricacies of the female psyche—and the female body."

"Whatever you say, Herr Lichtner. If you think you're doing your daughter a huge service by hurling her into bed with Dombrowski, who am I to disagree? Does that noble peasant of yours come with a brood?"

"That's the best part. Thaddeus has no progeny by his first wife Jolanta, who just died last year. Their children kept dying. The miserable woman looked exsanguinated when I saw her back in '82. She kept blotting her eyes and mumbling 'Maybe next time?' The last stillbirth finished her off."

"How convenient for Renate that he's unencumbered. No brats biting her ankles. No snotty noses to wipe. I imagine that hot-blooded Pole won't want to dillydally. He'll put Renate's womb to work. You still think it's such a brilliant idea?"

"The best idea I've had in years. And it just occurred to me on my deathbed. Renate and Thaddeus will make an idyllic couple. I'm sponsoring their happiness out of my pocket. I leave it up to you to see that my directives are carried out."

"Of course." Sebastian pinched himself. The conversation

had gotten out of hand. He should not have derailed what was meant to be a standard legal transaction. "It's not my place to advise you how to dispose of your daughter. Please forgive my crude violation of the contractual boundaries between us. In my two years of practice I've never witnessed anything of the sort. Forgive me."

Hermann stirred behind the curtain. "No need to apologize for your candor, Herr Messer. In our circles one doesn't often stumble across a genuine emotion. You're so fervent and opinionated, in spite of your upbringing. You throw a morsel of your heart into everything you do."

"It's grossly inappropriate."

"And endearing all the same. Alas, those qualities will fade away as you grow older. They're of no use to a lawyer. In time, you'll become jaded and methodical. You have your triumphs ahead of you, my boy."

My boy... Sebastian pulled out a handkerchief and blew his nose to mask a sob. Law school had not prepared him for that. He had tried so hard to keep his composure, and Herr Lichtner's speech pushed him closer to the precipice. Would another client ever refer to him as that? *My boy...*

"Back to business," Sebastian said, having finally cleared his nasal passages. "I assume I'll be the one breaking the news to your daughter?"

"I can think of no one more suitable for the task. Rest assured, Herr Messer, your efforts won't go unrewarded. I've set aside a severance for you. I don't want my death to impact your finances too drastically. I know I can count on your diplomacy when you speak to Renate."

"I believe she's out of town," Sebastian said. "The schoolmistress took the entire group to Alytus to paint cows. It's a yearly tradition. They aren't coming back until tomorrow night. My sister mentioned it in passing."

A whistling sigh escaped Hermann's chest. "So I won't see my daughter one last time."

"I can dispatch someone to Alytus to bring her here. I can even go myself."

"Don't bother. Perhaps, it's for the best that she's not here. Renate wouldn't get anything out of our meeting except for lingering nightmares. Just wait until she gets back from Alytus. There's absolutely no need to ruin her last excursion." Hermann called for the orderly. "Pauline! I'm ready for my dose of morphine! Make it a hefty one. Don't skimp, my girl."

The girl reappeared instantly, brushing past the handsome lawyer as if he was another piece of furniture. The hem of her skirt skimmed the tips of Sebastian's shoes. He caught a whiff of chlorine and musk. Underneath the ugly white cap her hair was curled and secured with sparkling pins. She brought in a syringe filled with murky concoction.

"Are you sure you don't want me to fetch a minister?" Sebastian asked.

"It's all right. I already met with one a few years ago, when Katherine died. I got a lifetime supply of ecclesiastic dogma. You're free to go, Herr Messer."

Sebastian did not need to be told twice. Retching into his sleeve, he bolted out of the infirmary, into the summer storm. Perhaps the tepid rain water would wash the rancid stench off his skin?

Left alone with the orderly, Hermann gestured for her to lean closer to him.

"Save the fabric," he whispered, his eyes fixed on the vault of the tent. "Don't let it go to waste. It came from my factory. See the stamp in the corner? Lichtner Textiles. It'll be a while before you see anything of comparable quality."

CHAPTER 3

Bloom Like a Rose!

Alytus—Frau Jung's summer home

Elsa Jung knew something strange was going on between Justine Koch and Marie Ostermann. The two friends had not said much to each other on the way to Frau Jung's summer cottage in Alytus. They had traveled in separate carriages and lodged in separate rooms. For the entire week they had eaten at the opposite ends of the table, avoided going to the washroom at the same time. On the morning of the departure, while their schoolmates were picking strawberries in the garden, Marie and Justine had an explosive quarrel, but when it was time to start packing, the two were found sleeping in the same bed, limbs and hair intertwined, their cheeks wet with saliva and tears.

Elsa Jung was enraptured by the resolution of their conflict. She had always encouraged this degree of closeness between the girls in her care. Her heart sang whenever she spotted her students sharing clothes, brushing each other's hair, weaving field flowers into each other's plaits, blotting their faces with the same towel or biting from the same apple. The more they enjoyed each other's company, the less likely they would be to seek out the opposite sex. By God, the world did not need any more debutantes or breeding cows. It needed more pretentious artists. While the rest of the female population was being groomed for domesticity, Elsa Jung was launching a counter movement—to drive her girls as far from the kitchens and nurseries as possible, preferably into the concert halls and art galleries. She strove to stomp out useless modesty while nurturing flippancy, impulsivity and egotism. Unsurprisingly, her favorite literary character was Miss Havisham.

Unlike her beloved Victorian heroine, Elsa was not a jilted bride but a two-time widow, presently married to an officer stationed in Bavaria. Having buried two husbands, she kept the third one at arm's length, refusing to follow Lieutenant Jung from one garrison to another, where her social circle would be limited to that of other military wives. And yet their childless marriage was strangely harmonious. They made it a point to meet at least once a year, on Christmas or Easter. Lieutenant Jung had his cadets in Munich, and his wife had her students in Vilnius. He taught his boys self-sacrifice and loyalty to their recently unified country, while she taught her girls self-indulgence and loyalty to their muse.

Elsa had one unquestionable advantage over Miss Havisham. Instead of just one ward, she kept more than twenty. The girls' families had no suspicion. She was diplomatic enough not to toot her agenda on every street corner or bite the hand that signed the tuition check. As far as the parents knew, Elsa Jung was helping their daughters preserve their German heritage in an increasingly Russified city. Kunstakademie von Jung was a unique establishment, officially it was open to girls of all nationalities, with the understanding that the instruction would be given in

German.

The school had started as a small studio above a flower shop on Castle Street and three years later had relocated to a two-level house in the merchant district. The seventeenth century building contained elements of gothic and renaissance styles. The ground floor contained the guest parlor, the drawing studio and the music hall. The lid on the grand piano was always open, so the girls could approach the instrument at any time of the day. The top floor was converted into the dormitory. The long balcony was equipped with a telescope.

Kunstakademie had at its disposal two Russian style line carriages with parallel benches and taut awnings that were used for long-distance excursions out of town. Every summer Frau Jung would take the girls on a retreat to her cottage outside Alytus. One of the recurring exercises was to paint the same landscape at different times of the day, capturing the shifts in lighting and the texture of the fog. Elsa felt that the bucolic setting would be conducive to forging bonds of artistic solidarity among her students. Her noble intentions invariably backfired. The quaint wooden cottage filled with girls at various stages of pubescent maturity would turn into a powder keg. If life at the boarding school obliged them to some rudimentary civility, the moment they left the city, the masks would peel off, revealing sardonic grimaces. Claws would start tearing through the lace gloves. Fresh country air made them vicious. In the balmy summer twilight religious wars would erupt.

Those girls who were Catholic belonged to St. Casimir's, the first Baroque church in Vilnius, built by the Jesuits in the early 1600s and distinguished by its majestic Roman-style dome. Those who were Protestants went to the Evangelical Lutheran Church famous for its magnificent organ concerts.

The one Orthodox girl, named Anastasia Gertz, had a Russian mother and an Austrian father. She attended the new St. Nicholas' that was rebuilt in the Neo-Byzantine style after the January Rising on the initiative of the general-governor Muravyov-Vilensky. The church served as another reminder of Russian domination in the city.

Frau Jung had vetoed all discussions on whose lineage was nobler, whose race was purer and whose faith was holier. The girls knew to avoid those subjects in the presence of their schoolmistress. Not all were equally fond of the czarist regime and the russification endeavors. Marie Ostermann, whose father took interest in eugenics and the writings of Francis Galton, insisted that Russians were mixed with Mongols and therefore not true Europeans, and that their religious practices were rooted in paganism as opposed to the true Byzantine Rite.

"We're living in a country ruled by Asiatic half-breeds," she whispered into Justine Koch's ear on the way to Alytus. "After three centuries under Mongols, Russians can hardly call themselves pure Europeans."

"Maybe that's what makes Russians so powerful, that drop of Genghis Khan's blood," Justine replied. "Maybe that's why Anastasia plays three musical instruments and can paint with her eyes closed. Russo-Germans are the new master race."

"This is heresy!"

"No more than that pseudo-Darwinian bosh your father reads."

"Well, if you are so enchanted by that Mongoloid mutt Anastasia, maybe you should sleep in her bed."

"Maybe I will."

"I hear she has a twin brother. You should marry him and have a string of babies with slanted eyes and flat noses."

The rest of the girls surmised that the recent rift between Marie and Justine had something to do with that heated exchange on the way to cottage. By the end of their stay in Alytus they appeared to have reconciled, judging from the way they caressed each other's fingers.

To make their ride back to Vilnius a little less dull, the girls needed to find another target. Who would it be this time? Renate Lichtner looked like a good candidate. That fifteen-year old blonde with perpetually pursed-up lips had not been pushed into the arena in a while.

Renate's schoolmates did not know what to make of her. She had the biggest fortune of them all, yet said fortune was relatively new. She could not boast aristocratic roots. Her parents were first-generation textile entrepreneurs who had managed to build a miniature empire. Renate had not grown up with an army of wet nurses, nannies, governesses and tutors. The Lichtners had raised their only daughter underfoot, on the factory floor. Since birth the girl had been surrounded by the noise of machines and the smell of dyes. The chemicals had hardened her skin and cooled her blood. She could afford latest fashions, yet she opted for plain frocks. Her hair, the same color and texture as the straw of her hat, was always coiled at the nape of her neck. A pair of gold earrings with demure amethysts constituted her only accessory. In short, Renate did not commit any sins typical for new money, thus denying her schoolmates what they craved most—a solid reason to ridicule her. Understandably, the girls could not forgive her that. Every clique needs a token laughing stock, and she would not provide a vital component to the formula. She'd elevated herself above the gossip, the intrigue, the manipulation—all the things that shape the character of a mature woman. Her extravagantly modern Vati treated her as he would a son. She did not need to rehearse female behavior. In a few years she would be reaping all the benefits reserved for men.

On the night of the departure, as Renate was putting away her combs and hairpins, Justine Koch brushed up against her.

"Aurelia Messer is telling me you're in love with a Jew."

"Aurelia dabbles in fiction, since her painting technique leaves much to be desired."

"Fiction, you say?" Justine folded her arms, letting Renate know that the interrogation was far from over. "Will you look me in the eye and tell me there's not a grain of truth to the allegation? She saw you two kissing on the corner of the Cathedral Square. What do you have to say in your defense?"

Renate proceeded to coil her braid. "I didn't realize I was on trial."

"Of course, you aren't. I think it's marvelous that you're in love with a Jew. Such a delectable scandal! Just wait until Frau Jung finds out."

Justine's juvenile giddiness mystified Renate. What was all the agitation about? Yes, she was fond of Benjamin, though calling it love would be an exaggeration. And yes, he happened to be a Jew, though his features did not exactly scream of his heritage. He had a straight nose, grey eyes and wispy light-brown hair to his shoulders. His face was not the first thing Renate noticed anyway. It was his hands and the grossly improper way they held the brush, much too close to the tip. Not to mention he was applying too much pressure to the paper. No wonder he kept ruining one sheet after another. There were five or six paintings at various stages of completion crumpled under his easel. His paints and his brushes were top quality, but his technique was abysmal. Renate had no idea how much instruction this boy had received, but he needed to be stopped before he ruined any more costly supplies. With an air of apostolic determination, Renate walked up to him and covered his fingers with hers, guiding the brush. Astounded, the young artist hummed and nodded, soaking in the criticism. After the lesson was over, they went for a walk. Benjamin shared that his father owned an upscale clothing atelier on Stikliu Street, and they belonged to a reform synagogue. He made it clear that he was very grateful for Renate's advice and intended to follow up. Before parting for the night, they exchanged a few sloppy, delicious kisses, but that was all. Of course, Aurelia, who had nothing better to do than spy on others, concocted a sensation about an illicit interfaith romance.

"So what's your next move?" Justine persisted. "Are you two going to elope to America? I hear the streets of New York are swarming with Jews. It's a sea of yarmulkes!"

Before giving her response, Renate tinkered with the collar of her dress. "Aurelia should really think twice before telling stories about me. Her brother works for my father. Next time you're gossiping behind the outhouse, remind her of that."

"I don't understand." Feigning stupidity was one of Justine's finest talents.

Renate stuck the last hairpin into her bun. "Since Vati keeps Sebastian employed, I don't think it would be wise of Aurelia to antagonize me of all people."

"Nobody is antagonizing you. Where do you get such ideas? We're all rejoicing for you. Of course, we feel a little hurt that you'd keep such news from us."

"I'm just saying there're many lawyers in the city fighting for clients. Sebastian isn't irreplaceable by any means. One word from me and Vati will drop him. Who'll pay Aurelia's tuition then? Frau Jung won't keep her for free."

Justine squinted, thinking of a venomous retort, but their schoolmistress' shrill cough interrupted the debate.

"Shame on you, ladies!"

Justine curtseyed and left the room giggling into her fist. Gouging such an intense reaction out of Renate was a major victory.

*****

"Fräulein Lichtner, have you forgotten the purpose of this retreat?" the schoolmistress said as soon as she and Renate were left alone. "It was to disengage from our prejudices."

"No, Frau Jung, I haven't forgotten, though it seems that some of the others have. I was minding my business, when Justine barged in."

"I don't care who started the quarrel. When I came in, it was your mouth moving, and the things coming out of it were far from kind."

"You have to speak to people in their own language. Forgive me my bluntness, but some of your students are hopeless. Even if you were to send them to a deserted island, they'd be bickering within minutes, and it wouldn't be over Renoir's latest masterpiece. Eugenics is the burning topic. If allowed, they'd spend their days measuring each other's foreheads and noses. You cannot change the stuff they're made of. You're a teacher, not an alchemist."

Elsa had always encouraged candor in her pupils, but Renate's explosive monologue took her by surprise. The girl had always been known for her equanimity.

"Deep breath, my dear." Elsa hugged her pupil by the shoulders and made her sit down on the wooden bench between two stacks of freshly washed bath towels. "What's gotten into you? You seem agitated."

"I didn't sleep well last night. Too much sunlight. I hate

the month of June. This past week dragged on forever. I'm ready to go back to Vilnius."

"Is there a certain someone you're impatient to see?"

Renate groaned faintly. *Mein Gott...* Did the rumor travel so quickly? Now her teacher was going to taunt her about Benjamin?

"Yes, there's one man I'm impatient to see—Vati! I haven't seen him for almost a month. First he was in Riga for two weeks, and then it was my turn to go out of town. It's the longest we've been apart."

"Which will make your reunion all the more joyous." Elsa was making every effort to sound soothing and cheerful. Renate's anxiety was beginning to infect her. "Think of how proud your father will be when he sees your latest series of drawings. I think this was your most prolific excursion by far. And no, I don't say it to all my students."

"Not to Aurelia Messer, I hope? You should've seen how she brutalized a perfectly good tube of ochre."

After a few moments of silence, Elsa gave her a sad, enigmatic smile. "There's something I wanted to show you."

Renate followed her schoolmistress up the stairwell to what looked like an abandoned artist's workshop. There were easels everywhere draped in cloth, blank canvases stacked against the wall, buckets with dried paint and melted candles.

"This part of the house is off limits for most," Elsa said. "My Julia used to paint here. She could stay in the attic for days, sleeping on a mattress in the corner." Frau Jung's deceased daughter was a forbidden subject, though all sorts of fanciful rumors circulated in regards to the nature of her death, from morphine overdose to suicide. "I want you to have Julia's favorite easel. It must be put to use. Your technique reminds me of hers. I feel like she communicates with me through your paintings."

It was no secret that Elsa, a nominal Lutheran, had been flirting with spiritualism since her daughter's death. She would not go as far as joining an occult society, but she had been studying the practices of the Hermetic Order.

Emboldened by the gift, Renate looked Frau Jung in the eye and finally verbalized the question that would hopefully put an end to all rumors. "What was the cause?"

"Pregnancy toxemia, the same disease that killed Charlotte Brontë. Did you know she's my favorite English author?"

"I thought it was Dickens, the way you quote *Great Expectations*."

"Mr. Dickens mostly bemoaned the plight of the deprived men. He didn't have much sympathy for the middle-class women. I doubt he would've found Julia's fate tragic. She died of natural causes in her soft bed." Elsa ran her hand over the faded patchwork quilt. "I never denied the suicide rumors, for marriage is just that—a slow suicide."

"If it's any consolation, I'm married to Vati's textile empire. You needn't worry about me. I'll die a rich virgin. Your easel is in safe hands."

***

When Renate and Elsa stepped outside into the yard, they witnessed a most peculiar scene between twelve-year old Sophie Goehl and nineteen-year old Inga Franke. The two were engaged in some sort of slapping game, or to be exact, Inga was doing all the slapping, punctuating it with jubilant exclamations. "Bloom like a rose! Be beautiful!"

The slaps must have been light and painless, because Sophie kept giggling, though her cheeks were quite red. Startled by the arrival of their schoolmistress, the girls halted the game.

"What was that I just witnessed?" Elsa asked indignantly.

"We're acting out a peasant ritual," Inga explained. "Our little Sophie has become a woman, so we threw a little initiation party for her, in the best Lithuanian tradition. She was the last of the innocents."

Elsa glared at her youngest student. "Fräulein Goehl, is that true?"

The twelve-year old nodded. "It happened this morning. When the washerwoman came by to strip the sheets, she told us how it's done in her village. Whenever a girl gets her monthly courses, her mother slaps her and recites those words. Since my mother wasn't here, I asked Inga to do the honors, because she's the oldest."

The flippant confession made Elsa shake her head in distress. "Shame on you for mocking the rituals of a subdued nation. Such callousness! I teach my students that there're no inferior cultures. Let's not forget that we Germans are long-term guests in this country. I don't expect you to adopt the customs of the people who'd lived here for centuries prior to our arrival, but at least have the decency not to mock them."

"We weren't mocking the custom!" Inga intervened. "On the contrary, we're honoring it. I've been dying to slap Sophie since we got here, and finally, I had a legitimate excuse to do it. Do you have any idea, how gratifying it was, how cathartic? See, this trip wasn't for naught. We've learned a new custom."

***

The ride back to Vilnius was surprisingly quiet, much to Frau Jung's relief. Having released their venom, the girls settled in for the night underneath wool blankets. There was no whispering, no giggling, only the rhythmical clacking of the carriage wheels.

Renate yawned and propped her head against Aurelia Messer's shoulder. "I heard there's a nursing program in Grodno. They're not particularly picky."

"Were you considering it for yourself?"

"No, silly—for you." Renate kissed the freckled cheek. "I don't see any exhibitions in your future. Frau Jung agrees. We had a candid discussion, right before she gave me her daughter's easel. Did I mention, she lets me call her Elsa in private? At any rate, she doesn't think your technique has progressed much. She won't be including any of your works in the next showcase. And, given that Vati has been thinking of replacing Sebastian with someone more seasoned, this is probably your last semester at Kunstakademie. That nursing school sounds good. Your late mother would be proud if you followed in her footsteps. There's no shame in emptying bed pans. I also hear those white aprons are very fetching. They add delectable curves to a stick figure."

A frail constitution was only one of Aurelia's physical flaws. She also suffered from a mild but vexatious skin condition that caused her nose, chin and earlobes to peel. Sunlight aggravated the symptoms, forcing her to stay inside during the day. Over the years she had conditioned herself not to scratch the affected areas. When necessary, she could exercise impressive self-restraint. As much as she wanted to sink her hands into Renate's flawless bun and yank out tufts of hair, Aurelia managed an acerbic smile.

"Why are you being so nice to me all of a sudden?"

"I'm always nice."

"Not to me. What made you change your tune?"

"Last Christmas I resolved to love my neighbor better." Renate wrapped one of Aurelia's auburn tendrils around her finger. "I'm only showing concern for your future, since you seem so preoccupied with my amorous escapades."

"When you marry your Jewish lover and settle in the ghetto above his father's tailor shop, I'll be sure to visit you."

"And if I see you selling rhubarb jam on the market, I'll be sure to stop by and say hello."

CHAPTER 4

Things They Don't Teach in Law School

Vilnius

By the time the two carriages returned to the school, it was already past eleven. All of the girls were asleep, with the exception of Renate and Aurelia, who had spent the past few hours wringing each other's fingers under the blanket. The game was becoming tiresome for both of them, as they were running out of acrimonies.

When they pulled into the courtyard, Aurelia craned her neck and spied an enclosed buggy drawn by a single horse outside the gate. Through the midnight fog she perceived the lanky silhouette of her brother. He was sitting on the doorsteps underneath a dim lantern. Something in his posture puzzled Aurelia. Sebastian had trained himself to keep his back straight at all times. He would not be caught stooping even in his own armchair by the fireplace. But now he looked like he had fifty kilograms worth of bricks piled onto his shoulders. Last time she had seen him so forlorn was when he had lost his pocket watch.

To get his attention, Aurelia put two fingers in her mouth and produced a shrill whistle that would put any street hooligan to shame. The drowsy girls in the carriage started stirring and rumbling. Sebastian lifted his head and gave her that look that could obliterate an entire Prussian army.

"What's the matter, dear brother?" Aurelia jumped down and threw her arms open. "No kiss for me? You smell like burned bratwurst. Did you spend the night at the new smokehouse?"

Sebastian walked right past her, avoiding eye contact. Aurelia was not his full-blooded sibling. She was a byproduct of his father's deathbed fling with a Lithuanian nurse—a most distasteful frivolity in Sebastian's eyes. The long-widowed Albert Messer had spent his last days at an elite tuberculosis clinic in Klaipeda, in the care of a certain wench with a broad frame and unabashedly Baltic name—Zivile Jocyte. The high-profile patients of predominantly German stock used the more cosmopolitan version of her name—Sybil. While compassion and delicacy were not her distinctive virtues, Zivile possessed enough physical strength to flip an ox, so the director of the clinic had kept her on staff for the hardest and the dirtiest jobs, the kind that nurses of German and Russian blood would disdain. Albert Messer had found himself in her red, chlorine-scented hands. The cocktail of fever reducers and cough suppressants had apparently killed his sense of decency, good taste, esthetic standards and racial pride, though it clearly did not decrease his libido. Sybil had probably added some ancient peasant aphrodisiac to the mixture. To make a long story short, Albert's last breath along with his last drop of his masculine seed went to her.

Before dying, he had made an honest woman of Sybil. Sebastian, who was ten years old at the time, had served as a ring-bearer at the bedside ceremony. Within six months the boy had lost his father and gained a wicked stepmother as well as a bratty little sister. Sybil, conscious of her immunity and impunity, had made Sebastian's life hellish. The memory of her cold metal ruler against the back of his head haunted him into adolescence. The boy had spent many a night at the chapel above the Gate of Dawn, praying to the Blessed Virgin to free him from his stepmother. The shrine featuring a Renaissance icon was said to possess the power to heal and liberate suffering innocents. And, behold! The Virgin had heard his pleas and granted his wish. Sybil had died on the eve of Sebastian's eighteenth birthday.

He had spent the week after the funeral purging the house of all traces of the witch, dragging dresses out of the wardrobe and dumping them into the rubbish bin outside the house. Disposing of his freckled seven-year old sister would prove a more challenging task. One night Sebastian had come home to find his study ravaged and his textbooks torn to shreds. Without a word, he had packed Aurelia's clothes and dropped her off at Frau Jung's boarding school with a tuition check and a note stapled to the collar of her dress. The following morning, he had departed for St. Petersburg to study law.

Nine years later, the Messer half-siblings continued being the bane of each other's existence. Sebastian continued paying his sister's tuition, however begrudgingly. It was a necessary expense.

Life at a boarding school seemed to agree with Aurelia. The girl did not mind the bland food or the stiff mattress. The freedom of movement justified the minor deprivations. Frau Jung did not nag her students to wear wool stockings in winter or eat beef stew. A young lady could survive on a slice of pumpernickel bread and a sip of black tea. Chronic hunger only fuels the creative process. The fuller the belly, the hollower the head. Elsa took pride in the fact that all her girls had narrow waists and thick portfolios, unconcerned that half of them showed signs of anemia. Slight pallor adds mystery to an artist's appearance. Aurelia, who had not inherited her mother's sturdy constitution, certainly looked the part. The painting smock draped from her bony shoulders in irregular folds, perfecting the image of a Bohemian waif. Her spine looked like a string of large pearls under her skin. That was Aurelia's main redeeming feature in Frau Jung's eyes, apart from, perhaps, her penchant for escapades. Her small, agile body was designed to squeeze into tight spaces. Her tiny pink ears with pointed tips and almost translucent lobes picked up the faintest of noises. Her amber eyes, the only tribute to her maternal lineage, saw very well in the dark.

Ubiquitous, elusive, indestructible, Aurelia always found out the news before anyone else did. If there was a fire or a robbery, she knew about it before the story hit the press. Like an adventurous hatchling, she would flee the coop every night and wander the farmyard in the dark, miraculously evading badgers and owls, only to return under the warm wing of the mother hen by dawn. If she ever got into trouble, she usually found her way out of it. Frau Jung had never needed to come to Aurelia's rescue. The girl took up so little space and consumed so little food, the schoolmistress had resolved in her heart to let her stay—as a pet—even if the tuition payments were to stop coming.

At the sight of Sebastian, Elsa forced a smile, one that did not reveal her teeth. He was one of her least favorite people in Vilnius.

"Herr Messer, what brings you here at this hour?"

"I've come to collect Fräulein Lichtner. I wasn't sure what time you were coming back."

"So you spent the night sitting at the doorstep?"

"What choice did I have? The door was locked."

"Would you like to come inside for a cup of tea?"

"No, we really should be on our way. Can you please tell her to hurry?"

Sebastian's random visit did not strike the schoolmistress as particularly odd. He had several clients in the area.

Renate did not need to be asked twice. "I'm ready," she chirped, jumping out of the line carriage. "I've everything I need."

She rejoiced at the prospect of spending the night at her father's house instead of the school dormitory. Had it really been a month since they last saw each other?

Before climbing into Sebastian's buggy, she waved at the schoolmistress. Elsa blew her a long-winded kiss. That flighty amicability of the gesture was tainted by some vague apprehension that evaded Renate but infected everyone else.

Little Sophie rubbed her eyes. "I don't like it," she droned sleepily, pointing at the buggy.

Inga, the nineteen-year old who had performed the slapping ritual on Sophie earlier that day, hugged her young friend. "Why not, *Liebling*?"

"It looks like a coffin on wheels. Too tight, and the windows too small. I don't think I'd like to ride in it, especially with that slimy fellow."

"That *slimy fellow* is one of the city's up-and-coming lawyers. Do you know how much his suit costs?"

"I don't like his mustache. It looks like he's been drinking hot cocoa and forgot to wipe his lips."

Justine laughed. "Ah, from the mouth of babes!"

"Sophie is no longer a baby," Inga corrected austerely. "She is a young woman as of this morning. One day she'll realize that someone like Sebastian Messer is quite a catch. Alas, he'll probably marry Renate." Inga surveyed her classmates. "Did anyone see how he squeezed her elbow when he helped her get inside? Men like him always try to marry their employers' daughters. Don't worry, Sophie, your day will come."

The twelve-year rolled her tongue out as if trying to cough up foul taste. "Blech! Men are revolting. If they are anything like Herr Messer, I'll become a nun."

"But you're Lutheran!"

"No matter, I'll convert to Catholicism, if it's my only way to stay clear of men like him."

Before long, the entire class was laughing, not because Sophie's comments were particularly amusing, but because the girls felt the need to dilute the foreboding.

***

There was so little room inside the buggy. Even two passengers as slender as Sebastian and Renate could barely squeeze in. The seat itself was a narrow leather-clad ledge.

With her drawings piled up on her lap and her travel bag clutched to her chest, Renate cast a glance at her companion. "So, how have you been?"

At first Sebastian pretended not to hear and remained in the same position, his forehead pressed against the foggy window. He would do anything to delay the imminent volcanic eruption even by a few seconds.

"Herr Messer, I asked you a question," Renate continued, "and not an overly intrusive one, I presume."

Sebastian stirred like a sickly pigeon. "I've been better."

"Oh well, there's always hope for tomorrow."

Sebastian's refusal to engage in a dialogue left Renate neither disappointed nor surprised. Whenever they were alone, the first and the last phrases usually belonged to her. On that night he was particularly scant with words.

After a few seconds of silence, Renate sniffed the air and frowned. "There's a smell of smoke. Or am I imagining things?"

"No, you aren't."

"It seems to be blowing from the north."

"Indeed, it is."

"It's not just wood. I smell traces of chemicals. Was there a fire?"

"A massive one." With each reply Sebastian was inching closer to the precipice. He wondered how many sentences it would take for them to get to the truth.

"That's where Vati's factory is."

"Was."

"Was? You mean he moved production to a larger facility? Don't' tell me...." Renate pried Sebastian from the window. "Vati went through with Bergmann's offer, didn't he? I told him it was a bad move. That man is a predator. I've seen that building. Sure, the ceilings are higher, but the ventilation and the lighting are poor. Vati knew I didn't approve, so he signed the deal while I was away. Now I see why you've been feeling rotten. Those realty agents must've put you through the wringer."

Ah, that look of deliberate denial! Those widened eyes the color of white currants. Those inflated nostrils frozen in anticipation. Sebastian would give three hundred imperial rubles to dump the burden of what he was about to do on someone else's shoulders.

"In moments like this," he began, laying his clammy hand on Renate's wrist, "it's vital to remember who you are and where you come from, so you can act with dignity."

"I don't understand your riddles." She pulled her hand away and wiped it against her skirt. "Can you get to the point, *bitte*?"

35

"Fräulein Lichtner, I need you to be an adult, for as of today, your childhood is over. A new phase in your life is about to begin. The Lichtner Textile Factory is no more. Your father sustained deadly burns in the fire. Thankfully, he lasted long enough to write a will and make sure that your interests are protected."

There, he got the words out. Sebastian was quite pleased with his delivery, actually. His voice did not falter once. Throughout his speech Renate had been rubbing her mouth with her fingertips and tugging at her lower lip. The girl was taking the blow far better than he had expected. No signs of hysteria so far. Perhaps, he had underestimated her.

"I'll give you a moment to digest the news." He fixed his vest and moved away from her as far as the dimensions of the buggy allowed. "Take all the time you need."

Renate began patting herself on the cheeks and whispering, "Wake up, wake up…"

Alas, Sebastian had spoken too soon. The worst was not over, far from it. The tempest was only approaching. Gradually her pats turned into slaps and her whispers escalated to shrieks. They burst out like cannon volleys out of her chest.

The throbbing in the Sebastian's right temple that he had been nursing for the past three hours became unbearable. He was not a sturdy man, and the thought of applying physical force to his dead client's daughter disturbed him, but he had no other choice, so he locked his arms around Renate, as she thrashed and kicked in his grip. The windows quickly fogged up from the struggle.

"Collect yourself, Fräulein Lichtner," he hissed in her ear. "You don't want the onlookers to get the wrong impression and call the gendarmes. The last thing I need is being accused of deviant acts. How will I then prove my innocence?"

Renate sunk her teeth into his thumb. Sebastian let out a profanity and released her for a second, only to grab her even tighter, this time placing his forearm under her chin and pushing her head backward. "Don't make me wring your neck, fräulein. That's not what your father sent me here for."

Eventually, Renate started running out of steam. Her tantrum was violent but short-lived. When she finally lifted her head, Sebastian found himself looking into a different pair of eyes than he did five minutes earlier. Those swollen eyelids, blood-laced whites and dilated pupils indicated that an earthquake had happened inside her head. The tectonic plates had shifted, altering her very countenance.

"I want to see Vati."

"Of course." Sebastian reached into his briefcase and presented a photograph of Hermann against the background of his factory. The picture must have been taken sometime in the early 1870s based on the fashion. "It's yours to keep. The rest of the photos perished in the fire."

She swatted his hand away. "It's just a stupid picture. It's not my father. You know damn well what I meant when I asked to see him."

"This is how he would've liked to be remembered."

"There's going to be a funeral, isn't there? I want to see the body."

"No, you don't. I saw Herr Lichtner at the infirmary shortly before his death, and it wasn't a pretty sight." Sebastian surmised his words were far from comforting. Pastoral care was not in his job descriptions. "The burial has taken place already. Your father didn't want any lavish pageantry."

"In that case, where *are* you taking me?"

"To a safe place in the countryside. You're going to stay

with a very nice gentleman, your father's trusted friend."

Renata let out a bigger growl. "Rubbish! Vati didn't have any friends. Friendship is for menial workers who congregate around a beer barrel after work, trashing their employers. People of Vati's caliber don't need friends."

Sebastian shrugged and fixed his tie. "You're entitled to your opinions, fräulein. I'm sorry, but I cannot reveal any more details. I'm only carrying out Herr Lichtner's will. It's not safe for you to stay in the city, with your father's murderers on the loose." He pulled out a flask from his pocket and twisted the lid open. "Take a sip, like a good girl. It'll help you sleep. There's no reason for you to stay awake. We have a long ride ahead of us."

Without asking what was inside, Renate grabbed the flask and gulped the content down. "Pleased now?"

No, Sebastian did not look pleased. "I said a sip. Not everything to the last drop. It's laudanum, for God's sake. Potent stuff."

"Well, it's too late." She threw the empty flask out the window. "If it kills me, all the better. At least I won't have to suffer your company, Herr Messer."

A few moments later she was asleep, with a thin stream of blood trickling down from her left nostril. Gingerly, Sebastian pulled out a handkerchief and blotted the blood from the girl's upper lip. He had to deliver the precious merchandise in presentable condition.

CHAPTER 5

Reverie

Stikliu Street—Jewish district in Vilnius

Benjamin Asher was sitting in the back of his father's workshop, tinkering with the sewing machine, tailoring a suit for his younger brother's upcoming bar mitzvah. The chore was a part of his complex punishment for missing most of the Shabbat dinner the week before. Ten days of house arrest. Ten days of cutting black wool and pondering various philosophical questions. Given a choice, Benjamin would have opted for a harsher but briefer punishment, like getting smacked on the knuckles, but Daniel Asher, the patriarch of the family, did not believe in corporal punishment. Instead, he inflicted mild psychological torture over a prolonged period of time.

Overall, Daniel Asher, fondly referred to as Tatti, was a peculiarly lenient father—as far as Jewish fathers went. He understood that a sixteen-year old boy could think of more exciting pastimes than watching his mother light candles, pulling apart stringy challah and reciting prayers. Benjamin's stifled yawns and furtive eye rolls during the ritual did not escape his father's attention. The boy, to his credit, tried hard to mask his boredom. He had enough respect for his ancestors and their customs, yet he clearly lacked the zeal and the fervor of his twelve-year old brother, who practically gulped the scriptures. Little Jacob, with his more pronounced Judaic features and dramatic inflection, would open his own rabbinical academy one day. Jacob needed no reminders to get dressed for the weekly walk to the synagogue and voluntarily buried his beaky nose in the Torah in anticipation of his upcoming bar mitzvah. Benjamin, on the other hand, was always the first one to bolt out the door after the closing prayers, anxious to get back to his sketches. Drawing was not considered work, at least not in Daniel Asher's book. He neither encouraged nor impeded his oldest son's artistic pursuits. Nothing significant would come out of them anyway.

Had the reason behind Benjamin's tardiness been truancy or petty hooliganism, Daniel would have given him a lukewarm chiding and left it at that. Not that the boy was prone to street mischief. Benjamin had never been caught smoking, making noise or damaging other people's property. No, this particular wrongdoing was considerably more disturbing. Benjamin had been sighted in the company of a fair-haired girl identified as one of Frau Jung's students. Reportedly, the two were laughing, holding hands and kissing, oblivious to the glares from the onlookers, or perhaps, relishing the disapproval, as adolescents are wont to. For that brief moment of defiant bliss Benjamin was now paying with his freedom, missing the longest and most glorious days of June.

***

The clock struck midnight, marking the end of Benjamin's arrest. Once again, he was a free man—at least until the next transgression. Instead of going to bed for the night, he went for a walk through the quiet, immaculately clean streets where the air smelled of jasmine and bittersweet chocolate. His childhood had passed here, to the sounds of violin and clarinet. If there were clouds thickening above the Jewish quarter, Benjamin was not conscious of that. Grandpa Isaac kept saying that the Jews of Vilnius had a better life before the Russians. The old man remembered the days of relative peace. Now *pogroms* were happening in various corners of the Empire. In 1881 a riot had broken out in Warsaw. The mob demolished Jewish businesses and homes adjoining the Holy Cross Church. Hundreds of families were left financially devastated and were forced into immigration to America. Grandpa Isaac insisted that the riot was engineered by the Russian secret police to sabotage the Polish-Jewish relations. Naturally, it was in the Czar's interest to drive a wedge between the two groups. It was only a matter of time before something similar would happen in Vilnius, which was called Jerusalem of the North.

Benjamin did not pay much heed to Grandpa's rants. Old people rely on tales of doom to capture the attention of younger family members. Those isolated skirmishes in Warsaw would not translate into anything major. Why all that talk about persecution and oppression? Benjamin certainly did not feel oppressed, having grown up in the posh enclave on Stikliu Street with a housekeeper and a cook. The women in his family had never touched a dishrag. No, their swift ivory fingers were meant for manipulating exquisite fabrics to create fashion masterpieces. Benjamin's mother Esther and older sister Leah were two of the most elegant ladies in the city, always modeling their own designs to prospective customers as they promenaded through the boutiques and galleries. Yes, they worked, but their work was clean, creative and well-compensated. Staying slim and youthful was one of the non-negotiable requirements. Esther, even after three children, could, with a corset, shrink her waist to nineteen inches. She was in her mid-thirties and strove to look at least a decade younger. No matronly frumpiness, no sullen scowls, no grey hair, burst capillaries, craterous pores or wrinkles were allowed in their trade. Esther would drench her face in cucumber juice and tint the tips of her eyelashes with indigo dye to bring out that sought-after pallor. Mother and daughter, who could easily pass for sisters, served as paragons of affluent merchant class womanhood, making every female in Vilnius between twenty and fifty want to dress, dance and laugh like them. Unsurprisingly, they did not have many close friends.

"Being gorgeous, witty and stylish surely is a lonely road," Esther would sigh to her daughter as they clanged glasses filled with kosher wine. "As gentiles would say, it's our cross to bear."

In the sixteen years of his life, Benjamin had never been to the poor parts of Vilnius, though he had heard stories from the cook about the squalor shacks along the railroad inhabited by day laborers, mostly ethnic Lithuanians and Poles, outcasts in the country that formerly belonged to them. Such a sad lot! Benjamin pitied them in absentia, on the instinctive level, but those feelings did not motivate him to any decisive action. He did not know what to do about those faint sporadic stirrings of his conscience. The compassionate streak in him had never fully matured. Rabbi Goldman, in his sermons kept making nebulous, cautious references to *mitzvah*, but not in the context of economic justice. In the affluent synagogue the Ashers attended, dwelling too much on the issue of material disparity would be a sure way to lose members.

Benjamin could not remember the last time he had made

his bed, let alone shined his shoes. Those functions were performed for him behind the scenes by people who wisely kept themselves inconspicuous, toiling like the elves from the Grimm Brothers fairy tale. The porcelain dishware from Dresden, the down mattresses, the brocade curtains, the silver candle holders were the attributes of belonging to the chosen tribe. Cultivating a sense of social awareness in his children was not one of Daniel Asher's goals. The poor were not to be despised, abused or provoked, but why should prosperous Jews concern themselves with the fate of destitute Poles? Their paths would never cross anyway. On what occasion should the coddled Asher children interact with the gentiles living by the railroad tracks?

Benjamin felt little affinity for his historical ancestors who had emerged from the desert. The cold foggy city was his home, the only one he had known. Sure, he had been called a *yid* on occasion. But then there was an endearing slur for a man of every ethnic group—*lech* for the Pole, *labas* for the Lithuanian, *katzap* for the Russian, *fritz* for the German. They were all inhabitants of Vilnius. They all rivaled, bickered, traded and partied under the same overcast sky. Still, there were some boundaries that did not get crossed, not without tangible consequences. Selling fancy hats, stockings and corsets to German women was one thing. Locking lips with them was a different story.

In Benjamin's defense, he was not the one who violated the boundaries. His boldest move was setting up his easel in a blaringly Christian quarter. Renate was the one who approached him. She also was the one who initiated the first kiss—Benjamin was fairly certain of that. There was no way to tell how many men she had kissed before him, but the confidence with which she placed his hands on her hips suggested that their encounter had been painstakingly premeditated. Perhaps, she had spent many hours practicing on a ripe tomato. Clearly, Renate was acting out a fantasy that had been brewing in her mind for quite some time. At least, that was what Benjamin wanted to believe. The idea of a German woman singling him out from the crowd and strategically ambushing him to satisfy her sexual caprices made Benjamin dizzy with vanity. A few times he had to halt and pat his burning cheeks. Could it all have been a case of mild intoxication from inhaling the paint thinner fumes? Life would be so much easier if he could write the experience off as an episode of temporary delirium. But no, there were witnesses, and rather vindictive ones, eager to report him to his father. He, Benjamin Asher, was a wanted man, a threat to convention. In the sixteen years of his life he had never had so many scrutinizing eyes on him.

Then he let his imagination fly with the impetuousness of Icarus. What would need to happen in order for him to marry the German heiress? For starters, he would need to convert to Lutheranism, or whatever form of Christianity she was practicing. Obviously, he could not expect her to convert to Judaism. Would it crush Tatti to see his oldest son turn his back on the faith of their ancestors? Not really. After a few days of frowning and growling, Tatti would probably shrug and accept the new way of things. The religion of the prospective daughter-in-law concerned Daniel Asher less than her financial status. A rich Lutheran is better than a poor Jewess. Tatti would be more upset to learn that his son was not planning on taking over the family business or even staying in Vilnius. Surely, Benjamin loved the city where several generations of Ashers had toiled and prospered, but he had no allegiance to it. He and Renate would run away to America, meet up with fellow-artists and establish a gallery in New York City. Of course, he would send gifts and postcards to his family in Vilnius. He would even pay for their transatlantic tickets.

Benjamin was flying through the alleys, his coat unbuttoned, head thrown back and feet barely touching the wet cobblestone. Before he knew it, he had crossed into the Russian quarter where many of the officials lived and all the signs were in Cyrillic. By then the lights were out in most of the windows. A few meters above his head, on a balcony, a couple was arguing in Russian. What a harsh language! Everyone says that German is terse and abrupt, but Russian is far harder on the ears, in spite of the defined consonants and melodic vowels. There is something sinister in that pristine clarity. For the first time, Benjamin felt something akin to discomfort from being in a foreign element.

His anxiety lasted but a few moments. The thoughts of his new German sweetheart flooded his consciousness again. This time those thoughts were marked by bold, unapologetic carnality. He was no longer preoccupied with how his affair looked to the rest of the world. He was more concerned with what Renate's body looked like underneath that puritanical linen frock. He had a suspicion she was dressing drably on a principle. Still, there would be no harm in presenting her with a fancy gown from Tatti's shop. No girl, no matter how progressive and enlightened, could resist one of Asher's creations. But first, he was determined to see her naked. Ah, the things he would do to that girl in the dark! He was already planning their next rendezvous. Of course, they would need to find a secluded place, a basement or an attic. Benjamin would not mind a few pigeons or rats. No doubt, Renate knew of such a place. She seemed resourceful enough. Hah! Rabbi Goldman would have a heart attack. There was no turning back for Benjamin.

He threw his arms around the lantern post and pressed

his sweaty forehead against the cool metal, an exquisite ache coursing through his loins.

CHAPTER 6

Apparition

A piercing moan interrupted Benjamin's reverie. That part of the city was laid out like a maze, which made it difficult to determine where exactly the sound was coming from. He could not even tell if the moan was produced by a person or an animal, but the infinite anguish communicated in that sound chilled his blood. He recoiled from the metal post and stepped into the street. He could hear the sound of hooves clicking. The wailing grew louder.

A few seconds later a slick enclosed buggy flew by, nearly knocking Benjamin off his feet. Through the foggy side window, but he caught a glimpse of a struggle. A fair-haired girl was flailing and gasping in the arms of a man. Her words were not making any sense. She was not imploring her captor to release her. Benjamin made out words, "Wake up, wake up!"

Paralyzed by the lurid apparition, he leaned against the wall of the building. A few seconds later he was sprinting behind the buggy, gulping the humid air with his mouth. The back window was shuttered, so he could not see what was happening inside, but he could still hear the girl's weakening pleas. Around the corner, he slipped on a wet cobblestone and fell flat on his face, scraping both elbows and knees. Grinding his teeth with pain, he watched the buggy disappear out of sight. His heart, lungs and limbs had not been trained for exertions of such intensity. He had spent too much time tailoring and painting. Even without the slip he would not have been able to outrun the horse.

The girl bore a disturbing resemblance to Renate. Benjamin hurried to shake off that idea. No, it couldn't possibly be her. She was in the countryside with her school. There are so many other blonde German girls in the city. It's not unusual for an infatuated man to see the face of his beloved everywhere. Renate was probably on her way back from Alytus. Tomorrow morning he would see her by the Gate of Dawn chapel, and they would resume their affair.

***

When he came home around one in the morning, limping, he found his father sitting in the living-room, a smoldering cigar in his hand. Benjamin could not remember the last time he saw his father smoking.

"Sit down," Daniel demanded.

In a fit of adolescent indignation, Benjamin threw his arms up. What have I done this time, Tatti? I thought my term of imprisonment was over. I went out for air. Is it a crime?"

Daniels shook his head and put out the cigar. "So you didn't hear what happened?"

"No. I spent the last ten days at the workshop, shackled to the sewing machine like a good Jewish son. No contact with the outside world."

"I'll need to find a new fabric supplier," Daniel said. "I have all these orders to fill, and I'm lucky if I have two rolls of linen in stock."

48

"What happened to the old supplier? He doesn't want to do business with you anymore? Don't tell me it's because of that incident on Castle Street. Did Lichtner break his contract with you because I kissed his daughter? I swear on my life, I'll never touch that German cow again. She means nothing to me."

"Lichtner is dead. He perished in the fire that engulfed his factory. The news is spreading. Nobody knows for sure who's responsible. This is why I asked you to sit down."

This time Benjamin complied. "Tatti... I had no idea."

Daniel examined his son's blood-stained clothes. "Who did this to you?"

"Nobody." Benjamin closed his jacket. "I slipped on a cobblestone."

"Are you sure?"

"I swear to you, Tatti, that's the truth. I didn't pick a fight with anyone, and I wasn't attacked. It was an honest accident. The roads were slick, and I—"

"Fine, I believe you," Daniel interrupted him wearily. "Still, I don't want you wandering the streets past nine o'clock. This city isn't what it used to be. Look what happened to Lichtner." Daniel snapped his fingers. "Which brings me to my next point."

Benjamin tensed up and assumed a more defensive attitude, sensing that his father was to present him with some outrageous demand. "And that point would be?"

"For the foreseeable future, it's best for us to lay low. If anyone asks you about our business dealings with Lichtner, keep your remarks to the minimum. That man had been good to us, and his departure won't go unfelt, but we must ensure the safety of the living."

"Understood. I'll do my best to pretend I'd never heard Lichtner's name. Anything for the family, right? Now, may I be excused? I need to wash my knees before the fabric sticks to the wounds."

Daniel nodded. "There should be some dressing gauze and a new bottle of iodine in the cabinet. Try to get some sleep. It'll make more sense in the morning."

Like hell it will, Benjamin thought grimly as he climbed the stairs into the bedroom that he shared with his younger brother. Jacob's expressive lips were moving in his sleep, reciting passages from the Torah, his swarthy face stamped with prophetic rapture. His skin the color of caramelized milk was perfectly clear. The pubescent process had not started yet. Would the boy manifest the same degree of piety two-three years down the road once the masculine instincts had set in? What kind of temptations did G-d have in store for this one?

The new bottle of iodine remained unopened. Benjamin could not muster the motivation to rinse and disinfect his cuts, so he just rolled up his trousers exposing his knees to air. Falling asleep was out of question. Every time he closed his eyes, he saw the image of the flailing girl inside the buggy. Now he knew beyond the shadow of doubt that Renate had been lost to him.

***

For Elsa Jung, learning about Hermann Lichtner's death was almost like becoming a widow for the third time. To her that man was much more than a paying patron. He embodied that cosmopolitan Aryan ideal, someone who could lead the entire race into the twentieth century. Perhaps, she was a little infatuated with Hermann. If not for her nominal marriage to Lieutenant Jung, she would have seriously thought of pursuing the textile magnate, even though he was considerably younger.

That night Elsa stayed in the music room, playing her favorite German tunes on the piano by candlelight. The students had tacitly agreed that there would be no acrimonious remarks, at least until the next morning. Instead of retreating into their rooms, they brought down blankets and pillows and camped out on the floor around the piano.

Marie Ostermann remembered she had an enormous illustrated Bible, still in its original gift wrapping from three Christmases before. It seemed like a perfect occasion to open the book for the first time.

CHAPTER 7

Delirium

Raven's Bog

Wake up, wake up... Renate slapped her cheeks a few times but felt no tingling.

The first thing she saw when she opened her eyes was the Blessed Virgin staring down at her from the wall. The holy image carved into a pine slab was framed by a constellation of loose amber nuggets. Renate had seen hundreds of such carvings at craft fairs all over Lithuania, and this particular icon was not the best executed one as far as technique was concerned. The craftsman had succeeded at giving the Virgin a strict and commanding countenance.

Compelled to make the sign of the cross under the steadfast gaze of those hooded eyes, Renate lifted her right hand and immediately got distracted by the fanciful embroidery on the sleeve of her linen shift gown. She was drowning in a thick goose down mattress, propped up on pillows and covered with a patchwork quilt that smelled of dried mint and lavender.

Having leapt out of bed, she was overcome by the sensation of floating. She heard the floorboard creak but could not feel the surface with the soles of her feet. Her heart was as numb as her body. The only identifiable emotion was a sense of detached wonder from being in a strange place that looked like a country cottage. The room was spacious and uncluttered, with plenty of sunlight coming through the windows curtained with wide strips of handmade lace. The walls and the ceiling were plastered with white clay. The furniture consisted of the tall wooden bed, a sturdy table and several giant trunks the content of which did not interest Renate. In addition to the carving of the Virgin there were several painted plates nailed to the walls, all floral patterns in orange and blue on black background, and a woven tapestry depicting a hunting scene. The color scheme made absolutely no sense. Clearly, no thought had been put into decorating, just random artifacts thrown in together.

Her box with paints and the easel gifted by Frau Jung were at the foot of the bed.

Having examined the rustic interior of the room, Renate unlocked the oaken door, thick and heavy enough to withstand an invaders' assault, and stepped outside. Judging from the position of the sun, it was about four o'clock in the afternoon. The first thought that came into her mind was that the rainbow had vomited all over the green fields. There was no more accurate way to describe these blotches of color splattered against the glistening grass. Dandelions, poppies, cornflowers, wild carnations and buttercups trembled in the wind, spouting golden pollen. Renate had never seen such robust petals and saturated colors in the city, not even at Frau Jung's summer house outside Alytus.

A winding clay road leading to the woods separated the estate into farmland and marshland, with potato and flax fields to the left and mossy bogs to the right. Wrens, buffleheads and flycatchers would spring upward from their camouflaged nests. Renate remembered her father telling her that in the eastern part of Lithuania you could have very dry patches next to very wet ones. It was not unusual to have sand, clay and swamp on the same square kilometer—a landscape artist's dream but a farmer's nightmare.

The steamy bog exuding the smell of mushrooms, rotting birch bark and clover was calling Renate's name. She longed to sink her fingers into the lukewarm muddy water. She lifted the hem of her night shift and stepped onto the grass.

A low-pitched growl started her. She glanced over her shoulder expecting to see a guard dog but instead saw a peasant woman with a comely toddler girl in her arms. Both were wearing puffy blouses and drawstring skirts of plaid wool.

"I wouldn't venture into the bog," the woman said in a language that sounded like a mixture of Polish and Russian. Renate guessed it was Belarusian, so common in the southeastern parts of the Dainava region. The peasant woman, judging from the condition of her skin, could not have been much older than forty, but most of her teeth were missing. She kept licking her thin lips with a smacking sound, akin to that of a fishtail makes against the water. "Go back inside, m'lady, lest yer wish to lose a foot."

Now Renate knew she was still dreaming. It was the same bizarre dream that had started in Vilnius. "What are you talking about?" she asked in Polish. "How would I lose a foot?"

"A bear's been comin' by from the woods."

"You're afraid the bear will maul me?"

The woman puckered spitefully. As if a noble predator like a bear would find the skinny German girl appetizing! "He'll ravage the bee hives and the raspberry bushes, and there'll be nothin' to put in yer tea over the winter, no honey or jam. So Master Dombrowski has bear traps set up."

The woman pulled up the hem of the girl's dress exposing a maimed foot with several toes missing. "Magda, my granddaughter, when she first learned how to walk, wandered into the field. I was pickin' apples at the orchard when we heard a snap and a horrid shriek, like nothin' we ever heard before. We were mighty distraught. Who'd marry a cripple? Master Dombrowski felt contrite and gave Magda a nice dowry."

"A dowry for a few toes..." Renate wondered how many other peasant women would deliberately send their children into the field for the same reason. "I suppose, removing the traps isn't a solution? That would be too easy, wouldn't it?"

"One doesn't argue with the Master," the woman said austerely. "The traps will stay in place for as long as he wills it. By the way, my name's Agatha. I cook for the family. Now, let's make yer decent for the Master, shall we?"

The woman put her granddaughter down and led Renate back inside the house. The crippled girl moved rather swiftly on her fours, faster than she would if she were to try hobbling around on her feet. Renate winced as she compared the child to a spider or a wild animal. The grunting noises she was making were not exactly human either. Perhaps, the girl was deaf too?

Agatha opened one of the trunks and pulled out a dress with a red bodice, puffy white sleeves and a plaid skirt. "Put in on, m'lady." She dangled the garment in front of the guest.

Renate was not in a hurry to comply, put off by the smell of moldy wool which reminded her of the elderly peddlers from the market in Vilnius.

"Whose is it?"

"It belonged to the late mistress."

After a few moments of hesitation, Renate finally

removed the nightdress and stepped into the dress. The prison of scratchy wool swallowed her whole, instantly aging her a good ten years.

"What's wrong, m'lady?" Agatha asked. "It's not to yer likin'?"

"It's a little loose in the waist." Renate tried to adjust the cross-stitched sash to give her figure a more flattering silhouette.

"Not for much longer. Before yer know it, yer will be with child, and the loose-fittin' dress will come in handy, sure enough. Master Dombrowski isn't one for wastin' time. He'll want to get busy right away. I predict 'twill happen by the harvest season."

So the toothless hag had quite a sense of humor. One would not have guessed by looking at her mien. As Mutti used to say, "A king is only as good as his jester."

Renate had no choice but make her peace with the frumpy dress. Now was not the time for acting fastidiously. Still, something needed to be done about her hair. The bun she had coiled at Frau Jung's cottage was coming apart, with frizzy tendrils sticking out everywhere.

"Allow me," Agatha volunteered. "I'll fix yer hair the way Master Dombrowski likes it. Yer must look pleasin' to him."

Renate abdicated and handed the comb over. The peasant woman seated her on the chair and started pulling out the pins from her tattered bun and combing through the knots, showing as much delicacy as she would be while pulling feathers out of a dead chicken. Renate tolerated those crude manipulations. She was not accustomed to being brushed by someone else, even though the other girls at Frau Jung's school would groom each other regularly.

"The late mistress had such nice hair," Agatha lamented. "As black and glossy as a raven's wing. Pure pleasure 'twas to comb and braid it. Yers is like straw, thin and brittle. Isn't much for me to tinker with, m'lady. Whatever they fed yer at that posh city school? Bunches of parsley and dried apples, I bet. No wonder yer nearly bald."

Renate did not respond. After all, it was just a dream. She was going to wake up any minute in her dormitory room.

"Have you prepared me for human sacrifice?" she asked, looking in the murky mirror. Agatha had parted her wheat-colored tresses in the middle and pinned the strands around the temples, letting the rest hang loose down her back. "Will there be a floral wreath and a necklace of wolf's teeth?"

"It's good enough for the master. He likes to wrap a woman's hair around his knuckles." Agatha shook her fist in the air, mimicking the gesture.

"Sounds like the incarnation of gallantry, your master."

The mirror caught the reflection of little Magda who had found Renate's box with oil paints and was smearing ochre all over the bedding.

"Shoo, get away from my art supplies!" Renate shouted, throwing the mirror onto the bed. "These paints cost a fortune. Agnes? Agatha... Whatever your name is! Tell her to stop touching my things."

"Idiot child," the woman murmured approvingly. It pleased her that her ragamuffin of a granddaughter had done something to annoy the haughty house guest.

"I'd like a word with Master Dombrowski now," Renate demanded. "Take me to him."

"I fear yer have to wait until nightfall. The master's out in the fields."

"Setting up more bear traps? God help those poor barbarians who dare to invade your village. It's comforting to know you're well-fortified."

Agatha scooped up her granddaughter. "I better go and

set the table for the master and his lads. Will yer keep yerself amused, m'lady?"

"I shall try. Are there any other places here I should avoid? There are no landmines or bear traps buried behind the barn, are there?"

"No, only cow droppings."

***

Having no idea how much longer the dream was going to last, Renate took the opportunity to explore the rest of the estate. Never before had she come in contact with genuine rural architecture. Frau Jung's summer home did not count, as it was built according to the standards of modern German engineering. It was only meant to look endearingly rustic on the surface. The schoolmistress enjoyed all the modern accommodations, including indoor plumbing and a nickel-plated stove.

The house at Raven's Bog appeared to have started as a simple one-level log cottage with a vaulted roof. Several annexes had been added to the original building over the years. The newer wood was noticeably stronger than that on the main house. Renate clicked her tongue disapprovingly. Not much effort was invested into renovating and fortifying the original structure. The foundation was beginning to slide. In a few years the walls and the roof would start collapsing. The housing arrangement itself struck Renate as odd. As far as she knew, the annex would normally be reserved for domestic servants. Field hands would be housed in separate huts on the same grounds as the barn animals. It seemed that at Raven's Bog everyone lived under the same roof. They probably ate at the same table too. Didn't the toothless cook say she was going to set the table for the master and the lads? Did they also bathe in the bathhouse at the same time?

Wouldn't that be hilarious—the lord of the manor and his lackeys whipping each other with leafy oak branches!

Vati had never as much as broken bread with his workers. Once a year, before Christmas, he would open a bottle of champagne on the factory floor and let his foreman fill the glasses. Anything beyond that would be unpardonable familiarity.

Vati... She would wake up and tell him about her dream, and they would laugh together.

***

At dusk, Agatha appeared on the front step, wiping her reddened hands against her apron, smelling of onions and potatoes.

"Is your master coming?" Renate asked impatiently. "I must've circled the house thirty times in the past hour."

The cook nodded in the direction of the clay road. Renate peered into the twilight and saw glowing dots emerging from the forest, like a swarm of fireflies.

"The lads must've stopped to fetch some lumber," Agatha said. "They'll be famished when they get here. Go inside, m'lady. It'll take them a while to unload the cart."

"No, I want to see what kind of lumber they got, oak or maple. I assume they'll be repairing the main house? About time. I can give your master sound advice."

Agatha dropped the dish rag and uttered what sound like a mild Polish profanity.

"Don't look at me like I'm mad or possessed," Renate said. "I know a thing or two about engineering. You know what that word means, don't you? *En-gi-neer-ing.*"

Agatha used another profanity, this time a stronger one, and disappeared inside the house. Renate remained on the porch and watched the glowing dots approach. In about ten minutes she started seeing the outlines of male figures and a cart drawn by a scrawny old horse. She heard the mournful creaking of the wheels against the gravel, the stomping of boots and rowdy voices. The men were singing a folk song, making no effort to keep the tune.

> *The horse is neighing, doliya!*
> *Beyond the little gate, doliya!*
> *Little sister we go, doliya!*
> *To open the gate, doliya!*

Renate had heard of the polyphonic choral tradition in the Caucasus Mountains where several melodies were sung simultaneously. That was not the case with those men. They would interrupt the song with bursts of guttural laughter and then resume.

When they approached close enough, she could take a look at their clothes. Most of them wore striped trousers with cloth belts, loose-fitting shirts with open necks, leather vests and knee-high boots with narrow tips. The degree of distress varied from one article of clothing to another.

The muddy cart loaded with lumber waddled through the gate into the barnyard. A shaggy dog of uncertain breed leaped off the planks and charged at Renate. She shuddered but held her ground, and the dog backed away after a few seconds of growling.

The torch-bearer leading the procession dropped the horse's reins and leaped up the porch to greet Renate.

"Fräulein Lichtner, you're awake! Don't worry about Milo. He won't bite."

Ah, so that's the master. Renate squinted to assess him. He was not the tallest or the brawniest in the group. He had a typical Polish face with high cheekbones and a straight nose, sufficiently pleasant though entirely unremarkable. His body, however well-proportioned and agile, did not make an instant impression of great strength. It was evident that this man worked with his hands, but he was no chainmail-clad giant of the fairy-tales who could lift a whole anvil with his index finger. His hair was the color of flax fibers and his eyes were the color of flax blossom—rather appropriate for the trade he was in.

"Excuse me, gentlemen," he said, glancing over his shoulder. "You can go inside. Don't wait for me. Agatha should have the table set up. We'll join you in a minute."

Now Renate was truly confused. What gentlemen was he referring to? She did not see any gentlemen, just a handful of peasants. They stood and gaped, propped by their pitchforks and scythes. When their master repeated the request, they started moving in the direction of the house. One of them started howling another song, and the rest of them joined in.

Left alone with Renate, Thaddeus squeezed her hands and lifted them, as if preparing to kiss them, but stopped half-way.

"Welcome to Raven's Bog, Fräulein Lichtner. Do you remember me? I came to your father's factory two years ago. My wife... my *late* wife was with me at the time."

"There were so many people coming in and out of Vati's factory. I cannot possibly remember all of them. Please, don't take offense at that."

She sensed that the sight of her wearing his dead wife's dress was disconcerting to Thaddeus.

"It's even better that way," he said, "to start our acquaintance afresh. We can discuss the particulars after supper."

***

The first thing Renate noticed when she came into the

61

dining-room was the table centerpiece—an enormous pig's head on a platter with a baked apple in its mouth. The head was staring at her with its slanted eyes.

It appeared that the people of Raven's Bog followed Lithuanian customs, at least when it came to seating arrangements. The master's place was at the end of the table facing the wall decorated by a small icon. Since Thaddeus had no son, the seat to his right was given to Antanas, a giant blacksmith in his mid-twenties with straight dandelion-yellow hair in a bowl cut and a massive crooked nose. His pregnant wife Bronia was sitting across from him, a freckled milkmaid in her late teens. She was Toothless Agatha's daughter and Lame Magda's mother. To help track of the servants' names, Renate augmented their names with titles. She was still thinking of a proper nickname for Bronia, whom she had just met. It did not escape Renate that the milkmaid's plain face was extremely animated. She blinked and smiled all the time, her eyebrows jumping up and down, her sharp nose twitching like that of a mouse.

"I knew we'd have a guest," she whispered to Renate across the steaming plates. "D'yer know how I knew it? The cat licked its paw facing the door. Cats never lie. We've kittens in the barn. Want to see them after supper? Two of are red with stripes and one pitch black. There were five in all, but one died and one got lost. We think the badger got him."

After saying grace, Thaddeus pulled the baked apple from the pig's mouth, tossed it up in the air, smiled and handed it over to Renate.

"Our guest of honor, for whose sake the boar was slaughtered, gets the first bite."

With all eyes fixed on her, Renate brought the apple to her mouth, bit into the withered skin, and put it down on the plate. Thaddeus began slicing bread and passing it around. The remaining loaf was left on the table, with the cut end facing the shrine.

Renate remarked that the solemnity of the meal mimicked that of a church service. She had expected the peasants to behave in a rowdier fashion at the table.

Lame Magda, who had stuffed herself on farm cheese and strawberries before dinnertime, was playing with her bread, poking holes in it with her index finger. Agatha whacked her granddaughter on the head with a wooden spoon.

"Idiot child! It takes both hands to earn bread, so yer must break it with both hands."

The girl must have gotten accustomed to receiving whacks, because she continued playing with her slice.

The servants drank slowly, passing the giant beer glass around the table. When it was Renate's turn to take a sip from the glass, she simply held it in front of her face for a second. The thought of coming in contact with the brim that had already been touched by so many lips made her cringe.

Before getting up from the table, Thaddeus smiled at the cook. "You've outdone yourself. There was an abundance of everything. The only food missing was bird's milk."

Agatha bowed her kerchiefed head. "To yer health, Master."

***

"You barely touched your food," Thaddeus said to Renate after supper as they walked outside into the farmyard. Most of the chickens had gone back into the coop. Milo, the shaggy dog had settled in its vaulted kennel.

"I wasn't hungry."

"Tomorrow morning you'll be. Just wait until you try Agatha's potato pancakes with buttermilk gravy and foxtail mushrooms. If I were Czar, I'd give out medals for making perfect pancakes."

Renate turned to face him. "Master Dombrowski, you shouldn't exert yourself on my account. It's not my intention to eat you out of your house. I don't want to abuse your hospitality."

The prudish inflections in her own voice surprised her. She was addressing her host as if they were standing in a parlor, not outside a barn. The effects of Sebastian's tranquilizing concoction were wearing off, and the reality in all its absurd horror was setting in.

Thaddeus scratched between his eyebrows. "Hmm... Exactly how much do you know about the arrangement between me and your late father? Did anyone give you the details?"

"Are you referring to flax trading?"

"I'm referring to the document your father composed on his deathbed, making me his beneficiary on the condition that I—"

"Oh, that? Agatha made a joke about it earlier today as she was helping me dress."

"Agatha is a great cook but not much of a joker," he said in his gentle back-to-business voice. "Fräulein Lichtner, as you may know, my first wife has been dead for eighteen months."

"Well, your servants act like she's still here." Renate was determined to cling to denial for as long as she possibly could. "Agatha still washes and presses her old mistress' clothes."

"My people were very fond of Jolanta." Thaddeus emphasized the word people. "Still, we're quite accustomed to funerals around here. How about I show you the family cemetery? Three centuries of history. The artist in you will appreciate the carvings on the tombstones."

"My history teacher told us about certain African tribes that dig up their dead and bring them to family gatherings." Feeling another scream rising in her throat, Renate sunk her fingernails into the rotting wood of the fence, bracing for the rapid reentry into reality.

"Your father believed the arrangement would benefit us both." Thaddeus was one of those people who use exaggerated politeness to mask his embarrassment in awkward situations. "What do you think of it?"

Still clinging to the decrepit planks, Renate threw hear head back. "Does it matter what I think? It seems like Vati has done all the thinking already. I didn't fight him when he sent me to that detention facility for the artistically deranged. Master Dombrowski, forgive me."

"What for?"

"I'm about to scream."

Thaddeus gave her a nod of approval. "Go right ahead."

"Be warned, I have a very shrill voice. The animals will be frightened."

"They're used to loud noises. I'll scream with you."

Thaddeus scooped her in his arms as he would an ewe and carried her back into the room where she had spent the previous night. For a few minutes he sat on the bed and rocked her, singing a pastoral ditty.

> *Again the blossoms of May*
> *Have decorated the meadows and valleys*
> *And fields and forests and old farmsteads...*
> *My native farm, tell me why I long for you so much?*
> *And why I love you like this?*
> *Perhaps it's only because*
> *I was bustling here when I was small*
> *And at the pure stream I played with my friends.*

Because I found my first love like an adorable rosebud
In a small hut of the native village...

"Please, put me down," Renate implored. The rocking sensation brought back the memory of her ride from Vilnius. "I'm about to vomit. Just don't tell me you'll vomit with me out of solidarity."

Thaddeus lowered her onto the bed. "I'll fetch you a bucket. I also might have something to calm you down."

"Hell, no... I'm not drinking any more potions or concoctions." Her eyes half-closed, Renate pointed at the image of the sinister Madonna. "Put that thing away."

"Don't you like her?"

"I don't think she likes me. I think she knows I'm a Lutheran. Just for tonight."

Thaddeus shrugged and pulled the carving off the wall. "Fine, I'll give it to Antanas and Bronia. Do you want the candles burning?"

"Yes, please." A second later she changed her mind. "No, you can blow them out."

On his way out of the room, Thaddeus lingered on the threshold, as if deliberating whether to articulate his thoughts or keep them to himself. "It's not deadly, you know," he said at last. "Heartache, I mean. Don't believe what poets say. I don't know anyone who's died of grief itself. And I've seen many people die."

Thaddeus closed the door and walked out into the yard. Through the shattered window, Renate heard the sound of a chain clanging followed by servile yelping. Milo must have crawled out of its kennel to lick the master's face one more time. With his mongrel by his side, Thaddeus resumed singing.

MARINA J. NEARY

Here joyfully passed
My youth—as a pearl.
A song resounded as an echo of lark over fields
Whenever I remember the early sunny spring morning
I long for that song every day.
There near the birches
Violin strings slowly tremble
The hymn of its notes is like forefathers' lament.
Like a friend who I love with all my heart
I will never ever forget the native village.

CHAPTER 8

Coffee and Croissants

Vilnius, Castle Street

There was a mischievous little demon living in the upper drawer of Sebastian's work desk. That demon kept planting copies of *Aušra,* translated as Dawn, the first Lithuanian nationalist newspaper that had been in circulation for about a year. In light of the press ban, the production was taking place in the town of Ragnit in Lithuania Minor which was under German control—Kaiser Wilhelm the Great could not care less what language his Baltic subjects spoke as long as they paid taxes on time. *Aušra* was the brainchild of Jonas Basanavičius, a young activist and proponent of Lithuanian National Revival. Basanavičius directed the editorial policies remotely from Prague and arranged to have copies of the newspaper smuggled into Lithuania. How would a copy of *Aušra* find its way into Sebastian's desk? Clearly, somebody regarded him as a viable convert.

On his way to the office, he tossed the paper in the rubbish bin.

"It's all a swindle, you know," he heard his sister's voice. Aurelia was standing by the curb, wearing the same clothes from the night before. "I'm talking about the hair-thickening lotion you've been splurging on." She approached her brother with the slow intentness of a prosecutor, hands locked behind her back. "That Jew who sold it to you is laughing all the way to the bank. And your Russian ice princess doesn't care about your appearance. "

Sebastian's jaw stiffened. How in the world did Aurelia know about Lydia?

"Get lost." He could not think of anything meaner to say.

"It won't solve anything, dear brother. I'm the least of your problems." She flipped a loose pebble with the tip of her shoe. "Even if I die tomorrow, you won't grow a luscious mane. Not that it matters to *her*. Your head could be smooth as an egg. That seasoned Russian shrew wants to know who your clients are and how much they pay. If she deems your income too modest, you won't stand a chance with her, even if you transform into Adonis overnight."

"What will it take to make you disappear?"

"Oh, just a bit of information about Renate Lichtner's whereabouts." Aurelia dropped her clownish mannerisms. "I know you're privy to every detail."

"You're daft to think I'll murmur a word of it to anyone, let alone you, of all people."

"Come on, big brother." She clasped her hands in mock plea. "You know I'll find out sooner or later."

"Why does her fate concern you so?"

"Renate is my friend. The rest of the girls worry about her too. They stayed up all night in the music room, listening to Frau Jung's gloomy etudes. Imagine suffering through six hours of Schubert?"

Now it was Sebastian's turn to play detective. "How would you know what they did all night? You weren't even there." His eyes wandered to the hem of her floral skirt that was covered in soot as if she had crawled over a pile of charred rubble. She must have visited the crime scene and tried sneaking inside the burned down factory. He would put nothing past her. She probably did not get very far, as the area was barred off and guarded by the gendarmes.

"What does it matter where I spent the night? I'm trying to get some answers."

There were two things Sebastian did not believe in: faeries and female friendship.

"Spare me the farce," he growled. "Your concern for Renate is about as genuine as that gold coin your mother tossed into the collection plate. I remember that Christmas of '72. Sybil took us to St. Stanislaus. When it was her turn to make a donation, she pulled out that counterfeit coin from the magic shop across the street."

Aurelia's frail shoulders shook with laughter, though there was no merriment in her eyes. "You're raving." She tucked a greasy red tendril behind her ear. "There was no magic shop within a ten kilometer radius of our house. And the three of us never went to church together. You made it up. Those thoughts are causing your hair to come out. Take your temperature."

Sebastian would not fall for Aurelia's provocations. The sneaky witch was trying to disorient him by jumbling his memories and make him question his sanity.

"Even a blind man could've told that the coin was counterfeit." He poked his finger into her forehead. "You Balts are tenfold more vile and treacherous than Jews. So don't tell me that you give a damn about Renate's fate. If I told you she was safe, you'd be dismayed. What you're hoping to hear is that she's suffering. That would be music to your ears. Nothing delights you more than seeing someone you've always envied fall. That's what you live for."

"Wrong. That's what *you* live for." In a swift movement, Aurelia closed her fist around Sebastian's finger and wrung it back, causing the joint to crack.

Sebastian blanched but did not make any noise, despite the pain shooting through his hand up to his elbow. "You'll pay for this."

Aurelia ended the torment promptly but continued holding onto his finger. "Unlike you, I'm content being a meager mite. Creatures like me live through famines, revolutions, epidemics. But you're spinning your wheels towards a precipice, dear brother. We know what happens to ambitious men. Want to end up like Hermann Lichtner?"

Hypnotized by his sister's grim prophecy, Sebastian stood silently, the image of his burned client resurrected in his memory. When he finally shook off the stupor, Aurelia was gone.

***

Passing by the Napoleon Bistro on Castle Street, Sebastian spotted Theodor Nekrasov, a ruddy twenty-three year old accounting clerk of Russo-German extraction who worked at the city hall. Theodor was enjoying a chocolate-filled croissant with coffee and flipping through a men's fashion catalogue. At this stage of agitation and angst, Sebastian felt a strong urge to talk to someone whose worldview differed dramatically from his own. Even though Sebastian did not think very highly of his pudgy acquaintance, he kept him around as a form of antidote. Theodor was a walking sedative, a valerian root tablet in the human form. Instead of agonizing over the meaning of life, he set realistic, achievable goals, like procuring a new cashmere scarf, or a new pair of leather gloves to match his shoes, or planning a trip to a sanatorium on the Baltic coast. His warm, cozy, roomy belly could accommodate an entire tray of freshly baked marzipan rolls. His modest intellectual appetite could be satisfied with a crossword puzzle and a short story from the *Niva* magazine.

All in all, Theodor had the languid appeal of a well-fed, well-groomed, well-behaved house cat. He enjoyed reasonable success with women, though they were not of the same caliber that would interest Sebastian. Unlike his ambitious friend, Theodor did not chase heiresses or rich widows. He was perfectly content keeping company with working girls—hospital orderlies, shop clerks and children's nannies. Occasionally he aimed as high as telegraphists and school teachers, who were considered in a different league altogether. It was not uncommon for him to be sighted strolling at the foot of Mount Gediminas with a housemaid on each arm. He seemed in no hurry to settle on any one in particular. His life was too plush, too sweet already. There was no pressing need to end his bachelorhood. He always carried a jar of minty lip balm in his pocket. He was arguably the most kissed man in Vilnius. Some would even go as far as suggesting that he got more than kisses, judging from that look of contentment and satisfaction on his face, but those were just theories. Theodor himself did not brag about his conquests. There were no scandals or dark secrets attached to his name. He always returned his lady friends home to their parents at a decent hour. As a result, he was always welcome at their dinner tables. The vast majority of the meals he consumed were cooked by someone else. There was no way he could eat that well on a clerk's salary.

At the sight of Sebastian, who looked like he never had time for a buttered baguette or a rendezvous, Theodor felt pangs of pity. An attorney's life is so frantic, so joyless.

"Join in, Messer," he greeted his friend. "Their strudels are out of this world. Try the one with strawberries and cheese. My treat."

Ignoring the amicable gesture, Sebastian pushed his fists into the tabletop. "Has Aurelia been pestering you?"

Theodor peeled another flakey layer from the croissant and shook his head. "I haven't seen your sister in weeks. She must be pestering someone else."

"You better be telling me the truth, Nekrasov."

"Easy, man. Don't rattle the table. You'll spill my coffee." The last thing Theodor needed was a stain on his light summer trousers.

"I've got no time for games."

"You never have time for anything. And why would I lie to you?"

"I don't know anymore." Sebastian shrugged and dropped into the chair across from Theodor. "Aurelia enjoys playing amateur detective, and so far you're the only person who knows about that widow in St. Petersburg."

Theodor dumped a third sugar cube into his coffee. "Are you asking me if I've been discussing your non-existent love life with your sister?" Fie! Theo had dance parties to attend, macaroons to eat, telegraph girls to fondle.

"I just know that my sister has a way of extracting information, distorting and spreading it. Somehow she found out about Lydia. She spreads rumors like rats spread plague. I really don't want to become known to the world as some desperate wife-hunter."

Theodor clicked his tongue. "That's quite a piquant scenario you've concocted in your head, Messer. Are you sure you don't have a fever?"

Sebastian felt his forehead. It was the second time someone was insinuating that he had a fever. Looking back, yes, he had been suffering from chills and general malaise.

"Just bear with me, Nekrasov, will you? I didn't sleep for

two days. You cannot blame me for my wavering trust in humanity. I just lost my most prominent client."

"So I've heard. God rest Lichtner's soul."

"He was gracious enough to give me a severance." Sebastian picked up a fork and began toying with it. "I just don' know what to do, Nekrasov."

"I already told you: try one of their strawberry and cheese strudels. For starters. Then you can try a slice of their quail egg quiche and barley soup for lunch."

Sebastian grimaced. "All you think about is food. It's like your brain lives in your stomach."

"I can't help it." Theo did not look offended in the least. "That's the way God made me."

"I'm asking you a serious question about my future. Maybe this disaster with Lichtner is a sign that I should give St. Petersburg another chance. Ever since the graduation I've been holding a grudge against that city."

"Come on, Messer, we've been through this a hundred times already." Theodor cleared his throat and assumed a lecturer's tone. "Those pompous snobs in St. Petersburg will hand you your diploma and kick you back to where you came from. You can work in any other corner of the Empire, just not in the northern capital. You see, in order to practice law in St. Petersburg you must be born there, in the right part of the city too, in the right family. Accept it!"

Sebastian shook his head in protestation. "No, don't ask that of me. I'm not ready to give up on my dreams."

"What's so remarkable about St. Petersburg anyway?" Theodor went on thinking out loud. "How many trips to the Hermitage can you make before those statues and paintings start blending into one? Just get an illustrated album. You'll have to put up with the arrogance and the prudery of the natives just so you can brag about renting a room on Nevsky

Prospect. Why bother? You could live like a king right here in Vilnius. Your father has already paved the road for you. All you have to do is stroll down that road in your fancy English leather shoes."

"It's not the same. I've milked this city for what it's worth." Sebastian winced as he loosened his tie. "I'm feeling stifled."

Theodor burst into chocolaty low-pitched laughter that resembled a cat's purr. "You've been practicing law for eighteen months, and you're already feeling stifled? Listen to yourself, Messer. You make it sound like we're living in some provincial dump. You think Vilnius is a second-rate city?"

"It's an *occupied* city," Sebastian emphasized gravely.

"Why should that matter? It was good enough for your father."

Sebastian reclined against the back of the chair and lolled his head back. "Something needs to happen in my life, something fundamental. I either need to find a prestigious position or make a stellar match, or both. I cannot see myself spend the rest of my life in Vilnius, handling small-scale patent transactions for local businessmen."

Theodor's saintly patience was starting to wear thin. Apart from his surname, he had no tangible ties to Mother Russia. All that talk around Sebastian's existential angst was interfering with his digestion. Internal venom corrodes the lining of the stomach, as any doctor will confirm. Theodor worried about his friend, who had grown thin and gaunt over the past two years. He could easily see Sebastian dying of a gastric ulcer.

"The best things in Russia are German," Sebastian resumed. "Before Peter the Great, Russia was a quasi-Asiatic wilderness crawling with bears and bearded peasants. And I, being German by blood, have as much right to enjoy the benefits of living and working in St. Petersburg as anyone. Wherever you turn, you can see that German touch. Why should I be banned from the very city that my ancestors helped create?"

Theodor spread his greasy fingers. "Because... because people are greedy bastards." He could not think of a better answer. "They steal each other's ideas and then ban each other all the time. How is it different from what's being done to Lithuanians? Vilnius used to be their city. Now all the signs are in Cyrillic. The younger generation doesn't know any different. But you think the old-timers were thrilled to see their homes pillaged? Yet I don't see you outraged by the way they were treated."

Sebastian hadn't expected a heated opus in defense of the Balts from his seemingly apolitical friend. "Oh, Theo, don't tell me you're one of those... sympathizers who read *Aušra*?"

"I'm not one of anything." Theodor threw his napkin on the table. "I'm a glutton and a philistine. Give me a juicy lamb chop and a buxom nurse, and I'll be content. In this sick and twisted world, my only loyalty is to my stomach."

"I can't believe my ears, Nekrasov. What made you change your philosophy? You always insist that the world is this glorious place."

"That's right. It is to me. I surround myself with delectable food and cheerful people, no matter what language they speak. Everyone likes bread pudding with berry sauce. You, on another hand, always seek new methods of self-torture. This is why you look like a skeleton dipped in wax." Theodor checked his pocket watch. "Now, I'm asking you one last time: do you want that strudel or not? I'm heading to the office in a minute."

Sebastian looked down at his chipped fingernails. "Fine, get the strudel."

***

Frau Jung ambushed Aurelia at the door of Kunstakademie. "Any news? Talk to me. What's that look on your face? I don't like it. Have you seen your brother? Did he say anything about Renate's whereabouts?"

Aurelia exhaled and pulled her bonnet off. "It'll take nothing short of Spanish Inquisition to make Sebastian talk. I'll try again. Aggressive assaults don't work on my brother. Slow corrosion is the key. If you follow and annoy him long enough, he'll start cracking."

Elsa cupped Aurelia's face. "I don't want you pressing Sebastian anymore. Just leave him alone for the time being. Don't be a nuisance."

"But I'm always a nuisance to him. It's one of my few guilty pleasures in life. He's so pompous, like a turkey." She stretched her neck and inflated her cheek. "Gobble, gobble!"

"I can imagine. But now isn't the time to awaken the vulture inside that turkey. If you must interact with him, make sure there're other people around." Elsa sighed and brushed Aurelia's hair back, revealing a tiny scar on her temple. "Remember the night your brother left you here?"

Aurelia frowned, straining her memory. "It was raining."

"It rains every other day, silly. What else do you remember?"

"The sole on my right boot was detaching. My stocking was wet."

"And... what else?"

"I wasn't feeling very well. My head was aching."

"Do you remember why it was aching? You had a gash along your hairline. When you stepped into the parlor and crouched by the fire, I noticed the crimson trails running down the left side of your face. You were wearing a plaid dress with a white lace collar which was stained in blood.

You were so very quiet and watchful. The older girls called Dr. Klein at once, and he applied stitches. Have you no recollection of that?"

"Not really. I remember the wet stocking, but not the doctor's visit."

"He gave you a light sedative so you wouldn't squirm, just a few drops of morphine. But do you remember how you got the gash in the first place? Your brother maintains it was an accident, that you tripped on a box and hit your head against the edge of his desk."

"It's possible." Aurelia shrugged, anxious to end the conversation. "The house was a mess after my mother's death. Sebastian was getting rid of her things."

"Somehow I'm not convinced that it was an accident. I've known you for nine years, *Liebling*. You're agile and balanced enough to be a tightrope walker. I'm certain it was your brother's handiwork. I still remember the expression on his face when he dropped you off."

Elsa walked over to the credenza where she kept her student's individual paper files and pulled out a letter dated 1875. The fragile paper bore a few brown stains that looked very much like dried blood. The schoolmistress handed the letter over to Aurelia.

Dear Frau Jung,

I am leaving my recently orphaned half-sister Aurelia Roberta Messer in your care. My current academic obligations preclude me from serving as her guardian, as I am bound for St. Petersburg to pursue a diploma in law. Aurelia grew up hearing Lithuanian. Our father had died before she was born. In light of her mother's pernicious

Baltic influences, Aurelia's German is quite poor. I trust that you will raise her with to respect her noble paternal heritage. It is my sincere hope that one day I may be proud to claim blood kinship to her.

Best regards,
Sebastian Adolf Messer

With a contemptuous chuckle, Aurelia handed the note back to the schoolmistress. "Pernicious Baltic influences... Lying bastard! Mama Sybil always pushed German on me above all other subjects. The language of the merchant class, she'd say. Was my German really poor when I arrived?"

Elsa hugged the girl impetuously. "I honestly don't remember. You didn't say much in the beginning. Just promise me you won't provoke your brother. I've already lost Renate. I couldn't bear losing another one of my girls."

Such fervent exhibition of tenderness left Aurelia feeling puzzled. She was not accustomed to Frau Jung paying much attention to her.

"Don't fret about losing me. I'll stay with you until I'm thirty-five. If my brother stops paying tuition, you can move me down to the basement where the cat lives. Together, we'll keep your school free of mice." Aurelia tensed up in Elsa's embrace. "May I ask you something?"

"Go on."

"Perhaps I shouldn't. You'll think me bold and presumptuous."

"I'd never think that of you. You can ask me anything."

"Next time you are purging your late daughter's inventory, do you think I could have one of her things?"

Elsa released her and backed away in horror. "Fräulein

Messer!"

Aurelia fanned her fingers in self-defense. "I'm not some sort of brazen opportunist who swoops down like a vulture on other people's sacred possessions. Renate told me about the easel you gave her as a gift. She bragged about it all the way home. If there're more things you're looking to get rid of, please keep me in mind."

CHAPTER 9

The Stone and the Oak

Raven's Bog

By the seventh day of her self-imposed confinement, Renate had filled out an entire sketchbook with images of infernal torments reserved for her father's murderers. Her mourning had taken an unexpected turn, one that left her with a mixture of confusion, horror and amusement. The screaming fit Renate had so dreaded never repeated. She could not beat another cry out even if she struck herself in the chest with a fist. Tears would not flow freely. Dry, silent rage set in, growing beyond the core of her heart, finding expression in the form of gruesome illustrations. She wondered how Vati would react to her recent artistic exercises. A balanced, cool-blooded German girl from the merchant class does not nourish such savage passions. But Renate was not even sure if she had a nationality or a class anymore. She had been pulled from her usual social environment. The term "German Heiress" no longer applied. Her new title would be "Polish Farmer's Wife". She had Vati to thank for the transformation.

Whenever she tried to picture what Hermann looked like

in his last hours, her imagination would not go past a certain point, as if some internal defense mechanism was at work. The images of his murderers were a different story. She could easily envision every pore, ingrown hair and bead of sweat on those scums' faces. Inventing exquisite tortures for them and fleshing them out in bold colors became the axis of her mental activity.

All that creative exertion made her hungry. She would not mind one of Agatha's rustic delicacies. A slab of calf liver dusted in flour and fried with onions sounded rather tempting.

On her way to the kitchen, Renate heard some strange groans and whispers. She pressed her ear to the closed door and recognized Agatha's loose-lipped murmur.

God, I am askin' you, nay, I am commandin' you through the Stone and the Oak: utter the word, stop the blood from runnin' out our master's veins, from temptin' the soul out of the body. You better tempt the soul out of the tree that has become parched, you better let the blood out of the grass that has been cut by a scythe.

When Renate opened the door, she saw Thaddeus sitting on the floor with his back against the wall, his shirt and pants drenched in blood. It was impossible to tell where the blood was coming from. Agatha was kneeling by his side, mumbling spells. Antanas and Bronia, their arms around each other, were observing the ritual from a slight distance. Lame Magda was picking her nose, rocking back and forth.

"What's all this?" Renate asked, grabbing an apple from the hanging basket. "How did Master Dombrowski come to be butchered?"

"It's nothing," Thaddeus whispered. "Go back to bed, Fräulein Lichtner."

"No, let me see," Renate insisted, her mouth full of apple.

"If your pregnant milkmaid can handle the sight, so can I."

At a closer look she saw that the blood was gushing from a wound on the palm of his left hand. Bronia, who was as talkative as her husband was taciturn, explained what had happened.

"So the master and Antanas were sawin' wood in the shed. The bench wobbled, the block slipped, and the blade went straight into the master's hand, rippin' the flesh and grazin' the bone." Bronia described the incident nonchalantly, as losing fingers, eyes and teeth was a trivial event on the farm. "My idiot husband was drunk. He crippled the master."

"Peace, Bronia," Thaddeus intervened. "Don't blame Antanas. I'm the one who offered him a swig of vodka. It wasn't even distilled properly. We shouldn't have been sawing so late anyway. And there wasn't enough daylight. I should've hung a lantern on the wall. Now I'm paying for my own lack of foresight. Same thing could've happened to Antanas."

Still chomping on the apple, Renate stood over him to assess the severity of the injury. "Well, this looks ugly enough. You need a doctor."

Thaddeus chuckled with his mouth closed. It was hard to tell if he was laughing or stifling nausea. Antanas and Bronia, emboldened by their master's example, also started laughing.

The nervous snorting sounds peeved Renate. "What's so amusing?"

"Don't take offense, Fräulein Lichtner." Thaddeus opened his inflamed eyes and glanced at her for the first time. "This isn't Vilnius."

"So I've noticed!"

"The nearest doctor is twenty kilometers away."

"Then you should send Antanas. It won't take him long to

get a horse and a cart ready."

"No, it's too late and foggy."

"Well, it's the least he can do for you after nearly slicing your hand off. With any luck, by tomorrow morning you'll get some earnest medical attention."

Thaddeus grinned through pain. "No worries. Agatha has everything under control."

"What exactly is she doing?"

"My mother is castin' a spell to slow down the bleedin'," Bronia explained. "When Magda walked into a bear trap, we did the spell, and that's how we managed to save a few of her toes. Otherwise she would've lost her whole foot."

Renate spat out the apple seeds and pushed Agatha aside. "I'll need a needle and some thread, something thin but sturdy. Sheep yarn won't work. We'll also need some hot water and something for the master to bite on."

While Bronia was looking for sewing materials, Antanas gave Renate a dirty dish rag. Agatha observed the commotion from the corner. She was not ready to take orders from a stringy-haired brat who had so rudely interrupted the sacred healing ritual.

"This'll have to do," Renate said, folding the rag and stuffing it between the patient's teeth. "Surgeon Lichtner to the rescue."

As she stuck the needle into the tattered skin, she began singing "The Faithful Hussar", a German folk ballad she learned from her father's workers.

> *A faithful soldier, without fear,*
> *He loved his girl for one whole year,*
> *For one whole year and longer yet,*
> *His love for her, he'd ne'er forget.*

This youth to foreign land did roam,
While his true love, fell ill at home.
Sick unto death, she no one heard.
Three days and nights she spoke no word.

Unable to see the servants' faces, Renate sensed that the sound of a foreign language disturbed them. Her song could have been a satanic incantation for all they knew. The main target of her aggression was Agatha, who had made her feel unwelcome since day one. Renate had not forgotten the ugly dress, the messy hairdo and the surfeit of disparaging remarks. There were twelve verses in the ballad. She sang the last one in a particularly sinister voice.

A long black coat, I must now wear.
A sorrow great, is what I bear.
A sorrow great and so much more,
My grief it will end nevermore.

Having finished sewing up the wound, Renate pulled the towel from the patient's mouth and blotted the sweat from his forehead.

"See? It wasn't so bad. Bismarck himself would've been impressed by your stoicism."

Thaddeus' dusty-blue eyes exuded a mixture of gratitude and confusion. "Who's Bismarck, again?"

It was an earnest question. Feigning ignorance was not in his nature. "You should rest." Renate rubbed his upper arm. "We'll talk about Prussian politics some other time. Would you like me to sit with you for a bit?"

"I'd rather go for a walk. It's awfully stuffy in here. I'm breathless and dizzy."

"It's from the blood loss. Your clothes are soaked. You

85

can expect to feel weak and sleepy for the next few days."

"I'd like to go for a walk all the same." His left hand in a sling, Thaddeus pushed his right hand against the wall, trying to stand up, which only exacerbated the vertigo. "Get me out of here."

Antanas and Bronia swiftly rushed over and helped him to his feet. Then Renate stepped in and offered her shoulder for him to lean on.

"I'll go with the master," she told the servants with a dismissive nod. "He promised to show me the cemetery."

CHAPTER 10

Atonement

My dear little son,
Little son—little apple,
What have you thought of,
What have you decided,
In your young days?
Little son—little flower,
Here are standing
Your parents
And older sisters
They want to... to talk.
Dear little son, wake up,
Talk in lovely little words,
Little son—little flower.
       —A Lithuanian lament

The family cemetery was three hundred meters away from the house, but it took Renate and her host at least half an hour to cover that distance. Thaddeus made frequent stops, doubling over and heaving, his hand still on Renate's shoulder. She could sense he was losing steam, as the grasp of his fingers was growing weaker and his walk sloppier. A few times he stumbled. The stains on the bandages indicated that his wound continued bleeding, though not as profusely as before the surgical intervention. Although conscious of his suffering, Renate refrained from suggesting that they turn around and go back. Thaddeus wanted to spend the evening at the cemetery, and she had taken it upon herself to escort him there. So she kept on walking, illuminating the path before them with a lantern. Milo, the shaggy mongrel was following them a few paces behind.

Without the rowdy peasants ruining the landscape, Renate could tune into the beauty of the night. A drowsy yawn of wind ran over the potato field, ruffling the leaves. The steaming bog was like a giant orchestra pit where toads, crickets and grasshoppers performed their crepuscular symphony. An entire civilization of flowers, birds, animals and insects emerged after sunset.

The cemetery was situated at the edge of the forest, with a steep ravine to the left and a stagnant pond to the right. The layout of the burial ground struck Renate as odd. Instead of one big fence encompassing the area, each grave had its own individual picket fence with a small gate. At the St. Bernard's cemetery in Vilnius where her mother was buried all monuments were made of stone or granite. The graves of the Dombrowski clan were marked with wooden crosses painted red and white.

Thaddeus headed towards one decorated with fir branches. Renate could not make out the name carved into the plate, but she assumed it was where his first wife was buried.

"Damn it," he muttered, resting his good hand on the fence.

It was the first time Renate heard him use a profanity. Thaddeus had always been mindful of his language. In retrospect, she realized that none of his servants cursed either. Did they adhere to the same rule when the master was not around?

"Are you in a great deal of pain?"

"Yes. But that's not what bothers me the most. I didn't bring anything for Jolanta. How could I forget? Stupid me."

"What do you normally bring—flowers, holy water?"

"A slice of bread with dried cranberries."

"Why bread? Wouldn't the birds eat it?"

"That's the point. She loved birds, my Jolanta. And they loved her too. They'd eat out of her hands."

Renate pictured the former lady of the house in her traditional dress sitting on a tree stump, her black hair streaming down her bosom and sparrows on her shoulders. The image was a little too sweet for her taste, almost sickening, like a honey-drenched dumpling, something straight out of a Lithuanian revivalist's fantasy. Someone like Dr. Wilczynski, a famous antiquarian and connoisseur of Baltic folklore, would probably beg the late Madame Dombrowski to sit for a painting. Such unpolluted rustic beauty enraptured city intellectuals who had never cleaned out a pigsty with bare hands.

A great horned owl flew over their heads carrying squirming prey in its claws. Renate hung the lantern on the stump of a giant maple tree and shifted her gaze to the row of four tiny graves that looked like ant hills with knee-high fences around them. So those were the Dombrowski infants.

"They all died shortly after birth, despite Agatha's efforts," Thaddeus explained. "God knows, she did everything in her power to save them."

Renate's stomach turned at the memory of the cook's mystical incantations in the kitchen as she was trying to stop the master's blood. "You let Agatha near your wife?"

"Oh yes! And I'd do it again. Her skill is in high demand."

"What skill? Chopping cow's liver?"

"No, midwifery. Expectant mothers from other villages come to Agatha. I'd put my hands into fire for that woman. I wouldn't trust anyone else to deliver my children. If Agatha couldn't save them, nobody else could."

The diffused lantern light streaming on his face erased the tiny lines around his eyes, enhancing the illusion of youth. He certainly did not look thirty. Renate would have given him twenty-four at most, so light and clean were the lines of his profile. *Mein Gott...* So young and already so many funerals under his belt! How many of those could have been prevented?

"Do you still grieve for them?"

"As much as a Christian man is allowed to."

Now that was an original reply. Did Catholics need a special dispensation from the Pope to grieve? She found that talking about someone else's suffering to be pleasantly distracting, if not healing. She did not care much for this man or his dead children, so she could indulge her curiosity without putting any additional strain on her heart. "Exactly how much would that be?"

"It's hard to tell. Here I am, thirty and without an heir. Of course, it's a disappointment."

Renate inclined her head. *Disappointment.* A peculiar word choice. Not sorrow or tragedy. She was still trying to wrap her head around the value system at Raven's Bog, where children's deaths apparently ranked on the same level as crop failures. Such accentuated deprecation of personal loss was a sign of solid moral grounding.

"I shouldn't liken my everyday frustrations to the sufferings of Christian martyrs," Thaddeus continued. "My private wound is no stigmata. Wallowing in sadness makes one idle and useless. And my people count on me for protection."

Renate smirked. "I'm afraid to ask what you think of me. I just spent an entire week in bed. In your eyes I must be a self-indulgent weakling."

"Oh no, you're no weakling." He wiggled the fingers of his injured hand. "Not after what you've done for me. Where did you learn to sew like that?"

"From Mutti. I've seen her work with fine leather. But don't be so hasty to praise me. You should still see a real doctor. You want to save your hand, don't you?"

"Obviously. For the sake of my people."

My people...

Contact with his wife's grave drained Thaddeus of whatever strength he had left. It was as if the remainder of his blood went into the mossy soil. Using her shoulder as a prop once again, Renate led him to the maple tree and made him sit on the exposed root.

"Some things still aren't clear to me," she said, fixing the sling to ensure that his injured hand was positioned at the right angle. "Who's the master here?"

"In the legal sense, I own this land. But in the eyes of God, these people have as much right to live here, pious and hardworking as they are. They weren't always free. Some of them still remember my late father and the old regime."

"I know history, thank you graciously. Many of Vati's friends were abolitionists. I've heard all about the landowners' atrocities."

"Imagine falling sleep and waking up to the sound of the whip cracking. My father acted like the Emancipation Act didn't apply to him. Some of the servants didn't even realize they'd been freed. He'd managed to keep the Czar's degree a secret for some time. I'm still amazed they choose to stay here. I wouldn't have lasted a winter without them. There're no shackles binding them to Raven's Bog. They could've burned the house down. What keeps my people tied to the place where they were abused and tormented?"

"Just don't get any ideas about loyalty or forgiveness." Renate stretched and wrapped the floral shawl tighter around her shoulders. "They don't know any different. I bet half of them don't even believe that cities really exist. If you tell them there're factories, shipping yards and guilds, they'll think it's some sort of devil's ploy to lure them away from the land. Tell me, what's the story with Antanas? Why do you dote on him so? He can do no wrong."

"It's true. I do protect Antanas—as an older brother should. We share a natural father."

"Oh..."

"Somehow our fates got reversed. Antanas should've been born a master, with an imposing statue like his. I look like a dwarf next to him. He's bright, dexterous, a fast learner and a patient teacher. He taught me everything I know about carpentry and blacksmithing. Physically he had an advantage over me, but not socially. My mother was the lady of the manor and his mother a thirteen-year old servant girl named Alesia."

"Was that an act of... subjugation?"

"According to my father, Alesia encouraged him. One day she just sat on his knee and pulled her bodice open. I heard him brag to the neighbor over beer, while the pregnant girl was right there, filling their jugs with beer. I must've been five or six at the time. Antanas was born in a stable."

"Like Jesus, yes?"

"Something like that. His early years were hellish. Growing up, he was no different from any other serf born on this farm. He got whipped and tied to the post often, even for a most trivial offense. One time I brought him water, so I was punished alongside him. We were both bawling in the rain. My mother made sure that both Antanas and Alesia suffered. The thought of her husband bedding a serf was unpalatable to her."

"Why, your story is worthy of an ancient Roman drama." Renate fanned herself with a burdock leaf. "A patrician's wife tormenting a slave girl and her child, locking them in a lion's cage while sucking on a ripe peach."

"But, that's all in the past." Thaddeus refrained from commenting on her reference to ancient Rome, as that subject was outside of his sphere of knowledge. "What's important is that the old ways are gone. And we have Russians of all people to thank for it."

"Why, I didn't realize the Czar was so popular in these parts."

"He's not. Nobody's denying the mayhem brought by the Imperial troops. But, thanks to them, Antanas is a free man. Not that I would've kept him indentured otherwise. I would've freed him anyway, even if the law hadn't changed. Perhaps, my life's mission is to atone for the crimes of my forefathers."

As much as Renate did not relish the idea of human beings buying and selling each other, she found Thaddeus' speech a little heavy on pathos.

"Maybe I shouldn't ask your opinion of my father. You probably think he was an avaricious tyrant who exploited former serfs."

"I don't think that at all. I'd been inside his factory. He had skilled workers operating high-quality machinery. He didn't just lift desperate beggars off the street who'd be willing to work in abysmal conditions for a few kopecks. God knows, there're factory owners who do that, but your father wasn't one of them. I'd never heard of anyone getting maimed on his premises. He was a most ethical employer."

"Just don't accuse him of being charitable or pious," Renate hurried to dispel the myth before Thaddeus placed a halo over her father's head. "Vati bowed to the God of Commerce. If he maintained decent working conditions, it wasn't because he was motivated by love of humanity."

Thaddeus spent a few more hours bleeding, sweating, reminiscing, grinding his teeth and apologizing, until he finally settled down with his head in Renate's lap and his wounded hand clutched against his chest.

"I'm not crushing you, am I?"

"Not at all." Renate was grateful that he stopped fidgeting and bumping her with his elbow. "You're light as a... sack of flour. Go to sleep."

"Yes, it's a perfect night for sleeping outside. I'm sorry if I stained your dress."

"You mean Jolanta's dress?"

"It's yours now. That's one bad thing about linen, it stains easily. I'll ask Agatha to get you another one out of the trunk. She had so many nice dresses, my Jolanta."

My Jolanta... Renate could not hold back a sneer. *My people... My Jolanta...*

Before drifting off into restless feverish slumber, he murmured his wife's name a few more times. His forehead and neck were dripping with sweat. Renate resisted the urge to blot his brow. She had already done enough for him for one night.

CHAPTER 11

The Last Summer Solstice

Vilnius, July 1884

Dr. Wilczynski, a retired surgeon and art collector, had resolved to enjoy what he suspected to be his last summer. Subtle warning signs had been there since winter. No, it was not the giant alarm bell blaring the rapid approaching of Thanatos but rather a dulcet chime telling him gently that his time was trickling out. He had seen enough patients in his medical career to know what vertigo combined with pallor and sudden weight loss meant. He could not point out any specific organ as the source of malady. It could have been his lungs or his liver. Even if some malignancy was slowly eating him up, he was not in any pain. Episodes of lethargy alternated with those of extreme alertness and creative yearning.

Jonas Casimir Wilczynski came from an educated and enlightened Polish-Lithuanian family in which arts and sciences were equally revered. He had graduated from Vilnius University, before it got shut down by the order of Czar Nicholas I. After practicing medicine in Warsaw for a few years, he had returned to his native Vilnius. At a time when vivid interest in ethnic history was bourgeoning in most of European countries, the destructive presence of czarist authorities in Lithuania was growing more apparent. With Catholic abbeys and parishes closing down, Wilczynski became consumed by romantic nostalgia for the Grand Duchy of Lithuania. Somewhere in the mid-1840s he had conceived the idea to assemble and publish a collection of images of the most eminent art and sculptural monuments in order to preserve them for posterity. He named his creation "The Vilnius Album". A fastidious maximalist, Wilczynski was not satisfied with the production quality of local lithographic workshops and had the album printed at the Lemercier Lithographic Workshop in Paris. The album itself consisted of six series, totaling three hundred and sixty images, interspersed with accounts of events of Polish and Lithuanian history. Unrivaled in its scope and artistic merit, the creation became a grandiose monument in Lithuanian graphic art. The iconic images of ornate churches, elegant coaches on the streets of the Old Town and graceful hunters on slender horses immortalized Vilnius as the capital of a subdued but undefeated country.

About ten years later he collaborated with two hundred other national history enthusiasts to form the Museum of Antiquities on the premises of the closed Vilnius University. The mission was to collect, expose and popularize artifacts tied to the country's past. Lithuanian patriots offered their personal collections and organized archeological expeditions to various locations of the former Grand Duchy at their own expense. The press ban of 1860s made it increasingly harder for Wilczynski to find contributors for his publications. His efforts to preserve what the czarist authorities had been trying to stamp out had lasted for forty years and were nothing short of heroic. At home, he spoke exclusively

Lithuanian.

On a rainy afternoon in July, while Wilczynski was organizing old correspondence with his former supporters, many of whom had been deceased for decades, the doorbell rang. The doctor wrestled himself out of the armchair, tightened the belt of his velvet robe and dragged his slipper-clad feet down the hall. Having delegated every other chore to the housekeeper, he insisted on answering the door himself on principle. He had resolved to perform that task until the bitter end. Whoever ventured outside on such a dismal day and trekked through ankle-high street puddles deserved his personal welcome.

When Wilczynski opened the door, his nearsighted eyes sparked with wonder and delight. The mysterious guest was a school girl, around sixteen or seventeen. The tattered umbrella with bent wiring did not do a very good job protecting her from the storm. Water was dripping from the tips of her auburn ringlets. An otherwise comely face was marred by slight irregularity of the skin tone with patches of red above her eyebrows and around her nostrils. As a doctor he immediately determined that she was lacking certain proteins found in dairy and pumpkin seeds. He would have to remember to suggest some dietary adjustments. Apart from that she was ravishing, endowed with the charm of a baby weasel with those clever beady eyes, a sharp nose, a long pliant neck and that air of waifish immediacy not yet hampered by propriety. Wilczynski noticed an embroidered sash peeking from underneath her jacket, a discreet implication that she belonged to the revivalist movement. Dear God, was he dreaming? It had been ages since he received a visit from a young lady, let alone one who appeared to be a fellow patriot. Having pursued and romanced some of the most exquisite women of Western

Europe in his youth, Wilczynski had retained his taste for the unembellished, slightly brusque Baltic type. Those Frenchwomen with their highly stylized mannerisms were too much like bleached flour. The girls who traced their ancestry to the bogs of Dainava had more texture. They wore their hair in loose plaits instead of chignons, did not powder over their freckles and were not afraid to use their teeth and nails during lovemaking.

"Good day, *širdelė*." Sweetheart. He used that Lithuanian endearment on all female specimens, regardless of ethnicity or social status. His formidable age of seventy-eight afforded him such harmless liberties. "What brings you here on a day like this?"

"I deliberately picked the dreariest day of the year." Her Lithuanian was grammatically correct, though her delivery tentative. "I knew this way I wouldn't be competing with anyone else for your attention."

"For you, *širdelė*, I'd interrupt an audience with the Governor himself."

The girl stepped inside, bringing the smell of chalk and paint thinner with her. Wilczynski noticed she was carrying a waterproof leather portfolio. "Your house looks like a museum," she said, looking at the framed lithographs that covered the walls of the hall. "Is there anything I shouldn't be touching?"

"You can touch anything you want."

"Do you even know who I am?"

"Of course, I do. You're an angel who came to whisk me off to heaven."

"Not just yet, sir. You aren't quite ready for heaven."

"An old man can only dream. If only I were sixty years younger..."

"You knew my late mother, Sybil Jocyte of Rambinas."

The doctor let out a nostalgic gasp. "Ah, you must be—"

"Aurelia Roberta. Before she died, Mama scribbled your name and address on a piece of paper and slipped it into my hand. I was seven years old at the time."

"And it only took you nine years to visit me?"

"Mama said not to pester you in vain, not unless my ogre half-brother made my life unbearable."

"And has he?"

"Very much so. But that's not why I'm here."

"Then why are you here, *širdelė*? If you need something from me, this is the time to ask. I don't expect to last much longer."

Aurelia unbuckled the straps of her portfolio. "A little bird told me you were acquiring Baltic landscapes, so I brought a few pieces that I painted during our last trip to Alytus. I thought you'd be interested."

Wilczynski cupped his cold wrinkled hand around her elbow. "Not before you join me for a cup of tea with cognac. My nephew brought me a box of candied pecans. I usually don't appraise art on the empty stomach."

Before Aurelia had a chance to accept his invitation, he took the portfolio from her and escorted her down the hallway. Physical contact with a young female body instantly invigorated the old doctor. His gait had not been that brisk in twenty years.

* * *

Wilczynski's parlor looked like no other in that neighborhood. Not that Aurelia had expected to see standard décor with brass cherubs or a globe on the fireplace mantle. The room was filled with random artifacts for many of which he had no use: an antique harpsichord, a broken typewriter with several keys missing, even a surgical bench. All the items of sentimental value that other homeowners would store in the attic were on display in Wilczynski's parlor.

The only ordinary piece of furniture was a sofa upholstered with burgundy velvet. In a corner of that sofa Aurelia noticed a peculiarly shaped spotted cushion. When she touched it, the cushion came to life and grew muscled paws. A pair of tasseled ears emerged, followed by white fangs. Before long the astonished girl was looking into the slanted eyes of a bobcat.

"Quite an alternative to a spaniel," she said, pulling her hand away.

"Have no fear, he's tame. His name is Vincas."

"How did he end up in your home? I read your article about respecting nature."

"I rescued him from a Russian official who'd gotten him as a kitten but then grown weary of the smell. The man's servant was peddling the beast on the market. There were quite a few bidding buyers, mostly interested in the pelt. So I stepped in. The peddler walked away with a stack of my rubles."

"Why didn't you release Vincas back into the wild?"

"Alas, it was too late for him. He wouldn't survive a day in the woods. He's been gentrified beyond redemption." Wilczynski scratched the bobcat behind the ears. "Isn't that so, old boy?"

The beast threw his head back and yawned. With a little encouragement, Aurelia reached out and rubbed him under the chin. "These creatures are known for bringing down prey twice their size. Aren't you in the least bit afraid that he might turn against you and break your neck?"

"It's always a possibility. Still, I trust Vincas more than I do my fellow humans."

"Mama would've never allowed me to keep such a pet," she said wistfully. "But then, we had Sebastian living with us, so we already had one creature with fangs under our roof."

While the housekeeper was boiling water for the tea, Aurelia played a few pieces by Bach on the harpsichord. To her surprise, the instrument was better tuned than the one at Frau Jung's school.

"It's yours, *širdelė*," Wilczynski said when she finished Minuet in G major. "You don't need to wait until I'm gone. I'll have it delivered."

Aurelia cracked her knuckles one by one. "Alas, I'll have no place to put it. I'm always a hairsbreadth away from being homeless."

The drinks arrived, served in tall clay mugs instead of dainty porcelain cups. Judging from the smell that filled the parlor, the content of cognac exceeded that of tea. The host and the guest sat on the opposite ends of the sofa, the bobcat between them.

"Speaking of your mother, have you been practicing her native language?" Wilczynski's tone suddenly became stern. "I detect pauses between certain words."

"Vilnius is the worst place to learn Lithuanian."

"Why, *širdelė*, it's a most insulting excuse. If you venture outside the city, you'll find the climate much different."

"If you are referring to those illegal barnyard schools popping up all over the countryside, I fear I'll have trouble getting admitted to one. They'll think I'm a czarist censor."

"You'll have to go farther westward, across the border to Klaipeda." Wilczynski wagged his hand, as if the task was as simple as crossing the street. "You're young, unencumbered."

"Where would I stay?"

"With your maternal relations. Of course, it may take some time for you to win back their benevolence."

Aurelia looked down into the steaming cup. "What did my mother do?"

"She defied the convention."

"By marrying a German?"

"By marrying too late, *širdelė*." Wilczynski added a thimbleful of cognac to his tea. "If you aren't in a hurry to go back outside, I'll impart a bit of your family history. The plot is worthy of a Jane Austen novel."

***

Zivile Jocyte's story, as told by Dr. Wilczynski

Zivile was born into a family of prosperous farmers. Being the oldest of four daughters, she enjoyed certain privileges. Her parents, Albertas and Egle were staunch adherents to the tradition and followed the strict principles of priority, which meant that Zivile's younger sisters could not even contemplate marriage until she was out of the house. According to the custom, she was the only one who could practice marriage-related magic, serve as a bridesmaid or attend church outings and youth dances. The three younger girls were banned from these festivities, lest Zivile should look like a spinster next to them. Her doting parents did everything to see her advantageously matched. They would dress her up in costly garments and request Sunday mass in her name. They would even hire beggars and traveling craftsmen to advertise her dowry. That dowry was handsome enough to make many a young bachelor look past Zivile's plain looks and ill temper. Of the four sisters she was the least attractive. As an artist, I've studied thousands of faces. There's no such thing as an ugly Lithuanian girl, not unless she deliberately makes herself ugly. Russians would say: "The first pancake always comes out lumpy." There's some truth to that. And while Albertas and Egle could do nothing to embellish their eldest daughter's masculine face, they could do even less to sweeten her temper.

One would think that with so few natural charms a girl would go out of her way to make herself pleasing to the prospective suitors. That was not the case with Zivile. She kept driving her suitors away. None of them was good enough for her. She saw no reason to settle. Is choosiness a luxury reserved for pretty girls only? It seemed that she would purposely sabotage her parents' efforts.

Having exhausted all their opportunities for marrying Zivile off, Albertas and Egle were faced with an unenviable dilemma: send her either to an almshouse or to America. Zivile could no longer stay in her parents' house. She was blocking her sisters' way to marriage. To everyone's surprise, Zivile left home voluntarily, thus relieving parents of the need to make a choice. This act, the very first selfless act on her part, stunned everyone. Instead of going to America, like others in her situation would, Zivile went eastward, to Vilnius. Her first job was scrubbing floors at the hospital where I was performing surgery. One day we started talking. I don't remember what prompted that conversation, but I do remember the wooden comb in her hair, an early courtship gift from a jilted suitor. She told me her story, how she grew estranged from her parents after they'd sunk so much money into matchmaking. It wasn't her goal to vex them. She simply didn't like any of the suitors. Besides, the prospect of spending her life on a farm didn't excite her. She was much happier in Vilnius, scrubbing floors.

There was no bitterness, no self-pity in her voice. Her crude candor moved me. She was no damsel in distress. I recognized potential in that girl and offered to pay for her nursing classes on the condition that she'd spend three years working for me. After fulfilling her obligation to me, she found a position at a tuberculosis clinic in Palanga. It was there that she met your father, Attorney Messer. He was fed up with the false pleasantries of the women from his own social circle. I understand why he would choose someone like Zivile to spend his last months with. His colleagues thought he had gone mad and blind. I say, illness had finally opened his eyes. Yes, I was present at their wedding ceremony in place of Zivile's father, who'd died by then. Little Sebastian was holding the rings. I still remember the boy's face. He tried to be brave and composed for his bedridden father, though his left hand was clenched into a fist.

***

"So the Lithuanian Cinderella turned into the evil stepmother," Aurelia said in response to Wilczynski's narrative. "I know it's tempting for you to idealize your protégée, but she'd been nasty to Sebastian. I'm paying for her crimes now. My brother hates me."

"I'm sorry to hear that."

"Don't be." Aurelia did not believe for a moment that the old man was sorry about anything. "After all, I owe my existence to you, Doctor. Without your patronage my mother never would've met Albert Messer. You played the role of her fairy godfather. Perhaps, you have some magic left to spare? Could you do for me what you've done for Zivile? I'm not asking you to introduce me to a prince or to turn my wet boots into glass slippers." She reached out for the portfolio. "All I'm asking for is your honest opinion."

She started pulling out her watercolors and charcoals and spreading them over the sofa. Wilczynski's gaze shifted from one landscape to another as he struggled to find traces of brilliance in Aurelia's work. Alas, all the fondness he felt for the spirited girl did not make her drawings more appealing in his eyes. He was mildly intrigued by some of them but not enraptured. As much as he hated to admit, Zivile's little girl was no asset to the Lithuanian artistic pantheon.

"Well?" she said impatiently. "Can you think of a suitable venue for my collection?"

Wilczynski shook his head. "I'm sorry, *širdelė*. I cannot help you."

"But what about your mission to discover new talent?"

"Alas, I don't detect much of it in your work."

Aurelia blinked a few times and tugged on her earlobes. Was her hearing deceiving her?

Was it the same man who called her an angel and offered his harpsichord? Were all those gallantries and compliments for naught?

"I realize my technique isn't perfect, but it will improve."

"Not significantly. I've seen enough paintings in my lifetime. Truthfully, you'll never rise above high-level mediocrity, even if you apply yourself. Stop wasting painting supplies, *širdelė*."

"Don't call me that." Aurelia began to frantically assemble her drawings. "I don't understand why you're being so cruel."

"It would be far crueler on my part to tell you that your work was exceptional. That would only perpetuate your delusion."

"But you helped my mother."

"Yes, I sent her to a nursing school, not a ballet academy. I helped her cultivate the talents she possessed, not the ones she lacked. You need pork to make sausage."

"I'm sorry that my... pork wasn't juicy enough."

That day would be eternally veiled in shame for Aurelia: she had allowed another human being to see her tears.

CHAPTER 12

If Not for the Golden Summers

Raven's Bog, July 1884

The weeks following Thaddeus' injury were trying for the inhabitants of Raven's Bog. Unaccustomed to idleness, the master drove everyone crazy with endless apologies. As soon as it became evident that he had dodged the risk of gangrene —all thanks to Renate's efforts to change the dressing frequently—his apprehension turned to ardent self-blame. Truly, he had picked the worst time to get injured, when every pair of hands counted. He still insisted on accompanying his men to the fields, even though he could not do any earnest work. Whenever he tried using his good hand, the exertion would cause the wound to start oozing again. Not to mention, he was still weak from the blood loss.

"Poor Antanas suffers the most," Thaddeus lamented. "He must work for two, all because of my recklessness and stupidity. I failed him."

The blacksmith was perfectly capable of leading the workers himself, and he did not mind the responsibility in the least, but Thaddeus did not see it that way.

"I know Antanas. He puts on a brave face for me, but

deep inside he's overwhelmed."

The temptation to peek under the bandages to check on the progress of healing was too strong. Whenever Renate caught him pulling his left hand out of the sling and trying to unroll the dressing, she reprimanded him as if she would a toddler. There was still a risk of infection, and Renate would hate to see her hard work to go to waste. She had not cleaned, sewn and dressed the wound for nothing.

When Renate suggested that, perhaps, he should try reading to fill his time, Thaddeus gave her a sheepish smile. After going through Jolanta's trunk, they found a few volumes of Adam Mickiewicz. For the first time in his life, Thaddeus read *Konrad Wallenrod*, an epic poem set in the 14th century Duchy of Lithuania written in protest against the late 18th century partition of the Polish-Lithuanian Commonwealth. The poem, consisting of six cantos, told the story of a fictitious Baltic pagan adopted and reared by his people's long-standing enemies, the Teutonic Knights. It was a lyrical exploration of ethnic and religious identity.

The unexpected pleasure Thaddeus derived from reading only exacerbated his guilt. If he got addicted to literature, it would be a disaster. He envisioned himself lounging in a hammock under an apple tree, indulging his intellect, while his people toiled in the fields.

"We shouldn't do this again," he told Renate as he handed the book back to her with a trembling hand. "It's sinful. I see why some people say that books are dangerous."

As aggravating as supervising his recovery could be at times, she was grateful that it provided a neutral conversation topic and bought her some time. As long as they discussed the healing of soft tissues and regrowth of blood vessels, they did not have to address Hermann's will and what it would require in order to put it into effect. Their relationship had started as that of a host and refugee and unexpectedly changed into one of patient and surgeon, but the game of evasion could not continue indefinitely.

Coming in contact with Thaddeus' blood had given Renate insight into his soul and deepened her conviction that they made of entirely different substances. The gap between them was not growing wider, just more apparent as the fog that enveloped them in the first few days had started to burn off. Renate admitted that he was not a born simpleton, just academically deprived and intellectually neglected. Alas, his parents had never bothered to expose him to sophisticated literature or progressive ideas. As result, certain parts of his brain were never awakened. Had anyone engaged him in stimulating discussions? Was his first wife a reader and a thinker? Based on the pristine condition of the book, it was safe to assume that Jolanta either took exceptionally good care of her miniscule personal library or she never accessed it at all. The latter possibility seemed more plausible. What if Thaddeus had been born in a worldlier, more refined and well-traveled family? Perhaps, there was hope for him yet. There were seeds of critical thinking in him. Would those seeds sprout one day? If Renate could convince him to pick up a book once, she could probably do it again. If she could salvage his hand, perhaps the same applied to his mind?

***

The process of pulling out the stitches was akin to that of unveiling a monument. Armed with a pair of scissors, the most appropriate tool she could find, Renate started pulling the thread from the freshly scarred flesh. All in all, she was pleased with the results of her novice operation.

He had lost some sensation and strength in the palm itself, but his fingers had retained their mobility and dexterity. He would not be able to lift heavy wood logs for a while, but he would be able to resume light carpentry.

"I'm a rude boar," Thaddeus said. "It occurred to me that I've spent the last two weeks apologizing to my people, and I haven't thanked you once."

"Please, hold still and try to be quiet."

Thaddeus complied and steadied his hand, but that only lasted for a moment. "You've averted a disaster. You've saved my people from a hungry death."

Renate broke from her task and looked up, hoping that eye contact would make him take her words more seriously. As soon as she lifted her face, he leaned over and kissed her on the corner of her mouth.

She dropped the scissors. "Jesus wept. You couldn't wait for me to pull out the last stitches?"

"I've waited long enough."

"Well, maybe you should finish the job yourself."

"No, I shouldn't be trusted with sharp objects."

With an incredulous frown, Renate picked up the scissors and resumed her task. In spite of her bourgeoning sympathy for Thaddeus and her desire to introduce him to great literature, she was not ready for the feeling of his flaxen whiskers on her skin. He snatched that kiss the way an ill-mannered child would snatch a chocolate truffle from a box or a cat would grab a slice of sausage from the table, without any fear of repercussion.

The kiss itself was not terribly executed, not too wet or invasive. At the same time, she got a strange feeling that it was not intended for her. The foggy wistful look in his eyes, as well as a faint aftertaste of vodka he had sipped before breakfast, suggested that he was seeking out his dead wife.

My Jolanta... My people...

With most of the thread removed, Renate rinsed the fresh

scars with witch hazel extract. "Just out of curiosity, who's been opening the vodka bottle for you while you were incapacitated?"

"I've been using my teeth. Antanas might have a stronger back, but I've been blessed with jaws of steel." Thaddeus laughed, and Renate joined him. For the first time in three weeks they were laughing together. Then his face assumed a serious expression. "I almost forgot. I have gifts for you."

Renate's heart sank. "No, you don't."

"Yes, I do. Wait until you see them."

***

The gifts consisted of an amber necklace and a German translation of Guy de Maupassant's *Une Vie*, a story of a naïve convent-reared woman and her road to marital disillusionment. Renate thought it was an odd choice of literature in light of their approaching nuptials. But then, of course, Thaddeus had no idea what the novel was about. He must have delegated the task of choosing the book to the shopkeeper.

As for the necklace, it was just about as exotic and exciting to Renate as a bear trap would be to one of Thaddeus' peasants. Amber was sold on every corner in Vilnius, and she had seen much better quality. What Thaddeus gave her was just a string of murky uneven nuggets. Nevertheless, she put the necklace on immediately. She did not ask him to help her with the clasp, because she suspected that he would seize the opportunity to kiss her on the neck. But the book... The book, she had to comment on.

"I daren't imagine how much this edition cost you. German translations aren't cheap, especially on gilded paper. You shouldn't have splurged."

"No, I wanted you to have it." Thaddeus placed his freshly

repaired hand on hers. "That first week, while you were pining behind closed doors, I went to the city on business. There's a new bookshop on Castle Street. The owner called the novel a masterpiece."

"I agree. I read it in the original last year when it first came out. Frau Jung ordered a shipment from Paris, the latest of Maupassant and Zola." Renate slammed the book shut and laid it aside. "However, I'm curious to see how badly the translator butchered the text."

Thaddeus disregarded her contemptuous remark. "So you speak French?"

"Among others. Languages have always come to me easily."

"That means you can learn Lithuanian and converse with the people in the village to the north of us. There're maybe two Polish speakers in all."

Renate reached out, as if to stroke his cheek, but then pulled her hand away at the last moment. "Why would I waste my time on a dying language?"

"Ah, but that's where you're wrong. Lithuanian certainly isn't dying out around here. It's very much alive, and it has at least six dialects."

"In case you haven't noticed, it isn't spoken by anyone who holds any real power."

"A language doesn't need to be spoken by politicians or academics to survive. It's the common people who keep it alive. Come with me, and I'll show you."

"I'd rather stay home and read the German translation of *Une Vie*."

"No, I insist. Spend the day with me before I return to work. It just occurred to me that you haven't seen most of the land in daylight."

He grabbed her hand and tried pulling her to her feet. In

his mind, they already were making excellent progress. Fräulein Lichtner did not slap him after the first kiss, and she did not turn down his gifts. They even engaged in an argument about books and languages. In time she would see that he was no simpleton. Thaddeus Dombrowski could carry on a conversation with a lady, thank you graciously.

Renate rubbed her temple. "Bother, I have this horrid headache."

"Ah, fresh air will cure it in no time. And if that doesn't help... I have another remedy." His eyes twinkled as he patted the inside pocket of his waistcoat. "Vodka."

"At nine o'clock in the morning?" Renate had a feeling she was not going to complain her way out of that excursion. Thaddeus continued pulling at her fingers with the persistence of a hound eager to go hunting. "Fine, I'll go with you. Just give me a chance to put on different shoes."

Suddenly, they heard screams from the farmyard. It sounded like a giant flock of crows flew over the house. Renate ran to the window and saw a mob of youngsters armed with sticks and belts chasing a boy around thirteen.

Thaddeus placed his hand on her waist. "This is my favorite part."

What happened next looked like some sort of punitive ritual. The crowd gathered around a wobbly bench covered with buckets and sacks of grain. The boy started jumping over the bench, while his peers were hitting him on the back with their belts and chanting. Renate did not understand the words, but it sounded like "Kill the bastard!" Eventually he ended up on the ground, and the battery continued.

"What crime did this poor devil commit?" she asked, sliding away from Thaddeus. "Did he steal a chicken? Violate a milkmaid? Well, are you going to just stand there? There's a murder taking place on your property."

"You're right," he said with a sigh. "I should do something."

When Thaddeus appeared on the porch, the mob felt silent and all the commotion ceased. At the sight of the landlord, the boys backed away from their victim. Renate gasped when she saw Thaddeus kick the youngster in the ribs a few times, extracting dull grunts. The boy's red face exuded a peculiar mix of agony and jubilation. It was hard to tell if he was begging for mercy or more abuse. What followed was even more bewildering. Having played his part in the execution, Thaddeus extended a helping hand and pulled the boy up into a brotherly embrace. The rest of the lads began to cheer. They picked up their battered peer and carried him off on their shoulders.

Thaddeus returned to the house glowing with pride as if he had brought down a wild boar or deflected a Viking invasion. Renate was awaiting an explanation.

"What the hell did I just witness?"

"An initiation rite into the youth community. Lads and maidens live in their own world governed by its own set of laws. They harvest, play, dance and court. That novice, Steponas, was just admitted into the inner circle. He's old enough for adult work: sowing, mowing, threshing and blacksmithing. His friends were only testing his physical maturity and endurance. Tonight Steponas will get drunk, and his name will be inscribed into the symbolic book. The welts and the bruises on his back will be forgotten."

"And why did you intervene?"

"My station obliges me. I'm not just the landlord. I'm also the oldest unmarried male. They locals have a word for it—bernas. It's my duty to make sure that the rites are carried out properly. Once I remarry, another man will take my place."

"I see," Renate replied, satisfied, if not entirely appeased. She remembered the slapping game she witnessed back in Alytus. Physical abuse appeared to be a fixed element in all coming-of-age rituals. She wondered what brides and grooms did to each other on the wedding night. "Well, are there any other... customs I should know about?"

"Many more." Thaddeus pulled her into a loose embrace and twirled her. "It takes a lifetime to learn them. I was born here, and I still don't know everything. I'm not of their blood. My line goes back to Warsaw. The difference is subtle but undeniable. Sometimes I feel like a guest at someone else's feast."

Renate pressed her fingertips into his collarbones, not as a display of amicability but as a last attempt to maintain some distance between them. She had allowed him to get this close to her. There was no turning back. It was going to be the new norm, this abundance of insinuating contact. She would have to get used to constant tapping and stroking from him. This man had a very intimate tactile relationship with the universe. He worked, learned and loved with his hands. No wonder the prospect of losing one of them terrified him.

***

At the crossroads about one kilometer south of Raven's Bog stood a meeting hall where youths from neighboring villages, children of landowners and hirelings alike, assembled under the same roof. The gatherings were open not only to active mate-seekers but to newlyweds who had not had their first child yet. The hall served a dual purpose as a massive workshop and a venue for festivities. Within those walls the line between toil and amusement blurred. The evening gatherings provided the youngsters with an opportunity to showcase their talents. The girls spun and embroidered sashes. The boys wove ropes and carved wood. In the middle of the room a dance circle was forming. The participants appeared to be guided by the same instinct as bees or ants. Several melodies were emitting at the same time, tangling together like yarn fibers. Some refrains did not even have words. They were imitations of bird and insect sounds.

When Renate crossed the threshold of the unevenly lit hall, her immediate impression was that of being inside a broken music box with gears spinning out of control.

"There's a different song to accompany every task," Thaddeus said, "from herding to ploughing, milling, spinning and weaving. There's a science to it. You don't sing oat harvesting songs while pulling buckwheat. You don't sing about herding oxen while pasturing horses. You don't sing about fish while hunting deer."

"It all sounds the same to me," Renate confessed.

"Give it time. Eventually, you'll be able to tell the tunes apart. The outsiders who pass through Dainava joke that people here sing more than they talk. Mothers bring their infants in wicker baskets to the fields. The little ones inhale these tunes along with the flower pollen."

Renate's gaze wandered to one of the dimmer corners of the hall that afforded some privacy. She spotted a couple engaged in amorous discourse. The girl was sitting on the boy's knee, while he was pulling flowers out of her wreath and planting kisses behind her ear. Both looked no older than fourteen.

"So this is where matches are being sealed?"

"This is nothing," Thaddeus replied with a wink. "You should come to the harvesting games. That's when the wild merriment begins. Lads put on horse masks and pester the girls, whipping them with juniper twigs."

"And if the merriment gets out of hand?"

"It won't. The young ones are prudent. They know when to stop."

"Do they? That Steponas fellow nearly got killed by his friends."

Thaddeus placed his hand upon his heart. "In my entire life I've never seen anyone get killed or maimed during an initiation game. Able-bodied men are worth their weight in gold. If the lads were to knock one of their own out of commission, it would mean more work for them. Take a look. Our young friend seems to be faring quite well."

Still wearing his sullied peasant shirt, the Steponas boy was standing on top of an ale barrel and singing in his cracking voice, accompanying his performance with rather lewd pelvic thrusts, much to the approval of the onlookers.

"What's he singing?" Renate asked.

When Thaddeus heard that question, his eyes filled with hope. "You... you want to know the words?"

"Don't get any ideas," she curtailed him. "I'm not falling in love with Lithuanian folklore, if that's what you're thinking. I was just curious about what the song was about."

"All right, I'll translate for you." Thaddeus encircled her waist and began whispering in her ear, punctuating the recitation with sighs.

If not for the golden summers,
If not for the blue cornflowers
We wouldn't have ended up here
Where the days pass by in grey.
So silently the summers crawl,
The blooming flowers wilt away.
Silently we wipe our tears
After burying our youth.

We will leave these crossroads
And everything we had -
The youth, the laughter, the tears
And the ones we loved.
I will depart one evening
And won't ever come back.
The cornflowers will blossom in blue
But I won't see them again.

When Thaddeus fell silent, Renate glared at him. "I don't believe you. These aren't the real words."

"Now, would a country boy like me be able to make up something so eloquent on the spot? This lament was written over decades of Czarist occupation. The tears mentioned in the song were shed by more than one person."

"Well, if the song is so melancholic, why was Steponas doing his lusty dance? He was mocking the suffering of his ancestors."

"Ah, but that's what they do. They scoff at their own tragedies. You mean to tell me that Germans don't do the same?"

"No, we Germans don't cry or laugh often. We've about as much feeling as sea bass. Besides, I don't think your question is fair. Germans aren't the subdued nation. We already rule a nice chunk of the continent."

"That's right, I forgot."

"We don't take up as much space as Russians," Renate continued, "but I believe we're superior to them. You don't see the Kaiser frantically imposing censorship and banning press. We have better things to do than stamp out small nations."

She stretched her arm out and made a sweeping motion as if she were spreading flour across a table. "All this doesn't bother Germans. It's endearing and inconsequential."

After observing Lithuanians for a few hours, Renate concluded them to be a paradoxical race. Everything they did seemed counter-instinctive at a first glance. A boy got thrashed by his friends just for turning thirteen, and then, as a sign of great respect, profaned a lament written by his long-suffering forefathers.

Having dismounted from the ale barrel, Steponas waved, directing the audience. Boys and girls swiftly formed two lines facing each other, joining outstretched hands.

"Look, they're about to do the rabbit dance," Thaddeus said. "They expect me to lead. I'm still their *bernas* and all. Come, join me."

Renate racked her brain trying to come up with a plausible excuse not to participate. She could not use her father's death anymore.

"I don't know the steps."

"It doesn't matter. Just follow my lead."

"But I'll ruin the dance for everyone."

"If you miss a step, nobody will remember. If you miss the whole dance, nobody will forget. Just pretend that you're a rabbit and skip."

He flung her into the sea of puffy embroidered blouses, sashes, plaid skirts and floral wreaths.

One of the older lads, a newlywed, started playing a *bandonija*, a type of button accordion. His wife sat on a low bench with a *kankles*, a five-string chordophone in her lap. After the first four instrumental bars, the dancers joined in.

> *A rabbit was running, dancing through the woods.*
> *He met a squirrel and lifted his cap.*
> *Good morning, squirrel, you shall be my kin.*
> *Don't get married—wait a little bit.*

CHAPTER 13

Dethronement

The third gift Thaddeus presented to Renate later that night was a ten-year old chestnut stallion by the name of Dragoon.

"He used to be Jolanta's," he said, running his fingers through the horse's mane. "She brought him in as a part of her dowry. He's not very fast, but he is quite strong. You wouldn't find a gentler, more docile beast. You can ride him around the farm like Jolanta used to. Maybe you can use him for your paintings. He'll stand still for you."

Renate never understood the appeal of horses. As an art student, she was expected to swoon over their grace and agility. Having done about a dozen watercolors featuring horses to appease Frau Jung, she was not looking forward to painting another equine.

"Go on, pet him, so he'll get used to your scent and touch." Thaddeus grabbed her hand and brought to Dragoon's shivering nostrils. "Aren't they soft? Truly, he's one of a kind."

Renate thought that Dragoon looked like every other horse. There was nothing unique about his coloring. She had seen richer chestnut hues and glossier coats. Dragoon's tail was sparse and brittle, his eyes inflamed and foggy, and his upper teeth yellow and chipping, the inside of his ears crusty with some sort of skin parasite. And that string of foamy slime hanging from the corner of his mouth! For an animal that occupied such a privileged spot in the master's heart, Dragoon looked rather neglected.

"Simply charming," Renate said, pulling her hand away and wiping it on her skirt.

"You like him, really?" There was timid jubilation in Thaddeus' voice.

"What's not to like? All that snorting and puffing is pure music."

"Thank God. Poor Dragoon was so distraught when he lost his old mistress. He drove her body to the cemetery. He's not very good with harness, but on the day of the funeral he allowed me to put the collar and the traces. Animals are so clever and perceptive. I thought it was important that he saw Jolanta laid to rest. Otherwise he would've thought that she'd abandoned him. He didn't eat or drink for a week. I spent several nights in the stable, praying to St. Francis to heal him."

Not the most skilled actress in the world, Renate struggled to keep her face from twisting into a contemptuous grimace as Thaddeus related the saga of his dead's wife horse.

"There's just one problem," she said. "I've never sat in the saddle in my entire life."

"I'll teach you," Thaddeus promised ardently. "Dragoon is a perfect horse to practice on. He won't throw you off, unlike some of the young stallions yet to be broken."

His smirk and the intent stare suggested he was anticipating some token of gratitude. Renate rose on her tiptoes and gave him a light peck on the scruffy cheek, suspecting that it would not be enough. As much as she wished for that to be the moment when they bid each other goodnight, she knew she was not going to get off easy. Thaddeus was not done for the evening. Having softened her up with presents, he felt emboldened to make the next move. The second kiss was longer and more deliberate than the one earlier in the day. This time he bit and pulled on her upper lip a little.

Renate realized she was not dealing with a skittish Jew boy whom she could easily shoo away if he crossed any boundaries but with a grown man twice her age who was accustomed to having his needs satisfied. The breeding season was in full swing. Master Dombrowski would not be excluded from the festivities of the flesh. Ready or not, Renate was expected to participate. Only a few weeks ago the conjugal bed with all its implications seemed eons away. Hermann had never brought up marriage in conversation and always seemed more interested in the continuation of his business than his bloodline. It had always been understood that her potential husband would be a fellow Prussian, or perhaps a Swede, but definitely a Lutheran from the merchant class. She had never gotten as far as attaching an actual face to the fitted charcoal suit, but she could clearly envision the cut of the vest, the pattern on the tie, the shape of the buttons. Yet there she was, in the hands of a benevolent but insistent peasant, a Pole and a Catholic. Sebastian's words rang clearly in her ears. *Your childhood has ended.*

Her lack of enthusiasm did not go unnoticed by Thaddeus.

"You feel flaccid." His tone indicated that he felt sorrier for her than for himself. The sullen girl did not know how to have a good time. "Do I displease you?"

"The only thing that displeases me is the German translation of *Une Vie*."

"Let's see if we can cheer you up." He retrieved the flask from the inside pocket of his waistcoat and pulled out the cork. The smell of spirit burst forth like a convict escaping prison. "Go on, take a sip," he said in the tone of a caregiver administering medicine to an ailing child. "You haven't had anything to drink all night."

Renate scratched her arms nervously. The feeling of cold glass against her lips brought back the memories of the night Sebastian drove her out of Vilnius. "What's in it?"

"Vodka."

"That's all? Are you sure? None of those herbal remedies mixed in?"

"On the graves of my children, I swear there's nothing except for pure old-fashioned vodka—as pure as we can make it on the premise."

Renate yanked the flask from his hand and took a few deep swigs of the liquid fire. It was not easy keeping a straight face with her tongue and gums ablaze. Her throat immediately constricted, all her instincts screaming against the substance. People of her race were meant to drink beer and Riesling, not this infernal beverage. But after the initial struggle with her reflexes she understood what Thaddeus meant. Fire began spreading through her insides, burning away tension and petulance.

"That's my good girl." He took the flask from her and drank a few mouthfuls. "Would I ever offer you anything harmful?"

"I have no idea what you're capable of, Master Dombrowski."

He immobilized her face between his calloused hands, looked into her blurry eyes and rubbed her flushed cheekbone with his thumb. "I know you've been going to bed with a cramp in your neck. I can tell by the angle of your chin. Sometimes prayer alone isn't enough to relieve the pain. That's why God gave us vodka. There's no shame in taking comfort in God's gift. Maybe I'll use vodka to baptize my future children."

Now, that was a fairly profane thing to come out of the mouth of someone who purported to be deeply pious.

"It would take a lot of vodka." The stacks of hay, the rusty ploughs and horse saddles started performing a circle dance. "*Mein Gott*, this is strong stuff."

Thaddeus unbuttoned his shirt and pressed her ear against his naked chest. "Hear that? I've only seen a physician once in my life, and he said he'd never heard such a strong heartbeat."

After a few seconds of listening to the dull rhythmical thumps, Renate straightened up. "Is there a reason you are sharing this with me?"

"Just a bit of reassurance. I don't want you to think that you're marrying a feeble old man. I intend on staying agile and industrious for another fifty years. You'll never be ashamed of me." He cupped her jaw with his mangled hand. "I want you to know that I'm capable of... great generosity." His voice was low and hoarse, as his gaze slid up and down Renate's exposed neck. "I cannot cover you with rubies, but I have other talents. My late wife had tasted of sorrow, but I made damned sure there was pleasure in her life. Until her last days, she was a very satisfied woman, my Jolanta."

My Jolanta. The wretched cow died a martyr's death on the altar of marital bliss, slowly exsanguinated by the repeated stillbirths. After each failed pregnancy, she kept coming back for more. Renate had no trouble believing that Thaddeus was telling her the truth. A primitive woman with primitive tastes. With no galleries or concert halls in the immediate vicinity, the poor thing clung to her spousal bed as the sole beacon of entertainment. The prospect of locking loins with a man like Thaddeus seemed like divine manna. No doubt, Jolanta thought she had married a prince. If Renate could miraculously purge her own head of all her prior knowledge and look at him through the eyes of a sheltered provincial Polish girl, she too would see a prince. Those clean Western Slavic features frosted in flaxen stubble and veiled in the smell of baked potatoes were designed to encourage frequent coupling. As a specimen of his race and class he was ideal. In order to get any pleasure out of intimacy with Thaddeus, Renate would have to forget her innate supremacy.

"So your love ditty has a few more verses?" she asked.

"Nah, the old ditty is finished. I'll sing a new one—if you're ready to listen."

Renate braced for the inevitable. What other part of his anatomy would he demonstrate next? But it seemed like Thaddeus was done showing off, at least for that night. He kept the rest of his clothes on and instead started fumbling with the tasseled drawstrings on Renate's blouse. She did not immediately recoil but she turned her head aside, much to his amusement.

"Bashful, aren't we?"

Bashful! Pig's arse! A German heiress would never blush before a Polish farmer... even if he had just pocketed her fortune.

"I know you're dying to inspect the merchandise," she slurred through her teeth. "Make sure there are no defects. It's not much different from choosing a horse at a market." With cottony fingers, she proceeded to untie the string of her blouse, fully intending to pull the garment over her head, but

Thaddeus stopped her.

"No need for that."

"Why not?"

"The straw is rather coarse. Your back will get scratched. Let's keep it covered."

When it came to little things, Thaddeus showed an abundance of common sense. He did not know much about rotating crops or keeping his servants in line, but at least he thought far ahead to protect Renate's skin. It was the first sensible thing she heard him say all day.

A minute later, she was sprawled on the straw on her back, with Thaddeus on top of her, planting his lips wherever he could. She continued turning her head from side to side to avoid being kissed on the mouth, but not because she found the idea revolting. Quite the opposite, reluctant as she was to admit it, that man ignited her physical curiosity. She did not protest when his hand slipped under her skirt and up her calf, but when he started rubbing the knobs of her knees, she squeezed them tighter together.

"I love someone else." She had to spout those words as a last stand.

"I guessed as much." Thaddeus did not seem surprised or dismayed. "But your father gave you to me, and not him. Dwelling on your first lover won't make your life any easier. I don't expect you to love me, but it would help if you at least liked me. Just a little?" He slapped her thigh, drawing a quick laugh of abdication from her. "Not even half as much as I like you."

Renate was dying to ask him what exactly he liked about her. Was it her stringy hair, her flat chest, her acidic personality, her crude surgical skill or her father's capital? In a way Renate was thankful to Thaddeus for not trying to be romantic or gallant. His nonchalant, good-natured carnality put her at ease.

For the first time, their lips joined in a deep, reciprocal, honest-to-God, grown-up kiss that instantly elevated Renate above her peers. She would bet that none of the girls at Kunstakademie had ever kissed like that in real life. They may have even practiced on each other, reenacting the scenes from the romance novels which Frau Jung despised. None of those girls had lain underneath a thirty-year old man. Renate promised herself she would survive the initiation into adult life with dignity befitting her Brandenburg lineage. If lucky, she would even get some pleasure from the process.

"We don't have a towel," she said when they broke away from the kiss. "Surely, there's an empty sack somewhere."

"We won't need it tonight. I won't take anything that cannot be given back, not before the wedding."

She stifled a chuckle. Of course! Disturbing the mechanical aspect of her maidenhood would tarnish his halo and compromise his soul. Drinking and mauling were allowed, but not consummation.

"Now, if there are things you've done with your first lover," he continued, "things you've been missing, I'd like to hear about them. I certainly don't want you to feel... deprived."

To Renate's chagrin, there was not much to report, no heroic tales from the battlefield. She suspected that Thaddeus figured out how meager her prior experience was and only asked that question to humor her.

"You were the one who told me not to dwell on him," she replied elusively. "Just do what you think is best. I give up."

It took just a few strokes across her loin to bring her to a place that in the past she could only achieve after forty minutes of manipulations and fantasizing. The confined anguish and rage of the past weeks burst forward in violent, vengeful ecstasy. And she experienced it in a drafty stable of all places, with a man who had given her a string of shabby gifts and speeches on atonement. How quickly he found the right key to her, without even trying.

As soon as her breathing evened out, Renate rolled over onto her side and buried her face in the hay. Next time she would have to be firmer, cooler and more resistant.

"You know women," Renate said after a few minutes of silence.

"I knew one woman well. I'd learned her tastes over the years."

"I suppose I'll be expected to learn your tastes as well."

"My tastes are quite simple." He passed the flask to her. "Here, you can finish the rest. There's barely anything left."

CHAPTER 14

Trepidation

"Think the master will marry that German bitch after all?" Agatha asked her daughter while they were kneading sourdough in the kitchen.

"Afraid so," Bronia replied, her rounded belly covered in flour. "He's been givin' her gifts, though she's been turnin' her nose on them. Last night he took her down to the meetin' hall, and then they locked themselves in the stables."

"Pf! That means nothin'."

"That means everythin', Mama, and yer know it." The milkmaid sighed and wiped her brow with the back of her hand. She had spent the morning stringing wild mushrooms and hanging the garlands to dry.

Agatha pushed her sticky fists into the tabletop. "Why wouldn't he marry that Korczak girl one village over?"

"The Korczak girl has no money. Sure 'nough, she's got long raven hair, just like the master likes it, but hair alone doesn't pay taxes. That German... bitch, as you put it, is what's keepin' us all out of the almshouse. If not for her dowry, we wouldn't see another harvest here. By fall we'd be roamin' the nearby farms in search of work."

Agatha's hands sank into the dough. "Says who? Where'd

yer get those ideas?"

"From Antanas." Bronia's voice broke as her colorless eyelashes fluttered. "Things got dire 'round here, Mama. Them officials were knockin' on our door."

"I didn't see no officials."

"The master kept quiet and prayed for a miracle. Like it or not, the German's here to stay. Yer better learn to be nice to her."

The cook exhaled and resumed kneading the dough, doing it with such ferocity as if she were choking an intruder. "Maybe she won't live long. Who knows?"

Bronia flushed and made a sign of the cross. "Have yer no fear of God, Mama?"

"Sometimes I think God turns a deaf ear and a blind eye to Raven's Bog."

Now Bronia was frightened in earnest. "Take it back, Mama! For the sake of yer grandchildren." Her eyes as wide as Imperial ruble coins, she continued making signs of the cross.

"Ah, don't tell me now the thought never crossed yer mind."

"I just don't want my baby to come out deformed or dead."

"Bah! The late mistress was a saint. Never blasphemed. A fat lot of good it did her! All her children were born looking as pretty as buttercups, and all died in my lap." Agatha spat into the scrap bucket. "Three years ago yer had a chance, idiot wench, and yer let it slip away."

"Aw, Mama..." Shaking her head, Bronia backed away from the stove. "Not this again."

Finished with the dough, Agatha started slicing apples for the pie. "That summer, when the first lady was bedridden, yer could've gone with the master to the hayloft." She pointed the knife at her daughter. "But nay, yer were fawnin' over that blacksmith. Too holy to lay with a married man, are yer."

Bronia tightened the floral shawl around her breasts. "Stop it, Mama. Master Thaddeus never fancied me... in that way."

"How'd yer know what men fancy? They're all animals. Yer pet and pinch 'em in the right places to get 'em goin'. Our god-fearin' master is no exception. He was lonesome and could use a little diversion. A smart girl would've grasped at that God-given chance. Yer could've born his child, and we'd be golden. We'd have a hut of our own with a shed and a water-well, a few pigs and chickens to boot."

"Think it's that easy, eh?" Bronia snapped her fingers. "Lay with the master and wake up with a crown 'pon yer head?"

"I didn't say it was easy. But yer never even tried. All that lofty business, purity and chastity, it's for the likes of Lady Jolanta. They don't have to spread cow dung over the potato fields. A milkmaid doesn't stuff her head with such nonsense. She grabs whatever floats down the river, and yer missed that load of booty. For that I'll never forgive yer."

"Never forgive me..." Bronia threw her arms up. "That's just grand, Mama. Keep tellin' yerself that I let a trunkful of gold slip away. What difference did it make for Antanas, bein' a landlord's bastard? He still got flogged and pilloried like any other serf."

"Master Thaddeus is nothin' like his father. He'd have taken care of yer."

"But he does take care of all of us. That's why he's marryin' that... Lady Renate."

Little Magda was sitting on a wooden stool by the oven, her mangled foot underneath her, her face stained with blueberry juice.

"Bitch!" she puckered as she pointed towards the stable. "German bitch."

***

Renate awoke to the sound of metal clanging. Judging from the brightness of the light breaking through the cracks in the walls, it was late morning. Thaddeus was nowhere in sight. To his credit, he had covered her with a horse rug and placed his bundled waistcoat under her neck as a makeshift pillow. Renate strained her memory, trying to replay the events of the previous night, but they all blended into one bizarre Polish-Lithuanian fairy tale in which horror and humor mixed together. Battling vague dread, she raised her throbbing head and inspected her clothes. The fabric was wrinkled but not torn. Buttons and strings appeared to be in place; no traces of blood on her skirt. Renate concluded her virginity was still intact. The same could not be said for her sanity. Not that sanity, at least in the German sense of the word, was a particularly useful virtue at Raven's Bog.

The hangover made the clanging sound coming from the smithy all the more agonizing. Ah, the price one pays for an evening of giddy oblivion! The moment she flung the doors of the stable open, the daylight slapped her in the face as an indignant mother would slap her wanton daughter who had spent the night gallivanting. By then it was probably close to noon. The cows had moved from the meadow to the bog for watering.

Renate tore a handful of mint leaves and stuffed them into her parched mouth to kill the vodka aftertaste, then took a gulp of icy water from a tin bucket. Her reflection in the quivering surface made her cringe. Who was that chewed-up waif with puffy eyes, cracked lips and straw in her matted hair? It was the new Renate, the one who had let a drunken

Pole squeeze her thighs. A girl without standards.

The metallic banging resumed with vengeance, like an entire brigade of demons hammering away. She tightened the laces on her ankle boots and headed towards the smithy, struggling to keep her gait steady.

At the entrance to the dark blazing cave, she paused, mesmerized by the form silhouetted against the flames of the forge. A leather apron thrown over his naked chest, Antanas looked like the Baltic equivalent of Vulcan. The smithy comprised a small autonomous realm, his temple where he was both the deity and the head priest.

"Where is the master?" she asked.

The blacksmith did not turn his head. Bowed over his anvil, he continued forging what looked like an iron cage.

Mein Gott, does anyone here speak a civilized language? I thought he understood Polish. She entered the smithy and positioned herself right in front of Antanas, within reach of the flying sparks. When he finally saw her, he put the hammer aside and grinned, revealing his crooked upper teeth.

"My work made me deaf. Step back, m'lady. The anvil gets pretty hot. If yer get branded, the master won't be pleased."

Renate realized she did not look very imposing in her present state. Not quite the lady of the manor. "Where is he now?"

"Out on business."

"When is he coming back?"

"How am I to know? I put new shoes on Dragoon first thing in the mornin', so you can practice ridin' him. Those were the master's orders."

Antanas turned around, letting Renate know the conversation was over. When she saw his back, her blood ran cold. There was not a patch of skin that was not scarred. Some lesions were pale and flat, while others dark and elevated, suggesting that the scar tissue had built over a prolonged stretch of time. So Thaddeus was not exaggerating when he described his father as a brute. She wondered where the beatings had taken place. Was it in the yard, in plain view of other servants, or inside the barn where she and Thaddeus had spent the previous night? Did the cold earth floor absorb the boy's blood, as the wooden walls soaked in his cries? The violent history of the place was sealed within each brick, each log. And yet, Raven's Bog was not any more cursed or haunted than any other rural estate. Before the abolition of serfdom, the indentured workers were whipped for the smallest offense. If the serf's facial expression was too merry or too gloomy, if he allowed the hunting dogs to come too close to the horses, if a work horse's tail brushed against the landlord's carriage, the overseer would put the birch rods to use. If the overseer was suspected of treating the peasants too mildly, he too would be whipped, often by the master himself. According to the law passed under Catherine the Great, a landlord convicted of beating a servant to death would be sentenced to a fine and religious penance. The mild punishment did not suffice to deter the nobility from homicide. Thousands had died of blood loss and infection. No peasant over the age of twenty-five could boast an unscathed back. Antanas was hardly an aberration. It just happened that his back was the first one Renate had seen up close. The blacksmith was an ambassador from that era. Instead of compassion, she felt superstitious fear. To have survived so many beatings one must have been superhuman. No wonder Thaddeus tiptoed around him. The yellow-haired giant with a scourged back was the true master at Raven's Bog.

THE GATE OF DAWN

***

Mounting Dragoon was about as thrilling as mounting a sagging couch. The docile animal did not respond to spurring, or rather, he had a delayed reaction. Thaddeus had not instructed anyone to give Renate riding lessons. He must have thought her clever enough to figure out the mechanics on her own. It did not escape Renate's attention that the saddle strapped to Dragoon's back was made for a man. It was not one of those dainty sidesaddles that would allow her to ride in a modest fashion without wrinkling her clothes. She had heard that in rural Lithuania women rode horses astride, a fact that astonished Russian travelers. All the better, she thought. The man's saddle freed her from the necessity to worry about posture and balance of weight. A feeble creature like Dragoon would probably get injured if a rider swung both legs to one side.

After a few tepid slaps and kicks, Renate was finally able to make the horse move. From her new vantage point she could see the expanse of fields, wetlands and meadows. For the first time, she heard the sleepy infertile earth speak to her. It was not an amicable address by any means, but rather a declaration of serene indifference. The fields, the bogs and the meadows were not welcoming her, but they were not banishing her either. *There's nothing for you here, but you can stay*, murmured the muddy brook.

The sound of Dragoon's snorting brought back the memories of the previous night. The old horse was the only living witness of their tryst. How many other couples had rolled in the hay underneath his steaming nostrils? By then the home-distilled spirit had worked its way out of her bloodstream, so she could examine the contradicting emotions Thaddeus stirred in her, leaving her exasperated and intrigued her at the same time. How could a man of such stiff piety possess such fine-tuned sensual intuition? As much as she despised his philosophy, she admired his kissing skills. Succumbing to the brash curiosity of one who had nothing left to lose, she was strolling down a mystical corridor. Having opened one door, she longed to see what was behind the next one. It was like tearing a rose apart, petal after petal. *He loves me, he loves me not.*

***

At dusk Thaddeus galloped through the gate, his face glowing underneath a layer of dust. With his sleeves rolled up and his flaxen hair combed back, he came perilously close to the swoon-worthy hero of a Polish historical novel. In that moment he embodied the lofty Slavic archetype hailed by authors like Adam Mickiewicz.

Startling a flock of white hens, Renate leaped to her feet. Thaddeus dismounted, dropped the reins and opened his arms. Truth be told, he had not expected to find her waiting for him at the gate. On his way home, he had wondered what mood he would catch her in upon return. The prickly and volatile German girl was still a mystery to him.

"Where were you all day?" she asked, her fingers rubbing the buttons on his vest.

"Oh, just taking care of a few matters. Estate related."

"Do you want to hear about my day? I tried riding Dragoon. I nearly broke his back. He must hate me."

"He'll get used to you. He stood idle for almost two years. Have you had supper yet?"

"I was waiting for you."

"You didn't have to. You should've asked Agatha to make you something."

"I don't think it would be proper for me to give out orders in your absence. I'm still a guest here."

135

"We'll take care of it soon enough."

"How... soon?" Her voice was faltered.

"Tomorrow afternoon. I spoke to the priest of St. Lawrence's. It's a quaint little church that hasn't changed much since Jolanta and I got married there twelve years ago. Everything's moving forward. I assume you have no objections?"

Renate could not believe he asked her that question. As if her objections made a smidgen of difference! As if Thaddeus in his infinite chivalry would pinch her cheek and put her on a train to Brandenburg with all her money. The man was a saint, not an idiot. There was no way in hell he would walk away from the fortune that landed in his lap. He had already laid his hands on her most intimate parts, and soon he would lay his hands on her money too.

"Sure, let's get the formalities out of the way," Renate replied on an exhale. "You've made all the arrangements. All I have to do is show up."

Thaddeus peered into her eyes, checking for traces of mockery but all he saw was sardonic resignation. "Do you have any last-minute thoughts?"

"I cannot get married wearing this." Renate pinched the sleeve of Jolanta's blouse. "And don't tell me there's a wedding gown sitting in your dead wife's trunk. I want something of my own, just for one day."

"Oh, you'll have a dress of your own, rest assured. The girls will see to that."

"What girls?" The thought of Agatha and Bronia preparing her for the altar filled Renate with dread.

"The ones you saw at the dancing hall yesterday. They'll know what to do. You'll be in good hands." Thaddeus looked over her shoulder and shouted to the stable boy. "Arturas, water my horse and steam up the bathhouse, will you? Make it hot as hell and throw some oak leaves in the tub." He returned his attention to Renate. "Sorry, I cannot get married with three layers of city dust on me. The place is teeming with Russians. I swear there're more of them each time I go to Vilnius. Not a single sign in Latin. Cyrillic everywhere. They'd rather speak broken Russian then pure Polish."

"Hmm, what's the world coming to..."

"This lad named Darius I knew years ago. Growing up we'd catch fish with our bare hands. Then he got a job in the city selling clerical supplies: stationary, calligraphy kits and other junk. When I stopped by his shop, just to say hello, he acted like he didn't know me. It's not that my looks have changed. He just wouldn't have any Polish spoken in his shop. A Mohammedan entering a church would get a warmer welcome."

Entertained by his agitation, Renate reached out and rubbed his cheek. "If you work yourself up into a stroke over it, it'll be one more Polish casualty." She was experimenting with different strokes and tones of voice, just to see what kind of effect they would have on Thaddeus. That night she was in a playful mood, and his gullible indignant heart made for a suitable toy. What would happen if she showed him a bit of sympathy and solidarity? "You shouldn't grind your teeth down over the czar's latest initiative."

"I'm not angry at the czar," Thaddeus said, his agitation subsiding. "I'm angry at the fellow Poles who have no pride in their roots and no loyalty to old friends."

"Ah, who gives a damn about those sellouts? You're about to rise above them all. How many of them can brag about marrying a German heiress? A few months from now, when we stroll down Castle Street after our honeymoon in Paris, decked out in the latest fashion, it'll be their turn to wave and beg us to come into their sorry shops. It'll be our turn to snub them."

Thaddeus responded with a noncommittal hum. He had trouble picturing himself wearing French couture. "First I need to scrub off that czarist grime. Will you help me?"

"It depends." She closed her mouth around his Adam's apple, sending a jolt through his body. "Will you spare some hot water for me? The wooden tub is built for more than one."

"Have pity, my girl," Thaddeus whispered as he backed away to conceal his obvious physical reaction.

"Oh, don't ask for pity now. You started it." Unmoved, Renate stuffed her hands into the spacious pockets of her skirt. "It's a little hypocritical to hide your urges after last night. Where is your bravado? Of course, it's easier to be free with a girl who's drunk. Well I'm sober now."

Blue smoke was coming out of the bathhouse chimney, spilling over the flax field.

"Let's go and test the water," Thaddeus said half-audibly.

They walked down the path leading to the bathhouse, embracing and tripping over each other's feet. The wooden hut was filled with thick fragrant steam. In a matter of seconds their hair and clothes became soggy.

Thaddeus threw his waistcoat on the bench and stood in the middle of the steam room, his boots planted on wooden planks. Something was bothering him.

"I owe you an apology for leaving you in the stable overnight," he said. "You were fast asleep, and I had no heart to disturb you."

Renate resumed kneading his face. "And I never thanked you for your gifts. If Mutti were alive, she would chide me for my rudeness. Exquisite gifts deserve exquisite gratitude."

"You're teasing me."

"Just a little." Aroused by her own game, Renate proceeded to pull the embroidered blouse over her head.

Thaddeus needed no further encouragement. Before long, they were standing in the giant wooden tub up to their waists in hot water with oak leaves floating about them. For the first time, they had the opportunity to take a good look at each other. There were no great surprises in store for Renate. Thaddeus looked pretty much as she had imagined him in all his well-proportioned but unremarkable masculinity. Apart from the healing gash on his hand, he had no scars or major flaws that would give him certain *Charakter*, as Frau Jung would say about her officer husband. If Thaddeus' father had ever subjected him to corporal punishment as he had Antanas, he had not left any marks. The skin on his face, neck and forearms had been subtly gilded by the sun, but the rest of him was quite pale. Renate could see herself falling asleep comfortably on his moderately muscled shoulder.

As for Thaddeus, he seemed rather ill at ease at the sight of his bride. His breathing quickened, but not with desire. The crease between his eyebrows deepened, conveying concern and remorse. He was accustomed to more voluptuous womanly forms. The homespun clothes added bulk and created an illusion of curves. It rattled him to discover an adolescent girl with narrow hips and small breasts lined with faint bluish veins.

"What's wrong, Master Dombrowski?" Renate slapped him on the cheeks lightly to drive him out of his stupor. "Is something not to your liking?"

"Have... have you been eating?"

"Yes, I've been eating Agatha's bland potato mush. No, I haven't lost weight. This is how I looked when I arrived here, and I'm not likely to get any larger, even if your cook feeds me bacon three times a day."

"I just want to make sure you're not ailing."

"My hips will never be as wide as a mead barrel." Renate drew a semicircle in the water in front of herself. "I take after my mother. She was tall and lean her entire life. If not for that stupid lung infection, she'd still be alive, as probably so would my father. Mutti never would've let him die like that."

Renate could not believe she had to justify her God-given physique. Ah, that was the detriment of being with a man who had only seen one woman naked. He only kept his dead wife's clothes so he could make prospective candidates for replacement try them on to make sure they filled them out nicely. The desire to say something venomous was overwhelming.

"A buxom woman can be sickly and barren on the inside," Renate continued, "while a twig can be as fertile as a sow. I promise I won't disappoint you the way Jolanta did. I'll give you ten children, just to prove you wrong."

Thaddeus knew he needed to act fast to fix his blunder. The girl was hyperventilating. The last thing he had wanted to do was insult her the day before the wedding, while they were both naked. It would take eons to win her good graces back.

The only remedy he could think of was to scoop her up and smother her with compliments. "Don't be angry with a crude village fool who's unaccustomed to refined beauty. I'm still learning my way around ladies of your rank."

Renate continued giving him a silent treatment, but at least she was not evading his kisses or struggling to get away. When Thaddeus eventually released her, she turned her back to him and submerged herself fully in hot water. When she came up for air a few seconds later, with leaves and pieces of bark in her hair, the look in her eyes suggested that she was not dwelling on his unintended insult.

"I promised to help you scrub off the city grime." She pulled a coarse towel off the hook and grabbed a fresh slice of pine scented soap. "You'll be cleaner than you've been in decades. Beware: we dainty German girls have rough hands. When I'm done with you, your skin will be beet-red."

Thaddeus responded with a rich low-pitched laugh, which reminded her of dark smoked German beer.

After the bath they lay down on a lambskin rug in a nest of fresh linen towels. The caresses resumed, with slight variations. This time around her reflexes were not slowed down by alcohol, so the sensations came through all the sharper and deeper. Her body remembered the succession of events. Every stroke was a step towards a peak from which she would eventually take a giddy, euphoric tumble. So she reclined and allowed Thaddeus to showcase one of his few talents—making her nerve endings sing. It was the least he could do after making her suffer through awkward conversations. Sinking her fingers into the moist lambskin, she suddenly became conscious of another desire—to overshadow her predecessor. She could not forget that patronizing concern in Thaddeus' eyes, and it still irked her. The night before he half-jokingly accused her of bashfulness, and then he questioned her fitness for consummation based on the width of her hips. She surmised it was not his fear of God or regard for propriety that kept him from plunging into full-fledged intercourse but the assumption that she was too juvenile and unversed. The idea of biting into a green apple did not appeal to him.

Suddenly, the roles reversed. As soon as her pulse resumed its normal rhythm, Renate embarked on a mission of self-advocacy. Her caresses became more aggressive and deliberate. She was about to clear up the confusion regarding her sexual maturity. The poor man would not know what hit him.

All along Thaddeus had been optimistic that his juvenile bride would thaw out and meet him half-way, but he had not expected it to happen so soon. Renate tucked her tangled wet tresses behind her ears and locked eyes with him for a second before her lips slid down his chest. The expression of blissful disbelief on his face was priceless. Lusty, excitable fool! He had no idea what he was about to inherit along with the money. A cynical heart and a dirty mind. A pristine unscarred womb and a warm eloquent mouth. All that in the skinny body of a fifteen-year old.

Thaddeus did not tell her exactly what he desired, and she did not ask him. Renate leaned on his cryptic nods and smirks, her own imagination and random bits of nighttime gossip she had picked up from her older schoolmates. It helped immensely that his body was beautiful. She could feel his ribs through the thin wall of muscle. There was no way in hell she would have done the same for a man whose flesh was not firm.

Alas, Renate's performance was over before she had a chance to demonstrate her most exquisite skill. The fireworks went off the moment the first spark hit the fuse. Nearly two years of forced abstinence had taken a toll on his self-restraint. Above her head Renate heard a profanity that sounded like a compliment.

Satisfied, she pressed her face against his concave, heaving stomach. At last, a semblance of power balance was restored. They were even.

CHAPTER 15

Amber Dust

Renate's wedding dress looked like a well-tailored nightgown with flowing sleeves. The embroidery was not as colorful and ornate as on a more traditional garment. The threading was pale-gold instead of cornflower blue and poppy red. The fabric itself was uneven—thin and transparent in some places and opaque and coarse in others.

Around ten o'clock in the morning a comely young Pole named Gabriela came to help Renate get dressed and braid her hair. The girl kept weeping.

"Is it another one of your customs to soak the bride's head in tears?" Renate asked.

"I weep because this dress was made for my older sister Martha."

"What happened? She didn't like it?"

"She drowned in the lake one week before the wedding. They never found her body, just a pair of her woven slippers on the shore and a bead necklace. The priest recited prayers over the water, and we sent wreaths with candles afloat. I'd gladly keep the dress for myself, but Mother says it's cursed and shouldn't be kept in the family."

Renate laughed. "Sure, let someone else inherit the

curse."

"You've nothing to fear, my lady. The curse won't take hold since you're not related to us by blood. The dress has been soaked in holy water, dried in the sun and given away, so the curse is broken."

Renate wondered if the entire episode had been staged as a prank, so strong was the element of rural melodrama. The chilling saga of the drowned bride sounded too much like something Agatha would tell her toddler granddaughter before bedtime. Balts and Poles were notorious for incorporating fables and practical jokes into their wedding celebrations.

As Gabriela was weaving the last ribbons into the bride's tresses, two more girls arrived, Sabina and Klaudia. They looked about fourteen. Sabina wound a coral string around Renate's neck, and Klaudia crowned her with a wild rose wreath. They dusted some white powder over her cheeks, stained her lips with beet juice and blackened her eyebrows with charcoal, turning her face into a mask. Hearing the high-pitched trio brought back memories of Kunstakademie. How distant that world seemed now! What would Frau Jung and her students think of her now if they saw her wearing this mummer's costume?

Gabriela hugged her from behind and whispered, "Master Dombrowski is waiting."

Renate looked out the window and saw Thaddeus. He looked like a dashing outlaw with his neck scarf and slick knee-high riding boots, the stuff of adolescent fantasies. The fact that he had actually made an effort to get a quality shave for the occasion moved Renate to the core. He must have paid a barber to remove that chronic peachy scruff. His flaxen hair was slicked back, exposing a high youthful forehead. In that moment Renate was as conscious as ever of the venom radiating from the female guests. Master Dombrowski, a king in body and soul by local standards, was taking a foreign bride. The hostility thickened when he extended his hand and called out.

"You look astonishing, fräulein!"

Renate acknowledged the compliment with an understated bow, her head already weighed down by the wreath. Instead of running towards him, she walked slowly, with a queenly resolve. They linked fingers, and he paraded her around the yard in an impromptu polonaise, the only Polish dance she knew how to perform as it consisted primarily of slips and dips.

"Thank God she's a German," Gabriela whispered to her two younger assistants. "This way we don't have to feel guilty about hating her. Imagine if he picked one of us? It would be the end of our friendship."

The two younger girls brought their flowered heads closer to Gabriela's. Renate continued dancing. When her gaze accidentally fell upon her bridal party, she saw three ruddy faces with fake smiles plastered over them.

***

Before the trip to the church there were a few last-minute customs to observe. Since the bride and the groom both had no living parents, the rituals involving the in-laws had to be altered or omitted altogether. To Renate's pleasant surprise, Agatha was not standing in for Thaddeus' mother. The honor was given to his fifty-year old aunt Monica who had traveled from Vilnius for the occasion, a lethargic blonde with cold sinewy hands and lilac mist wafting about her. In accordance with the custom, she shared her fondest memories of Tadek, as she called her nephew, pinned a flower to his lapel and presented with him a rosary as a symbol of God's blessing.

Without engaging in familiarities or making the speech longer than it needed to be, Lady Monica was merely performing her duty.

"Do you have more relatives like her?" Renate asked Thaddeus as they were walking to St. Lawrence's with Gabriela and the two flower girls in tow.

"No, she's the last one. My father's twin sister. Never been married, hence she still carries the family name."

"Well, I like her."

"I knew you would. She always looks like she's carrying sour cranberries in her mouth. Don't get too excited. Aunt Monica isn't long for this world. Her lungs are failing, if you cannot tell by the color of her skin. Coming here was a huge feat on her behalf. It's probably the last trip she'll ever make out of the city. I do regret that you don't have any relatives by your side."

"That's not true. Vati is with me. As long as I have access to his money, I feel his presence."

***

St. Lawrence's was a quintessential rural Lithuanian church. The axe was the primary tool used in its construction. Unlike the rest of wooden chapels, St. Lawrence's did not bear a single hint of Baroque influences. There was an unusually spacious separate bell tower with a tent-like roof covering an open gallery. Both buildings were painted a rich green, making them blend with the lush vegetation. The most striking element of the church's interior was a red pulpit with frescos featuring the Acts of the Apostles. The carved images of angels and seraphs were true masterpieces of folk art. The organ chamber also contained a large painting of Mary in an ornate frame. Right by the altar there was a group sculpture depicting the burial of Christ.

Since the bride was Lutheran, Father Nicholas stripped the ceremony of all opulence. He did not want to waste precious candles and incense on a couple that he perceived as mismatched. He could not remember the last time he was asked to marry a Catholic and a Protestant. With a stiff face, he recited the benediction through his teeth as the newlyweds exchanged rings. The choir consisting of three adolescent boys closed the ceremony with a hymn. The piece consisted of five verses, but the boys performed only two.

Renate did not mind the brevity of the wedding ceremony any more than she minded the dryness of Aunt Monica's speech. So far they were moving through the rituals painlessly. She knew there was more in store.

At the doorstep of the church, Gabriela presented them with a basket with polished stones with various character traits of the newlyweds inscribed on them, from honesty to jealousy, to hot temper, to melancholy. The idea was to sort through the stones, discard the bad ones and keep the good ones. In the old times the stones were considered messages to the gods. Father Nicholas condoned this tribute to the pagan lore as long as it was performed outside the sanctified walls.

"I don't know what genius wrote these," Renate muttered, picking through the stones. She knew enough Lithuanian to be able to identify separate words. "There's not a single trait, good or bad, that applies to me. Not much of a choice, is there?"

Thaddeus came to her aid. "I think I've found something that applies to us both," he said, pulling out a small flat stone with *tamprumas* inscribed upon it. Resilience.

"A rather bold choice. I don't think one can claim to be resilient until having lived to the age of eighty."

"We've made it so far, haven't we? Let's hold onto this

stone. And if time proves us wrong, we'll discard it."

***

When the newlyweds returned from the church, Monica greeted them at the gate with a tray containing bread, salt and wine diluted with water. The bread symbolized life, as salt did bitter moments and the rose-colored drink was to wash everything down. Before Thaddeus and Renate were allowed to enter the house, they were required to pass a number of challenges. The groom was expected to navigate an obstacle course with a blindfold over his eyes while carrying his bride who in turn would coach him where to tread. The path was covered in boulders, ropes, wooden wedges, fir branches and cracked barrel pieces.

"When I did it twelve years ago, I tripped over a rock," Thaddeus whispered as he pulled his neck scarf to cover his eyes. "The guests were in stitches. Jolanta walked away unharmed, while I had to dance all night with a bleeding knee. I count on your mercy, fräulein."

"One cannot go wrong taking orders from a German general," Renate said, her arms around his neck.

She did not need to have the significance of the ritual explained to her. She knew that Baltic women enjoyed greater authority within the family unit than their Russian sisters. For a young husband, that temporary surrender of control to his wife served as an exercise in humility and willingness to compromise. It was one ritual Renate did not want to omit, one prank challenge she did not want to fail. Ignoring the howls of the guests', she navigated Thaddeus in a low, steady voice. He either deliberately ignored her instructions or truly did not know right from left. A few times he came close to tripping and dropping her. Of course, the slippery soles on his new boots did not help.

"Be thankful there isn't a bear trap at the end of the path," she whispered in his ear as she pulled the blindfold off.

Before putting her down, Thaddeus gave her a deep, demonstrative kiss, the kind he could not give her at the altar in front of Father Nicholas. The pressure of his smooth, painstakingly shaved chin brought back a disconcerting memory of Benjamin and the kisses they had exchanged in front of the Gate of Dawn. The sudden flashback startled her; she had not thought of the boy since she left Vilnius. Perhaps it was the trace of German cologne by Mäurer & Wirtz that every urban bachelor wore. Thaddeus must have procured it from the same vendor who had sold him the German translation of *Une Vie*. One thing was undeniable: on that day Thaddeus did not look or smell like his usual self. Renate felt like she was kissing a different man.

Sprinkled with yellow chamomile petals by the two flower girls, the newlyweds made their way to the clearing behind the house where the banquet was set up. Renate took a moment to admire the sturdy oak tables that were designed to withstand a great deal of fist-smashing. Each table had a designated bottle master who was responsible for making sure that everyone's chalice was filled.

After the first round of drinks, Gabriela began agitating the female guests to perform the circle dance around the bride. All that was required of Renate was to sit on a chair with her back straight, while the girls twirled around her in a dervish of plaid and stripes and sang.

> *Dear hop, dear hop, you green one,*
> *When you, the green one, have been planted*
> *My dear mother has been raising me.*
> *When you, the green one, have been winding round,*

I have been weaving my braids.
When you, the green one, have been plucked,
I, the young one, have been married out.

Around midnight the guests gathered around a bonfire. Gabriela passed a cup with amber dust, urging the guests to sprinkle it on the flames and make a wish for the newlyweds. It was an invitation for an old Baltic ancestral spirit to care for the young family.

When the weary guests started retreating to their sheepskin beds under the apple trees, Renate gave her husband a quizzical look. "They aren't going home?"

"The festivities aren't over. Tomorrow morning the revelry will resume with vengeance."

"There's... there's room for vengeance?"

"Always! You haven't seen half of it. Lithuanian weddings last for two days. Today was a lovely mixture of sacred and profane, tomorrow will be mostly profane. With the blessings and the amber sprinkling out of the way, it'll be prank after prank. An accordion player in a donkey costume will rouse everyone with his wake-up serenade. Except a few black eyes and knocked out teeth. Then everyone will reconvene for some cabbage soup with duck blood and melted butter."

Renate took a moment to process the list of the ingredients and winced. "*Mein Gott...* Sounds awful."

"A perfect hangover cure! Then the guests go to the bathhouse and cool off in the lake afterwards or just get a bucket of icy well water dumped on them. Still, everyone's favorite part is putting the matchmaker on trial. Since we don't have your German attorney friend present, we'd have to pick another victim to stand in. The guests will sentence him to death by hanging, and he'll start reciting his own obituary, then you as the bride will save him and present him with a red sash, which he'll have to wear for the next month."

As Thaddeus was describing the traditional pranks, Renate detected an air of boredom and annoyance in his voice. He did not sound very keen on going through the rites. Timid hope stirred within her heart.

"Are you trying to tell me something?"

"We don't have to stay for the second act." He began fiddling with the ribbons in her braid. "We can disappear in the middle of the night. It's our turn to play a prank on the guests. They won't miss us one bit, I assure you. The party will go on without us. These people know what to do. Since when do you need the newlyweds to enjoy the wedding festivities?"

Renate liked the sound of it. "Where were you thinking of going?"

"To a secret place." He drew her closer and kissed the tip of her ear. "If you're not too tired, I'll make it worth your while. You've been practicing riding, haven't you?"

"If spurring Dragoon counts."

"Forget Dragoon. You're ready for the real thing."

***

By one o'clock at night, when all the guests were asleep, the newlyweds were galloping towards the woods. The two black stallions retired from the Russian cavalry were gifts from Aunt Monica. Everyone else had brought embroidered towels, painted carving boards and shiny knives. Did they think Thaddeus was running a butcher's shop?

Renate was not accustomed to riding at such speed. The slick beast underneath her had been bred and trained for battle. Clutching at the silky mane, her heart thumping with terror and thrill, she followed a few meters behind her husband. It did not occur to Thaddeus to slow down or at least glance behind. He expected Renate to keep up the pace.

When they were passing the family cemetery, Renate threw a quick glance at the patch where her predecessor and the four infants were buried. She thought that the cross on Jolanta's grave looked a little crooked, as if someone had tampered with it. A large horned owl was sitting on the fence like a guardian spirit.

They rode through a gradually narrowing corridor of ferns and wild raspberry bushes. The smell of pine sap, moss and crushed berries filled the air—the smell of Baltic legends.

For the next five minutes Renate rode with her face down and her eyes closed to avoid being blinded by a branch. With every leap of the horse the foliage seemed to be getting denser. When they reached a clearing, Thaddeus halted the horse. "We're here."

Renate opened her eyes and saw the outline of a wooden hut with a vaulted roof and a stubby chimney, just like something out of a Baba Yaga fairy-tale. She ran her fingers over the ornate carving on the window shutters.

"You built it yourself?"

"Not exactly. I found it in disrepair years ago, when Milo was but a pup. We were running through the woods during a thunderstorm and stumbled across this hut. The door was open, so we just came in. There were some broken jars and dead mice, all veiled in spider web."

"Weren't you afraid of finding the owner's skeleton?"

"Bones don't frighten me, nor do ghosts. Clearly, the hut had been waiting for me. Over the next few months I had done some repairs, first the floorboards, then the door. Whenever I had a free moment, I would take my dog, a sack of tools and head into the woods."

"So this is where you brought your first wife on your wedding night?"

To her surprise, Thaddeus shook his head. "Jolanta didn't know about this place, one of my few secrets. I tell you, it's hard to keep secrets from someone you've known since the dawn of your life. You're the first woman I've brought here."

Renate did not believe him for a moment, and yet she appreciated the white lie, as it was intended to make her feel privileged. After all, she had spent the last month wearing another woman's hand-me-downs.

While Thaddeus was starting a fire inside a tiny rusty stove, Renate unsaddled the horses and tied them to a tree. The impeccably groomed and disciplined stallions knew what was expected of them. For the first time she came close to understanding why some people swooned over those animals.

Behind the hut she found a bubbling stream. Cupping her hands, she scooped some icy water to wash the paint off her face. The wild roses in her wreath had begun to wither, so she tossed it into the water. The colorful ribbons followed. One by one, she released them into the stream. The bead necklace would have to be returned to Gabriela. The hem of her gown was stained with dirt, grass and wine. Her feet were throbbing, even though she had not done much dancing that night. She kicked off the leather sandals with hempen ties and stepped into the water knee deep.

"It's time," she heard her husband's voice behind her back.

CHAPTER 16

Elysium

August, 1884

For the next three weeks the newlyweds moved on horseback through the woods and fields, stopping at neighboring settlements where Thaddeus' friends lived. Young Master Dombrowski was highly esteemed in the ranks of the rural Polish gentry, even though he was one of the poorest. While his legendary impracticality served as a subject for good-natured jokes, his kindness and humility made him a welcome guest in the most prosperous of households. The news of his marriage to a German heiress spread through the nearby estates, stirring a mixture of fascination and disbelief. It was a Cinderella story with the roles reversed. Everyone was dying to see the enigmatic princess.

Thaddeus was showing off his new wife as he would a prized breeding mare. His friends scrutinized the circumference of Renate's hips. Those people possessed just enough tact to choose their words but not to control their facial expressions. With standard salutations out of the way, their gazes would immediate shift to the parts of the bride's anatomy responsible for procreation. Everyone knew the tragic story of Thaddeus' first marriage and sympathized with his plight. They wondered if the lanky fifteen-year old could satisfy his desire for children.

"My father was murdered," Renate announced to Michael Zielinski, their first host over dinner, "burned to death inside his factory. That's how I ended up here." She wanted to get the introductions out of the way. "Feel free to share the story with your neighbors, so I don't have to repeat myself. You can even add a few fanciful twists to the story. I'm sure by the time it circles back to me, it will be unrecognizable."

The flabbergasted host stuck his fork into a cube of white chicken meat and did not ask Renate any questions for the rest of the night.

Thaddeus' friends marveled at her masculine posture, her wry sarcasm, and above all, her ability to dominate conversations without saying much.

By the end of the third week the names got all scrambled in Renate's head: Zielinski, Kowalski, Bargowski, Kramarz, Rozpondek. Their living-rooms were decorated in the same style. Most of them had modest libraries. One home had an upright piano, though it was horribly out of tune. After extensive cajoling from the hostess Renate played a waltz.

"Marvelous!" Madame Rozpondek's oversized rings clanged as she clapped. "Simply enchanting. Who wrote it?"

"Your fellow countryman, Frederic Chopin. It's one of his most prominent pieces, actually."

"Well, would you mind playing it again, so we could all dance?"

"Alas, Madame." Renate closed the lid on the piano and pushed the bench in. "My performance was an insult to his genius. Poor Chopin must be tossing in his grave in Paris. By the way, did you know he requested to have his heart ripped out and returned to Warsaw in a jar of alcohol? That's right. His sister Ludwika did the honors. Imagine traveling across Europe with your brother's pickled heart? At any rate, you need to fix the C sharp key."

The hostess blanched at the lurid tale and never asked Renate to play again.

Thaddeus worked hard to keep his pride in check and keep his head from exploding. His fifteen-year old wife looked like a marvel of sophistication in her moss-green bustle gown with a standing collar and her blonde hair in a low slick chignon in contrast to the appallingly philistine ringlets of the hostesses. The gown was a gift from Madame Kowalski, who had originally bought it for her eldest daughter only to discover that the boarding school diet had doubled the girl's waist circumference. So the matron made a timid suggestion for her young guest to try on the dress, swearing up and down that it had never been worn before. Renate accepted the gift all too eagerly—she had not worn such a meticulously tailored garment in ages. Of all the hostesses, Madame Kowalski became her favorite. Renate got the impression that the Kowalskis were one tier above the rest of their neighbors in terms of refinement, worldliness and affluence. Falcon's Cliff—that was the name of their rural estate—was one of several properties. They bought the farm on a whim without any expectation of monetary return. They just needed a picturesque sanctuary to detox between the ball seasons in Warsaw. At the same time, the Kowalskis did not flaunt their superiority to their provincial neighbors. The lakefront picnics at Falcon's Cliff drew dozens of guests each summer.

Their all-embracing cordiality, however, did not extend onto the domestic help. In fact, there was one thing all households had in common: the servants actually behaved like servants. They were paid fairly, in some cases generously, but they would not think of sitting at the same table as their owners of the house. While Renate was playing piano at the Rozpondeks' parlor, they listened to the music from the hallway.

"Is Thaddeus an admirer of Count Tolstoy?" Regina Kowalski asked her in a discrete whisper one night over a card game.

Renate raised her rounded eyes at the hostess. "Is this a joke, Madame?"

"I wasn't asking whether or he's read *War and Peace* but whether he's adopted those egalitarian ideas. It seems to be the latest fashion among the Russian aristocracy."

"I assure you, Madame, my husband is neither fashionable nor aristocratic. These ideas aren't coming from Count Tolstoy."

"But he lets his servants use his towels, doesn't he?"

"Not just his towels but also belts, socks, scarves, hats, gloves. The washerwoman launders everything in one barrel, hangs out to dry and then dumps everything into one pile, from which the servants help themselves to whatever they need on any given day. Sometimes I'll see the stable boy with one brown sock and one grey. They all smell the same."

Regina Kowalski covered her mouth with an ace of hearts. "You want this radical nonsense to stop, don't you?"

"Do you have any advice for me?"

"I predict that once Thaddeus has children of his own, his affections will shift in the right direction. I'm not saying he'll stop infantilizing his servants altogether—old habits aren't easily obliterated—but it'll get better." Regina leaned in with a conspiratorial glow in her feline eyes. "I placed a little bag with mint and sage under your pillow in the guest bedroom."

Since Renate was not the blushing or giggling type, she

responded with a dry nod. "Thank you for your hospitality, Madame." *I shall be thinking of you as I perform my wifely duties tonight.*

"At any rate, I'm glad to see Thaddeus in pragmatic German hands," Regina resumed. "Not to speak ill of your predecessor, but Jolanta nourished his lunacy. She loved him a little more than a harmonious marriage calls for. Don't repeat her mistakes, dearest. If you behave like a breathless star-struck ninny around a man, if you drink in every idiotic proposition that rolls off his tongue, it'll lead him to believe that he can move mountains. And in the end, the mountain will crush you both."

Renate laid her cards face down, stretched in her velvet-padded armchair and assumed her usual Spartan posture. "You needn't worry, Madame. I'll be sure to clip his wings before they take him to dangerous heights."

In the first three weeks of her marriage Renate learned a great deal about her body's abilities—and its limitations. To her husband's chagrin, she could not reach the peak of bliss more than twice in a row. Her vessel of sensuality was quick to fill. After a certain amount of vigorous caressing she would stop responding. As much as she wanted to meet him half-way, her anatomy did not cooperate. Eventually she would lay back and surrender her body to his gratification. After eighteen months of abstinence, Thaddeus plunged into his spousal privileges full force, giving Renate no time to refuel between the episodes. The energy that he would normally invest into his flax fields was now being poured into lovemaking. His young wife's waning ardor left him visibly perplexed. Renate gathered that he was accustomed to having his advances met with more enthusiasm. Jolanta must have been one lusty sow, always ready to welcome him between her thighs. She and Thaddeus must have broken quite a few bed frames.

"What's the matter?" he kept asking Renate. "Don't you like me?"

"Of course I do—in moderation. Too much firewood kills the flame."

"We can try something else."

"We've already tried everything, including a few things that the Church frowns upon."

One could not fault Thaddeus for being unimaginative. He certainly had enough tricks in his arsenal left over from his first marriage. Renate was beginning to wish he could be more like the inconsiderate, callous men who did not care for their wives' pleasure. Then she could just lay back, let him have his way with her and not engage in laborious discussions.

"Bored already?" he asked.

"Not bored—satiated. Remember those wild mushroom tarts they served at our wedding? Two was all I could eat. Even heavenly things should be dispensed sparingly."

"I think I've found the answer to your coldness. It's your age. Women don't blossom until they are in their thirties."

"Don't begrudge me my youth. You knew I was fifteen when you married me."

He patted her on the hip. "You're right. We have plenty of time, *kumpela*."

The Polish word for lady-pal was what he had settled upon, an ambiguous and not terribly obliging endearment. He did not call her *kochana* for beloved or *złota* for treasure. Renate had no pet names for him at all. Calling him Tadek was the pinnacle of familiarity on her part. Even so, she used the diminutive form of his name sparingly, as she believed it reduced him to the rank of a stable boy.

After one month of touring the neighborhood estates

Thaddeus began showing signs of restlessness and remorse.

"We should start heading back soon," he said one August evening, shielding his eyes from the crimson glare. They were standing on the porch of the Bargowskis' house, sipping mint tea from the same cup. "You know I cannot be away from the farm for too long. My people need me."

Ordinarily, any reference to the "people" would make Renate's teeth ache, but she was actually looking forward to going back to Raven's Bog, as it would mean a respite from her husband's advances. Reengaging in physical labor would take his attention off the conjugal bed. With any luck, the frequency of couplings would be reduced to twice a day.

CHAPTER 17

Revelation

Raven's Bog, early September, 1884

Before retiring the bustle-gown into the lopsided oak wardrobe Renate ran her hand one last time over the luxurious fabric and the shiny opal buttons. God alone knew when she would have an opportunity to wear it again. The pseudo-honeymoon was over. The drudgery of her sleepy rural ever-after was about to resume. The Kowalskis had already moved to their Warsaw residence for the next six months, and Renate could not think of any other families she was absolutely dying to visit. She suspected the feelings were mutual—she had done a marvelous job alienating the hosts with her haughty demeanor and her cryptic jokes.

Goodbye, little dress.

The tender moment was interrupted by her husband's frantic shout. "Come quickly, *kumpela*." Thaddeus burst into the room, panting and raking his hair with his fingers. "Something awful happened while we were away."

"What is it?" she asked without turning around.

"Antanas injured his foot. He's in a great deal of pain."

"Did he walk into bear trap?"

"No, he stepped on a nail in the dark."

Ignoring his wife's growls of protest, Thaddeus dragged her outside towards the smithy. The place smelled like vodka and blood. A couple of dirty bandages were scattered all over the stone floor. Antanas was sitting on a wobbly stool in front of the cold furnace, his left foot wrapped in rags and propped on a log. The injury had not knocked him out of commission altogether, so he was busying himself by sharpening a sickle. Like a wounded animal, he had retreated into his cave to recover.

"Back from yer honeymoon already?" The sudden intrusion did not make him too happy. "We didn't expect yer until harvest time."

Thaddeus knelt in front of the blacksmith to take a closer look at the injury. "You don't have to put on a brave face in front of us, Antanas. We're family. It's quite apparent that you're in a great deal of pain." Still kneeling, he glanced over his shoulder at Renate, who was standing at the threshold, holding a handkerchief to her nose. "It just happened two days ago. I had a bad premonition. It's my fault. What was I thinking, leaving him in charge for a whole month?" Thaddeus grabbed the end of the bandage and started unwinding it. The smell of sweat, blood and pus grew stronger. "No worries, my good fellow. Lady Renate will patch you up in no time. Won't you, *kumpela*?"

Renate did not say anything. At the sight of the blacksmith' swollen foot she doubled over and retched.

Antanas caught a glimpse of her spilling breasts and snickered all-knowingly. "Easy, m'lady. Don't endanger yerself on my behalf." He then nodded at Thaddeus. "Master, yer better tend to yer wife. I'll be fine. I heal quicker than a mongrel."

Leaning against the wall, Renate dragged herself outside

and collapsed on a stack of hay. Thaddeus followed her.

"I didn't realize you cared so much for Antanas, *kumpela*. I can clearly see that the sight of his suffering distressed you. He's become like a brother to you, hasn't he?"

"Don't ask me to do it again," she slurred into the handkerchief. "Just because I repaired your hand, it doesn't mean that I'm prepared to nurse your servants' feet. I'm not looking to fill the role of the village healer. If you're so worried about your blacksmith losing his foot to gangrene, find a real doctor. Just leave me out of it."

Renate spent the rest of the afternoon in bed, battling recurring episodes of nausea. The image of the blacksmith's pierced sole had long since faded from her memory, but the physical symptoms persisted. Worst of all, she could not find a comfortable position. After ten minutes her limbs would cramp up. Her breasts burned and ached. The linen blouse rubbing against them felt like emery paper. She could neither sleep nor pry herself off the mattress. Some malevolent internal force kept driving her body into that state of restless lethargy. If Renate was in the least bit superstitious, she would have guessed that one of the Polish hostesses had given her the evil eye.

Before supper, Thaddeus came in to check on her.

"I took your advice, *kumpela*. I don't want anyone to say that I don't listen to my wife."

Renate raised her matted head from the pillow and fixed her foggy eyes on him. "What now?"

"I found a doctor for Antanas, a medical student, to be exact. He doesn't have his diploma yet, but he surely knows his stuff. Remember Peter Bargowski? His son Janek was visiting. What a stroke of luck! He examined the wound, cleaned and dressed it properly. Antanas is out of danger. You don't have to worry about him anymore."

"What a relief," Renate fell back against the pillows.

"The Bargowski boy is still here. He's staying for supper. If you want to talk to him about your ailments, maybe he'll give you some of his fancy city concoctions."

Renate let out a sigh of doom that could turn the Gediminas Tower.

"I don't think this life is agreeing with me: the air I breathe, the water I drink, the language I hear, the linen I wear. I cannot turn my head without feeling sick to my stomach. I've never been so sick in my life. What are you smiling about?"

Instead of concern, Thaddeus' face expressed jubilation.

"What a dolt I've been!" He threw himself on the bed next to Renate. "I'll ask Arturas to slaughter a boar. No, I should probably help him. I'll hold the boar, and he'll slit its throat. We'll have a pork feast lasting a whole week!"

"Ugh... must you mention pork to me?" She covered her face and began to wail. "I know the truth now. You poisoned me, didn't you? First you pocketed my money and then decided to dispose of me. You couldn't just choke me and dump my body in the bog. That would've been too merciful. No, you had to drag me back only to poison me."

Convinced that her meltdown was a prank, Thaddeus trapped her in his arms over the blanket and rocked her from side to side. "Yes, *kumpela*, I poisoned you—with my lust. Our efforts were rewarded. All those tumbles in the hay weren't for naught. I'll tell Antanas to build a new cradle. It'll keep him occupied while he's recovering."

Renate stopped wailing and peeked through her fingers, but Thaddeus had already left the room. He was on a mission to slaughter a boar.

***

September, 1884

The following weeks passed in a fog of relentless nausea, smell of smoked pork and slow-burning complacency. Renate absorbed the news of her impending motherhood without any indignation. It did not occur to her to mourn the meager remnants of her freedom. Her plush unencumbered adolescence had ended back in June. There was nothing left to mourn of her old life. However, there were still ladders to climb and battlements to storm. From day one she sensed that the faceless, nameless entity inside her was more of an ally than a burden, as it gave her more influence over her husband. It was two of them against him. Renate looked fifteen years ahead and saw a sovereign blonde girl named Katherine, with a knack for languages, numbers and formulas. Together, mother and daughter would bring some semblance of social order to their household and restore the natural hierarchy as intended by the God of science and reason. They would cure Thaddeus of his disease and bring Raven's Bog into the twentieth century. Maybe, just maybe, they would build a small mill. By using the knowledge Renate had absorbed in those years of walking the workrooms of her Hermann's factory, she would be resurrecting Vati. Katherine would know her noble grandfather. The thought of any subsequent children that could potentially be born in those fifteen years did not cross Renate's mind. Whenever she envisioned the future, it was just her and Katherine. Those thoughts made the fatigue and the aches bearable. If Thaddeus did not like her designs, he could always go back to his little hut in the woods.

In the meantime, his behavior was that of obsessive dotage. His commitment to satisfy her every whim sent him barging into the room twenty times a day, disrupting her rest.

"Go on, tell me what you want," he would say. "I'll see that it's done."

Every time he asked her that question, her mind turned blank. The things her heart desired could not be provided instantaneously. She had more long-term goals than fleeting whims. Her interest in food still faltered, though her interest in conjugal activities had returned with vengeance. Even when she was too sluggish to get out of bed, she would grab Thaddeus by the front of his shirt and pull him on top of her. There was very little talking. They communicated in hums, moans and gasps. For once, her sexual appetite matched her husband's. Harvesting was in full swing, and Thaddeus spent the most industrious hours of the day under the blanket with his wife instead of toiling alongside his field hands as he had been doing for the past twelve seasons. Days would go by without him mentioning "his people" to her. Words like "beloved" and "treasure" started slipping into his vocabulary.

"I do have one wish," she told him one evening as they were putting their clothes back on after messing up another set of sheets.

"Anything, *kumpela*."

"I'd like a real honeymoon."

"But we already had one—as real as it gets. The most important goal is accomplished."

"Still, I'd like to go to Stockholm, ideally before I get enormous. I want my picture taken on a boat in front of the Royal Palace, and I don't want the Dombrowski heir obstructing the view. You can leave Antanas in charge."

"Stockholm..." Thaddeus winced, as if the word cut into the roof of his mouth. "But that's so far away. Besides, we don't speak Danish."

"One: Stockholm is in Sweden. Two: it's not that far away. Three: one can get by speaking German. Unless, of course, you find it demeaning to rely on your wife for translation."

There was no venom in Renate's voice. She had already made peace with her husband's ignorance of geography. To him, Sweden and Australia were equally remote from Raven's Bog, and therefore equally foreign and dangerous.

"I don't mind you translating for me," Thaddeus said.

"Then what exactly concerns you?"

"It's the money," he admitted reluctantly. "It would be a considerable expense."

"What about my inheritance? We cannot indulge ourselves a little. Come on, Tadek, just a touch of decadence. Vati would've wanted me to have the kind of honeymoon I deserve."

He pulled her close so that their temples were touching. "About that, *kumpela*... Remember how I told you that we had a few rough years? Well, that string of crop failures left us on thin ice."

It suddenly occurred to Renate that they were having their first candid conversation about money. "Exactly, how thin?"

"We fell behind on property taxes. The collectors kept a close eye on the estate and sent reminders now and then. As time went on, those letters became more frequent and... more eloquent."

"Well, what exactly did they say?"

"Ah, the usual... 'If you won't take care of your property, we'll find someone else who will.' They even brought a prospective buyer from the city. He wore a top hat and wouldn't stop twirling his pocket watch on a chain. You know how officials are, always putting on a show like fighting cocks. Why that frazzled look, *kumpela*? It's all in the past.

Our home is safe—thanks to your father. You wanted to know why we couldn't afford a trip abroad. It's only fair that you should know where the money went."

There, he said it. The young wife seemed to be digesting the news better than he had expected. Renate's face blanched slightly, though its expression did not change.

"I need to go," she muttered, slipping from under his arm.

"Where? Supper will be served in an hour."

Renate put on her ankle boots, jerking on the strings. "Since we aren't going anywhere in the near future, I'll try my bloody best to enjoy this land you saved with my father's money."

She ran out of the house towards the stables. Thaddeus made no effort to stop her, but a wrinkle cut across his brow. Dear God, what was that madwoman up to now?

***

Young Arturas, a twig of mint in his mouth, was humming a melody to a young male foal that appeared sickly. The song of healing, a mixture of a Christian prayer and a pagan spell, had worked on other farm animals.

Then the master's wife barged in and yanked the leaves out of his mouth.

"All right, where are the good horses?"

"They're all good, m'lady."

"Don't play idiot with me, boy." She seized him by the front of his shirt, causing his cap to fall backwards. "You know damn well which horses I'm talking about. Where are the black stallions we got from Lady Monica two months ago?"

"Oh, those? The master sold 'em to the Zielinskis down the road. Haven't yer heard? Their two daughters came back from convent school. They'll be courtin' this season. The master said them horses were no good for ploughin', just huntin' and ridin' fer fun. And there ain't no fun to be had 'ere at Raven's Bog, just earnest work."

Renate's vision clouded with tears of rage. Her stallions, as exquisite as black pearls, carrying two flighty Polish nitwits! With one shove she sent the stable boy flying against the wall lined with rakes and shovels.

After about a minute of pacing up and down the row of cells, she singled out a young smoky cream mare named Gita and seized her by the muzzle. "I'll take this one!"

Still dizzy from the fall, Arturas raised his index finger. "I wouldn't do it, m'lady. I ain't done breakin' 'er yet. She's feisty, that one."

"In that case we're well matched. She hates this place as much as I do."

Panting and licking her lips, Renate placed her foot in the stirrup. Gita let out a neigh of protest and recoiled. The stable boy made a sign of the cross. "You'll crack yer head, m'lady."

"Then Master Dombrowski can wipe my splattered brains off the floor."

On the third attempt Renate was able to mount the temperamental mare. The creature did not need spurring. Having realized her freedom from the narrow cell, Gita bolted out of the stable and galloped across the potato patches, kicking up loose soil. A few field workers craned their necks and pointed fingers at the new mistress of the house charging towards the woods, her loose hair mingling with the horse's mane.

"You'd think a Saracen army was after her."

"The master surely knows how to pick 'em. Horses, I mean."

The two boys bumped elbows as a sign of solidarity. This was promising to be an entertaining harvest season. Lady Renate had already become a subject of many jokes. Those jokes would keep them warm all winter long. After a stretch of austerity and bereavement that had plagued Raven's Bog for the past few years, this was a welcome change of mood.

***

After about ten minutes of wandering aimlessly through the empty house, Thaddeus took refuge in the kitchen. Agatha was adding the last pinch of thyme to the beef stew.

He plopped himself on the bench between two large jugs of malt brew. "You don't mind if I sit here for a while?"

"Yer the master," was the cook's reply. "Don't need to ask me for permission."

"But this is your domain, Agatha. I'd hate to be in the way. God, I hope I did the right thing by telling Lady Renate about the taxes. There was no delicate way to explain where they money went. Now she's furious with me, and rightly so. What do you think of all that?"

The cook folded her enormous red paws beneath her apron.

"And what makes yer think that ole Agatha has any business offerin' her opinion on the lady of the house?"

"I don't know. Because you have an opinion on everything, and you're seldom wrong."

"Well, Master, I pray I'm wrong this time. 'Tis one hell of a mess you've got yerself in with Her Ladyship. She's bound on makin' yer suffer for every ruble yer took from her."

Lame Magda crawled from under the bench and latched onto the master's leg like a tick. She had very strong fingers and sharp nails. Thaddeus was very fond of his niece, one of his very few blood relatives. As the girl was getting older, the deformity of the foot and the limp were growing more noticeable, exacerbating the guilt he was feeling. The money he had set aside for her dowry was sacred. He would sell half of his land before he touched what was Magda's.

"Come to Uncle Tadek." He grabbed her by the underarms and pulled her into his lap. She felt heavier than she looked. "What do you think, little one? Will there be a cousin for you next year?"

Magda began pulling on his cheeks with her dirty fingers. Her nose clogged with snot, she was huffing through her mouth. Thaddeus noticed pieces of chewed-up sunflower seeds trapped between her teeth. An outsider would find this little creature as esthetically appealing as a wet mutt, but to Thaddeus, whose vision was clouded by guilt and paternal bereavement, she was nothing short of a blooming water lily.

Before putting the child down on the floor, he kissed her greasy crown and presented her with a painted whistle in the shape of a cat, a jocose souvenir from his honeymoon. One of the Kowalski children had slipped it into his pocket prior to departure. A shrill warble instantly filled the steamy kitchen. Agatha shook her head and cursed into the pot of stew. Now the entire household would go to bed with a splitting headache.

When the workers started assembling around the table for supper, Thaddeus glanced out the window anxiously. Marital conflicts were new territory for him.

"I wonder what's taking her so long."

Agatha gave his hand a warning squeeze. "She'll be back when she gets hungry." On a rare occasion she would push the already tenuous boundaries and assume maternal authority over her susceptible young master. "Have some pride. If yer run after her now, yer will surely look like a fool."

"I *am* a fool, and everyone knows that already."

Thaddeus sighed and pulled the curtain over the window to avoid the temptation to keep looking outside. That night the dinnertime grace sounded rushed and dispirited. The master sliced the bread and forgot to pass the plate around. Reclining against the back of the bench, he studied the water stains on the ceiling. The half-butchered loaf sat in the corner of the table until Antanas kicked his brother's foot under the table. Thaddeus trembled, let out a sigh and reluctantly resumed his duties as head of the household.

Twenty minutes into the meal, Milo started barking and rattling the chain. Thaddeus went out on the porch and through the twilight saw a slender shape moving towards the house. At a closer distance he recognized the unbroken young mare. The empty saddle had slipped to the side. The reins were dragging on the ground. Renate was nowhere in sight. Having examined the horse in lantern light, Thaddeus noticed signs of struggle and battery. Gita's right ear was bleeding, and the eye was swollen. When he patted her on the neck, she responded with indignant neighing and recoiled, leaving Thaddeus bewildered as he was disturbed. The injuries could only have been inflicted by the rider. Having already antagonized every human member of the household, Renate had moved onto the animals. But where was she, and in what condition?

"Forgive me, dear girl," Thaddeus whispered to the mare when he finally was able to seize her by the reins. "Your troubles aren't over for the night."

The thought of taking the agitated horse out for another ride made him nervous, but Gita was the fastest and the sturdiest one.

He took Milo off the chain and gave him one of Renate's sashes to sniff. The dog made an eager hunting companion and a vigilant sentry, but searching was not his strongest talent.

Thaddeus did not ask any of the servants to accompany him, and none of them volunteered. They carried on as usual. As soon as the sound of his footsteps faded, the rumblings started. Everyone's attention turned to young Arturas, since he was the last one who spoke to Renate.

"Did she say where she was goin'?" Antanas asked.

"Yer think she'd tell?" The stable boy was huffing, fighting back the tears. "Now the master will shoot Gita. I just started breakin' her."

Bronia and Agatha started patting the boy on the back, assuring him that Master Dombrowski would do no such thing, as a fine horse like Gita was worth ten German bitches.

***

Riding over the hills and ravines, Thaddeus kept praying to St. Francis, the patron of animals. While the young mare was begrudgingly compliant, Milo's senility was becoming more apparent by the minute. The fourteen-year old mongrel did not understand what the master wanted from him, why he took him out in the dark and why he repeatedly shoved the strange piece of cloth in his snout. As they got closer to wetland patch that lay past the cemetery, Milo started moving in circles, panting and whining. A few times he plopped down on the wet grass, looking his master in the eye and wagging his tail.

"Work with me, old boy, just for tonight," Thaddeus implored the four-legged guide. "We must find her and bring her home."

The dog was growling at what looked like a stack of very fine yellow straw tossed over the rocks. Thaddeus raised the lantern to illuminate the area better and saw a heap of plaid fabric soaked in muddy bog water. A bright paisley shawl was draping over a dead branch.

Thaddeus did not dismount at once. He spurred the horse gently to take a few steps forward and called out his wife's name. He could now see the outline of her half-submerged body. She was lying on her side facing him, her breathing shallow but steady and her eyes wide open. Thick blood was oozing out of her mouth and nose.

Thaddeus jumped off the horse, his boots landing in mud ankle-deep. When he flipped Renate over to her back and elevated her head, spilling lantern light over her face, she looked right through him. Her one pupil appeared wider than the other. Her left foot looked twisted and swollen. Without making a sound, Renate allowed Thaddeus to lift her up and prop her in the saddle. She was able to keep her back straight, though her head bobbed forward.

Having caught the scent of the offender, Gita started pounding the ground with her hoof. It took Thaddeus a fair amount of whispering and patting to placate the animal. He proceeded to lead the horse by the reins with his wife wavering in the saddle.

As they got closer to home, Renate started emitting a faint droning sound. Thaddeus could not tell whether she was moaning or singing. There was a definite melody. Perhaps, she was singing the pain away.

The servants watched their master pull his wife off the horse and carry her across the threshold. Bronia held the door of the bedroom open, but her intervention went no further.

Without examining the extent of Renate's injuries, Thaddeus laid her on the bed with her shoes and clothes on. He feared that one careless move would exacerbate the damage. Standing over her, his arms crossed, he finally broke the silence.

"What were you thinking, wrestling with a horse? Arturas was mortified. I saw him shaking in the corner of the stable. The poor boy probably thought I was going to shoot Gita and banish him."

"That would be a daft thing to do." Renate looked down with theatrical self-disdain. She spoke clearly, even though the left side of her jaw was swollen. "You shouldn't dispose of valuable assets, the horse and the boy." She crumpled the bloodied handkerchief and threw it at her husband. "Dirty thief..."

"That's me, all right." Admittedly, it brought him relief to see that she was well enough to carry on a fight. "To be fair, I didn't take anything your father didn't give me along with his blessings. Nor have I spent his money frivolously on drinks and... women of questionable character."

"Whores." Renate gave him a slow deliberate blink. The man's prudishness was truly mind-boggling. "You should call things by their proper names. Your tongue won't turn black. You can rinse your mouth with holy water later on. But who'll rinse your sticky hands and your treacherous self-serving heart?"

"I used the money to save my home, which, incidentally, is now your home too. You've made it abundantly clear that it's not to your liking. I was to tell you more about my plans, but you didn't let me finish. Now that the debts are paid off, I can focus my efforts on making the farm profitable again."

"That'll never happen. Two-three years from now you'll be exactly where you started. You know that. My father's money bought you some time, but sooner or later you'll be in need of another heiress."

Despite the pain spreading through her limbs, Renate was feeling strangely victorious. At last, she had cracked

Thaddeus' saintly shell and lured his true colors to the surface.

"I've no time for this," he muttered, buttoning his coat.

"Bosh. You have all the time in the world. You've just run out of arguments. And now you're running away, because you don't want to admit your defeat."

"No, truly, there's no time to lose. You need a doctor. It'll probably take up most of the night looking for one. Janek Bargowski is back in Warsaw."

"There's no need for a doctor. I know what's wrong with me: a sprained ankle, two bruised ribs, and perhaps, a mild concussion. Whose brain wouldn't benefit from an occasional jostle? In Antanas' words, I heal quicker than a mongrel."

"It's not just your life that I'm concerned about. Forgive me if I sound self-serving, but I'd strongly prefer not to lose another child."

***

Left alone with her injuries, Renate gave herself permission to groan and even curse. She was using German words she had heard from her father's employees. New epicenters of pain kept flaring up throughout her body. The most worrisome was the spasm below her navel.

Agatha and Bronia were folding linens in the hall. Renate could hear every word.

"Think she'll miscarry?" the milkmaid asked her mother.

"I suppose we'll know by tomorrow mornin'."

"That would make the master mighty sad."

"Still, I say 'tis better to miscarry early on than give birth to an idiot. Remember Basia, the Zielinskis' maid?"

"The one with a nose like a spud?"

"Yah, that one. She married a leather smith. A bull-calf got loose and knocked her off her feet. Seven month later she birthed a son with clubbed feet shaped like hooves. The wretched babe ne'er spoke a word. He went through life mooin' like that damn bull that attacked his mother. That's what they called the lad, Jurek the Bull."

The load of local folklore was too much for Renate's ears. She grabbed a clay jar and slammed it into the wooden stand. "Come here, you two!"

Feeling no sense of urgency, the two women waddled into her room and stood at the foot of her bed.

"I realize I cannot keep you from badmouthing me," she said. "At least have the decency to keep your voices down. If you continue peeving me with your fables of mooing idiot children, you'll find yourself without a roof over your lice-ridden heads."

Agatha's sagging breasts heaved underneath her blouse as she cackled.

The hag's lack of concern mystified Renate. "If I were you, I'd start bundling up my rags for the road. Thaddeus loves me, and he'll do anything to keep me happy."

Bronia sat on the edge of the bed and squeezed Renate's ankle through the blanket.

"The master doesn't love yer."

"That's what your unlettered lot wants to believe. Like it or not, I'm here to stay."

"Time will tell."

The milkmaid's ruddy face exuded more pity than malice. Like her mother, Bronia did not seem in the least worried about her future at Raven Bog.

"I suppose I'll have to make most of this dunghill," Renate continued, her gaze wandering over the walls. There was just enough air in her lungs for one final attack. "I have plans for this place, big plans, that don't include people who annoy me. Once I get back on my feet, I'll convince Thaddeus to tear down the ugly clay huts and build an elegant villa. We'll staff it with literate, well-mannered servants. You're on thin ice, dearies."

"Master Dombrowski doesn't love yer," Bronia repeated in the same flat voice, as if Renate's entire tirade had escaped her ears. "Surely, he's nice to yer, but he's nice to everyone, even the tax collectors. That's just the kind of man he is. But he doesn't love yer like he loved the old mistress. If yer give him a child, maybe he'll warm up to yer."

CHAPTER 18

Black Ink, Lilac Satin

Vilnius, Stikliu Street—March 1885

The spring of 1885 was filled with promise for Esther and Leah Asher. Having spent most of the winter in Paris, mother and daughter returned to Vilnius with trunks full of fabric samples and latest couture patterns. As soon as the frivolous souvenirs from the Rue de la Paix were distributed, the two started preparing for the spring showcase. Every March the atelier hosted a miniature gala frequented by the wives and daughters of local merchants and officials.

The highlight of Leah's stay in Paris was meeting a very promising bachelor by the name David Kravitz who imported French fragrances into the major cities of the Russian Empire. He said he was going to be passing through Vilnius on his way to Moscow and promised to attend the fashion parade at the atelier. At first, Leah was skeptical. An entrepreneur of his caliber probably had "a wife in every port". But then, a week before Passover, she received a telegram from him saying that he was at a trade show in Riga and would not mind swinging by Vilnius. Leah spent the day twirling around the house, tripping over furniture and giggling, clutching the telegram to her warm virginal bosom. David was magnificent, except for two minor flaws: he kissed with his eyes open and did not keep kosher. In his defense, sticking to the rabbinical diet would be next to impossible given his lifestyle. He spent too much time on the road, traveling from one posh metropolis to another. He was constantly dining with distributors and shop owners. Most of them loved pork, and they taught him to love it too. As for gawking during intimate moments, how could he let a ravishing creature like Leah out of his sight even for a second?

"He's really coming," she kept saying to her mother. "My King David! And I've nothing to wear, as usual. Perhaps, I should greet him naked."

"Settle down, you vain hysteric," Esther curtailed her. "The man is a bacon-gobbling blasphemer."

"Don't be a prude, Mamah. You'd latch onto him yourself if you weren't married."

Instead of slapping her brazen daughter, Esther giggled into a peacock fan. "Haven't you read Honoré de Balzac? A woman doesn't blossom until her late thirties. Here, take the fan. It'll go with your emerald dress."

"But that dress is from last year's collection! The buttons on the cuffs scream '84."

"You don't want David to think you're trying too hard. Back to business. Have your brothers assembled the podium? The doors open in less than ten hours."

Leah's shoulders fell. "They haven't even started. Benjamin has been painting, and Jacob has been praying. You think they care about the family business?"

"We cannot trust Jacob with a hammer and nails. Go find Benjamin, grab him by the scruff of his neck, and tell him that if he doesn't get the podium assembled and draped by noon, he'll spend the next month scrubbing floors at Rabbi Goldman's house." In times of crisis, Esther demonstrated Napoleonic composure. "And if that doesn't motivate him, tell him we'll cut his allowance and confiscate his painting supplies."

***

Faking early symptoms of consumption was hard work indeed. It involved remembering to cough at regular intervals, complaining of fatigue and shortness of breath and asking to be excused from the dinner table early. Everyone in the Asher household knew that Benjamin was not really sick, at least not physically. Yet, something was clearly gnawing him from the inside, some juvenile ennui. His parents were optimistic that the mysterious malady would eventually run its course.

"You should either die or get back to the land of the living," Leah said, standing over his bed. "Nothing is more depressing than having a living corpse in your house."

A pile of watercolor paintings on the desk caught her eye. With lukewarm interest, Leah flipped through them. All paintings depicted the same architectural landmark, the Gate of Dawn and the chapel above it, from different angles, at different times of the day.

"Look, if you're having a spiritual crisis," she continued, "if you want to become a Christ follower, just say so. You know our parents don't care. Even Grandpa Isaac has given up on you. What's more distressing is that you haven't brought a single ruble into this household. How many of your masterpieces have you sold?"

Benjamin sat up on the bed, his unwashed long hair a Bohemian mess. "You'll have your bloody podium. Just show me which fabric you want for the drapery."

As they approached the workshop on the ground floor

where the fabric was stored, Leah picked up on some rather suspicious rustling and scratching noises coming from within.

"Rats," she whispered. "Told you we had rats. See, this is what happens when you leave half-eaten biscuits by the sewing machine."

Leah had been begging her father to get a cat, one of those fancy white Angoras she had seen in every fashionable household in Paris, but Daniel feared that the cat would jump on old Isaac's chest at night and smother the old man.

What Leah saw inside the workshop surprised her. A skinny redhead in an ill-fitting frock was standing over an ironing board, trying not to burn a hole in a starched petticoat.

Leah wrinkled her aristocratic nose and hissed at Benjamin. "What's this?"

"Your new assistant."

"I didn't ask for one."

"Yes, you did. For the past year you've been moaning to dump the dreary tasks on someone else. This girl agreed to serve finger sandwiches and beer tonight for a nominal fee. It'll give you more podium time. See, I do care about the family business."

"So you bring this street urchin under our roof and leave her unattended with costly supplies? How do you know she's not a thief? What if she steals a roll of my finest brocade? Where did you find her anyway?"

"Just outside Frau Jung's school."

Suddenly everything made sense to Leah. "Another German? *Oy vey*... You and your Aryan fantasy."

"This one is half-Lithuanian."

"Even better! We all know how much the Balts adore us. This one must be really down on her luck if she agreed to the job."

"Her older brother is a total ogre. He keeps hoarding her share of the inheritance until she turns eighteen."

"And you gobbled up her weepy damsel-in-distress story?"

"It's the truth. I know her brother and what he's capable of. Does the name Sebastian Messer mean anything to you?"

Leah winced as if she had just witnessed a dog run over by a carriage. "Oh... So she's the infamous half-breed? I don't envy her—or him for that matter. Is this your mitzvah for the day? Keeping a starving art student out of the whorehouse?"

Benjamin leaned closer to his sister and lowered his voice, even though Aurelia could not hear them. "I confess my motives aren't entirely selfless. I want to be on friendly terms with Aurelia, because her brother is my only link to Renate. He knows where she is."

"Not again... Don't tell me you're still moping over that Lichtner girl. She could be abroad, for all we know."

"Or just a few kilometers away."

Leah was the only family member privy to her brother's ill-fated tryst. Benjamin had confided in her a few days after Renate's disappearance. As much as his sister relished taunting and patronizing him, he knew he could count on her not to blabber his secrets to anyone. Even though the nature of her work bound her to pragmatism, Leah understood the piquant allure of an interfaith romance.

"If your Aryan muse wanted to be found, surely she would've given a sign by now."

"Unless she's held against her will."

Leah gave him a light slap on the back of his head, kicking his hair up. "Someone's read too many Alexandre Dumas novels. Now stand back and let me take it from here." Clicking her heels, she walked up to the uninvited guest.

"Fräulein, you don't belong here."

"Well, I cannot leave now," Aurelia retorted, flexing her lower back. "Your brother's already paid me, and I've already spent the money. I fear this transaction cannot be reversed."

Leah produced a Cheshire Cat's smile and stretched both hands forward. "Perhaps, my message wasn't clear. When I said you didn't belong here, I was referring to this grim workshop. A beauty like you belongs on the podium. I could use a redhead in the showcase."

Benjamin slapped his forehead. Could his sister be so cruel? Indeed, she could! She would never miss an opportunity to tease a penniless German girl.

In the meantime, Leah snaked her arm around Aurelia's waist. "Come with me, my puppy. The wicked fairy will turn you into one delectable bitch. The dogs in the crowd will be salivating all over you. But first we must powder your nose. It's so red and peeling. Did you stick it in a kettle full of boiling water?"

Before succumbing to Leah's advances, Aurelia cast a quizzical glance at Benjamin.

"You're in good hands, fräulein," he assured her. "My sister is a miracle worker."

***

Leah's latest creation was a two-piece dress in lilac satin with a back-shelf bustle. The bodice was draped up at both sides and worn over a matching underskirt, the neckline as wide at the bust and narrower at the shoulder.

"You don't have to keep up the façade around me," Leah said, sticking a silk flower into Aurelia's hair. "I have you all figured out."

"Do you?"

"My dear, I've traveled Europe. Don't expect me to

184

believe that my brother was the one who solicited you. He knows better. It was you who latched onto him, wasn't it?"

"Does it matter how I got here?"

"Not really. What matters is how you'll be exiting. If you're looking for a rich Jew, you've come to the right place. Tonight the studio will be swarming with them. Many of my father's friends would like a juvenile German mistress. If you're lucky, they'll pay for your art supplies."

***

Castle Street

"My name is in the news." Sebastian waved the latest edition of *Aušra* in front of

Theodor's face. The two friends were having afternoon coffee at Napoleon Bistro. "I don't know what it says, but I doubt that the content is flattering."

The mysterious troll had struck again. Another edition of the Lithuanian nationalist paper had been slipped into Sebastian's desk drawer. This time his name appeared on the front page, circled with a red pen.

Theodor, who had grown up with a Lithuanian nanny and understood the rudiments of the language, scanned the article.

It has been nine months since the destruction of Hermann Lichtner's textile factory, a former beacon of industrial success, and no criminal charges have been filed to date. The Russian authorities appear to be in no hurry to bring the arsonists to justice. A prosperous German establishment was an eyesore for the Czar's agents. Incidentally, a new textile factory has opened just a few hundred meters from the old one. The owner, a Muscovite by the name of Alexander Naumov, seems all too happy to employ Lichtner's former workers and take advantage of their knowledge of the machines imported from Brandenburg as well as the methodology developed by the late entrepreneur. Sebastian Messer, Lichtner's attorney and the executor of the estate, has yet to comment on the subject. He is the only one privy to the whereabouts of Lichtner's surviving daughter. In light of Messer's slavish loyalty to the crown, one cannot help but wonder how much money he received for keeping his mouth shut and cooperating with the authorities to cover up his former client's murder.

"Well, Messer, now you're an Imperial celebrity," Theodor summed up, folding the newspaper. "What are you going to do about it?"

Sebastian shrugged with affected indifference. "Not a thing. Nobody with an ounce of intelligence reads this drivel. It's not even a legitimate enough publication to merit a rebuttal. This pseudo-exposé is but an amateur crime feuilleton, cheap anti-czarist propaganda."

"If it's garbage, then why did you show it to me?"

"So we could laugh at it together."

"Yet you don't look very amused, Messer. You look rather tense."

"I always look tense." Sebastian began murdering the pastry with a fork. "Don't give me that accusatory stare. My specialty is patent law, not criminal justice. It's not my job to go after Naumov, even if he had a hand in the murder, which is entirely possible in this God-forsaken city, but so far we have no proof. Lichtner made it clear he didn't want any criminal charges filed. It's my job to see that my dead client's wishes are honored and his daughter is kept out of public eye. I'm sorry I cannot indulge your curiosity."

Theodor added more cream to Sebastian's coffee. "Settle down, Messer. I'm not accusing you of anything. I'm just worried about you. The last year has taken a toll on you."

"And that's why I'm going to St. Petersburg in June," Sebastian announced, pushing away the plate with the brutalized pastry, "to catch the white nights. A few outdoor concerts, a ride on a steamboat down the river... Of course, I'll need a new summer suit. I think cream or beige would look good on me."

Theodor's mouth started salivating. Next to gourmet food, fashion was one of his favorite topics. Finally, his friend was talking about something pleasant.

"I hear there's a showcase on Stikliu Street. We should go. The entrance fee includes food and drinks. So even if you don't walk away with the suit of your dreams, you'll get a light supper out of it."

Sebastian grimaced. "Asher's Atelier? I'm not looking for a rabbinical prayer shawl."

"You know damn well there's much more than a stack of yarmulkes to be found there. Last season I bought a plaid vest from them, and I'm still getting compliments on it. When was the last time you got a compliment?"

Sebastian knew what his friend was really asking: *When was the last time you lay with a woman without paying an hourly rate?* The anemic lawyer did not have a straight answer for that question. There were a few perfectly hospitable brothels in Vilnius, mainly catering to imperial soldiers and transient merchants. In the twenty-eight years of his life, Sebastian had been to such an establishment only once, and the experience had left a lasting sensory trauma.

THE GATE OF DAWN

His culprit was unfashionable squeamishness that stemmed not so much from any moral convictions but rather from a heightened sensitivity to unpleasant stimuli. The sight of garishly painted half-naked whores with distended breasts, the smell of bodily fluids, cigars and cheap apple wine, the sound of accordion ballads punctuated by guttural exclamations, all that had shaken up Sebastian's delicate nervous system. Aside from his mortal fear of catching a disease, he worried that interaction with whores would deepen his general antipathy towards women and render him impotent. On some level he associated the brothel employees with his stepmother, the biggest whore of all as far as he was concerned. If he stood any chance of marrying well and actually making that marriage tolerable, he could not allow himself to become a hardened misogynist. He had to safeguard whatever tenderness and respect he had left in his heart towards the opposite sex. For the past few years he had been relieving his tension in chilly, teeth-grinding solitude while fantasizing about his aloof Russian widow. In his fantasies Lydia Vishnevsky was fully clothed and engaged in some sort of cerebral activity like transcribing music or assembling a photo camera. It took that image specifically to get his body to respond. That was the spectrum of his sensuality. He had not been touched by a living, breathing woman since his university days.

His first love, Elizabeth, was a few years older and married to his economics instructor, Professor Suhanov. Unlike most women from her class, she was no ordinary parlor cow who spent her time gossiping and squandering her husband's money. Elizabeth actually had a position at the university as an associate librarian. The affair had ended as suddenly as it had started, and Sebastian could honestly say that it was his only gratifying, albeit shattering, erotic experience. The lady possessed that perfect combination of frivolity and self-control, warmth and egotism. During lovemaking she did not thrash or roar. She twitched and squeaked like a mouse. But those movements and sounds were perfectly natural and sincere. Sebastian knew she did not feign ecstasy to patronize a green boy she was dallying with. He felt like a man. No, take that back—he felt like a god! And then she broke it off, without excessive tears or pompous speeches on duty and sin. Her suffering was as evident as Sebastian's. Between dry farewell kisses, they made a provisional pact. "If my husband dies before me, and if you're still free, I'll be yours," she said. They both knew that scenario was not likely to transpire. Suhanov was still relatively young and in good health. Not that Sebastian would wish premature death upon one of his favorite instructors. Dear God, what a loss it would be for the University. No, the Professor's life and reputation had to be protected at all costs for the sake of the hundreds of young men who looked up to him. Suhanov was cultivating the next generation of lawyers, officials and entrepreneurs who would lead the Russian Empire into the twentieth century. What are two selfish amorous hearts against hundreds of future careers?

Sebastian derived somber satisfaction from knowing that he had martyred his love on the altar of the Empire. Yes, he still recognized Christian standards of conduct, even if he did not always adhere to them. Now he was faced with the tricky task of picking up the pieces and getting himself to a place where his sexual appetites, moral convictions and career ambitions could be in agreement. The experience with Professor Suhanov's wife had ruined him. Of course, there are men who can go back to eating tripe after having tasted filet mignon. Sebastian was not one of those men. He would rather starve. With Elizabeth almost certainly lost to him, Lydia was the next best thing.

"I don't care for... compliments," he finally said.

"If you're so dead to the world, you should've become a monk." Theo's plump, nimble fingers began twirling the butter knife. "The Ashers use only the most delectable female subjects in their fashion parades. Last time I met two chorus girls from the Imperial Ballet School. I took them home, and they performed a little *pas-de-deux* for me. In the morning I escorted the two lovelies to the train station and promised to come to one of their shows."

Sebastian glared at his friend with a mixture of contempt and envy. He knew the fat boy was not making the story up. Of course, Theo did not mention the two ballerinas' names, so that made his behavior more gentlemanly. A flippant Epicurean like him was incapable of intense, exclusive attachments. Instead, he kept an ever expanding legion of omnivorous female friends who were always eager to show their goodwill by giving him discrete and noncommittal groin rubs.

"Fine, you've convinced me," Sebastian said. "I'll go to the showcase with you."

***

Stikliu Street—Asher's Atelier

The first sip of kosher wine felt a little surreal to Sebastian. After all, he was introducing his finicky palate to an entirely foreign substance. A hardened beer drinker, he was not used to such sticky sweetness. Still, it was the only alcoholic drink served at Asher's Atelier, and he would feel like a fool staying sober for the night. He had to admit, however reluctantly, he was actually enjoying himself. He could see why Theodor was so enthusiastic about this place.

They had arrived unfashionably early. Theo had insisted on being the first one to get through the door and assault the table of food. That was his plan. Smoked fish tartlets always went fast, and Theo could not fathom trying on clothes on an empty stomach. All that buttoning, unbuttoning, tying, layering and turning in front of a mirror burns a lot of energy.

By eight o'clock the showroom was bustling with patrons and photographers. Daniel Asher, dressed in a charcoal tail suit, was greeting visitors at the door and handing out freshly printed catalogues with the highlights of the new season's collection.

A tall dashing gentleman in his early thirties was passing around tiny vials with shiny labels. He explained that those were complementary perfume samples from Paris. He introduced himself as David Kravitz, a friend of the Asher family, who traveled all the way from Riga to support the lovely Leah and enhance the success of the showcase.

"This particular scent is called Conqueror," he said to Sebastian as he slipped a vial in his hand. "Its top notes are rosemary and salt water. It hasn't yet been released. I got an advance sample from the manufacturer. How would you like to be the first man in Europe to wear it?"

In spite of being tipsy, Sebastian saw right through David's act. "I bet you say that to everyone."

"A little bit of healthy skepticism is good. That's why I've singled you out. My intuition for character is just as keen as my sense of smell. When I look at you, I see someone rational, disciplined and victory-oriented."

"These qualities apply to most men in this room."

"You were born to wear this scent. Open the vial and tell me if I was wrong."

When Sebastian pulled out the cork plug and held the vial

to his nose, he was immediately transported to a courtroom in St. Petersburg. Enveloped in blue light breaking through the vaulted window, he was standing before the judge, arguing the biggest intellectual property case of the decade. Sebastian could feel authority and triumph coursing through his veins. The perfume dealer was a sorcerer, no doubt. He could read people's thoughts and tap into their deepest ambitions.

"Nekrasov, you have to try this."

Theodor was nowhere in sight. Having finished stuffing himself with finger sandwiches, he was probably behind the curtain in the dressing booth, groping the models as they were getting ready for the fashion parade. He was on friendly terms with the Ashers, so they allowed him access to the girls.

Around nine o'clock Esther came out and delivered a speech about her recent expedition to Paris. The fiddler started playing a slow droning melody that did not overpower the voice of the hostess. One by one, the models emerged from behind the curtain and twirled on the podium beneath the giant chandelier. The first one was a buxom blonde with a contrastingly stern frozen face, laced up to the chin in chocolate velvet. The second one was a brunette draped in red and green tartan wool. With each new appearance, the outfits kept getting progressively more revealing and suggestive. The last model in the parade was a fragile redhead sporting a profusion of frills, swags and ribbons in lilac satin. The upper part of her face was covered by a demi-mask.

With a swift flutter of her fingers, the redhead unhooked waistband causing the bustle skirt and the petticoat to collapse. The girl remained standing on the podium, flashing a pair of rose-pink drawers with lacy knee bands and white silk stockings. Showcasing undergarments to the audience was not all that uncommon during a fashion parade at Asher's Atelier, though usually such bold displays were saved until the very end. To avoid overexciting the male patrons and enraging their wives, Esther and Leah had deliberately picked a girl who was not overly voluptuous. This one was barely out of adolescence, with boyish hips, stick-thin limbs and an underdeveloped bosom.

When Sebastian saw a birthmark on the girl's right calf showing through the stocking, his mellow joviality vanished, giving way to rage.

He grabbed her by the wrist, dragged her down from the podium and ripped the mask off her face. The fiddler played a few more bars of the tune and then hid behind the curtain. A collective gasp ran through the lines of patrons. Was it part of the performance?

"I knew it!" Sebastian shouted. "My sister, dressed like a cheap vaudeville whore."

Aurelia cocked her head and burst out laughing. "So I'm your sister all of a sudden?"

Sebastian's reddened eyes scanned her from the silk flowers on her head to the tips of her satin shoes. "You're every bit like your bog-dwelling mother. Perhaps, instead of paying for your education, I should've sent you to a brothel. That's where you'll end up anyway."

Theodor, his mouth still filled with pickled herring, tried to squeeze his full belly through the crowd towards the podium. "Messer, for the love of God... Stop!"

Sebastian proceeded to wring his sister's wrist. A thin amethyst bracelet broke, and the tiny nuggets scattered all over the floor. With his free hand he started pulling pins and flowers from her hair, calling her every dirty name in every language he knew. The flabbergasted patrons did nothing, so absurd was the scene before their eyes.

The visiting perfume merchant was the first one to come out of his stupor. He grabbed a candle holder and struck the drunken German between the shoulder blades. Sebastian collapsed with a groan. David Kravitz took a bucket with half-melted ice and dumped the contents over Sebastian's head.

"You won't insult a woman on my watch. And you won't disrupt my friend's event." With a leonine air, David surveyed the audience. "All right, who brought this clown here?"

"I did," Theodor replied contritely. The crowd parted for him, and he was able to enter the scene of the crime, nearly slipping on one of the ice cubes. "I shouldn't have allowed him to drink all that wine. He's not used to grape beverages."

"You're a good man," David validated him. "Now get your friend out of here before I call the gendarmes."

***

The theatrical manner in which David had dealt with the rowdy German raised him to new heights in Esther's eyes.

"I was wrong about him," she told her daughter after the crowd had dispersed. "He's a real man after all. Of course, he'll probably never set his foot here again. He must think we run a freak show."

"I'm sure he's seen worse, Mamah. He'll be back with more perfume samples and, maybe, a diamond for me."

"Impudent girl!"

"Like mother, like daughter." Leah unclasped her lapis medallion necklace and dropped it into a velvet pouch. "I must say it's exhausting, wearing so much jewelry."

Esther tapped her lightly on the back. "You better go check on our patient. See what you can do for her. I feel so sorry for that creature."

"You cannot feel sorry for everyone, Mamah."

Aurelia was sitting in the coatroom of the atelier, still sporting the ill-fated lilac ensemble, her swollen wrist wrapped in a towel. Despite the tear trails on her copiously plastered face, her expression was triumphant. Benjamin was keeping her company.

"Keep the outfit," Leah said, half expecting a refusal. "Unless you think it'll bring back bad memories... in which case it would be perfectly logical to leave it here. I won't take offense, truly. I'm sure there are plenty of interested buyers."

"No, I'll take it," Aurelia replied. "I assume the boots, the gloves and the hat are included?"

"Of course... A dress without accessories is like steak without sauce. Is there anything else my family can do for you before you... go home?"

"A dose of morphine, perhaps?"

Leah lifted the edge of the towel to examine the extent of the damage. There was considerable swelling and bruising. "Benjamin tells me you're an art student. What if your technique suffers?"

"I'd call it a blessing! I've been waiting for a legitimate excuse not to pick up the loathsome paint brush again. When my teacher sees my mangled hand, she'll stop demanding results from me. Then I'll be free to pursue my true passion— military journalism. Next time the Czar picks a fight with Turkey, I'll be there, on the front lines with a helmet and a typewriter."

"I see..." Leah wondered if Aurelia needed to have her head examined. Even the most progressive girls who managed to soldier their way into journalism were restricted to society reporting, covering the latest in food and fashion. But the Russo-Turkish conflict? Of course, with a body like that she could disguise herself as a boy. Stranger things had happened. "I'll go and fetch some morphine."

The moment Leah left, Aurelia moved closer to Benjamin. "Now, getting back to our original conversation..."

He shuddered, as if awaking from a daydream. "Ah?"

"You should stop looking for the Lichtner girl."

"But I love her."

"Nobody can help you with that."

"I have a feeling she's thoroughly wretched, wherever she is."

"Or, she could be deliriously happy. Have you considered that possibility?"

CHAPTER 19

Penance

Raven's Bog—spring, 1885

On the first day of Easter the boys from the nearby villages assembled for the ritual of *lalavimas,* which involved walking through the neighborhood, caroling. They stopped by each house to wish everyone a good year, harvest and health. Marriageable girls stood on their porches as the boys performed a special song, *lalinka,* wishing them luck finding good husbands.

Renate absorbed the sounds of spring festivities from her bed, to which she had been confined since her duel with an unbroken horse back in September. Thaddeus had spent the night after the accident searching for a doctor. One of the neighbors had finally pointed him towards a retired hospital orderly, a Polish woman by the name Angniezska who was renting a patch of land and a hut from the Rozpondek family. The lady was nearly deaf and blind, but she was all science with a touch of cosmic fatalism, no mystical folklore. At least she did not make any false promises. Having poked the patient in the belly with her cold fingers, she concluded in her sleepy croaking voice that the fate of the fetus was in

God's hands. If the bleeding and the cramping would not subside, the womb would eventually expel the little tadpole. There was nothing to be done to reverse or speed up the process. As long as no fever set in, Renate would be able to resume her wifely duties within fortnight. The ribs and the ankle would heal on their own.

Before leaving, Agniezska patted Thaddeus on the cheek with her wrinkled claw.

"It's all right, sonny. The Lord is merciful. I see the guilt in your eyes. Don't chastise yourself too harshly. You're not the first man to beat his pregnant wife."

As much as Renate wanted Thaddeus dead, the outrageous accusation prompted her to set the story straight. "He didn't lay a finger on me. I fell off a horse." It was not Thaddeus' image that she worried about but her own. Did she, Hermann Lichtner's daughter, look like someone who would take abuse from a man?

The woman's lips stretched in a patronizing smile. "Sure, sweetheart, tell that to your mother. You cannot fool old Agniezska. But you're a good woman to defend your husband. Try not to provoke him next time."

When the old woman departed, Renate and Thaddeus locked eyes and started laughing at the agonizing stupidity of it all. Rather, she was laughing, and he was merely mimicking her out of solidarity. By then Renate's prevalent emotion was embarrassment. Her behavior had been unworthy of a balanced, calculating German woman. She should not have gotten so angry with someone who was not her equal. Thaddeus' actions, however displeasing to her, were consistent with his moral code. What did she expect? Asking a man who had no ambition or wanderlust to appreciate the Royal Palace in Stockholm was just as unreasonable as asking a barnyard rooster to fly across the

Neman River. It was not the rooster's fault that God had not made him a falcon, just as it was not his fault that he had been given a white peahen in marriage. They were grossly mismatched in every way except one. And now they were going to have a child together—God willing. Renate prayed for a favorable outcome. She did not want to think about the alternative and what it would do to Thaddeus. Losing another child would only fortify his sense of martyrdom. It would give him one more excuse to recite a speech on the self-indulgent nature of grief. He would become even more pious, more devoted to "his people". *Mein Gott, lass die Kaulquappe zu leben.* God, please let the tadpole live.

And God answered her grumpy prayer—reluctantly and not immediately. After a few nerve-racking days of checking the nightshirt for traces of blood, the pain finally abated. It kept its distance as long as Renate stayed idle. The moment she would exert herself in any way, the spasms would return, driving her back into bed. Pain kept her on a short leash. It became her invisible, ubiquitous prison guard.

When the carolers were passing through Raven's Bog on Easter, she did not even peek out the window, even though Thaddeus hinted that it would be appropriate for her, as the lady of the household, to hand out cake and painted eggs to the carolers.

As her belly swelled, her limbs grew thinner and weaker, to the point where she could not brush her hair without her arms cramping up and trembling. She spent the last two months of her pregnancy in a hazy restless slumber, inertly gulping Agatha's potions that smelled like moss and oak bark. At first Renate took pleasure in aggravating the old woman by making her run errands, but eventually even that game lost its appeal.

She did not see much of Thaddeus during that time. He

had rejoined his workers and spent his days hammering and sawing. His infrequent visits to his wife's bedside lasted a few minutes and ended with the routine pinch of the cheek and a kiss on the forehead. His latest project was to build cages and populate them with domestic nutrias, beaver-like animals imported from South America. Their neighbor Zielinski had pitched that idea to him, swearing that nutrias were a most profitable investment. Their dense glossy fur was all the rage. The females were very fertile and could produce two or three litters a year. Zielinski went as far as selling Thaddeus his first pair of albino nutrias at what he claimed to be a fair price. The animals lasted less than a week. One morning the stable boy found them with their bellies up.

"Stupid me," Thaddeus lamented to Renate. "I totally forgot that those creatures needed a water basin to splash in. That makes sense, as they live near rivers and lakes in the wild. They must've died of thirst. I haven't told Zielinski yet. But I'm glad I built those cages. They weren't a complete waste. We'll fill them with Angora rabbits. Tell you what: once you're back on your feet, you can take over that venture. How does that sound? Jolanta had her bee hives, and you'll have your rabbits. Nutrias you have to kill for the pelts, but Angoras you can you keep alive forever and just shear them. You could probably do it yourself. I'll ask Antanas to sharpen the shearing scissors. Of course, the trick is not to stab the animal. Rabbits do kick and wiggle, so you may need to tie their hind legs."

The most torturous part of the confinement was being forced to listen to the cries of Bronia's infant son Edgaras on the other side of the wall. The baby, who had arrived in February, possessed an unusually strong, piercing voice that could penetrate even through the thickest barriers. Renate had not seen him, but she detested him already. Her imagination, fueled by Agatha's potions, conjured a giant red-faced monster. She could not hide from the loathsome sound, even by sticking her head under the pillow. One time she pleaded with Thaddeus to have Bronia and Edgaras moved into another part of the house, but he declined her request. The other rooms were not as well heated, and the little one would catch a cold. He also emphasized it would be good for Renate to get used to the sound of an infant wailing.

***

One mid-April morning Renate felt an overwhelming desire to rinse out her paint brushes, which had been sitting in a tin bucket without use for months. The last time she had tried to paint was right before Christmas, but her brain, eyes and hands had refused to talk to each other, so she had abandoned the unwashed brushes and a few crumbled sheets of ivory paper in the corner underneath the orphaned easel. Agatha had avoided setting her foot in that corner during her daily visits, as if that part of the room was a shrine to some unholy entity. Renate had spent most of winter and a good portion of the spring staring at that depressing composition, a testimony to her failure as an artist. Suddenly, scrubbing the dried watercolors off the fine sable hairs seemed like the most important task in the world. She added clean water to the bucket and started swooshing the brushes vigorously. The front of her nightdress quickly became stained with patches of green and blue, but she did not care.

Spreading the freshly washed brushes on the windowsill to dry, Renate remembered her mother's final days, that fragment of time between the initial onset of the influenza symptoms and the dinner party which smoothly transitioned into a funeral. Before dropping dead, Katherine had cleaned and organized her jewelry, sorted out her sewing tools and oiled up the sewing machine. Apparently, she did not want to leave a mess behind and inconvenience the survivors. Mutti had always put her obligations above her own wellbeing. That explained her ridiculous premature death.

A startling epiphany avalanched upon Renate.

I'm going to follow Mutti! Today is the day.

The sharp spasm in her back affirmed her premonition. The pain was nothing like the sporadic cramping she had been enduring for the past seven months. It was no longer the stern prison guard but the executioner himself dragging her to the scaffold.

Leaning against the windowsill, she glanced at the carpet of snowdrops and buttercups covering meadow. *A bloody nice day to die!*

The very idea of exiting the physical world did not stir any protest in Renate's heart. Her self-preservation instinct had been drained and gnawed down by the months of isolation and malaise. But damn it, she was going to exit on her own terms, with dignity becoming of a Lichtner! Not in that bed, surrounded by *those...* people. She would follow in the footsteps of solitary wild animals.

Renate slipped out of the house without any trouble. Thaddeus was in the fields with his men planting potatoes. The women were inside the chicken coop picking a hen for slaughter. There was nobody to stop her. Propped against the wall was a rusty plough covered with a large piece of grass-stained sackcloth. Renate draped the cloth around her shoulders to make herself less conspicuous against the landscape. A figure in white would be easier to spot. Careful not to make any noise, she started trekking towards the bog. It was a strange feeling, trying to run without seeing her feet. Could that grotesque bloated shadow be hers? Contact with the soil gave her an instant jolt of energy. At least, nature was on her side. The solidarity of the elements was only her consolation prize for the past ten infernal months. In the meantime, the spasms kept getting more frequent and intense. Renate had heard that there is a flush of euphoria before one draws the final breath. Who had told her that? Benjamin! According to Jewish beliefs, when a righteous person dies, there is no pain, only a kiss. Alas, she was not Jewish—or righteous for that matter. No, she was going to die a classic Christian death, shrouded in agony.

The belt of snowdrops spun around her as she collapsed with her back against a giant mossy rock by the rim of the bog. It looked like a safe, private place to die. With a slab of softened bark between her teeth, she reclined and simply allowed the pain to plunder her insides.

CHAPTER 20

Elation

Young Arturas was basking in his first romantic victory, his adolescent ego soaring above the bogs and meadows—he had managed to conquer a privileged older woman.

How did it start? To show his appreciation, Master Dombrowski had excused Arturas from field work for an afternoon and even allowed him to borrow his old hunting rifle. The boy realized very quickly that the rifle was completely useless. So he wandered through the woods in the company of Milo, soaking in the dewy breath of the spring soil. Passing through a clearing, Arturas spotted Klaudia, the middle daughter of Adrian Baginski, who worked as a gardener for the Rozpondeks. Klaudia had come to the woods in search of wild strawberry bushes with the intention of digging them up and replanting them in her backyard; her family loved berry jam.

Judging from how the fabric of Klaudia's skirt skimmed her legs, Arturas deduced that she was not wearing a petticoat. The realization made his skittish heart thump harder. At the same time, he remained conscious of Klaudia's superiority. In addition to being two years older, she was from a clean, solid Polish family. Arturas was an orphan and a Balt. Clearly, that girl was out of his rank. That spring day, however, he felt strangely inspired and emboldened. Perhaps, the spores and the pollen he had inhaled possessed some fortifying powers helping him summon the audacity to talk to her.

"Well, g'day to yer." He tipped the bill of his cap, pleased that his voice had deepened in the past few months. Arturas was rather tall for his age and broad in the shoulders. Klaudia did not need to know how old he was.

Her fist on her hip, the girl surveyed the stable boy and puckered. "Look at you, with your dog and gun."

Arturas let out an indistinct hum. Technically speaking, neither the dog nor the gun belonged to him, but Klaudia did not need to know that either.

"What yer got in that basket?"

The girl lifted the lid and showed him the tender green bushes she had picked. The content of her half-unlaced bodice fascinated him more than that of the basket.

"Think they're perky enough?" Klaudia asked, fingering the soft stems.

"I'll say..."

"You don't think they'll shrivel up? Good." She closed the lid. "I better get home and start planting."

"I'll walk with yer," the boy volunteered. "So yer won't walk alone."

Klaudia pulled one of her braids across her mouth and giggled. "Why, are you afraid I'll get lost? Are there robbers and goblins on the loose? And what about your hunt?"

"Nay, I'm done for the day."

"Already? You haven't even started. I didn't hear any gunshots."

"That's because I didn't see anythin' good to shoot." Arturas shrugged with affected spite and looked away.

Keeping up those benign lies for the sake of maintaining his strapping grown-up image was proving to be a challenge. "I, too, should be headin' home."

"How's your master? I haven't seen him since the wedding."

"All right, I s'pose." Arturas adjusted the gun strap on his shoulder. "Drinkin' a lot. I've been countin' them bottles in the cellar. I don't recall him drinkin' half as much after Lady Jolanta's death. How's your family?"

"My big sister Maria is moving to the city."

"Oh... Has she got a husband there?"

"Nay. She'll be working for a dentist."

"A what?" Arturas inclined his ear. He had never heard that word before.

"A tooth doctor, silly. Ever seen tools for pulling teeth? They look like farming tools, only smaller and sharper. Tiny rakes, axes and shovels to dig up inside your mouth. The chair alone looks like something from the witch-hunting days. You know what Maria's departure means for me?" Klaudia put the basket on a tree stump and spun, her plaid skirt fanning to expose supple ankles. "I can start going to dance parties and kissing lads."

"Can I be the first one to kiss yer?" Arturas heard himself blurt out.

What did he have to lose? What was the worst thing that could happen? She would slap him and go home alone. He was not prepared for what was to follow. Klaudia stopped spinning, took a few wobbly steps towards him and fell against him, her arms draping over his back.

"Thought you'd never ask, foolish man."

Man... By God, she called him a man! Too bad his parents were not alive. How proud they would be of him for having sacked such a tasty wench. He was going to marry Klaudia, no question about it. He was going to do things to her, mysterious grown-up things that Master Dombrowski did to his wife. But first they needed to get the first kiss out of the way.

Their soft freckled noses bumped against each other a few times while they two of them were trying to figure out a perfect angle for a kiss. When their lips finally met, Arturas dropped the rifle. The firs and the birches twirled around him in wild circle dance. In that moment he was thankful that the loose-fitting trousers allowed room for his expanding manhood.

As his arousal was reaching its peak, Klaudia suddenly pulled back.

"What's wrong?" Arturas asked, panting. "Let's keep goin'. Don't yer want to?"

"I heard something. A cry, a moan... It was coming from the bog."

"Must be a crane."

Klaudia shook her head, making the fuzzy braids dance. "It didn't sound like a crane or any kind of bird. Sounded more like an animal, a wounded one. Didn't you hear anything?"

No, not Arturas. A grenade could have exploded above his head, and he would not have noticed. "So what if there is some dyin' beast? What does it matter? To hell with everythin'!"

He pulled the tasseled strings of her blouse, exposing the pulsating caves above her collarbones. By then the wool bodice had come completely undone. Klaudia did nothing to stop him. She waited for his next move. Holding the girl's braids with one hand, he ran his free hand over the engorged mounds of her bosom crowned with what looked and felt like acorn caps.

"We have to see what it is," Klaudia said. "That cry won't let me rest."

"Yer teasin' me. I bet at the next dance yer won't even look my way."

Klaudia pinched his crimson cheek and tied the strings of her neckline. "I'm not teasing you, I swear. I just want see what's in the bog. Then... then I'll be all yours. I'll show you whatever you want to see, greedy man."

There. She called him that name again, and Arturas believed her. He was confident that Klaudia would keep her word and let him indulge his curiosity.

Arturas fixed the belt on his oversized trousers. "I'll come with yer."

He picked up the useless rifle and whistled to summon the dog. Milo looked puzzled and restless. Over the past few months his condition had further declined. He had started dragging one of his hind legs, and his tail wags appeared weaker.

"Lead the way, old boy," Klaudia said, realizing the futility of her command. The dog was going to go wherever his senile brain was going to take him.

Arms linked, the youngsters crossed the clearing and headed down towards the wetlands.

Suddenly, Klaudia halted and pointed in the direction of the massive rock protruding from the water. "Holy Mother of God... What did I tell you? It wasn't a crane."

Arturas followed her index finger and saw a half-naked woman with her back propped against the rock. Her wrinkled nightdress was lifted to her hips, exposing pale legs smeared in blood. Between them there was a squirming red lump. The woman's face was covered by tangled blonde hair, yet the boy instantly recognized Lady Renate. Having seen enough corpses in his life, he knew that the ashen skin tone was not a good sign. He removed his cap and mouthed a prayer.

The shaggy mongrel dashed forward as fast as his rusty hip sockets allowed. The youngsters followed. Arturas sighed with relief when he saw that his master's wife was still alive. Her eyes closed, she was wincing and licking her lips.

Klaudia swiftly picked up the squirming morsel and used the hem of her skirt to wipe the wrinkled face. "A boy," she announced. "Do you have anything sharp on you, like a penknife?"

Arturas patted his pocket and pulled out a dull shaving razor that he used for carving toy boats out of tree bark. "Will that do?"

The girl snatched the tool from his hand and sliced the slippery cord connecting the infant to his mother.

"He's not breathing very well," she said. "There's fluid in his nose. I don't like how blue his toes are. Who knows how long he's been lying there. Before long, ravens would be pecking at him. They love fresh meat."

In the thirteen years of his life Arturas had seen many a newborn foal, but he had no idea what human babies were supposed to look like. "What are we to do now?"

"You tell me." Klaudia shrugged and returned the blade back to Arturas. "You know your master. Whose life matters more to him? We cannot get them both to the farm." She allowed the boy a few seconds to deliberate. Then, seeing that he was not ready to give her a definitive answer, she made the decision for him. "Fine, I'll run the baby to the farm, and you stay here with Her Ladyship."

Klaudia laid the baby in the basket on top of the strawberry bushes and closed the lid to protect him from the insects. Before taking off she bent down and gave Arturas one more kiss which he returned with fervor. In fifteen minutes he and Klaudia had gone from mere acquaintances, to lovers, to partners in rescue.

Crouching in front of Renate, Arturas tapped her on the cheeks a few times. "M'lady? Are yer awake?"

She opened her eyes, sank her dirty fingernails into the boy's hand and unleashed a torrent of German profanities. At least, they sounded like profanities to Arturas.

Careful to avoid contact with her skin, the stable boy rolled the nightdress down to cover her legs. "Be still, m'lady. Help is on the way."

With a look of profound disgust, she released his hand and fell back against the rock.

***

"I have an heir," Thaddeus declared as he brandished the bottle of vodka infused with mint and honey. The servants had heard the same speech four times already, and in all cases the celebration had proven premature. Still, they would never decline sweetened vodka in the middle of a work day. God willing, fifth time would be the charm. So they drank to the health of child. The mother's name somehow got omitted, and Thaddeus made no effort to remedy the oversight. The focus was entirely on the newborn.

Agatha was the only one who did not put on airs or take a single swig of the concoction. She stood apart from the rest, arms folded and eyes burrowing into the jubilant master.

When the workers began returning to their chores, Thaddeus pulled her aside. "I know what's on your mind," he said. "You're chastising yourself for leaving Renate unattended. After all, it was your duty to look after her. You must think I'm angry with you. Don't think that. Today is the most victorious day of my life."

The cook did not look terribly contrite. "It gives me no

210

pleasure to say this, Master, but yer wife isn't ripe for motherhood." She made a fist, as if catching an invisible fly. "Not to ruin your cel'bration.... I knew a girl like her who lost her wits and dumped her baby in the well."

Thaddeus ran his hand over his forehead, slicking his hair back. "God love you, Agatha. There's a tall tale in every village."

"This one is true. It did happen, on Kowalskis' property."

"That wretched girl was probably unwed, a child herself."

"No, she was nineteen and married. She seemed like a good girl, clean and quiet, made a livin' with needlework. Yer should've seen the portrait of the Blessed Lady she'd embroidered. It hung at the sacristy at St. Lawrence's. When Father Nicholas heard 'bout her evil deed, he tore that portrait down and burned it. He wouldn't have his church tainted by the craft of a baby killer."

Thaddeus put his hands on her shoulders. "You're worrying for naught. Renate isn't capable of such atrocities."

"Nobody knows what a woman can do if a demon lodges in her ear. I'm not sayin' yer wife will drop yer son in a well. But there's more than one way to harm a child. She mustn't be left alone with him."

***

When Renate regained consciousness, it was already after dark. To her great dismay she discovered that she was in the same loathsome bed where she had spent the past seven months, under the same patchwork quilt. The sensation of throbbing tautness in her belly had been replaced by an equally unpleasant sensation of looseness. There were no more kicks and spams, only painless twitches below the navel. So the restless tadpole had been extracted from her belly. She remembered washing her paintbrushes, running across the field towards the bog and being slapped on the

211

face by the stable boy. She made no further attempts to reconstruct the events of the past day. Those memories were not of the kind she would cherish.

Something was scratching her left wrist. Renate pulled her hand from underneath the quilt and saw an amber bracelet crafted by the same sloppy artisan as the necklace Thaddeus had given her as an engagement gift the year before. The surge of annoyance made her temporarily oblivious to the burning wound between her legs. At that moment nothing seemed more urgent than getting the ugly bracelet off. She began looking for the clasp but could not find it. There was one continuous metal chain with murky nuggets woven through.

"There's no clasp," she heard her husband's voice above her head. "We put the bracelet on you while you were sleeping. Antanas helped me close the chain shut. This way you'll always keep the bracelet on without any danger of losing it—as a reminder of this glorious day."

Renate would gladly kick that radiant face. "I want this thing off, understand?"

Undeterred by her rejection of his gift, Thaddeus sprawled on the bed next to her with his muddy boots still on. "You must be curious about the child. He's sound asleep. Bronia has fed him. When he wakes up, we'll be happy to show him to you. Here's a surprise: he has dark hair. Wonder where that came from..."

"That's because I kissed a Jew before I married you."

Taking advantage that the covers were limiting her mobility, Thaddeus patted her on the thigh. "Ah, *kumpela*, I'm glad you're making jokes again."

"I wasn't joking. I really did kiss a Jew. So don't be surprised if our child develops a hook nose and an affinity for algebra."

"Oh, Dominik will do great things."

Renate ran the tip of her tongue over her parched lips. Naturally, none of her numerous caregivers had thought of putting a pitcher of water within her reach. "Dominik, eh?"

"Why, is something wrong with that?"

No, Dominik was acceptable. A strong, neutral name of Latin origins. At least it did not reek of bog water like Gintaras or Algimas.

"Wasn't it a bit hasty on your part, naming our son without asking me?"

"It's another burden off your shoulders, *kumpela*. You've done the hard work. Leave the trivial decisions to us."

"Why Dominik? Why not Benedict or Francis? I'm just curious."

"Dominik was the name of Agatha's son who died in infancy. I thought it would be a respectful gesture to name our firstborn in his memory."

Of course! Renate knew there was some weepy backstory involving one of the household members. "I bet she's smacking her gums in delight, that usurping witch."

Thaddeus stood up and tucked the blanket around her legs. "Still grumpy, eh? The worst is over, *kumpela*. You can start riding Dragoon again. The old boy will be waiting for you when you're ready to get back into the saddle."

The very mention of the saddle made Renate shudder. Only a hopelessly thick-skulled man could make such references to his wife who had just given birth.

"Here's random question for you," she said. "Why is Bronia feeding my son?"

"Because she has enough milk for two. She doesn't mind at all."

"What if I mind?"

"Why would you?"

"I just don't know how clean she is. Bronia does dirty work all day."

"I assure you, that girl keeps herself very clean in the right places. Her children are very sturdy. They never get colds or fevers."

"What if she drops Dominik on his head?"

"She won't. Bronia is a seasoned mother. She's done it twice already. Her children's skulls are intact."

"Let's not forget, her own daughter is missing a part of her foot."

"That was my fault, not Bronia's, as it's been explained to you already. Bronia's mothering skills are beyond reproach. She's a natural nurturer."

"Unlike me, of course. I'm suitable for incubating your offspring but not for rearing it."

Thaddeus squeezed her feet. "We're just trying to make your life easier, *kumpela*. You've been through an ordeal and deserve some respite. You've been encumbered by the child for the past nine months. There's no harm if someone else looks after him. Go and do something self-indulgent."

"Like what?" Renate gave him a murderous stare. "Shearing your damned Angora rabbits on which you'd spent the last ruble of my inheritance?"

"That's not what I meant. You're welcome to go to the city and visit some old friends."

"So you're no longer afraid that my father's murderers will corner me? Of course, I'm not worth much anymore. My fortune's been squandered. There's no profit in burglarizing a gutted house."

Renate started kicking under the blanket, but Thaddeus tightened his grip on her ankles.

"You haven't recovered from the shock yet, *kumpela*. A change of scenery will do you good."

"You took my money and my child, and now you're sending me into the world in peace? Weary of my company already? Why, you're the most unscrupulous crook of all! My father might've been blind, but God isn't."

Thaddeus interrupted her tirade with a rough end-of-story kiss, that of a man who would not have his jubilation tainted by a tantrum from his little wife.

The taste of honeyed vodka did not escape Renate. The obscene tragicomedy of her life was far from over. Dying of blood loss in the bog would have been too easy.

CHAPTER 21

Visitation

Vilnius, Kundstakademie von Jung—June, 1885

Marie and Justine knew things were looking bleak for Frau Jung when she chose not to walk Dr. Klein to the door. Since late spring the schoolmistress had been suffering from lack of energy and appetite. It had started with gnawing pain in her right side and persistent nausea. The symptoms suggested something more serious than seasonal ennui. When her skin and the whites of her eyes started turning yellow, the two girls called the physician, who had an unrivaled talent for delivering bad news with style and elegance.

After thirty minutes behind closed doors with the patient, Dr. Klein finally emerged, blotting his forehead with a handkerchief. "Your teacher would like a word with you."

"That awful jaundice will pass, won't it?" Marie asked. "Surely, a few teaspoons of calendula extract will put her back on her feet. Did you leave the medicine for her, or should we run to the apothecary's shop?"

Dr. Klein promptly blocked the surfeit of questions. "Forgive me, but I must hurry to another appointment. Frau

Jung does have a few legal matters to discuss. Attorney Messer can be more useful to her than I at this point."

The door slammed, rattling the Dresden figurines on the mantelpiece. The girls were beginning to regret their initiative to seek medical counsel for their schoolmistress. Now it was their duty to manage the consequences. Fingers intertwined, they walked into Frau Jung's room. She was sitting on the edge of her bed wearing a roomy bathrobe over her nightgown.

"Come here," she summoned them. "Do you know how proud I am of you?"

Weighed down by anxiety, the girls sat down obediently one either side of her, trying to avoid contact with her clammy yellow skin.

"Dr. Klein is such a haughty, callous man," Justine said, "badly dressed, too."

"If you didn't like what he had to say, we can call someone else," Marie proposed.

Elsa drew them into a feeble embrace. "I have no reason to doubt Dr. Klein's diagnosis. And no, I didn't like what he had to say." She took a few seconds to collect herself. "I count on you to make sure that your younger schoolmates finish their education. Our school will continue to operate until we fulfil our obligations to the girls whose parents have paid the tuition in advance. My failing liver shouldn't mark an end of an era. If the parents get the impression that the ship is sinking, they'll demand refunds, and that'll be the end. We cannot let that happen. *Verstehensie?*"

The girls hummed in unison. The idea of being hugged by a dying woman filled them with a sort of squeamish terror, even though they knew the disease was not contagious. They were ready to agree to anything in order to be released from her embrace.

***

Later that night, after everyone had settled in, the doorbell rang. Marie peeked through the glass window and saw a slouching matron in a frumpy dress, her puffy face framed by stringy wheat-colored tresses.

"Can I help you?" Marie sounded a little abrupt. After the tribulations of the day she had no patience left.

Brushing past her, the visitor stepped over the threshold and collapsed on the sofa across from the fireplace. "I'm dying of thirst. A bite to eat would be nice too. Come on, you know where Frau Jung keeps her biscuits."

"You... you cannot be here," Marie said, astonished by the intruder's audacity. "I've no idea who you are."

"Quit feigning ignorance. I couldn't have changed that much."

Marie peered into the swollen face and gasped. "Fräulein Lichtner!"

"Dombrowski since last July." Renate held up her hand to show the thin wedding band. "You can tell Aurelia that I didn't run away with a Jew after all. I ended up marrying a Pole. Now, if you bring me a cup of tea and some biscuits, I'll tell you what I've been doing for the past year, so you can relate the embellished version to the rest."

Renate kicked off her ankle boots and unbuttoned the collar of her dress, soaking in the familiar smells and sounds. The drawing room was exactly as she had left it, every chair and flower pot in the same place.

About ten minutes later Marie came back with a mug of mint tea. Justine was tiptoeing behind carrying a tray with open sandwiches. Both girls took great care not to make any noise with Frau Jung resting behind closed doors.

When Justine saw her old schoolmate, the tray wobbled

in her hands. *Mein Gott, what a dismal sight... Is that what marriage does to a girl?*

The sight of ingenuous supper revived Renate. "*Danke schön.*" She rubbed her fingers together. After a few bites, she pushed the tray aside. "I would've been here sooner, but the lame horse kept puffing, drooling and stumbling."

"Since when do you ride horses?" Justine asked. "I thought you hated them."

"Well, I had to overcome my distaste for many things. Dragoon was a wedding gift. The minute I rode that stupid creature through the gate, he started fighting me, as if some invisible rope kept it tied to the barn. Luckily, I saw a family of farmers heading to the market, so I sold Dragoon to them cheaply. I should've asked for more, but I had no time to bargain. What they gave me was enough to pay for a coach ride to the city."

"You look good with your hair down," Marie remarked, running her fingers through Renate's brittle tresses.

"Yeah, the old witch who cooks our meals took away my hair pins. She probably uses them for her satanic rituals."

"I'll give you a dozen of mine," Justine said. "Your old room is empty now. Anastasia moved to Moscow with her family after Christmas. We'll give you some fresh sheets."

"Sounds heavenly," Renate exhaled, rubbing her knees. "What I really need is a bath, to get the smell of the farm out of my skin."

***

The lavender bath relieved the ache in Renate's joints but not in her heart. She kept thinking about the trip she was going to take the next day, her main reason for coming to Vilnius. She was not interested in rekindling camaraderie with her former classmates. Those duplicitous gossips had not changed one bit, still encapsulated in their pseudo-

Sapphic realm. Renate knew that her pathetic condition delighted them. Malevolence stood behind their exaggerated hospitality and friendliness. Naturally, they wanted to keep her around just to scrutinize her figure. How gratifying it was for them to see a former golden girl, who in the past had snubbed their alliances, dethroned and humiliated.

After a sleepless night, she headed to the site where her father's factory once stood. Since she had not seen Hermann's body or been present at his funeral, visiting the ruins of his demolished empire would be the closest thing to paying last respects. Images of charred pillars and chipped brick had plagued her dreams for the past year.

The recurring nightmares could not possibly prime her for the shock of seeing the flat empty space. Whoever had been assigned the task of cleaning up the debris had done an exceptional job. There was no scar, not a scab left on the surface, no evidence of the factory having ever been there. She closed her eyes, trying to reconstruct the Grecian outlines of the factory with workers streaming in and out, but all she saw was the black void. Originally she had planned on visiting St. Bernard's cemetery—it was her educated guess that Hermann had been buried there, not too far from Katherine—but the bewildering discovery made her change her itinerary. Clearly, it was not the best day for chasing ghosts.

The few rubles she had left from the sale of Dragoon were burning a hole in her pocket. She was dying to spend them on some knick-knacks, something entirely useless and tasteless. It had been so long since she handled genuine Vilnius produced junk. The amber trinkets Thaddeus had given her did not count. The artisan district on Castle Street was calling her name. She bought a bright floral shawl with glass bead tassels and a pair of beaver trimmed gloves from an old gypsy woman. Then she stopped by a vintage boutique and bought a used Parisian parasol. It was in great condition, apart from a few inconspicuous coffee stains. Her last purchase was a burlesque bonnet decorated with peacock feathers. The garish accessories did not match, but she did not care. The old Renate, the skinny morose girl in a beige frock no longer existed. She had been replaced with a vulgar woman in a clownish getup, who ate macaroons out of a paper bag and licked her fingers.

On the south side of Vilnius' only remaining city gate she spotted a miniature sidewalk exhibition. It was a place where the most desperate and dejected artists congregated to commiserate.

A row of watercolor paintings depicting the Gate of Dawn and façade of the chapel caught her eye. The two-dimensional rendition looked vaguely familiar. She had seen that sloppy technique before. But then again, there were so many incompetent amateurs trying to peddle their work. In all honestly, the most skillful element was the painter's monogram in the lower right hand corner—B.A.

"The entire collection goes for fifteen rubles," she heard a young male voice. "I'd prefer not to separate them, if at all possible. They'll grow wistful without each other, like siblings."

"I wouldn't know anything about that," Renate replied. "I'm an only child, and an orphan to boot. I must say, there's a certain freedom that comes with it."

Shifting the angle of the parasol, she looked into the artist's grey eyes and nearly dropped the bag of macaroons. Standing before her was Benjamin Asher. The recognition was instantaneous and mutual. The dashing young Jew had not changed much in the past year, except that his hair had gotten longer. He was still wearing the same fashionably distressed bowler hat and a silk neck scarf. Renate realized that her appearance had undergone a more drastic transformation.

Benjamin stepped out from behind the stand, knocking off a few of his ill-fated paintings. "Fräulein Lichtner... I must be dreaming."

Abandoning his display, he grabbed Renate's hand and led her into the chapel upstairs. On the way upstairs she stuffed the bag with the macaroons into a rubbish bin. She suspected that the conversation was going to involve some intense hand-pressing, and she did not want her fingers to be sticky.

The noon mass had just let out, and the organist's bench was still warm. It was the only place to sit in the entire chapel. The architects had opted for leaving as much free space as possible. Having spent the whole morning walking, Renate welcomed the opportunity to give her feet some respite.

"Why didn't you look for me?" she asked in a tone more jeering than accusatory.

"I did."

"Not hard enough."

"What was I to do? For months I shadowed Attorney Messer. I even befriended his sister. I consulted every detective novel under the sun. Why didn't you write to me? You knew my address. One line from you, and I would've dropped everything."

"Keep your voice down. We're in a house of worship, remember? I was only teasing you. Sending a letter isn't as easy as it sounds. There's no post service where I live. I'd need to go to the nearest town. You think my husband would allow me to send anything without reading it first?"

Benjamin's heart sank. Of course, there was another man

in the picture. ""How did you manage to escape?"

"Apparently, I lost my relevance," Renate replied with a shrug. "Master Dombrowski has no more use for me. He pocketed my money and has spent it already. Now I'm a thorn in his side, upsetting the bucolic flow of life. If I suddenly vanished, he'd probably be relieved. There's just one minor twist. I have a son. They're keeping me away from him, but I'm not ready to relinquish my claims just yet."

"Do you miss him terribly?"

"I don't remember what he looks like, to be honest. Still, it's a matter of principle. I went through great pains bringing that boy into this world. I fully intend to use him as a weapon against my husband, though I'm not quite sure how." Renate stroked her chin pensively. "Right now it's the only thing keeping me afloat. You think the Blessed Virgin will offer guidance? She's a mother after all. Or would she think me too belligerent?"

Benjamin took a few moments to formulate a response to Renate's tirade. They were sitting in one of the holiest Christian places in Northeastern Europe, and she wanted a Jew's point of view. "My religion doesn't teach forgiveness," he said at last. "We sons of Israel are a vengeful, greedy lot. We understand money and violence. Although, I've been toying with Christianity."

Renate could not suppress an outburst of laughter. That was classic Benjamin! Toying. Always toying. With watercolors, violin, German women, Christianity. A sheltered, flighty dilettante eager to take a bite out of every forbidden fruit, only to spit it out later on.

"I've actually made some progress on the artistic front," Benjamin said. "I remembered your advice on diluting the paint. In the past year I've spent many mornings on the banks of the Neris River. I could hear your voice scolding me.

A few of my landscapes are at the Public Library now. I didn't get paid for any of them, but at least they are on display. I'd love your opinion. Though, you'd probably critique them to shreds."

"I'm no position to critique anybody." Renate pulled the bonnet off her head. "I haven't done much painting in the past year. A few charcoal sketches don't count. Doodling and dabbling, that's all it was. Frau Jung would be disgusted, after all the work she'd put into me. At any rate, tell me more about your flirtations with Christianity."

"I've been poking in and out of the chapel between masses. I was just curious if the Blessed Virgin would grant a lapsed Jew one wish."

"Well, did she?"

"You're here, aren't you?"

"One year too late! Who's counting?"

Benjamin took the liberty of slipping his arm around Renate. "There's an old bookstore a few blocks away, one of the few places where you can still procure texts in Lithuanian. The owner keeps a stack of them in the back room. You need a password to gain access to the forbidden collection."

"Where are you going with this?"

"I'm renting a studio on the second floor with a few friends I've made. We're all pitching in to provide a safe place to work, away from naysayers. If you want to, I can make you a copy of the key, so you can... come and see me from time to time. I'd like that very much."

There was no delicate way of responding to Benjamin's proposition, so Renate took his hand and laid it upon her breasts. "They're still filled with the milk intended for another man's child. In case you haven't noticed, I'm not a fifteen-year old heiress. I'm a lactating cow whose calf was taken away."

"I don't care," he said with boyish obstinacy. "It's not too late for us to reclaim what's ours. While you're busy waging a war against your husband, can't you carve out some time for love?"

"That's what you're saying now. I don't know how many naked women you've seen in your life, but trust me when I say that seven months of bedrest didn't bode well for my figure. If you saw what's underneath this dress, your ardor would surely cool."

CHAPTER 22

Wolf Hair Beneath the Skin

Raven's Bog, June 1885

"That old boy was a family member," Thaddeus said when he learned about Dragoon's fate. "How could you sell him to complete strangers? Did you at least tell them what kind of oats he likes? He has a sensitive stomach. What if they turn him into smoked sausages?"

"It's more merciful than letting him rot away in a stable," Renate replied, laying out her new purchases on the bed. "I needed money."

"Then you should've asked."

"See, that's where you're wrong." Renate pointed the tip of her new parasol to his chest. "I shouldn't have to ask for money. And I shouldn't have to ask for permission to see my son. To make a long story short, Dragoon was my horse. I disposed of him as I deemed fit. That necklace you gave me isn't worth much. Besides, you urged me to do something self-indulgent. Since you haven't lifted a finger to brighten my existence, I took matters into my own hands."

"Forgive me, *kumpela*. I've been inattentive and negligent."

Renate dismissed his apology. That man who lived in constant state of contrition did not think twice before saying he was sorry. To him it came as naturally as breathing.

"I wanted to share something with you," Thaddeus continued. "The day you left Dominik started running a fever. His head felt like a baked potato. Agatha and Bronia wiped him down with a damp cloth and gave him oak bark tea, but nothing seemed to help. So I knelt and promised Our Lady that I'd build a chapel on my land in her honor if she healed my son."

"Be careful with your promises, Tadek. I guess now you'll have to uphold your end of the bargain. We'll have a chapel sitting on the bog—an ideal spot for a house of God!"

"It should've been done long ago." Thaddeus continued talking to himself, ignoring his wife acrimonious remarks. "My people have been complaining that the nearest church is several kilometers away, and it's a burden to travel there during winter. It's about time we built a chapel on our property."

Renate sprawled on the bed amidst her new trinkets. The shawl and the bonnet still smelled like the coffee shop on Castle Street.

"So, what will it look like, that chapel of yours? I hope it's better than the glorified outhouse where we said our wedding vows. Have you consulted an architect? You'll also need carpenters and painters—assuming this endeavor isn't one of your vodka-induced fantasies. If you want to do this properly, it'll cost you. Skilled tradesmen don't come cheaply."

"I don't need any architects—or carpenters. I'll build it with my own hands."

"It took you three months just to repair the barn."

"My people will do the work—with God's help."

"I see. So you'll build a chapel every time our son gets a runny nose? I have a feeling that by the time Dominik grows up we'll have a miniature Vatican around us."

***

Before going to bed, Renate stopped by the annex where Antanas and his family lived. Locking doors was not something that was practiced in a house where all possessions were presumed to be communal. Before Bronia had a chance to intervene, Renate grabbed Dominik from the cradle and held him to the light to take a closer look at his features. The last time she had seen his little face it was still red and scrunched like a withering apple. Feeling his mother's unfamiliar touch, the baby started squirming. After a few awkward minutes of trying to pacify him, Renate laid him back in the cradle and turned to Bronia.

"I heard my son had a fever while I was gone. Is that true?"

The milkmaid nodded. "He coughed and retched, sure enough, but then he broke a sweat, and the fever came right out, and he suckled heartily."

"So, what did you try on him, leeches from the bog? I saw red marks on his neck."

"Those marks were there when he was born, m'lady," Bronia assured her with a stutter. "Stork bites they call them."

"Stork bites? That's rich! I saw my son before I left, and there were no marks on his neck. I think you and your mother have been trying your witch spells and potions on him. In a civilized household, someone like you wouldn't be allowed near a child. Those fit to mind cattle shouldn't be trusted with children. An enlightened father would engage a trained nurse and a governess for his child. In the city you'd be arrested for your tricks."

The milkmaid crossed herself. "I swear, m'lady, we did nothin' of the sort. No spells, no potions and no leeches. May the Lord strike me if I'm lyin'!"

Renate interrupted her with a sonorous slap. "Stupid cow!" She was not going to wait for the good Lord to strike the milkmaid. "I leave for a few days, and you nearly kill my child in my absence."

Having never been struck before by the lady of the house, Bronia had not cultivated the cowering reflexes. The sudden blow left her lower jaw unhinged. Renate raised her hand to strike the girl again, but Agatha intercepted her hand in mid-air.

"No need to get agitated, m'lady," the purple lips smacked.

The sheer ferocity of the cook's grip was astounding. Renate knew Agatha to be an extraordinarily strong woman, one who could give any man a run for his money, but it was the first time she saw that strength put to use. Those hands could do more than just chop beef for stew. They could maim and kill. Renate sensed there were primal forces at work, instincts that transcended social hierarchy. Driven by an ursine urge to protect her daughter, Agatha would not hesitate raise her claw against anyone, even the lady of the house.

"Back to yer husband, m'lady," she said, releasing Renate. "He's been pinin' for yer."

***

The altercation with the cook and her daughter left Renate dizzy and subtly disoriented. Thaddeus did not ask her about the origin of the bruises on her wrist. Taking advantage of his wife's catatonic state, he started making amorous overtures.

When she felt his hand stealthily kneading the small of her back, she shuddered. "Don't start. Not now."

Thaddeus disregarded her rebuke and continued making advances with escalating insistence. Using the weight of his body, he wrestled her onto the mattress. The smell of alcohol on his breath seemed stronger, suggesting that during Renate's trip to the servants' room he had taken a few more sips from the bottle. Dear God, could that thirty-one year old child be left alone for a minute? She whipped him across the face with the shawl.

"It's been too long, *kumpela*," he rumbled, undeterred by the lashing of glass beads across his eye. "Much too long. Surely, your battle wounds have healed by now."

It suddenly hit Renate that they had not been intimate since last September. Where does the time fly? Having kept dutiful distance throughout his wife's pregnancy, which was a titanic exertion on his part, Thaddeus expected Renate to resume her bedroom obligations.

"For God's sake, get yourself a milkmaid," she pleaded, knowing that Catholic principles would never allow Thaddeus to take that route. "I don't mind if you keep a whole stable of wenches. Just leave me alone. I'm not spending another winter in bed."

He covered her mouth with his hand. "Hush, *kumpela*. It won't come to that. I'll be careful."

At some point Renate realized that giving in would be more dignified than keeping up the resistance. Wiggling and clawing at his face or trying to bite his hand would be downright pathetic. After all, Tadek's actions, however distasteful, were in no way criminal. He was merely exercising his spousal rights after a lengthy period of forced abstinence. Being mauled by a drunken husband was something that every married woman endured on occasion.

No sooner than she resolved to take his assault with stoicism, something bizarre and utterly humiliating happened. She felt her body responding with unprecedented ardor. That crude, beastly side of Thaddeus that she had never seen before piqued her fancy. If all his lame attempts at arousing her in a gentle and respectful manner had the opposite effect, the moment he applied violence, the torch in her lower belly blazed up. Wildfire ran up her spine. Intertwined in a cheerful mazurka dance, hatred and lust sored towards the ceiling.

Would Thaddeus keep his promise to hold back? Naturally, he did not. That man was not trained in exercising self-control in such matters. With a victorious grunt, he flushed all those months of sensual frustration right into her.

Clutching the wrinkled shawl, Renate wondered if Thaddeus would apologize for his intemperance, but the apology never came. He took a few more sips from the vodka bottle, turned his back to her and fell asleep. At least now she knew where she stood and what his promises were worth.

Trapped between the wall and her snoring husband, Renate composed an inventory of the losses she had incurred in the past year: her father, her fortune, her familiar circle, her figure, her son. Now she had lost all remnants of dignity. And yet, wallowing in self-hatred would not be productive. She would have to scavenge for materials to rebuild her internal fortress.

***

The next morning Renate started packing her bags for Vilnius.

"Have a safe trip, *kumpela*," Thaddeus said with conspicuous relief in his voice. Life on the farm was so much harmonious without his volatile wife in the picture. Apart from Dominik's illness, those few days of Renate's absence had been delightfully tranquil. In a perfect world Renate would stay in Vilnius for most of the time and stop by once in a while to ease the ache in his groin. "I hope you do something enjoyable."

"It's not a question of enjoyment." There was nothing left to pack, but she continued tinkering with the items in her bag to avoid looking at him. "I have an obligation to fulfill. My teacher is gravely ill."

"Can't those city quacks do anything for her? I thought they were supposed to be miracle workers."

"Dr. Klein had the decency to give her an accurate diagnosis. Anyway, I don't see myself sitting at her bedside, stroking her hand. Frau Jung needs help running the school."

"I commend your devotion, *kumpela*."

"Don't get too excited. I'm not moving out for good."

Once again, Thaddeus took refuge in awkward laughter. "On a serious note, I don't want you going to Vilnius alone. I'll send Antanas to escort you."

Renate's smoothed her nightdress over her postpartum belly. "In my current condition I'm not likely to tempt any predators. I don't need a bodyguard."

"But you need a driver. You cannot continue stealing horses from the stables. There's an old carriage in the barn, spacious enough for two people. It hasn't been used in ages. I'll ask Antanas to repair the axle and grease the wheels."

The fact that Thaddeus did not rush to negate her claim of undesirability took Renate by surprise. She would have expected at least a nominal objection.

"What is Antanas going to do in Vilnius while I'm attending to my business?"

Thaddeus drummed his fingers against the headboard.

"Perhaps, he could make himself useful at the school? That's an idea. Antanas cannot remain idle for long. He grows restless. Besides, some extra money wouldn't hurt. I'll write a recommendation letter for him. If Frau Jung has any odd jobs that require a pair of man's hands—"

Renate stopped him from going any further. "I cannot present someone like him to Frau Jung. It would be cruel to both parties."

"You're being needlessly harsh, *kumpela*. Antanas won't be giving a lecture on art theory or a piano recital. His appearance and manners are perfectly suitable for fixing a leak in the roof."

Renate looked at her husband, for the first time that morning. "The building is filled with wicked girls running through the halls in their undergarments. A man would have to be either a saint or a eunuch to stay focused on his work with so many bare legs brushing past him. Do you really want to subject his soul to such savage temptations?"

CHAPTER 23

Hands Don't Lie

Vilnius

On the way to the city Antanas racked his brain, trying to understand what transgressions was he being punished for. The Baltic Vulcan had been removed from his sacred smithy and demoted to the insulting rank of a coachman. His hands ached for the hammer and the anvil. Instead of doing earnest work he had been trained for, he was driving that insufferable shrew. All the lashings he had endured in his childhood did not leave him feeling so humiliated. At least, physical pain served as an affirmation of his masculinity. The mental anguish from being hurled into an element foreign to him was much harder to manage.

"Have you been to the city before?" Renate asked him about forty minutes into the ride.

Antanas continued to feign deafness. Even though his face was stiff and expressionless, Renate sensed that underneath he was seething. "I asked you a question in a language you understand. I just wanted to make sure you knew where we were going."

He cleared his throat and spat over his shoulder. "I was

given orders to drive yer and keep Yer Ladyship safe. Keepin' yer amused isn't included."

"Orders? My husband doesn't give out orders. It's not in his nature."

"These are farm horses, used to pullin' a plough down a field, not a carriage down a highway. It's not easy task to keep 'em on a straight path, m'lady. If yer keep distractin' me, we'll surely crash."

He dropped the reins and pulled out a hand-rolled cigarette. It took him several attempts to light the tip, as the wind kept blowing out the matches. Having finally succeeded, he inhaled a few greedy puffs, as if his very life depended on it. Renate quickly became shrouded in corrosive smoke. She knew it would be a bad idea to ask him to hold off, so she covered her nose with a handkerchief for the rest of the trip.

When they rode into the city, Renate had no choice but break her silence and help Antanas navigate through the streets. The horses, unaccustomed to congested cobblestone roads, became even harder to control, neighing and recoiling every time another carriage passed by.

"You can drop me off here," Renate said when they reached Castle Street. "Frau Jung isn't the only person I plan on visiting. I have a few other friends."

"As yer wish, m'lady..."

He maneuvered the carriage into a vacant spot along the sidewalk. Renate slipped off her seat on the pavement and grabbed her travel bag. Antanas looked like he had every intention of accompanying her.

"You don't need to follow me around like a dog," she said. "Your job is done. I know the city. I was born here."

The blacksmith spread his legs like a sailor on the deck of a rocking ship. "Sorry, m'lady—Master's orders. He told me not to let yer out of my sight."

Renate realized that a change of strategy was in order. She dropped her condescending air and produced a conspiratorial smile, as if they were partners in crime.

"You shouldn't take your master's orders word for word. I doubt that he'll expect a copious report of my activities. As long as you bring me home in one piece, who cares about the details?" Renate leaned in and tapped his arm. "Here's a proposition: give me a little breathing room, and I'll make sure you have the best meal of your life at the tavern of your choice."

Her touch sent a jolt of rage through the blacksmith's body. That smirk, that wink... In spite of his peasant roots, Antanas was perceptive enough to see Her Ladyship's true motives. Through the veil of familiarity, he sensed her disdain. No, that woman was not trying to forge a pact of camaraderie. Her goal was to get rid of him. And she thought him pathetic enough to betray his master for a pitcher of beer! *Like a dog.* Those were her words.

"The master's given me money for food," he growled. "I'll be feastin' for a week."

The last statement was a lie, and they both knew it. Before sending his wife to the city, Thaddeus had given her a few rubles with the assumption that she and Antanas would be eating together. It had not occurred to him to give his servant a separate allowance. With Renate holding the purse strings, Antanas depended on her for nourishment. Having not eaten anything since early morning, he was famished. Normally around this time he would be sitting down for a hearty mid-afternoon meal of smoked pork and potato pancakes topped with sour cream and dill. A tempest was brewing in his stomach, and the smell of freshly baked meat pies emanating from the nearby tavern was not helping his composure.

"Don't be stubborn," Renate said softly, slipping a few coins into his breast pocket. "My husband made me promise I'd feed you well. That was the arrangement."

This time Antanas did not protest. He blinked and accepted the money along with defeat.

"Good boy," Renate praised him. "I know you're not used to eating by yourself. It must feel odd, sitting at the table all alone in a strange city. I'm sure you'll make friends soon enough." She nodded at a handful of construction workers who were taking a break from repairing the façade of the book store. "Look, there're some nice lads around your age who speak your language having a jolly good time. Go over and say hello. I'll meet you out here in a few hours, and we'll go to Frau Jung's for the night."

***

The walls of the stairwell leading to the second floor were covered in charcoal smudges and paint splatters. The wooden railing felt sticky to the touch. It seemed that the crew maintaining the storefront on the bottom floor did not venture into the space above.

When Renate rang the brass bell, subdued grunting emanated from the inside, but nobody came to open the door. Finally, after several more attempts, a man in his mid-thirties poked his greasy-haired head into the hallway.

"What are you looking for?"

"I'm here to see Benjamin Asher."

The man grinned, exposing sharp crooked incisors. Combined with the prematurely greying mane and scruff, they gave him a resemblance with a wolf. "Another one, already? He's still tinkering with the one who came this morning. He's popular, that Jew."

"It's all right, I can wait." Well, at least she had the right address.

"No, if you and Asher made plans, he should kick the other one out. We haven't got the space to accommodate an entire harem."

"He wasn't expecting me, actually. It's a surprise."

"Grand. Asher loves surprises." The man laid his hairy claw on Renate's shoulder and pulled her over the threshold with the nonchalant determination of a wolf dragging its prey into a cave. "Hey, Asher, you filthy Christ-killing fucker! Fresh meat has arrived. C'mon, I'm tired of entertaining your bitches for you. There's not a drop of booze in the house."

Renate took a moment to survey Benjamin's new creative arena. It consisted of one drafty and poorly lit room with mounds of junk totally unrelated to art piled up against the walls. It would not surprise her to see a dead mouse. In the middle of the room, on an island of splattered tarpaulin, a wobbly easel was set up. It looked like it could collapse any second. Instead of a traditional painter's smock, Benjamin was wearing a butcher's apron.

The model enthroned on an empty produce crate was a scrawny girl with a disproportionately large nose and acne scars covering her hollow cheeks and sharp shoulder blades. After taking a quick look at the canvas, Renate gathered that the artist was not striving for realism. This was clearly not a study of irregularities of the human skin but rather an exercise in downplaying the flaws. Benjamin had added a few curves where there were none, made her hair longer and wavier, her lips brighter and fuller, her nose shorter and sharper. The girl shivering on the box in front of him was not the girl on the canvas. Embellishing was a lucrative skill. If Benjamin managed to master it, he would be rolling in gold. Merchants and officials would commission portraits of their wives from him. *Flattery will get you everywhere, mein Freund. It's the overly honest artists who end up starving.*

"Enough for today, Egle," he said. "We'll continue tomorrow."

The girl jumped off the box, slipped a loose-fitting summer dresses over her head, shoved her bare feet into clunky shoes and scurried out of the studio. The werewolf followed behind her.

"You didn't have to get rid of her," Renate said when she and Benjamin were alone. "I was tickled to see you in action."

"No, Egle needed to go. She has... other commitments. Besides, the lighting isn't right."

"The lighting is irrelevant for what you were trying to achieve. It's the draft in the room that bothers me. Did you see the goose bumps over the poor girl's body? Rule number one: if you cannot pay your models, at least provide bearable conditions. I realize we all suffer for our art, but you don't want Egle's death on your conscience if she catches pneumonia."

Benjamin brushed his hair back, staining his forehead with paint. "Is that what you came here for, to point out my shortcomings?"

"Well, you better get used to it—if we're to be together." Renate dropped her bag on the floor and sat down on the vacated crate. "It's a charming little rubbish bin you've got here. I can see us having many lovers' quarrels within these walls."

Benjamin looked around dissipatedly. "Forgive me. I've got nothing to offer you."

"So you want me to leave?" She ran her hand over the buttons on her dress. "Have you changed your mind about giving me a copy of the key?"

"That's not what I meant!" He sat down on the floor in front of Renate. "I wanted to say, I can't even offer you a drink. I had half a bottle of claret stashed away behind the can with paint thinner, but Jonas finished it off. He's one of the gentlest souls I've ever known. We met at a craft fair a few months ago. He's twice my age, but we get along splendidly. He's a real satyr. There's just one problem: it's not safe to leave alcohol with him." Benjamin babbled breathlessly, his voice growing softer with each syllable. "I still have a tiny flask of honey liqueur in my coat pocket. My riotous uncle slipped it to me as a prank gift for Hanukah last year. It tastes like sweetened pine sap."

"I'll try some," Renate said, savoring her last minutes as a dutiful wife.

She was not in a hurry to leap into Benjamin's embrace—before letting her go to the city, her husband had ravaged her repeatedly. Her breasts and thighs were covered in bruises, and the thought of another man laying his hands on her made her wince. Renate could easily go without intercourse for the rest of the year. She knew she was going to sleep with Benjamin eventually, just not right away. In the meantime, it was gratifying to see the delusional young artist grovel at her feet.

***

The city spun around Antanas as he stood in the middle of Castle Street, looking utterly ridiculous in his rough peasant clothes. As much as he abhorred the idea of being bribed with his master's money, the smell of meat pies and the fizzing of freshly brewed beer overrode the sense of loyalty.

The foreman of the construction crew approached him. "Why so grim, brother?" His dialect sounded different from the one Antanas was accustomed to. "I've been watchin' yer for the past half hour, and yer look like yer encircled by demons."

"Escortin' a German bitch all day wouldn't make yer grim?"

The foreman and his lads burst out laughing. Antanas sensed that their laughter was rooted in solidarity rather than contempt. But there were ten of them and one of him. The village blacksmith could not help feeling outnumbered.

"Yer know what I think, brother?" the leader of the pack said in a grave voice. "I think yer lust after that blue-blooded bitch. Yer want some of that blue milk runnin' out of her tits. 'Tsall right. Lads and I won't judge."

Those were the last words to come out of the foreman's mouth before the blacksmith punched him in the teeth. The rest of the workers howled and tightened their circle, just in case. It was highly unlikely that an earnest brawl would break out in broad daylight in the middle of a busy street. The place was teeming with gendarmes, imperial overcoats looming behind each corner.

Deep inside, Antanas knew that the comments were innocuous, but the trip to Vilnius had left his nerves tethered taut, and a single spark caused a massive explosion. The innuendo hurled at him was completely absurd. His hatred of the German Bitch did not have an element of frustrated longing. If presented with an opportunity to bed Lady Renate without any consequences, he would decline. She really was not to his taste, even without taking her rotten character into the equation. Antanas was not tempted by her looks. She was no match for his sweet industrious Bronia, who managed to stay trim even after two children. The German Bitch looked like a stretched out potato sack draped over a shovel. What did Master Dombrowski see in her? And to think how close she had come to dying in childbirth! Why did she bounce back at the last moment?

Just a few seconds after knocking his offender down, Antanas stretched his hand out to help him up.

"Not one for jokes, are yer?" The foreman spat out a lump of bloody saliva, his lower lip swelling rapidly. "I could use a pair of hands like yers on my team. Hands don't lie, brother. By the way, my name is Simonas."

CHAPTER 24

The Witch Who Stole the Harvest

Rambynas Hill, Lithuania Minor,
Prussian territory—June, 1885

Summer seemed to have bypassed most of Lithuania
Minor that year, resulting in a string of crop failures. Anxiety
engulfed the settlements on both sides of the Neman River.
The only oasis of fertility was Fox Glen, a farm at the foot of
Rambynas Hill. Mysteriously, the lady of the manor, Vitalia
Jocyte had not been seen in weeks. The farm practically ran
itself. It was as if the land was sucking the strength from the
woman who owned it.

The neighbors did not know what to make of Lady Vitalia,
an aloof old maid who fancied herself a widow since the
death of her childhood sweetheart. Her social class was just
as ambiguous as her marital status. She wore traditional
homespun garb, but her languid manners and snippy
inflections befitted a provincial aristocrat. She played a
number of musical instruments that were common in the city
but not in the countryside. Her collection contained a real
concert clarinet in lieu of the more traditional Lithuanian
analog called *birbynė*. God only knew where she had

procured those instruments and who had taught her how to play them. Still, Vitalia's most bewildering attribute was her youthful appearance. According to the baptismal records, she was forty-two, yet she could pass for someone in her late twenties, so smooth was her skin and so vibrant was the copper of her hair that she wore in a crown braid. The more benevolent neighbors attributed her freshness and slenderness to the fact that she was not encumbered by familial obligations. The less benevolent ones simply called her a witch.

A few days before the Feast of St. John, she received an unexpected visit from a scrawny girl who claimed to be her niece Aurelia, the daughter of her late sister Zivile.

"Be thankful you haven't inherited your mother's boning," Vitalia said, scrutinizing the freckles on the visitor's upturned nose from across the table. "You must take after your father."

"I never knew my father."

Vitalia's mouth rounded. "Oh, so you must be—"

"A bastard? No, I'm an heiress, albeit a dispossessed one," Aurelia explained, not in the least bit offended by the presumption. "I won't get my share of crown jewels until I turn eighteen. To put your mind at ease, my parents were lawfully wed, though only for a few months. My father died before I was born."

"I see. Zivile did him in. That blood-sucking witch..."

"Hardly. My father was dying anyway. They met at a tuberculosis clinic where she was working as a nurse."

"The poor devil must've been deaf and blind."

"Not just any poor devil—an attorney, one of the most prominent ones in Vilnius."

Vitalia shook her elaborately braided head. "Who would've thought? My horse-faced, rotten-tempered sister marrying a gentleman! The whole family thought she was out of her mind, turning down all those farmer boys. In the end, she got her prince."

"A widowed king, more like it," Aurelia clarified gently. "He was a good twenty years her senior."

"Poor kitten, bedding a rich old man for three months. Zivile did the right thing to get out of this manure pit. Maybe I shouldn't berate my home like that. We were lucky to have the most lucrative estate in the region. Still, we don't get many attorneys passing through the village. This land has nothing to offer except for sunflower seeds and honey. You still haven't stated your business."

"I'm here to fulfil a deathbed promise to my mother's benefactor, the man who paid for her education. I don't suppose the name Jan Wilczyński means anything to you? He disparaged my painting but praised my writing. Before he died, he instructed me to come here and write an article about the summer festival. A posthumous commission, if you will."

"Understood." In reality, Vitalia did not fully understand her niece's desire to reconnect with her heritage. It seemed as frivolous and absurd to her as a moth crawling back into its cracked cocoon. "If that's what you're after, you've come to the right place. In a few days the hill will be swarming with mummers. Just be careful. The men let their hands wander."

"I'll consider myself warned." Aurelia lifted her dainty tea cup. Porcelain was a rarity in that part of the country. Most inhabitants of Rambynas Hill drank out of sturdy clay mugs. "You know something about wandering hands, auntie?"

The hostess stood up to refill the kettle. Her foggy wandering gaze got hooked on a cracked plate above the stove.

"When I was your age, I fancied a lad, a miller's son

named Jurgis, yet I couldn't marry him because of the stupid custom. I was the youngest of four and had to wait for my turn." Vitalia spoke hastily, anxious to get the story out of the way. "My sisters stood in my way. First your mother, then Inga, then Beata. The lad decided he couldn't wait any longer and married someone else. I continued running into him at the market, in the fields. He found it was easier to pretend he didn't know me. By the time all three sisters were out of the house, my parents were too damn old and feeble. So it fell on me to care for them and keep the farm running. I suppose I could've married after my parents' death, but by then I was past my prime. No young man would take me, even with all the land I owned. The only men who showed interest were widowers with broods from earlier marriages, and I didn't want some other woman's brats running around my property. I would've made an exception for Jurgis, though. Had his wife died before him, I would've taken him in a heartbeat, even with all his debts, ailments, rancid habits and six children. For twenty-five years I nursed that smolder of hope that we might come together. He died earlier this spring. Drink killed him. The mother of his children scowls at me whenever she sees me. I'm his widow as much as she is. I'd have loved him longer."

***

Situated on the right bank of the Neman River, Rambynas Hill was the last remaining sacred place of the Balts. An old pagan altar stood atop the hill until the early 1800s, when the hill was eroded by the river. The holy mountain was shrouded in many legends featuring Perkunas, the god of Thunder, and his consort Laima. During the middle Ages, Crusaders attacked the land imposing their faith onto the locals and attempting to destroy the old beliefs. Although the Lithuanians adopted the Christian faith, they continued worshipping the ancient gods of their forefathers, making offerings at the great altar stone and washing themselves with the holy water on the mountain. According to the legend, prosperity would never leave the region as long as the stone stood in place. If a stranger's hand dared to touch the sacred stone, the mountain itself would vanish into the depth of the river. The prophecy was fulfilled when a German villager named Schwartz who was searching for a milestone for his mills split the altar stone. The mountain indeed started to go downhill to the Neman River, and crop failures started plaguing the region. In spite of those misfortunes, the inhabitants continued to come to the old shrine site for the midsummer festival to plead with the old deities. The festivities included searching for fern blossoms at midnight, jumping over bonfires, greeting the rising sun and washing hands in morning dew.

Dressed in the homespun apparel from her aunt's chest, Aurelia followed the procession of young girls carrying flower wreaths towards the river. She had originally intended on watching the festival from a distance and writing down her observations, but at the last minute decided to infiltrate the crowd for a more authentic experience. It was her first time wearing the traditional clothes of her maternal ancestors. Her late patron, Dr. Wilczynski, had shown her sketches of the colorful, intricately ornamented garments from the eastern regions. The dress she was wearing differed from the ones in Wilczynski's album. The Lutheran influences in the west steered the people of Klaipeda region to seek modesty and simplicity. Adapted from the urban fashions, the darkened fabrics and slimmer cuts were fetching in their own subdued elegance. The men standing on the banks of the river wore dark blue or black caftans and long trousers tucked into leather boots.

The very atmosphere of the festival also had a somber touch. An uninformed bystander watching the ceremony could easily take it for a funeral. The celebrants walked with their heads bowed and hands locked behind their backs. Aurelia wondered if such demeanor was typical for western Lithuanians, or if it had something to do with the recent crop failures.

Walking next to her was a dark-haired girl who could not have seen more than ten winters, yet had eyes of a vindictive old hag who had survived at least three drunken husbands. Those eyes, the color of rusty nails, burrowed into the intruder.

"How come I've never seen yer b'fore." Numerous throat infections had left the girl's voice squeaky and sour. "Not from around here, are yer?"

"No, I've come all the way from Vilnius."

"Thought so. Yer talk funny. I bet yer hang 'round Russians all day." The gap between the girl's charcoal eyebrows narrowed. "What yer doin' here?"

"Visiting my aunt."

"Who's yer aunt?" Questions kept shooting like arrows.

"Lady Vitalia Jocyte of Fox Glen."

"Ah, the witch who stole the harvest! She's the only one who prospers while the rest of us are hurtin'."

Aurelia leaned closer to the girl and whispered over her wreathed head. "Didn't you hear? Her chickens lay golden eggs, and the honey in her bee hives turns to amber."

The girl's mouth twisted into a spiteful sneer. "She couldn't have my father, so she put a curse on him. He drank himself to death. We all heard her cacklin' with joy! If that wasn't 'nough, she put a curse on all her neighbors, killin' their crops and animals."

Aurelia realized the girl was referring to Jurgis. "Perhaps, it's in my power to reverse the spell." She pulled a few small coins from her bodice and tossed them into the waters of Neman. "You think Russian gold will appease the goddess?"

The innocent proposition made the child all the more furious. "Yer aren't welcome here, witch!"

The procession stalled, as a ripple of excitement ran through the files of drowsy celebrants. Finally, something interesting was happening at Rambynas Hill—a stranger being accused of sorcery!

A weary-looking woman in her mid-forties stepped forward and intercepted the fuming child. "Hush, yer devil spawn! Is that how yer treat visitors?"

The superstitious fear in the woman's eyes did not escape Aurelia.

"Don't worry, I don't possess any supernatural powers," she said, holding her hands up in the air to show that there were no diabolic marks on her palms. "Black magic skipped a generation in my family. I'm not here to poison your water supply. And if I talk funny, it's because the language is dying out in the east, thanks to the Czars. You don't know how lucky you are to live under the Kaiser."

The villagers stared at her the pompous girl with a weird accent. To most of them Kaiser Wilhelm was up there with Perkunas, the God of Thunder.

As soon Aurelia realized she was the center of attention, she flexed her shoulders and lifted her chin. "Your monarch is enlightened and wise, a model European," she said with an air of apostolic pathos. "He doesn't stomp out languages and customs. Czar Alexander is a tyrant, even though he's styled 'Peacemaker'. True, he hasn't waged any major wars. He's too busy subduing the Northeastern Province. Alexander III won't rest until he reverses every progressive measures of his assassinated father. This very moment, he's imposing Orthodoxy upon Catholics, destroying the remnants of the German, Polish and Swedish institutions, banning Jews from the rural areas. When people speak the same language and practice the same religion, they're easier to control."

Half-way through Aurelia's tirade, the villagers started grumbling, anxious to resume the procession towards the top of the hill where the tables with food were set up. The smell of roasted lamb was streaming into the valley, and many of the villagers had not enjoyed a rich meal since last summer.

**

Ingrida—that was the name of Jurgis' widow—spent the rest of the day making sure that the young guest from Vilnius wanted for nothing. Aurelia's attempts to persuade the inhabitants of Rambynas Hill that she was not a witch were only partially affective. People did not want to take any chances. Malevolent forces had to be placated on the holy day. Ingrida took Aurelia to scavenge for the nine healing herbs called Kupoles after the goddess of all vegetation, who dwelt in the blossoms in summer and in snowdrifts in winter. Having collected the plants, the women used them to decorate the festival pole near the grain fields. Two days later the plants would be removed and fed to the farm animals and hung inside barns until Christmas to ensure the health of the livestock. Bunches of St. John's Wort would be placed behind the pictures of saints inside the homes of the villagers.

This interweaving of Christianity and paganism was not a shocking discovery for Aurelia. Dr. Wilczynski had told her about the practices in which the solstice pole and the cross became interchangeable. Celts, Slavs and Scandinavians had similar customs.

By nightfall, the somber ambiance of the earlier ceremonies began dissipating. Bonfires started erupting along the banks of the river. Aurelia observed the festivities from the hilltop where she had taken refuge while Ingida was not looking. It was time to relieve her extravagantly tolerant hosts. Besides, she wanted to capture the panoramic view of the valley. The flowers in her wreath were starting to wilt and shed petals. Pollen was settling on the sleeves of her embroidered chemise.

A pair of lean muscular arms encircled her waist from behind.

"Where have you been all this time?" a youthful male voice whispered in her ear. "I've been looking for you everywhere. My heart jumped when I heard your speech by the river."

"At least someone was listening to my rant," Aurelia replied without turning around to look at her captor whose accent sounded similar to hers. "My public speaking is as laughable as my painting. That's why I write."

"I knew it." Still hugging Aurelia from behind, he took her hand and held it to the light. "I spotted the ink stain on your finger."

"It's an old stain. I haven't written since I got here. I hope to have something for the editor of *Aušra*."

"So we're colleagues!"

The embrace tightened. Aurelia felt warm frantic puffs behind her ear. "What's your pen name?" she asked.

"I won't reveal it until my style improves. But my real name is Marius."

Marius... Aurelia immediately thought of the character from Victor Hugo's *Les Miserables*. She rotated in the youngster's embrace to face him, impatient to see if the real image matched the one she had conjured in her head. It pleased her to discover that her intuition had not failed her. Just like Hugo's hero, this Marius sported that fresh-from-the-barricades countenance: glistening eyes with dilated pupils, concave cheeks, a narrow prominent nose, unkempt dark curls.

"Were you at Wilczynski's funeral?" he asked. "I could've sworn I saw you. A beautiful face like yours isn't easily forgotten."

CHAPTER 25

The Imperial Spoon

Vilnius—June, 1885

The heartfelt letter of recommendation from Thaddeus ended up sitting in the blacksmith's breast pocket unopened. Since that fateful encounter with Simonas and his crew on Castle Street, Antanas had been working steadily under the supervision of his new best friend. There were several construction projects happening at Old Town, and the foreman could use every skilled pair of hands.

Simonas and his family rented an apartment in an industrial tenement near the river. The back room was reserved for the men on his team. Most of them were from out of town, working seasonal jobs to support their families in the countryside, and they appreciated the opportunity to save on lodging. At the end of a work day they had a place to wash up and spend the night. They used the side entrance and made sure to stay as inconspicuous as possible. On occasion, the foreman's wife Rasa would bring them trays with leftovers and a pitcher of beer.

Rasa worked as a cook for a Russian official who was wealthy enough not to keep track of the produce that was entering and exiting the kitchen. She would buy the freshest, costliest ingredients on the market, use half to prepare a meal for her employer and take the rest home. The lads would eat and drink in thankful silence. Sometimes they would play cards before going to sleep, but never for money. Drunkenness, bullying and petty theft had no place under that roof. Simonas imbued them with the idea that they were respectable tradesmen and were expected to behave accordingly. If during the day his men could exchange lewd jokes, at night they were expected to mind their tongues. He had two young daughters on the other side of the wall.

The pseudo-egalitarian dynamic between the foreman and his subcontractors reminded Antanas of Raven's Bog: same communal food tray and mixture of Polish and Lithuanian. There key difference was that for the first time in his life he was getting paid with real money, not just free meals, fraternal pats on the back and words of gratitude. Ah, the exhilarating feeling of rubles of in his hands!

Unlike Thaddeus, who had a talent for turning money into ashes with one touch, Simonas actually knew how to grow capital. A child of former serfs who had moved to the city after the Emancipation Reform, he was a first generation entrepreneur.

The men Simonas recruited were eager workers, but they knew nothing about prospecting or negotiating. They relied on the leader of the pack to provide work for them. Simonas did not worry too much that one of his former protégés might split from the pack and become a direct competitor. There had been one lad named Valdas, slightly inclined to insubordination, who got caught one day talking to a shopkeeper, offering his services as a carpenter at a low price without going through Simonas. That night Valdas did not return to the tenement by the river. The rest of the crew did not ask what had happened to their comrade, though it was hard to ignore the empty cot with a sack full of dirty clothes underneath. To curtail speculations before they started spreading, Simonas gave his men a terse explanation.

"Valdas has made his money and went home. He didn't need his old clothes. He can buy himself new ones."

Even if some suspected there was more to the story, they chose not to dig any deeper. They had a good thing under their foreman's wing. Valdas was a rash, ungrateful idiot. After his departure, the crew became even more tightly knit.

The incident had gone totally unnoticed by Antanas, who was still reeling from the novelty of having money. His hands were itching to spend it on some pleasant frivolity, something that had hitherto been out of his reach. The basement of the book store on Castle Street contained a room with used toys scavenged from affluent households. To Antanas that room was an enchanted kingdom and each toy an animate being with its unique history. One day during an afternoon break he went there to pick a few gifts for his children. He bought a porcelain princess for Magda. The lace on the doll's taffeta dress was coming apart, but the chestnut silk of her curls was still lustrous. He remembered something Lady Jolanta told him before dying, "If a girl plays with beautiful dolls, she'll grow beautiful." His second purchase was a train set for Edgaras. The locomotive had one of the headlights missing, and some of the wheels were not spinning properly, but still, it was the most sophisticated plaything Antanas had ever laid his hands or eyes on. Truth be told, he wanted that train for himself. It would be a while before Edgaras was old enough to appreciate it. After paying for the gifts, Antanas asked the shopkeeper to hold them for him under the counter. He did not want to take them back to the foreman's house for fear of unleashing a torrent of ridicule.

The shopkeeper gave him a sympathetic wink. "Perhaps, I'll give them to the young lady for safekeeping?"

Antanas frowned. "What young lady?"

"The one you serve, the pretty one."

"Yer... mistaken," the blacksmith said. "I don't serve any ladies. I'm a free tradesman."

"That's odd. I'm quite positive I saw you dropping one off not long ago. I'm very good with faces, and there're hundreds of them passing by my window each day. She comes here every night after dark to see an artist renting the loft upstairs. Sometimes she stays overnight, and they go out for coffee across the street in the morning."

"Yer mistaken," Antanas repeated austerely. "I don't know any coffee-drinkin' ladies."

"So be it," the shopkeeper conceded. "I'll hold your purchases for you."

Telling the shopkeeper he did not know Renate was probably the first conscious lie he had uttered in the twenty-six years of his life. In the past, he had been able to provide simple answers to simple questions, like how many chickens had been killed by a badger or how many rows of potato had been struck by a blight. There had never been any need for him to distort the truth. Suddenly, he felt the solid ground beneath his feet turn to quicksand. He had not seen Renate since the day of the arrival. To the best of his knowledge, she was staying at the art school, caring for her ailing teacher. Now that he possessed additional information about her nocturnal activities, he was not sure what to do with it.

He rejoined the crew and spent the rest of the day focusing on his task to keep the disturbing thoughts at bay. His comrades did not notice any changes in his demeanor, as he tended to be taciturn.

At dusk the foreman nudged him. "Dine with us tonight."

At first Antanas did not understand the nature of the invitation. He was already taking his meals in the backroom with everyone else. Then it dawned on him that his new patron was insisting on a private audience. Antanas was actually going to sit at the table with Simonas and his wife. He needed a clean shirt for that.

The real shock came when he saw the dinner table covered with a pristine white cloth and furnished with a multitude of sparkling spoons, forks and knives. At Raven's Bog, the most popular eating utensil was one's own hand. Whenever Agatha served soup, he would slurp it straight from the bowl and pick out the chunks of meat with his fingers. Scooping it with a spoon took too long. Using a knife and a fork at the same time was a feat he had not attempted before. The first dish Rasa served was a thin crepe with sour cream and caviar. Antanas was faced with the task of figuring out a way to slice the crepe into pieces without making a mess. As if out of spite, the knife was amazingly dull and made a squeaky noise against the plate.

"Enjoyin' yerself?" the foreman asked.

"Aye, that I am."

"Then why yer keepin' yer head down?"

Antanas looked up and forced himself to make eye contact with his host. "Still tryin' to make friends with the knife." Admitting ignorance of table etiquette was the easy part. "I'm used to handlin' big tools—saws, hammers, pliers."

"No need to keep yer head down with me, brother. I'm not the Czar."

"But yer surely live like one."

"Yer can live like that too." Simonas reclined in his chair. "Who says yer can't? I've been watchin' yer, brother. This can be yer life two-three years from now."

Antanas did not know whether he was being praised or mocked. To play it safe, he shifted the conversation back to Simonas. "So, how'd yer get all that stuff?"

"From Rasa's employer. That Russian sonofabitch pisses gold, I swear. His wife likes novelty. She can't bear lookin' at the same curtains for more than a few months. Everythin' from the last season gets discarded—and intercepted by Rasa. Her Ladyship tires of things quickly. Thankfully, she's more loyal when it comes to people. My wife's been cookin' for that family since '79. Her Ladyship doesn't mind if Rasa brings our girls to work. In fact, she lets 'em play with her jewelry box. Last week Solveiga, my four-year old, came home with a big red stone on a chain 'round her neck. I got worried for a minute that we'd get accused of theft, so I sent my girl back to apologize. Her Ladyship just laughed and told Solveiga to keep the necklace. *It's only a garnet*, she said. She always purges her home before some important guest comes to visit. So we keep the best of what she throws out, and sell the rest. See this silverware set? Imperial edition, with the Czar's portrait engraved."

Having forgotten all about the messy crepe on his plate, Antanas was listening to the foreman's narration. How often does a Lithuanian strike a goldmine like that? Simonas made it sound so easy, making money by reselling discarded luxury items. All it took was latching onto a rich Russian family. Settling down in Vilnius was not nearly as difficult as Antanas had thought. He could continue working for Simonas and move his wife and children to the city. Bronia could get a job similar to Rasa's. True, cooking was not her specialty, but she could learn a few recipes from her mother. But then Antanas thought of his master. How would Thaddeus handle their departure?

"Yer shouldn't be so harsh on that German Bitch," the

host added. "If not for her whim, yer never would've come to the city. We never would've met."

"Oh, I still hate her." The foreman's reference to Renate uncorked the flask of anguish in Antanas. "She keeps insultin' my wife, callin' her peasant cow and such. Oh, and Bronia's the one nursin' the master's child. The German Bitch will have nothin' to do with her own son. She's made everyone's life livin' hell."

Simonas swirled his spoon in the cold cucumber soup. "Yer know there're places where men can put obstinate wives. Surely, yer master knows of them."

"Yer jokin'!"

"I'm not. Indeed, there're such places. Last year I worked on summer house for a banker whose wife was one crazy shrew. He had her put away. Never had a rainy day again, clever bastard! So, not all is lost, brother. It's all about pullin' the ragweed out of yer life."

Something about the way Simonas uttered the word "ragweed" made Antanas think that the foreman was referring to a larger entity, not just the hysterical wives.

"I know a thing or two 'bout ragweed. I grew up on a farm, remember?"

"Good. There's plenty of ragweed in this city, stealin' sunlight from the rest of us, suckin' nourishment from the soil."

"Ru-ru... Russians, you mean?"

"Jews." Simonas stuck his fork into a slab of fried pork.

Antanas had never met a Jew in his life. To him they were mythical creatures, like faeries and goblins with their pots of gold with tightly sealed lids. Thaddeus had never spoken ill of them.

"Can't do much 'bout Russians," Simonas continued, his mouth filled with pork. "They're here to stay. And they're the ones keepin' us employed. Jews, on another hand... It's partially our fault. We've allowed their horde to grow too big. Too much of the city's capital is tied up in their shops. Our Russian mates are tryin' to crack down on them. You see Jews fleein' to America by the boatful, but not fast enough. The country we're buildin' here has no place for vermin. Time to smoke 'em out of their rat holes."

The foreman's tirade left Antanas with a strange feeling, as if he had received another round of lashes. The old scars on his back started burning again. His grave offense was that he did not know the enemy and had nothing valuable to add to the conversation. So he returned his gaze to the bottom of the soup bowl and kept quiet for the rest of the meal.

When Simonas went to refill his tobacco box, and Rasa started cleaning up the table, Antanas did something that something entirely absurd that contradicted all his principles —he took one of the smaller tea spoons and slipped it into his pocket.

CHAPTER 26

Ugly Petras

Rambynas Hill, Lithuania Minor—late June, 1885

"Would you like a sinister tale?" Marius asked Aurelia as they lay in each other's arms on the banks of the Neman River. "I know one that's been frightening the children of Rambynas Hill for the past decades."

After a week of relentless advances from Marius, Aurelia had finally surrendered, even though her original plans did not include a torrid fling. All her previous adventures, all her sneaking and sleuthing in the alleys of Vilnius, had lacked the amorous component. Neither fashionable nor voluptuous, she did not entice the opposite sex. A scrawny tomboy with a chronically peeling nose and coltish mannerisms, she had preferred observing other people's romantic affairs to having her own. Everything changed on the night of the Feast of St. John when Marius ambushed her on the hilltop. The dark-eyed, greasy-curled journalist worshipped her as if she were Goddess Laima herself. He did deliciously obscene things with her, the kind that the girls at Frau Jung's academy discussed in subdued whispers.

"Once upon a time, there was a landlord," he continued.

261

"Let's call him Adomas. His frigid and barren wife could not produce him an heir, so his attentions shifted onto a comely maid name Greta. Before long the girl fell pregnant. The landlord's wife, a staunch keeper of morals, kicked Greta out of the house, to set an example for the rest of the servants. For months the hapless girl roamed the countryside, moving from village to village, hiding in the barns by night, eating whatever scraps were discarded. One midsummer morning she made a nest in the bog and birthed a boy as handsome as the young woodland god Velnias. She named him Aras, meaning Eagle. As soon as she clutched the hungry babe to her breast, another wave of pain came, and her body expelled a hideous being, her second son. Even the mischievous bog nixies scattered at the sight of him. Every limb was crooked, every feature was deformed. Greta fled in terror with Aras in her arms. She left her handsome son at the doorstep of the church and ran off, never to be seen again. That day Adomas came to mass. When the landlord beheld the boy's features, he recognized him as his own. His wife did not object, though she looked particularly sullen that day."

"And the deformed son?" Aurelia asked. "Was he just left in the bog to die?"

"Patience, my love." Marius had been using that word consistently since the night they met. "The deformed child was found by a witch named Vaida who lived in a cottage near the bog. He was so perfect in his ugliness that he made her black heart sing. She rejoiced in him more than Adomas rejoiced in his handsome son. Old Vaida adopted him and named him Petras, for the lad was sturdy as a rock. She taught him all her wicked tricks, all her pernicious spells. He knows how to conjure the water sprites and make them dance to his song. To this day Ugly Petras haunts the countryside, rummaging the barns and the chicken coops where his mother once found refuge. His first retaliation was against his natural father, Adomas. The haughty landlord took leave of his senses and hanged himself on a cherry tree."

"And Aras? Was he next?"

"No. The handsome twin proved to have a noble and charitable heart. And though Aras never met Ugly Petras, he sensed that he had a brother, and always left a pitcher of ale and a slice of ham on the porch for him. Petras gobbled up the treats and cast spells of protection upon his brother's estate. Since then no drought, no pestilence has plagued the land. Can you guess what the name of the estate was? Fox Glen."

"What a marvelous little tale. Do you tell it to every girl you seduce?" Aurelia raised her head from his chest and resumed a more businesslike attitude. "It should be published in the next edition of *Aušra*. A few pencil illustrations wouldn't hurt. I'm going to Bitėnai village, to see the editor."

"I'll come with you." Marius squeezed her wrist, as if he was afraid that she would run away. "I'm dying to meet the pompous man who keeps rejecting my articles."

***

Two days later, they were standing inside the home-based editorial office of Martynas Jankus. Aged twenty-seven, Jankus was the most prominent Prussian-Lithuanian activist and one of the founders of *Aušra*. Apart from graduating from a primary school in Bitėnai, the man was largely self-educated. In addition to supporting the paper financially, he contributed pieces under various pen names including V. Giedris, Martyneitis, Bitėnų Merčius, Gyvoleitis. He maintained close ties to the Lithuanians in America. In his opinion, having allies in the New World was of the utmost importance to the nationalistic movement in Europe.

Jankus greeted Aurelia but ignored her male companion.

"So you must be Dr. Wilczynski's famous protégée." His nearsighted eyes narrowed critically, and his chin dropped, making the neat dark beard appear more pointed. "In his last letter he told me you'd be coming. You have new material for me?"

Aurelia handed over her notebook. "I wrote a feature on the Feast of St. John. It would be grand to have a camera next time." She nodded in Marius' direction. "This young gentleman is an ardent supporter of your newspaper. If you decide to publish the piece, I insist that you credit him as well. He helped me write it. Anyway, I hope the article meets your standards."

Jankus took a few moments to scrutinize the content of the notebook. "My standards aren't unreasonable. I'm working with rather limited print space. My publication has reached a point where the contributors outnumber the subscribers. Trust me it's not a good place to be. I don't know how much I can continue doing this."

Aurelia's heart sank. Dr. Wilczynski would be devastated to hear the news. "Is there anything I can do?"

"Maybe. When are you going back to Vilnius?"

"In a few days."

"Can I trust you with a delivery?"

"You can trust me with your life, Master Jankus."

The editor nodded at a stack of books sitting on his desk. "There's a bookstore on Castle Street with a horse's head engraved above the entrance. When you come in, tell the man behind the counter you'd like to see the brass globe. He'll walk you to the back room."

Aurelia took a moment to process the request. "You... want me to smuggle the books across the border?"

"I realize it's not a glamorous task, but someone has to do it. The load isn't as heavy as it looks. If your friend is truly an ardent supporter of my initiative, he won't mind helping you." It was the first time Jankus acknowledged Marius' presence. "You can pretend to be lovers. The gendarmes don't bother young people who hold hands and kiss."

The aspiring journalist flashed a seething glare at the editor. "We don't need to pretend to be lovers," he said, throwing his arm around Aurelia. "We're getting married."

CHAPTER 27

Midnight Sun

Vilnius—St. Petersburg—late June, 1885

The best things in Russia are German.

Sebastian Messer kept repeating those words like sacred litany while lounging in the dining car of the St. Petersburg-bound train. The tepid summer wind breaking through the rolled down window blew his freshly washed and pomaded hair. Theodor Nekrasov was sitting across from him, chewing a stale caviar sandwich and washing it down with flat champagne. The menu left much to be desired, but Theodor did not complain, since Sebastian was paying for the meal.

Prior to departure they had made a list of concerts and exhibitions to attend. Both were wearing cream summer suits with cerulean vests and beige ties. Sebastian knew he looked far more dashing than his pudgy companion—light-colored clothes flatter a slimmer figure. The trip was not about Theo anyway. To be fair, he made a tolerable companion, as long as he did not draw too much attention. How would his signature fat cat charm work on the girls of St. Petersburg? Sebastian had his eyes set on a loftier prize—Lydia Vishnevsky. Having done his share of detective work, he knew which venues the philanthropically inclined widow would be attending. He had also rehearsed a few phrases to melt her heart. Attorney Messer was on his way to reclaim what was rightfully his.

What would Russians be without Germans? The hardcore Slavophiles could glamorize and glorify their quasi-Asiatic roots, embracing mysticism and rural life while rejecting rational thought and industrial progress. And yet, the Czars would always turn westward whenever they needed an innovator.

Peter Carl Faberge, the Dresden-educated jeweler, had been designing jewelry for the Russian Imperial family, capitalizing on the elements of the eclectic Art Nouveau. Alexander Poehl, a graduate of Giessen University, had been running the city's most prominent pharmacy and supplying the Court with medicine as well as teaching at the Military Medical Academy—achievements that had earned him a hereditary title and a family crest. Franz San-Galli, the Pomeranian entrepreneur, had built his fortune through manufacturing equipment for water supply, heating, and sewage systems. In addition to having patented a radiator, he produced decorative wrought iron and helped install gas lighting to the streets of St. Petersburg. Adolf Marks, another Pomeranian, had established *Niva*, the most popular weekly magazine in the Empire. Yes, it takes a German to cover Russian news.

***

Baltic Train Station, St. Petersburg

The moment they stepped off the train, a whirlwind of mirth swept them up and carried them down the platform teeming with university students at various levels of intoxication, confection vendors and accordion players.

Chorus girls from the Imperial Ballet School were handing out leaflets advertising the upcoming performances at the Mariinsky Theatre. As Theodor was paying for a bag of sugarplums, he felt a kiss on his cheek, and a second later, another one on his neck. He recognized Liz and Cat, the two ballerinas in whose company he had experienced some of the most erotically charged moments of his life. He nearly dropped the bag of sugarplums. His portly body sandwiched between two lithe dancers, he huffed and grunted with pleasure.

"You must see us in *La Bayadère!*" Liz tweeted, attaching a tiny bouquet of forget-me-nots to his lapel. "We're in the third row of the chorus."

"We'll sneak you backstage," Cat added, "so you can meet the rest of the troupe. Ekaterina Vazem is going to be there, the original prima."

The euphoric reunion was rudely interrupted by Sebastian's stern rebuke. "Nekrasov!" he barked. "I didn't bring you here so you could indulge your porcine appetites."

Theo reddened in the face and crushed a sugarplum between his teeth.

***

Alexandrinsky Theatre, St. Petersburg

About thirty minutes into the charity concert Theodor was ready to eat the glossy booklet. The elderly Adolf von Henselt, a Bavarian-born virtuoso and former court pianist, was giving a solo recital to benefit the widows and orphans of the Russo-Turkish war of the previous decade. Theo feared that the grumbling in his stomach was interfering with the performance. St. Petersburg was turning out to be a total disaster on the gastronomical front. He'd not had a proper meal since his arrival. Sitting on a hard, uncomfortable chair, he was daydreaming about the quaint bistros of his native Vilnius, the warm flaky croissants, the succulent quiches and the rich tarry coffee. Not that finding good eateries in St. Petersburg was a problem. He just never had the time to sit down, being constantly jerked around by his friend. The two were always on the run, going places where Sebastian felt he needed to be. Theo's stomach longed for Bistro Napoleon on Castle Street, and his loins ached for the dressing room of the Mariinsky Theatre. Liz and Cat were probably changing into their gauzy costumes, packing their cute little tits into pink corsets. He would give anything to squeeze those tits for good luck. Instead, he was stuck at a boring concert, playing the proverbial Sancho Panza to Sebastian's Don Quixote.

During the intermission Theo headed towards the refreshment stand in the foyer. A line was already forming in front of the champagne fountain. If he was lucky, he would get another stale caviar sandwich.

About ten meters away from him, Sebastian was talking to a statuesque brunette in her mid-thirties who was draped in burgundy taffeta. The virginal contours of her bosom suggested that her body had not been through childbirth. So that must be the elusive Lydia, Sebastian's proverbial Golden Fleece.

"Madame Vishnevsky, you stand out in the crowd like a cognac diamond in a pile of semi-precious gemstones. It was such a marvelous idea to invite von Henselt."

"Well, Adolf and I are old friends," the lady replied. "He's officially retired from the big stage, but he agreed to play for a good cause."

"Oh, Madame, there's no lion you couldn't tame."

The fan of black swan feathers fluttered in Lydia's hand. "Herr, Messer, have you been to the masquerade in Peterhof?"

"Not yet, I'm afraid. It's my first outing. To be truthful, I came here seeking medical care for a close friend," Sebastian spoke with affected reluctance. "He has an advanced stage of consumption. He's given up all hope, but I insisted on taking him to St. Petersburg. The train ride was taxing. Still, I couldn't bear the thought of him wasting away in his bleak Vilnius flat."

"I'd like to visit your friend," Lydia said in a tone of belligerent determination.

Sebastian did not expect for the conversation to take that turn. "That's awfully charitable of you, but I... I don't think he's up for visitors."

"I'm not just any visitor. I'm an ambassador of faith. There's one passage in the Bible that I'd like to read to him. Herr Messer, I demand that you take me to your ailing friend. Where are you lodging?"

"At that... that dingy little hotel on Ligovsky Prospect." Sebastian bit his tongue. Dingy and Ligovsky Prospect did not belong in the same sentence. "It's not really a hotel in a traditional sense. It's an old flat that's being rented out by the owner. No amenities apart from a bathtub. My friend just needs a quiet place to rest until the doctor can see him. The wait can take a few weeks."

"What's the name of the doctor? I can talk to him and convince him to make your friend a priority."

The questions kept coming. Sebastian realized he was lying himself into a corner. "His name is... Dr. Astahov."

Lydia ran her exquisite hand over her brow, straining her memory. "The name doesn't sound familiar. And I'm very well connected to the medical community."

"That's because... Dr. Astahov doesn't practice in St. Petersburg. He's from Moscow. He's here visiting family. He doesn't want to announce his presence for fear that patients will flock to him. He promised to make an exception for my friend. It's such a delicate matter, shrouded in secrecy."

"But why? Consumption isn't syphilis. There's nothing shameful about it."

"I know, but my friend is a very private and proud person. He hates being regarded as an invalid. Really, the best thing you can do for him is pray."

Lydia intertwined her long fingers over the sparkling amethyst broach on her belt. "I'll request a service in his name at St. Vladimir's Cathedral. Of course, I'll need his name."

"You can call him... Andreas. It's not his real name, but God will know for whose health you're praying. Now, if you excuse me, I'd like to make a donation."

Sebastian dashed across the foyer, pulled Theodor out of the buffet line and dragged him into the coat room. "She didn't see you, did she? Please, tell me she didn't."

"What's wrong? Is there a wine stain on my tie?"

"No, you fool! Did you see the lady I was talking to? It's *her*. I finally got three minutes of private conversation. Tremendous progress! I need you to go back to the hotel and stay there. As of today, you're dying of consumption."

Theodor patted his belly. "We just got here, and I'm already dying?"

"Yes. And you'll die for real if you don't follow my instructions. Tomorrow I'll bring Lydia for a visit. You'll stay in bed and look very, very ill. Cough and moan."

The clerk scratched the back of his head. "I don't know how convincing I'll be. I wish you'd given me some notice. Perhaps, I could've lost some weight. I'm not good at impromptu performances."

"There's no time for that. Look, Nekrasov, it's the most important trip of my life."

Theodor adjusted the belt of his trousers. He was relieved to have Sebastian's permission to leave the concert early. "I suppose I should get into character."

Before marching to his deathbed, he stopped by the Mariinsky Theatre to see the two ballerinas, just in time for the second act of *La Bayadère*.

***

Imperial Public Library, Nevsky Prospect

The story of Sebastian's mysterious ailing friend moved Lydia Vishnevsky to the core of her heart. She insisted on continuing the conversation after the concert. They spent the rest of the evening on the mezzanine of the Imperial National Library, reviewing the latest publications on the treatment of tuberculosis. The exhilaration Sebastian felt from closeness to Lydia dwarfed any remorse. For a middle-aged woman, Lydia possessed a surprisingly pure and trusting heart. It did not occur to her to question the young German's motives. She assumed the story was true. Before long, Sebastian started believing his own lie. He and Lydia were on a mission to save his friend. *Mein Gott*, she was so virtuous, vulnerable and loaded with money. Every breath she took was worth ten imperial rubles. This combination of refinement and humility likened her to the character of Madame de Tourvel from *Dangerous Liaisons*.

"I was wrong about you, Herr Messer." Lydia lifted the gaze of her innocent hazel eyes off the pages of the medical journal. "When we were first introduced, I took you for one of those egotists who only cared about status and prestige."

Sebastian spat out an unnatural chuckle. "Status, prestige? Bah! My father spent his best years chasing those chimeras, and what happened? He died with a gold-digger at his bedside. I assure you, Madame, I'm nothing like my father."

"I'm relieved to hear that. It would pain me to see a quality citizen perish before his time. Isn't it heavenly that our paths crossed?"

"Oh, Madame, it's... cosmic serendipity."

"I want to share something with you that I've never shared with another man."

"Please, do, Madame." His voice was warm and dulcet, like freshly brewed tea with clover honey and cream. "I'm so honored to be your confidant."

"As you may know, my late husband left me... quite comfortable. God didn't bless us with children, so there's nobody to inherit it."

Sebastian clicked his tongue. "What a dreadful disappointment. I mean... It's God's will. Surely, the Almighty has other plans for you."

"My plan is to donate my fortune to the church. I've already spoken to Father Theodosius about it. Herr Messer? You look pale. Perhaps, you need some fresh air. We've been sitting here for hours."

Suddenly lightheaded, Sebastian laid his hand on Lydia's shoulder. "Wait, Madame. Don't take any headlong plunges."

"I've thought about it long and hard. Count Tolstoy did it. To this day he looks back on his denouncement of worldly pleasures as a singularly liberating act."

"But must you..." Sebastian blinked, running his thumb over Lydia's clavicle. "Must you relinquish everything at once? Why cannot you continue organizing charity concerts and photography classes for orphans? The church is full of corrupt, manipulative people who press in the right places to awaken feelings of guilt."

The widow made a sign of the cross. "Don't blaspheme,

Herr Messer."

"I'm not speaking against God, Madame. In fact, it was God who sent me here to prevent you from making an irreversible mistake. I'm merely questioning the motives of the clergy. Those bearded men cannot be trusted. Sure, I'm a Protestant, but I know a thing or two about Orthodoxy. How can you be sure that they'll use your money honorably? Is this what your husband would've wanted?"

Lydia's firm unused bosom rose and fell underneath a thin layer of lace. Rapidly pooling tears made the tiny lines around her eyes more noticeable. "I've no idea how Alexei envisioned the next... forty or fifty years of my life." Her melodic mezzo-soprano broke. "All I know is that his fortune is like a beacon for predators. No matter where I go, his former friends ogle me. They keep asking me how I'm doing, feigning concern. I want to dispose of the money and disappear from the city, settle where nobody has heard my family name. Why am I sharing this with you? Because you're an outsider. You're not stewing in this caldron of vanity and intrigue. Your motives are pure. How can I tell? By the way you dress. This suit of yours is from the last season. Nobody wears cerulean vests anymore."

"Oh?" Sebastian's heart skipped a few beats. "I mean... Oh! That's right. I don't care about fashion. I'm just here to help my friend."

"When Alexei was ill, do you think any of his friends came to visit?" The pitch of her voice continued rising. "They did— to check how quickly his condition was deteriorating."

Sebastian took that opportunity to draw Lydia into his embrace and plant a quasi-platonic kiss on her hairline. "There, there, Madame. Your late husband's soul needs prayers, not tears. Let's pray together. I'll go first, in German. *Vater unser im Himmel, geheiligt werde dein Name...*"

CHAPTER 28

The Gilded Bear Trap

Rambynas Hill—July, 1885

When Aurelia announced that she was leaving Fox Glen, she could not tell whether her aunt was relieved or saddened. The spinster's eyebrows twitched, though the rest of her face, wreathed in copper braids remained frozen.

"I knew you'd get bored," Vitalia said. "You see one festival, and that'll suffice for the rest of your life. It's always the same every year, peasants walking in circles, tossing twigs into the bonfire."

The girl threw her arms around her hostess. Vitalia, who had not been hugged since adolescence, did not know how to respond to this impetuous familial gesture. Finally, she was able bring herself to tap her niece on the shoulder blade. The barriers that had been built over the course of decades could not be broken overnight.

Aurelia fluttered out of the house, her knapsack bobbing against her back and the ribbon of her straw hat flapping in the wind. Vitalia peeked through the lace curtains into the yard and saw a lanky disheveled youth standing underneath the apple tree with a cigarette in his teeth. At the sight of the girl, he assumed a militant posture and extended his hand to her. Ordinarily, the sight of someone else's happiness, the kind she had been denied, would send Vitalia through a wringer of bitterness, but this time the prevalent emotion was alarm. There was something unsavory about that male specimen. A hardened misanthrope, Vitalia Jocyte was accustomed to thinking ill of people and expecting the worst, but her niece's mysterious companion gave her a jolt of antipathy like she had not experienced in a long time.

"Let's try to catch the two o'clock train," she overheard him say to Aurelia. "I'd like to be in Vilnius by nightfall."

***

"That Jankus fellow really owes me," Marius muttered on the way to the railroad station as he was dragging an old suitcase filled with banned books. Aurelia had deliberately picked a carrier that was on its last breath, with broken latches, the two halves tied together by a rope, with colored rags spilling through the crack. The gendarmes would be more likely to search a neat, inconspicuous bag. "I just don't trust him."

"You don't like his taste in literature?"

"I didn't like how he was burrowing you with those lecherous beady eyes. Nobody ogles my woman like that. I don't want you going to his house alone again."

Aurelia wiggled her fingers, trying to disengage them from his grip. His obsessive jealousy was beginning to wear her out. It was no longer amusing or endearing. "What do you want me to do, disguise myself as a boy?"

"Very amusing."

"It's not my fault that most book smugglers happen to be men. This... revival isn't exactly dominated by petticoats. I don't get to choose my comrades or superior officers."

"So Jankus isn't to your taste?"

"He's all right, I suppose. Except for that beard."

You aren't to my taste either, she was tempted to add. So that was what it felt like to have a lover—a warm, sticky, talking shadow following you around, disrupting your thoughts? After the first round of lovemaking on the banks of the Neman River his enigmatic appeal had started waning. The only reason Aurelia had given into his advances was because she had never been coached on how to reject a man properly. She could not wait to get back to Vilnius and disappear in the familiar labyrinth of alleys and sewers. They would drop the delivery off at the book store on Castle Street, and then she would steal away. He would never find her. No more joint ventures. She operated much better on her own. Most men were only good for one thing: lifting heavy loads. Well, this particular specimen was not even good for that. He resented every kilogram of the forbidden cargo he had been entrusted with by Jankus. So much for suffering for the cause. He was an amateur, not a martyr.

"Remember the editor's advice: we must behave like newlyweds." Marius reached into his pocket and pulled out two makeshift wedding rings.

Aurelia hastily snatched one from him before he endeavored to slip it on her finger himself. The skin under the metallic band immediately started burning and itching. Her hand suddenly felt heavy and sluggish.

"This is where all talk stops," she said, when they finally reached the train station. "Walls and wheels have ears."

After paying for the tickets, Marius pulled Aurelia into a telegraph booth. "I need to send a message to my brother in Vilnius. I'll tell him to kick out the tenant. That drunken bastard hasn't paid rent in three weeks. We'll need the extra room. My woman and I won't be sleeping in the hall."

Aurelia thought it would be best not to argue with him in order to make the next five hours of the train ride as painless as possible. Fortunately, Marius could only afford traveling second-class, which meant they would have to share the compartment with other passengers. She prayed he had enough self-restraint to control his ardor in the presence of strangers.

Her prayers were answered. A family of four walked into the compartment and occupied the leather-padded seat across from them. The patriarch had the austerity of a Lutheran minister. Aurelia saw the edge of a leather-bound Bible protruding from his pocket.

"Good thing we've eaten at the station," he muttered to his wife in German. "The prices at the restaurant car are insane."

"I don't know how fresh the food is," the woman said. She fixed the unadorned bonnets on her young daughters and gave each a red apple.

After hearing Lithuanian for two weeks, Aurelia leaped for joy at the sound German. "You all look so elegant," she addressed the family. "The four of you belong in a picture book. Are you going to a wedding?"

Four pairs of Prussian blue eyes turned to her. The two girls froze in the same pose, their teeth stuck in the apples.

"We're going to a funeral," the father replied as soon as he got over the initial shock of the stranger's unceremonious intrusion. "My brother-in-law."

"Accept my condolences," Aurelia said. "I hope his passing was a peaceful one."

The man glanced at his wife, as if asking for her permission to carry on the conversation. The woman shrugged with the signature Lutheran stoicism.

"Actually, it was quite sudden and brutal," she imparted.

"My brother was stabbed in the chest several times and dumped into the river. It was no ordinary robbery. His wedding ring and his pocket watch were still on him. Whoever killed him didn't bother to remove his valuables." Seeing Aurelia's blanched face, she added, "I don't mind talking about it. In fact, it's my duty to warn fellow Germans. It's the least I can do for poor Fritz. If you have any relatives in Vilnius, tell them to watch their backs. There's a killer on the loose going after Germans. Last year it was Lichtner, and now it's my brother. Obviously, we're no longer welcome in Vilnius." She turned her attention to her youngest daughter. "How is your apple, *Liebling*? Not too sour, I hope. Your Uncle Fritz loved apples. When we get home, I'll make you his favorite strudel."

Aurelia wondered what kind of sedatives the woman was on, to be able to deliver such an explicit narration. "What was your brother's occupation, if you don't mind me asking?"

"Fritz was selling surgical equipment to dentists. He spent much of his time on the road. He died in Vilnius, of all places—on his day off." Once again, the woman shifted her attention to her oldest daughter. "Are you listening to what Mutti is saying? There's no reason for a Prussian to leave the Kaiser's domain."

***

Marius had spent most of the ride sleeping, or at least pretending to be asleep, with his head in Aurelia's lap. When the train reached Vilnius, he leaped down onto the platform with the swiftness of a weasel and received her in his arms.

"I just want you to know: the past two weeks have been heavenly. They'll live in my memory until I die."

His words left Aurelia a little perplexed, as they sounded like a prelude to a farewell. Could it be that the hothead had come to his senses? So all that talk about him kicking out the delinquent tenant to make room for her was not serious? They could even stay friends and joke about their tryst on the banks of Neman.

"Thanks for helping me with the baggage," she said, trying to wiggle her way out of his hug. "I couldn't have dragged all those books by myself."

"I love you, I swear." He exhaled into her neck. She could feel the moisture of his tears. Or maybe it was saliva.

Looking over Marius' shoulder, Aurelia saw three gendarmes walking down the platform towards them. Since 1871, the Special Corps of Gendarmes had enjoyed the right to investigate both political and criminal cases. The Corps consisted of the high-ranking officers who had already proven themselves in the regular army.

"I didn't know you had friends in uniforms," Aurelia said.

"There are many things you didn't know about me, my love." With one swift move he yanked the knapsack off her shoulder and pushed her towards the gendarmes. "Gentlemen, meet lovely Aurelia Messer, a boisterous young rebel who delivered an ardent speech against the Czar before a crowd," he said in flawless Russian as he pulled out several editions of *Aušra* from the knapsack as material proof. "From hereon I leave her in your capable hands. Officer Rudenski, she's all yours."

"Well-done, Panaev," the officer said as he handcuffed Aurelia. "Fräulein Messer, you are under arrest for sedition and violation of the censorship law."

It took Aurelia about ten seconds to process the situation and regain her footing. So, her intuition had not failed her. Right from the start she had felt that something was amiss about her new comrade. She had heard of the Secret Guard members infiltrating various revolutionary cliques and posing as sympathizers, but she had not expected that they would go after someone of her meager caliber. The good news was that she would no longer have to endure Marius' suffocating company, his sticky hands, his repetitive caresses and compliments. The bad news was that the latest audition of *Aušra* would never reach the hungry readers. The aloof editor would never trust her to run another delivery for him —if she were to walk away alive. According to her loose knowledge of the judicial system, she was looking at fifteen lashes and two to three years of hard labor. She was fairly confident in her ability to bear the punishment with dignity. Her pain threshold was rather high. Later on she could flaunt her scars to her former schoolmates. Those squeamish cows, Marie and Justine, would swoon with envy.

"My brother is an attorney, you see," she said, turning her nose up. "I know the laws. You cannot arrest me for a speech delivered on German soil."

"Ah, but you're on Russian soil now." Rudenski waved a copy of the newspaper. "Possession of printed materials in Lithuanian is a crime around here."

Aurelia could tell that Rudenski was good at his job. It took her breath away how swiftly and efficiently he managed to handcuff her, without any unnecessary harshness. That man must have arrested many female criminals in his lifetime.

"Can I pick you as my executioner?" she pleaded. "If I'm to be whipped for my naughty deeds, can it be by you?"

"As much as I'd love to whip a ravishing minx like you with my own hands, I'm afraid it won't come to that. Given your noble birth, tender age and fragile physique, I predict the judge will give you a few months at the Lukiškės detention facility. What you've done is but a caprice of a misguided child. In my humble opinion, it is your brother who deserves to be whipped, shackled and shipped to

Siberia."

For the first time since her arrest, Aurelia came close to tears. Was that all, three short months with petty thieves and unregistered prostitutes? The Lukiškės prison had been converted from an earlier Roman Catholic monastery in 1837. For almost fifty years the minimum security detention facility had been serving the miscellaneous needs of the Russian authorities. Aurelia's punishment lacked grandeur and pathos. Three months at Lukiškės was the equivalent of standing in the corner for an hour or being sent to bed without supper.

"Your informer friend hasn't reported half of my transgressions," she said to Rudenski. "Smuggling anti-Czarist literature is only a small part of what I do. I'm an anarchist of the most dangerous kind. I know how to make hand bombs and mix slow-acting venoms. I deserve to be punished on par with the rebels of '63."

Rudenski leaned in, his lush Cossack mustache brushing the tip of her ear. "Fräulein, I see you didn't get enough spanking as a child. If upon release you still think you merit a harsher punishment, I'll be glad to oblige."

CHAPTER 29

The Last Bottle of Kosher Wine

Stikliu Street, Vilnius—July, 1885

Grandpa Isaac's seventy-fifth birthday party was a smashing success, with gourmet food and light-hearted fiddle music. The entire second floor of the Asher's Atelier was decked out in miniature lanterns, flower garlands and silk ribbons streaming down from the balcony. The Stikliu Street had not seen such a soiree in a decade. Leah was the flamboyant genius behind the extravaganza. The oldest of the Asher children was at the peak of her creative glory. She had just sold three of her dresses to a banker's wife and accepted a marriage proposal from her perfumer beau. Among the things that David Kravitz loathed most were temperance and mediocrity. It was under his influence that Leah decided that Grandpa Isaac deserved something truly spectacular rather than another dull family dinner.

Per Leah's instructions, the musicians played a cancan. Her four female cousins, their ages ranging between ten and fifteen, dressed up in ruffles and feathers, lined up in a row and kicked up their skinny legs.

Amidst all the merriment, the guests did not notice that

the birthday boy had been in a dismal mood all night.

"This is my last birthday party," he sighed, tears dripping into his grey beard. "Great misfortunes are heading our way."

"Don't be a spoilsport," Leah chided him. "Crying on a night like this? You've had too much to drink."

"Or not enough," Esther said as she refilled her father-in-law's glass. "Tatti, won't you raise a toast?"

Isaac's trembling sinewy hand pushed away the glass. The substance it contained was not kosher wine but ordinary champagne that the girls had brought from their last trip to Paris.

"Where's Benjamin?" he asked suddenly. "I was going to give him my watch. Since my days are counted, it should go to my eldest grandson."

Leah and Esther exchanged perplexed glances. They had not seen Benjamin in hours. He had taken advantage of the festive commotion and snuck out early.

"He's probably across the street, fetching some kosher wine for you," Leah said at last. "He'll be back any minute."

Esther linked arms with her daughter and pulled her aside. "I do worry about your brother. What if he's fallen with a rough crowd? It's the last thing we need. Did you see that purple mark on his jawline? It's not just a smudge of paint. It's a real bruise. He must've gotten it in a brawl."

Leah responded with a mysterious sneer. "I assure you, Mamah, he got it under much more pleasurable circumstances."

"Do you have any idea who she is?"

Even if Leah knew, she would not betray her brother's secret. "It's definitely not Rachel Kaufmann or Miriam Gewirtz. Both are still here at the party, probably looking for him this very moment."

A crease cut across Esther's powdered forehead. "I just

don't want my little boy to catch syphilis at his tender age. He's been consorting with those models. *Oy vey!* They're walking cauldrons of disease. That's how Goya lost his hearing, you know."

Leah fought to stifle a laugh. "Don't be daft, Mamah. Comparing our untalented, delusional Benjamin to Goya?"

"Syphilis doesn't care about talent... or lack thereof."

"Fortunately, Benjamin has a seasoned, thoroughly rotten friend who personally inspects those sluts for health before passing them on to his protégé. If it's any comfort, I have reasons to believe that Benjamin is being monogamous. Earlier today he begged me to sell him a hat I made for the showcase. Blue velvet would look stunning on a blonde! I basically pocketed his monthly allowance. Would he go for such sacrifices if he wasn't serious?"

The alarm in Esther's eyes escalated. She was not sure what was worse, her little prince carousing with a dozen infected models or getting serious with a blonde.

***

Castle Street, Benjamin's art studio

For the first time since Dominik's birth Renate could look in the mirror without cringing. The damage childbearing had done to her appearance was beginning to reverse. Her body was regaining its former contours. The milk in her breasts had finally dried up, and they stopped throbbing and leaking. The facial swelling was subsiding. She could finally see the definition of her cheekbones. Clarity and pallor were returning to her complexion.

"I don't know where I can wear this hat," she said about Leah's creation. "If your sister spots it in the crowd, she'll know the truth immediately."

285

"I think she already knows," Benjamin replied.

"Well, Master Dombrowski is still in the dark. He thinks I've been sitting at my teacher's bedside all this time."

Benjamin was learning to take Renate's casual reference to her husband in stride. In the young man's mind, the Polish peasant remained a quasi-comedic figure, an annoying though not insurmountable obstacle.

"Besides," she continued, "I don't have a dress to go with the hat. All my frocks are so hopelessly bleak and plain." Poor Frau Jung would be mortified if she saw one of her most promising pupils pouting and prancing in front of a mirror. "Do you think such a dress exists?"

"The dress is in progress. Give me another week or two. Leah's been working on her latest Parisian-inspired masterpiece. I saw ten meters of turquoise velvet delivered to the shop. If you want to be the first one to wear the dress before it debuts in the showcase, just say a word. I'll see that you are the most glamorous woman in the city."

Renate shook her head, making the peacock feathers dance. Benjamin's adolescent devil-may-care bravado was both endearing and distressing. They had been lovers for a month, and Renate was only starting to enjoy intimacy with him. The first few attempts were rather deplorable. Benjamin was clueless and impetuous. His technique, or rather lack thereof, was shaped by sporadic encounters with models. Those women were mostly factory workers, accustomed to rough treatment from their men. They appreciated every word of flattery, every bite of roast beef sandwich, but did not expect to be satisfied in bed. They moaned and quivered in hopes that the two nice gentlemen would invite them back. Renate had resolved to break her young lover of his bad habits and teach him to be more like... Thaddeus. Learning about the pleasure wells on her body was one good thing that came out of her marriage. It would be stupid to let that knowledge go to waste. She dispensed instructions, and Benjamin carried them out with varying degrees of success. Luckily, he was an eager student and soon learned what a genuine female climax felt like.

In early July the book store directly beneath their love nest had been raided by the gendarmes. The owner had been arrested for collaborating with book smugglers and selling literature in Lithuanian. Stacks of old editions of *Aušra* had been found underneath the counter. Fortunately, the gendarmes had not thought of raiding the upstairs loft.

"Would you be as gallant to me if I were Jewish?" Renate asked suddenly. "Would you be just as eager to fulfil my whims if our love affair was public and sanctioned?"

"I've never had a sanctioned love affair, as you put it."

"You mean to tell me your zealous parents haven't appointed a perfect little Jewish bride for you?"

"You're misinformed," he said with a slight tremor of his voice. "We don't travel in Orthodox circles. The Ashers have been making their own matches for generations. My sister found that Kravitz fellow all on her own. It would be good for the family business to add a perfume dealer to the mix."

Renate nodded through his speech. "In other words, the reason why you don't have a fiancée is because you haven't succeeded in any trade?"

"My parents have given up hope by now. I never had much luck with women from my own tribe. They want someone frugal, industrious and level-headed, and I'm none of those things. I'd make a terrible husband for a Jewess. Perhaps, my destiny is to be a perfect lover for a married German woman."

***

THE GATE OF DAWN

Stikliu Street

On his way home, Benjamin stopped by the apothecary shop to pick up some valerian root drops for his grandfather. He felt it would be an appropriate appeasement gesture after his abrupt departure from the party. The gendarmes patrolling Stikliu Street seemed a little more agitated than usual.

"Where have you been, Benjamin?" he heard a trembling voice behind his back.

It was doe-eyed Rachel Kaufmann, an iconic merchant class Jewess, a woman of valor from the Old Testament. *A price above rubies...* A few months ago, right before Renate's reappearance in his life, Benjamin had kissed Rachel at a dance, and ever since then he had been paying for that fleeting indiscretion. Since then she had been shadowing him, her eyelashes weighed down with moisture, always looking for an excuse to touch him in a Torah-acceptable way. Irritatingly pious and accomplished in every applied craft from sewing to jewelry-making, she would have made a perfect wife for young Jacob. But, as fate would have it, her heart desired the oldest of the Asher brothers. The concept of casual kisses was foreign to her. She took everything too literally. Benjamin could not think of a delicate way of communicating his lack of interest in her. Simple avoidance did not seem to work. If anything, it fueled Rachel's fantasies even more. Leah had caught her going through the collection of wedding dresses. Perhaps she believed that if she stalked Benjamin long enough, he would eventually break down and propose to her.

"We've been looking everywhere for you," she said, touching his shoulder.

"A rabbinic 'we'? Are you speaking on behalf of God's

chosen?"

Rachel pulled her hand away with an air of infinite pain. "How can you jest at a time like this?"

"Did I miss another religious holiday? Maybe I've been spending too much time with Catholics and Lutherans." Then Benjamin remembered that he was dealing with someone who did not have a sense of humor. "Forgive me, Rachel. I can see you're trying to tell me something very important. Who's looking for me?"

"My family and yours... whatever is left of it." She muttered the last words so softly that Benjamin's ears did not register them.

"Can you repeat what you just said?"

Rachel bit into her lower lip. "You don't know anything, do you? We better sit down."

She took him by the hand and led him to a bench outside the apothecary's shop. Reluctantly, Benjamin followed. Of course, the Kaufmann girl was talking in riddles on purpose to prolong contact with him. If she wanted to tell him something in confidence, she had surely picked the least private place imaginable.

"I don't have much time," Benjamin said. "I'd like to be on my way home. Grandpa Isaac needs his medicine."

"No, he doesn't!" She shook her head vehemently. "Medicine won't do your grandpa any good."

"Why?"

"Because he's dead! He died shortly after the attack on your house."

Benjamin sprung to his feet. "Enough! I realize humor isn't your talent."

"You think I'm joking? What I'm telling you is the truth. It's God's will that you should hear it from me."

Benjamin's facial expression unchanged, though his

breathing quickened.

"After the party," Rachel continued, "someone broke the window on the first floor and threw several burning kerosene bottles in. Within seconds the workshop was on fire. It's a miracle everyone survived—except for your grandfather. His heart gave out. It wasn't the heat or the smoke that killed him. It was the terror. He whispered, 'Remember Warsaw.' Then his body went limp."

CHAPTER 30

The Last Pack of Cigarettes

Stikliu Street, Kaufmann Jewelry shop

With their own home rendered uninhabitable, the Ashers took temporary refuge with the Kaufmanns down the street. The jewelers gave their displaced neighbors a large room on the second level of their house. It was there that the Ashers were observing Shiva, the seven-day mourning period during which the immediate family of the deceased stayed inside with all mirrors veiled.

Young Jacob, who had remained composed through the ordeal, took it upon himself to see that all rituals were observed. He was the one who served as the *Shomer*, a "watchman" over his grandfather's body. The fourteen-year old was in his element. *Tahara, Chesed Shel Emet, Shiva, Shloshim, Matzevah.* Religious jargon was like oxygen to him.

Benjamin had been laid up with a fever since the day of the funeral. He stayed in the darkest corner of the room under the blankets, his face turned to the wall, refusing food or drink. His parents suspected it was his way of avoiding interrogation about his whereabouts on the night of the fire.

Not that convicting and executing him was a top priority for Daniel and Esther. The two were at odds for the first time. Esther insisted that the whole family should just move to America and start afresh there. Things were not going to get any better in Vilnius. Daniel, on another hand, felt it was their duty to stay and hold their ground.

Leah was like a bee trapped inside a matchbox, buzzing frantically, looking for someone to sting. The stuffy room had only one window overlooking the cobblestone back alley lined with rubbish cans and old crates. Each time Leah parted the curtains, she would see the same bleak picture.

"Do you expect to see the Louvre, my dear?" Esther sighed. "You know if you pinch yourself hard enough, you'll wake up in Paris?"

"I'm not in denial, Mamah. This dingy room is real. So is the ugly dress I'm wearing."

That poorly tailored mourning atrocity of black wool with a high neck came from Rachel Kaufmann's closet. With her entire wardrobe destroyed, Leah had to rely on her hostess, which was the most humiliating part of the experience. To be indebted to the Kaufmanns, of all people! But then, the Kaufmanns were the only family to offer shelter. The rest of the neighbors offered little more than a few sympathetic gasps. David was out of town on business. Would he still want to marry a girl whose family business had gone up in flames?

When Rachel brought a tray with food upstairs, Leah pulled her into a corner. "If I didn't know any better, I'd say you were the one who started the fire."

The stupefied hostess backed away. "What are you talking about?"

"You enjoy having my brother all to yourself, don't you? The divine prankster, has delivered the man of your dreams straight under your roof."

Rachel placed the tray on the table. "You don't mean it, Leah. Obviously, you're still in shock. In time God will heal your wounds, and you won't remember these hateful words. True, I've never seen Paris. I may be a coddled mouse in your eyes, but I do love your brother."

Leah came close to retching in face of such self-denying piety. "I guess people aren't exaggerating. You really jumped right out of the Scripture, to put us all to shame. A price above rubies... And your father knows a thing or two about rubies. You deserve better than Benjamin. My brother is a useless dreamer. But you'll find that out in time."

***

When Rachel left, young Jacob lifted his glistening eyes from the Torah.

"I know you're dying for a cigarette," he said. "You should go outside. God won't get angry, but our hosts might."

Leah kissed the boy on the crown through the yarmulke. "You'll make fierce competition for Rabbi Goldman one day."

She went downstairs and sat right on the steps of the porch, not caring if the ugly dress got dirty. The half-full box of French cigarettes was one of the very few possessions that had survived the fire. The box had been sitting in the pocket of her raincoat that she threw over her nightgown before running out of the house. For Leah, smoking had not become a physical addiction yet. It was a diversion, another way to emulate the fashionable Parisian women. After eating the bland lukewarm food at the Kaufmanns' house for the past few days, she was craving a taste of her former life.

The rain had stopped, and heavy fog set in. Leah could not see the tips of her shoes. In spite of the humidity, the cigarette lit immediately, and tingling bitterness filled her throat. If Reuben Kaufmann, the patriarch of the family, caught her smoking on his porch, he would undoubtedly confiscate the entire box. Leah inhaled greedily, each gulp like an inward sob. A high-pitched sneeze interrupted her reverie. A fair-haired girl around Benjamin's age emerged from the fog and stood in the shaft of light falling from the street lamp. Leah scanned the visitor from head to toe and suddenly burst into surly laughter.

"What do I see? It's the ghost of the Lichtner Empire, the textile princess, in flesh and blood! Hold that pose. Let me take a good look at you."

"There's not much to look at," Renate said.

"Now, don't be coy, my little marzipan cookie. There's plenty to look at. You've been eating well for the past year. Look at your matronly curves!"

"I heard what happened to your family."

"So you scurried to our part of town like a rat across a gutter." Leah squinted and blew a puff of smoke into Renate's face. "Bet you have some poignant message for me, a morsel of wisdom. After all, both our fathers had their businesses burned down. The only difference is that mine is alive, and I should be thankful for it. Did I get most of it?"

"I'd like a word with Benjamin."

"Not possible, I'm afraid."

"Well, it was worth a try." Renate reached into her purse and pulled out a broach and handed it over to Leah. "I wanted to return something of yours. It was a gift from Benjamin."

Leah hesitated to take back the family heirloom tainted by German hands. "I've been wondering what happened to it. So you're the one who's been marking his neck with love bites."

"The last few came from me," Renate confessed. "Anyway, I just wanted to return the broach."

She turned on her heels, but Leah's voice halted her.

"Did I say you were dismissed? I wasn't finished. What happened to us has nothing to do with you. It wasn't some sort of reprisal, if that's what you're thinking. We had plenty of enemies, like any influential family. If you have any fantasies about being Helen of Troy, get them out of your head. It's not in your power to ruin one of the Ashers, even someone as stupid and careless as my brother."

ꝀᕼAPꚍER 31

The Skin on the Forbidden Apple

Lukiškės Prison, a suburb of Vilnius—August, 1885

After six weeks of eating prison gruel, Aurelia could not look at it without nausea. Having always been relatively unfastidious when it came to food, she suddenly developed intolerance to that colorless, tasteless mush.

Those retching attacks did not go unnoticed by her cell mate, a young Russian streetwalker named Annushka who was imprisoned for failure to carry the yellow ticket. With prostitution legalized under Nicholas I, there were over a thousand operating brothels in the major cities of the Empire, ranging greatly in price and class. For a young love-peddler, working in one of those establishments was the most desired arrangement. Some of the girls, however, ended up in solo practice, either because their obstreperous personalities made interaction with colleagues difficult, or because they felt they could make more money working independently. Many relied on male managers or "cats" to drive business. Annushka's offenses included consorting with a "cat" and failing to keep her medical passport up to date. It was her third stint at Lukiškės.

Annushka boasted large square teeth and gorgeous wheat-blonde hair that she kept in a loose braid. Practicality and candor were her finest qualities.

"Try jumping off the table," she said after Aurelia threw up her breakfast again. "Works for me every time."

"Will that settle my stomach?"

"It's one way to get rid of what's causing the sickness. Sure, you may cramp and bleed at first, but it's a hell of a lot safer than going to some granny with a knitting needle."

Still heaving, Aurelia glanced reproachfully at her new friend. "You know I love you all the way to Moscow and back, but please, don't talk to me in riddles. What granny? What knitting needle?"

Annushka crossed her plump arms. "You're the one talking in riddles and playing games with me, dearie. I can see right through you. We're made of the same stuff. Life isn't over just because you got knocked up while making rounds through the barracks."

Aurelia was getting tired of telling her story over and over again. "For the hundredth time, I'm not a prostitute. I'm a political enemy, a regicide in training. In the good old days, I would've had my tongue cut out, my knuckles broken and been exiled to Siberia."

"That's right, dearie, keep talking." Annushka's bulbous nose twitched in contempt. "Before you came, we had a girl who claimed she was Catherine the Great. Syphilis was slowly cooking her brain. She'd break into those rants at night."

***

One day Aurelia received a surprise visit from Marie and Justine. They came to deliver the news of Frau Jung's death.

"It happened while you were in Rambynas," Justine said. "The doctor was a little surprised. He thought she would last through the fall."

"She wasn't making much sense towards the end," Marie added. "She was mostly ranting about her dead daughter. At any rate, we're the provisional government." She slipped her arm around her companion. "We're not taking any new pupils at this time. When the youngest ones graduate, we'll shut the doors for good."

Aurelia took a moment to process the news. A vagabond at heart, she still thought of Kunstakademie as a semi-permanent asylum where she could change her clothes and catch a few hours of sleep between her escapades. The world outside the prison walls was moving at a faster pace.

"Big changes are coming," Marie said. "Supposedly, the bustle is on its way out. In a few years, straight skirts will be all the rage. Same with German. It's becoming irrelevant. Russians are taking over."

"You can thank Czar Alexander for it," Justine snickered. "Marie and I will have to find new jobs—or husbands. Preferably Russian."

Feeling another wave of nausea, Aurelia stood up from the bunk bed, turned her back to the visitors and retreated into the corner of her cell towards the washing basin to splash some water on her face.

"Come back, you!" Marie called for her. "We didn't just bring bad news. Wait until you hear about the latest scandal, featuring your very own brother."

Her hands still dripping, Aurelia glanced over her shoulder. What Marie said made no sense. Sebastian involved in a scandal? That neurotic prig would sooner die than be spotted wearing a demoded scarf, or a tie that did not match his socks, or his hair parted on the wrong side.

Wiggling with excitement, Justine cleared her throat. "You know how your brother went on a wife-hunting expedition with Nekrasov in tow, that fat boy who keeps local bakeries in business? Well, apparently your brother ordered him to stay in bed and feign illness. Eventually Nekrasov got fed up with his confinement, announced that he was miraculously cured and joined a boating party. Naturally, he became the crowd's darling, which made Sebastian livid. After a few bottles of champagne, all hell broke loose. Your brother punched Nekrasov and sent him flying overboard, straight into the frigid waters. That marked the end of their friendship. They traveled back to Vilnius in separate train cars. Nekrasov fell ill with pneumonia after his dip in the Neva. He just got out of the hospital. Your brother made a royal ass of himself."

***

The most entertaining part of Aurelia's imprisonment was her weekly appointment with Officer Rudenski. Although it was not customary for members of the security police to interact with inmates over the course of their incarceration, Rudenski continued seeing her under the pretext of conducting further investigation. Between appointments, he would sneak apples, biscuits and censorship approved books into her prison cell.

"If you give me the names of your partners in crime, I might be able to shorten your sentence," he said during the first session.

"There are no partners. I don't like to share my glorious martyrdom with anyone. Nor am I in a hurry to get out. I rather like it here. Annushka is a riot!"

They enjoyed a few laughs behind the closed doors. One time Aurelia sketched his portrait in exchange for a bag of walnuts. Some of their conversations were serious. Rudenski was privy to the details of the recent skirmish on Stikliu Street. The thickening tension between Christians and Jews concerned him. He wondered how many more attacks would happen in the coming year. Policemen in other cities were starting to look the other way, coming to the aid of the Jewish citizens too late or not coming at all.

The spunky rebel maiden had left quite an impression on the gendarme. He was so used to handling the dregs of society, and Aurelia did not resemble the other detainees. She was a fountain of vivacious sarcasm in the desert of obligate austerity. He gulped from that fountain. His teeth were touching the skin on the forbidden fruit without breaking it.

"A most peculiar thing happened this morning," he told her one day. "A German girl just turned herself in, claiming she murdered her employer. She keeps ranting in her native language. If you could translate for me, I'd be most grateful."

Aurelia stretched on her cot. "Are you offering me an interpreter job? My services are rather costly."

"If you cooperate, I'll shave a week off your term."

"You know I'm not tempted by an early release, not enough to collaborate with Russians," she snapped her fingers, "whom I still, by the way, regard as the enemy."

Rudenski sat down on the edge of her cot. "What about our bourgeoning friendship?" He took hold of her skinny ankle. "Surely, you don't consider me an enemy. Don't look at it as fraternizing with Russians. The case concerns the death of a certain German by the name Hermann Lichtner. This is your chance to be a part of a murder investigation."

"I thought the Lichtner case was closed."

"Between us, it was never opened." He gave her ankle another furtive squeeze. "If anything, it could help you with your novel. Give you some material."

Ah, the novel! Aurelia had told Rudenski about her plans to write a contemporary mystery in Lithuanian and have it published abroad.

"Fine. I'll do it."

Rudenski led her into the interrogation room where he and Aurelia had shared so many hearty laughs and traded so many dirty jokes.

The German girl was stiff and blue in the face, like in the last stages of hypothermia when all shivering stops. Aurelia sat down on the bench next to her.

"What's your name?"

"Frieda. Frieda Zweig."

"Nice to meet you, Frieda. So you're a murderer, eh?"

"An accomplice to be exact." The girl locked her hands and slipped them between her twitching thighs. "It wasn't my idea. I just... played my part."

"When did it happen?"

"Last summer."

"And you only came forward now?"

"I'm gravely ill." Frieda coughed into her sleeve. Aurelia could tell she was not faking. The tiny droplets of blood looked real enough. "I don't want to go to hell."

"You'll go to jail first—if they convict you, of course. Before Divine Judgment, there's a secular trial. Tell me about your employer. Was he a beast?"

"No, Herr Lichtner was the best employer a girl could ask for. I didn't want to do it, but they made me. One night they ambushed me in the yard. They threatened to go after my family if I didn't play along."

"These men, what did they look like?"

"I couldn't see their faces in the dark."

"What language did they speak?"

"Broken German." The girl held her breath for a few seconds, then shook and produced another portion of bloody mucus. "I think they were Russians. They told me to go into

301

the bleaching room and scream for help. They'd take care of the rest. They assured me I'd be unharmed. Sometimes I wish I'd perished that day with Herr Lichtner."

***

"What are you going to do about this mite named Frieda?" Aurelia asked Rudenski as he escorted her back to the cell.

"I honestly don't know yet." With his hand on her elbow, he tried to slow down her pace to prolong their time together.

"Won't you take her into custody? That would be a logical first step."

"I have to think about it."

"What's there to think about? She practically turned herself in."

"The girl's lying. Not about the illness. That part I have no trouble believing. Her confession was a little too smooth, too rehearsed. I'm just not convinced that Russians were behind Lichtner's murder. I'd venture as far as suggesting that the arson was orchestrated by fellow Germans. They'd do anything to cast a shadow upon Russians."

Aurelia halted and raised her eyes at the gendarme. "Even murder one of their own?"

"I've been doing this for quite some time. Things are never as they seem." Rudenski spoke in a stealthy, melancholic whisper, his fingers sliding up and down Aurelia's bare forearm. "There are several clandestine wars going on, not just between native Russians and western transplants. There's also an internal war in the German camp, a battle for supremacy. A man of Lichtner's prominence had ill-wishers among those of his own stock. I bet it was another German who struck the match. It could've been one of his competitors, or perhaps, a jilted business partner. The mastermind behind the plot managed to kill two birds with one stone: obliterate Lichtner and put Russians under suspicion. It's like a smallpox vaccine. You introduce the disease to generate immunity to it. You get low-grade fever and localized scarring, but the lifelong benefits outweigh the vexatious symptoms. The German merchant community is stronger than ever. Lichtner's death was a small price to pay."

Overcome by a sudden surge of fatigue, Aurelia grasped onto the bar of her cell. What Rudenski had imparted was too much too digest at once, largely because it actually made sense. Embarrassment avalanched upon her, as martyr's bravado drained from her heart. She made a laughable detective with her utter lack of peripheral vision. All her sleuthing had been distressingly one-sided. For the past year she had been on a quest to expose Lichtner's murderers, all that time presuming them to be Russian. She had not contemplated the possibility that the strike might have come from within the German circle. To add insult to injury, Officer Rudenski was so infuriatingly courteous, attentive and sympathetic, confiding in her as he would in a true investigation partner, an equal. He did not know half of her ludicrous endeavors. She had not merely smuggled the banned newspapers—she had actually contributed articles, abysmal articles, written in a juvenile, flamboyant style. A delusional waif, who thought she had carved an apostolic niche for herself!

"I need to lie down," she murmured. "I assume you don't need me anymore."

CHAPTER 32

Road to Valhalla

Northern Vilnius—September, 1885

Renate took refuge in Šnipiškės, a quiet suburban settlement on the north bank of the Neris River, named after a rich merchant who had received the plot of land from Grand Duke Vytautas. There had been talks about expanding the village into an industrial center, but so far Renate could see no sign of commercial explosion. It was a sleepy heaven inhabited by lower middle-class families and elderly couples, free from the drama and the excitement of the Old Town. The brightly lit galleries, dance halls, ateliers, book stores and flower stands seemed worlds away. Instead of the fancy bistros there were a few two-story taverns that served filling, unimaginative food—chicken cutlets, cold beet soup, boiled baby potatoes with dill. The dishes reminded her of those served at Raven's Bog, but she ate them without fear, as they were not prepared by Agatha's hands. She could actually picture herself renting a room above one of those taverns and living there indefinitely in anonymity and obscurity. Since Frau Jung's death she had felt no attachment to Kunstakademie, even though she continued spending her nights there and helping Marie and Justine. The last piece in the mosaic of her adolescence had been shattered.

One September evening she stayed out longer than usual. An early autumn chill was descending upon the city. The fog was not thick enough to fully conceal the celestial bodies, only to mute their glow and soften the silhouettes of the buildings. The moon, like a lantern through a veil, spilled a platinum trail over the rippling water.

On her way to the cabriolet stop, Renate saw a drunk sprawled on the bench under a lamp post. Something about him made her pause and take a closer look. She regretted not having her sketchbook handy. The man made for a colorful subject with a vodka flask protruding from the pocket of his finely tailored but wrinkled and dirty waistcoat. The tattered shoelaces were untied, dirty dress socks showing from under the trousers. His taste in clothes was as exquisite as his taste in alcohol was cheap. Having examined his angular features, Renate recognized Attorney Messer. It had been over a year since their last encounter. Oddly, the sight of him did not aggravate the bleeding of the old wound. In that moment Renate did not see the callous messenger of her father's death, just another disturbed soul seeking refuge in the September twilight.

"*Guten abend*, Herr Messer."

Sebastian stirred and opened his eyes. He did not expect to hear German in that part of town. "Why, I feel like I died and went to Valhalla," he said breathlessly. "Am I dreaming? Come closer, let me touch you."

Renate sat down on the bench and gave him her hand. He pulled off her glove, spread her fingers like a fan and examined each one of them closely. "Yes, she still paints. There're traces of watercolors under her fingernails."

After indulging him Renate withdrew her hand. "What

brings you here?"

"I'm developing a taste for sleeping under the stars like a gypsy. At the rate my clients are dropping, I'll be homeless by the end of the year. You should stay away from me. Haven't you heard? I'm homicidally inclined."

"What a delightful coincidence! There're rumors circulating about me too. Shall we compare notes? You go first."

With a moan of exasperation, Sebastian pulled himself up into a sitting position. "Never trust any person who's universally loved. I'm referring to Nekrasov, the walking ganache cake. I invited him to join me on a steamboat cruise down the Neva, out of the goodness of my heart, and he made vulgar advances at a noble Russian widow, smearing his minty balm all over her. What was I supposed to do?"

"So you rushed to the lady's rescue, Teutonic knight that you are?"

"Well, the onlookers didn't think my behavior very knightly. Nekrasov provoked me on purpose, and when I lost my temper, he assumed the role of a victim. Fifteen years of friendship flushed down the gutter. Deep inside, I never believed that two people of different stock can be friends. When you go to a butcher's shop you don't see filet mignon placed next to flank steak, do you? How can a lawyer be friends with a clerk?"

"You thought you two were an exception?"

"We both were alone in this world," Sebastian continued. "Nekrasov's parents died within a year of each other, so he went to stay with his Russian great-aunt. The place smelled like cat piss and dried violets. The old maid was deaf and blind. He could've hosted an orgy at her house, and she wouldn't have noticed. Yet Nekrasov took the path of petty bourgeois diligence, taking low-paying clerical jobs. He was so damn pleasant, polite and punctual. He became a communal pet, always was wagging his tail, eager to do tricks for a treat. Tavern keepers would feed him leftovers. No wonder he got so fat! Tailors would give him botched garments their customers didn't want. His closet is full of hand-knit scarves, mittens and socks. He hoards them as tangible reminders that he's loved. Now, has anyone shown me a fraction of that love? I was an orphan too, in case people forgot. My situation was far direr than his. Instead of a senile auntie I had a sadistic stepmother. Yet I suffered in silence. Why? Because I had some pride left. Fishing for handouts was beneath me. What are you smiling about?"

"My smile is a sign of affirmation that I'm on your side—even if you do possess a murderous streak."

"Forgive me." He rubbed his forehead languidly. "I was so absorbed in my own rant that I didn't give you a chance to tell your story. What have you been up to?"

Renate adjusted her posture. "To summarize my past year in one sentence: my Polish husband is married to his Catholic guilt, and my Jewish lover is betrothed to his Semitic doom. Enough said?"

"And then you stumbled upon a drunk German." Sebastian sighed sorrowfully. "I've ruined your evening stroll. Honestly, I'm not as drunk as I look."

"I better get back to school," Renate sighed. "The trick is to slip in after everyone goes to bed but before Marie bolts the front door for the night. For whatever reason she won't give me a copy of the key. Cabriolets should still be running."

"I'll escort you." Sebastian started fumbling with the buttons of his waistcoat. "It's getting dark. I promised Hermann Lichtner that I'd look after you."

She took another look at him and shook her head. "No, I should be the one escorting you. In this state you won't make it very far. What if a prospective client sees you? Perhaps you should stay put until your head clears."

"All alone, on this bench?" Sebastian sounded like a terrified child.

"Whatever happened to the gypsy in you? Come on, I'll take you home."

Wretched as Sebastian was, the thought of being indebted to a sixteen-year old girl did not sit well with him. "There's a tavern called The Golden Goose half a kilometer from here. It stays open until four in the morning. Would you be up for a late supper? My treat."

Truthfully, Renate was not dying to get back to Kundstakademie. They linked arms and started making their way down the pebbled path towards the cluster of flickering lights. Helping Sebastian keep his balance was proving to be more difficult than she had imagined, in spite of his slenderness. He kept dragging his feet, tripping frequently, pulling on her arm.

When they were less than a hundred meters away from their destination, Sebastian halted, panting like a sprinter after a race. "I cannot do this anymore."

"Don't be a sissy. We're almost here."

"I must get it off my chest." He turned to face her. "Come home to your own kind. Forget the Poles and the Jews. Stop wasting your time on these inferior races and find yourself a deserving lover. Germans were made for each other—or Russians."

With every syllable, his face leaned closer to hers.

"Actually, I've considered swearing off men altogether. I've thought of converting to Catholicism and becoming a nun. There's a quaint little convent outside Kaunas."

"What a waste it would be." Sebastian reeled her into a sweaty hug. "I know there's a perfect man for you out there."

"Out there?" she nodded towards the river. "All I see is just murky water. Where is that man you're referring to?"

"Right in front of you, blind woman. Kiss me. Prove to me that you're on my side."

His request was so absurd that Renate felt compelled to indulge it. Brushing his oily whiskers upward, she gave him a superficial peck on the lips. "There. Will that be enough to assure you of my solidarity?"

No, it was not enough for Sebastian. He ripped into the woman in front of him, teeth, nails and tongue. Renate sensed the desperate of a drowning man taking his last gulp of air before submerging forever. The meticulously constructed albeit fragile façade was crumpling away faster than the water swirling under the bridge. In all likelihood, it was not Sebastian's first binge.

"Have pity on your delicate German kidneys," she said when they finally pulled out of the kiss. "They weren't designed for Russian spirits."

Wheezing through his nostrils, Sebastian nodded and buried his head on her shoulder. It looked like she was not going to have dinner that night after all. But how could she abandon that hungry, frightened boy who was burping and sniffling in her arms. What if he stumbled and fell into the river? A warm tingling sensation ran through her dry breasts, as her repressed maternal instinct spilled forth. The tenderness she could not lavish upon her son she ended up lavishing upon her twenty-eight year old lawyer.

CHAPTER 33

Imperial Autumn

Lukiškės Prison—October, 1885

Aurelia's release was as random and anticlimactic as her arrest. One morning she simply heard the same guttural voice grunt, "Out you go, Messer!"

She lingered a few more minutes on her cot, clutching her wrinkled ransack. Annushka had been released a few weeks earlier, thought it was only a matter of time before she would be arrested again.

"Just don't trespass on my turf when you get out," the veteran whore said with a meaningful wink. "By the way, that surly gendarme is sweet on you."

Rudenski did not come to see Aurelia off. In fact, he had not come by since the meeting with Frieda. Perhaps, it was for the best that he kept his distance. He must have figured out that Aurelia was useless to his investigation, so he spared her the embarrassment. She mentally thanked him for his tactfulness.

Once the heavy prison gate shut behind her back with a cold clang, she did not immediately flee to freedom. Instead, she sat down on the curb, like a wounded pigeon. After three months of being locked up in a dim, moldy cell, it took her a few minutes to get acclimated to the sensory stimuli of the outside world. Her eyes closed, she rocked back and forth, absorbing the sounds of the street: the clopping of horses' hooves, the chatter of vendors, the sleepy sighs of the autumn wind, the rustling of maple leaves.

Suddenly, a strong smell of fried dough reached her nostrils. Aurelia opened her eyes and saw a freshly baked marzipan roll right under her nose. Not questioning where it came from, she started pulling it apart and stuffing the warm flakes into her mouth.

"Don't choke," she heard a voice above her head. "I brought you a jug of coffee."

Her cheeks still filled with sweet dough, Aurelia looked up and saw the face of the man her brother had attempted to drown.

"Hello, Theo. You look... different."

Indeed, his appearance had undergone a noticeable transformation following his bout with pneumonia. His ruddy cheeks had waned and deflated. His belly had shrunk. There was very little of the former Epicurean left in him.

"Have a sip." Theodor opened the coffee jug. "It should still be warm."

"Why are you being so nice to me, after what Sebastian had done to you? Marie and Justine told me everything, how it took the divers three hours to fish you out of the icy waters. My brother is a rabid beast who should be locked away."

"For his own safety, more than anything," Theo chuckled light-heartedly. "In spite of my dip in the Neva, I enjoyed St. Petersburg. Though it sounds like your summer was even more eventful than mine."

Aurelia brushed the crumbs off her skirt. "My teacher died while I was away."

"Your friends told me."

"They're not my friends. I suppose I'll have a temporary

home until the school closes for good. It just dawned on me that I haven't seen much of the world beyond the boarding school and the prison. So here I am, aged seventeen, with a criminal history and a bastard growing in my belly."

Theodor took the declaration with a straight face, though his gaze wandered downward to her midsection.

"Who... who did this to you?" A second later he backed away. "Never mind. You don't have to answer. I have a general idea."

"I must say, the Balts are curiously tolerant in dealing with unwed mothers," Aurelia contemplated out loud, playing with her shoelaces. "At Rambynas I saw a girl with a stalk wreath on her head, tied to the door of a church. That was the extent of her punishment. Of course, she won't be allowed to rejoin the youth community in her village, but there won't be any shunning either. Her station would be similar to that of a widow." Her greasy trembling fingers found Nekrasov's hand. "Can you tell I'm a bit nervous?"

Theodor wiped her fingers with his handkerchief and proceeded to knead them. "No need to be nervous. I saw the latest financial statements. The city isn't doing too badly. There's a new French café at the very end of St. George Avenue. You have to try their raspberry mousse torte. I've been enjoying the balmy weather. We've had a real imperial autumn. Pity you had to miss the first half of it."

Nekrasov had not changed that much. He still derived pleasure out of simple things like fresh pastries, optimistic financial forecasts and warm weather.

"Be honest," Aurelia said, pulling her hand away, "what are my prospects of finding employment?"

"My Russian great-aunt Adelaide could use a companion." He came back with an instant answer. "In fact, it's one of the reasons I came to see you."

"That was before you knew about my interesting condition."

"Your condition doesn't change anything."

"So your aunt doesn't care that I'm a wanton mutineer of loose morals? She must have an open mind."

"Her mind is gone. That's the beauty of it. Her hearing is better than her eyesight. She likes having Dostoyevsky read to her. *Brothers Karamazov* is next on her list. You think you can endure hours of Russian literature?"

***

Golden Goose Inn, Šnipiškės

The morning after their night together, Renate fully expected Sebastian to revert to his aloof, arrogant self. Mentally preparing for a wry it-meant-nothing and don't-get-any-ideas speech, she stood in front of the mirror and buttoned her blouse with the imperturbability of a veteran adulteress. Having betrayed her husband once, she felt there no more barriers left to break. Another fleeting affair would not bring her soul any closer to damnation. Except, her tryst with Sebastian was a reprisal against Benjamin rather than Thaddeus.

She was grateful that the delicate blouse for which she had paid a fortune was not wrinkled or torn. At least Sebastian had respect for her wardrobe. Having finished dressing, she started twisting her hair into a bun. With her mouth full of hair pins, she had a legitimate excuse for keeping silent.

"I remember when you were this tall," Sebastian said, holding his hand about three feet from the ground. "Recall that Christmas party at the Ostermanns' back in '74? You had chocolate torte crumbs all over your plaid dress. Such a shrewd, vindictive little girl."

Renate nearly swallowed one of her hairpins. That wistful, sentimental tone was entirely out of his character.

"You must mistake me for someone else. I hate chocolate torte—or plaid for that matter. And Vati was never friends with the Ostermanns. They're a sneaky, hypocritical lot. The girl you saw at the party wasn't me."

"I'm fairly certain it was you. At any rate, I meant what I said last night."

"You said many things, Herr Messer. Do you remember half of them?"

"Come on, I wasn't that drunk. I merely suggested that you try loving a fellow German for a change. Tell me, did you notice any difference? What did it feel like to be with someone who's made of the same fabric as you?"

You're all made of the same fabric, Renate wanted to say. *You're all pretty much the same in the dark.* So far she had slept with a Pole, a Jew and a German. She had not tried Lithuanian yet. A brutal Baltic giant would be a nice treat. Antanas, perhaps? She had seen him ogle her on occasion. Using all the knowledge she had gained over the past year, she could show the burly blacksmith some serious ironworks. Then her erotic curriculum vitae would be complete, and she could join the convent in clear conscience.

CHAPTER 34

The Pact of Silence

Raven's Bog—September, 1885

Building a house of worship proved to be only a fraction more complicated than building a barn. Ironically, it was the first endeavor that did not turn to ashes in Thaddeus' hands. When the word got out that a chapel was being constructed at Raven's Bog, support started pouring in from the neighbors. The Rozpondeks engaged a young architect. Even the Kowalskis sent some money from Warsaw towards the materials. Benedict Korczak, a local iconographer, volunteered his services to paint the interior. His philosophy was that a rural chapel should be sturdy and simple on the outside and exquisitely decorated on the inside. Thaddeus was basking in everyone's goodwill. For once, his secluded, sleepy estate became a center of inspired activity.

Antanas had been back for a week, hiding in his smithy, avoiding the contractors. His behavior did not strike Thaddeus as odd, as the blacksmith had always been shy around strangers. Perhaps he needed to reconnect to the soil and the familiar elements after his stint in the city.

Still, the most pleasant part of the construction was interacting with Benedict's sister Emilia, a buxom brunette in her early twenties with large luminous eyes, a sharp upturned nose and a puffy mouth the color of overripe cranberries. She served as her brother's assistant, mixing paints and washing brushes. While the iconographer and the architect were taking measurements for the altar, Emilia showed Thaddeus a few sketches.

"I propose a nautical theme technique used in coastal towns," she spoke in her melodic voice. "If you tint the windows blue and paint the floor a sandy white, the sun breaking in will make the sanctuary look like the bottom of the sea. Or we can paint the walls the color of melted butter, with moss-green accents along the ceiling, and the ambiance will be that of a misty forest, especially with incense burners in each corner. The possibilities are endless. I wouldn't recommend mosaic floors. They're more suitable for larger urban churches. Remember, the goal isn't to compete with St. Anne's but to create a unique sacramental place that will reflect the spirit of your people."

Mesmerized, Thaddeus spent more time looking at Emilia's face than he did at the sketches of saints. "I could listen to you all night." He propped his chin with his fist. "Where did you learn all this?"

"While traveling. Sometimes you have to visit dozens of monasteries to distill ideas for a single panel. You cannot imagine the theory and the planning behind the simplest of murals. Last time Benedict agonized over the color scheme for a rosette window and finally settled on royal blue and purple. The area around the altar looked like a lilac garden."

The women of Raven's Bog served the newcomer their signature dinner of mushroom soup and potato cakes. Halfway through the meal Agatha got weepy and mentioned without lowering her voice that Emilia with her shiny black hair reminded her of the late Lady Jolanta. The young guest possessed enough tact to let that comment slip past her ears. The women continued fawning over her, refilling her plate and her ale glass. They even allowed her to hold Dominik. The baby yanked the amethyst pin on Emilia's bodice and slammed the moist palms of his hands against her bosom.

"Such a sturdy, observant boy," she said to Thaddeus. "Give my compliments to Dominik's mother. It's too bad she didn't join us for dinner."

Thaddeus raised his eyebrows and drummed his fingers against the tabletop. "The boy's mother is in Vilnius, tending to an ailing friend." Emilia did not need to know every detail. "Well, I hope to meet her soon. I heard she's an artist?"

"Not *that* kind of artist. She doesn't do religious stuff. I mean, she sketches churches, but she doesn't appreciate iconography or stained glass. She's a Lutheran. I don't think you'd have much in common."

"Yer Ladyship can visit any time she likes," Agatha interjected with a servile bow.

Emilia handed the baby over. "You'll be seeing a lot of me in the coming months. Thank you for the dinner."

***

After the contractors had left, Thaddeus stepped outside to clear his head, his euphoria quickly turning to melancholy. He had allowed himself to enjoy Emilia's company a little too much, and the tone of voice when he spoke about Renate's art was a little flippant. He had no right to mock her in front of another woman. Renate was still his wife, even though he had not seen her for months and had no idea when and if she was coming back. He needed to put the lid back on the jar before any more steam escaped.

Passing by the smithy, he heard sobs and groans. Fearing that Antanas had dropped the hammer on his foot or inadvertently poked himself with hot iron, he flung the door open. The blacksmith was sitting on top of the anvil, clutching his head. The origin of his pain was clearly not physical.

At the sight of Thaddeus, he slipped to the ground into a kneeling position. "I'm a murderer," he roared into his master's boots. "An old man's dead because of me. Now the authorities are lookin' for me."

Thaddeus tousled the blacksmith's hair. "Your head's burning, Antanas. Too much time in front of the furnace. Take a break and get some fresh air. I'll show you the bell for the chapel. It's not huge but it's loud."

Antanas slammed his fist into the dirt floor. "There weren't s'pposed to be any deaths. 'Twas s'pposed to be just a warnin'. I did as I was told. But the old Jew died of fright. That makes me a murderer."

The blacksmith's behavior was utterly bewildering, all that groveling and howling. Thaddeus started getting nervous. "I know how vivid some nightmares can be. I've had a few."

"No, 'twas real."

Since Thaddeus was unable to pull Antanas up to his feet, he knelt down himself, so they could be on the same level.

"Look at me. You're my brother. If you had blood on your hands, it would've appeared on mine as well. I know your heart. It's one of the noblest, bravest, purest hearts to ever beat. Some dark spirit came over you, making you believe those horrid things about yourself. I don't believe a word of it. I'll pray for you, my brother, so the Lord will restore your clarity of mind."

Antanas backed away from his master and plopped down on a pile of straw.

"Any man can become a murderer," he said hoarsely. "It's

so easy. Yer don't know what yer capable of 'til yer try it. I wasn't a thief either, yet I stole a spoon from the foreman's table. 'Twas all a part of his plot. He left the spoon in plain sight to see if I'd take it. Arson is an art, he said. Those who master it can make good money." Antanas shook fistfuls of straw above his head. "And I got weary of livin' in poverty, on this damned barren land! There yer have it, master. I've learned to steal, burn and murder, but I haven't learned to keep secrets from yer. And now, wi' this knowledge, tell me if yer want me gone. I'll take my family and vanish. Yer won't be burdened with a criminal in yer home."

His eyes still on Antanas, Thaddeus took a sip from the vodka bottle. "Don't be stupid, baby brother. You're not going anywhere."

"Didn't yer hear a word of what I said?"

"I did. But I'll pretend I didn't. Let's keep it that way. It's partially my fault. Remember what I said? Your crime is my crime. I shouldn't have sent you to the city. My wife told me you wouldn't withstand the temptation."

At the mention of Renate, the blacksmith's eyes blazed up again.

"She's wicked woman, yer wife. She doesn't love yer."

"I know. Still, that doesn't make her wicked."

"She's with another man, master. I've seen them t'gether. Whenever yer think she's visitin' her old school friends, she's really trystin' with her lover. It's the same German who brought her here. And before him, there was a filthy Jew! She's betrayed yer not once but twice."

Thaddeus gulped the rest of the vodka and ruffled the blacksmith's hair once again. "Well, that's not your cross to bear. You have your own, baby brother. I cannot protect you from God's judgment, but I'll do my bloody best to protect you from the authorities."

¢ℏAPⱢER 35

Unveiling

Vilnius, St. George Avenue—October, 1885

Theodor kept his promise to Aurelia and took her to the new French café on St. George Avenue, despite her lethargic protestations. He made her try the famous raspberry mousse torte, and she agreed that it was rather divine. Since Theo barely touched his portion, she gladly finished it and drank the remains of the frothy coffee from his cup. He looked as distracted as his companion. For once, his mind was somewhere other than the plate.

Theo had some good news to impart: he had been promoted to senior clerk. At least now he had a desk next to a window so he could see daylight. His new role afforded him a small budget to hire additional help. With all the new construction happening in the city, he was up to his ears in numbers and receipts. He was thinking of offering the position to Aurelia, knowing it would be a rather daring move. The labor laws explicitly barred women from government office jobs. In cities like Moscow and St. Petersburg, it was impossible to find a female stenographer. Perhaps, the rules were not enforced as strictly in the northwest? Theo wondered how his supervisor would react to his proposition to hire a seventeen-year old with a criminal record. The proposition seemed viable for its sheer absurdity. It was his duty to at least attempt to help Aurelia, whatever meager influence he possessed. The vacant, disoriented look in her eyes worried him. A girl with such a fragile moral core, who skipped from one obsessive idea to another, was a magnet for predators and manipulators. She went from being a painter, to amateur detective, to a book smuggler and anti-czarist agitator. What costume would she try on next? The chances of her ending up back in prison or in some piggish man's bed were alarmingly high. Watching her lick the spoon absentmindedly, Theo felt the nerve endings that had until then been dormant beneath the skin awaken.

When they left the café, it was raining. Theodor insisted on giving his raincoat to Aurelia. It was a genuine honest-to-God Mackintosh imported from England. They walked under the same umbrella, their fingers intertwined over the cool metal rod. The sidewalk was slippery from the wet maple leaves, so the two had to lean on each other for balance.

Theodor was wearing an unseasonably light summer suit. It did not seem to bother him that the cuffs of his trousers were covered in dark splatters from the puddles.

"Sebastian was right: a suit does look better on a slimmer figure." He proudly patted his deflated belly. "What do you think? I rather like my new shape. Your brother had actually done me an enormous favor. I spent an entire month in bed, unable to eat."

"I bet you charmed all the nurses. Those poor girls probably couldn't get any work done, prancing around your bed around the clock."

"They offered me all kinds of delicacies, but I had no

desire for them."

"The nurses or the delicacies?"

"Both. When you spend a month on your back, staring at the hospital ceiling, and your mortality tickles your feet, you start reappraising your life. Before the incident on the steamboat, my world revolved around rolls and croissants. I'd sell my soul for a raisin scone. Not anymore. I lost all interest in baked goods. Sebastian had helped me break my marzipan addiction. Suddenly, my horizons expanded. I've been reading Dostoyevsky. Speaking of which, have you and Auntie Adelaide made any progress on *The Karamazov Brothers*?"

"We reached the part where Alexei gets kicked out of the monastery by his elder. Trouble is your auntie keeps confusing the brothers. She insists that Dmitry is the atheist, and I keep correcting her. Dmitry is a sensual pig, no doubt, but it's Ivan who openly rejects God."

"Which brother is your favorite?"

"Probably Pavel, the sullen epileptic who collects and hangs stray cats. Though, I had to skip that part for your auntie. She loves cats, and her heart would give in if she heard about Pavel's atrocities." Aurelia sighed into the elevated collar of Theo's raincoat. "At any rate, that's my recent dabbling into the mystical Russian soul."

"*Crime and Punishment* is next on my list." Theodor boasted. "And after that? *Poor Folk* or *The Idiot*."

Aurelia pressed his fingers as a warning. "Be careful. At this rate you'll turn into a violent anarchist."

"Maybe that's what I was destined to become."

"It's a quick way to land in prison."

"So? Every young person should serve time. Two years of labor camp. It should be made compulsory. It builds character."

"While destroying your joints and your tooth enamel." Aurelia could not tell if Theo was joking. "Your sentence will probably be harsher than mine, given that you're a man. Think of what you'd be giving up."

"Think of what I'd be gaining." Theodor drew a deep breath and lifted his gaze to the dome of the umbrella. "I've spent my entire life avoiding conflict, playing the role of the Shakespearean Benvolio. As a schoolboy, I always was the one passing out bandages to my fellow students after schoolyard brawls. In the twenty-five years of my life I'd never been struck—not by a parent, or a teacher, or a peer. There's something unnatural about that, having no enemies. Your instincts become atrophied. You cannot become a fully empathetic person without tasting of antagonism. Your brother was the first person to punch me. That was my belated initiation into manhood. When you flail your arms in cold water, it's both sobering and liberating. Oddly, I feel closer to Sebastian now than when we were on speaking terms."

They reached the west end of St. George Avenue and stood on the corner of the bridge over the Neris River.

"What do your girlfriends think of your transformation?" Aurelia asked, examining his sharpened profile in lantern light. "How do they like the new Theo?"

"I haven't been making rounds through my usual venues. In fact, I'm planning on dismissing my old harem. I hope to stay on amicable terms with most of them. There's only one woman in the entire city whose opinion matters to me."

Aurelia's eyes turned as wide as imperial rubles. "Is this possible? Theodor Nekrasov is in love!"

"Most irrevocably," he confirmed, looking straight ahead. "Surprised?"

"I'm always the last one to find out. When did this

abomination transpire?"

"It's a fairly recent development. I haven't trumpeted my love to the world yet."

"And does she reciprocate?"

"Time will tell. I haven't made an official declaration to her yet."

Holding onto the slippery railing, Aurelia arched her back and giggled. "The world's turned topsy-turvy. Won't you give me her name? Do I know her?"

Theo turned to face her. "She's probably the only girl in Vilnius I haven't kissed yet."

Under the weight of his intent stare, Aurelia laughter dwindled to a whimper. "*Mein Gott...*" She looked down at the tips of her soaked ankle boots, struggling to digest the insinuation. A reformed fat cat and an alley stray! "Well, what are you going to do about it?"

Theo reached into his pocket and pulled out the jar with the minty lip balm. Aurelia stopped him before he had a chance to open it.

"I don't think so," she said, pushing his hand away. "I don't want to taste the same lip balm every other woman in Vilnius has already tasted."

He shrugged and threw the jar over his shoulder into the river.

CHAPTER 36

Hunting Phantoms

Vilnius, November 1885

Tracking Benjamin down became a new obsession for Renate. Every lithe man with longish light-brown hair dressed in a velveteen suit made her pulse escalate. There was no more tenderness left in her heart for him, but she could not get over the cowardly way in which he dropped her, without as much as a note ending with "don't think ill of me". There was nothing she desired more than for her old lover to spot her with his replacement. Just seeing Benjamin twitch in discomfort would give her immense pleasure. She deliberately went places where she was most likely to run into him.

Sebastian did not understand why she kept dragging him to dance halls and student art exhibits. Such odd choices of entertainment for a woman of mature taste. Then he reminded himself that she was only sixteen. That was the price of getting entangled with someone so juvenile. Still, it amused him to see the vengeful determination in her eyes every time she grabbed his hand and pulled him into a crowded venue. She would always run one step ahead of him, head thrown back, like an opera prima donna making an encore stage entrance.

Indisputably, they made a striking couple. Sometimes Renate would pause in front of a shop window and admire their reflection. *Brandenburg doesn't produce ugly people.*

One time Renate really did see Benjamin inside a chocolatier shop. He came with his mother and some young Jewess who was clearly not his sister. The girl dressed older than her years and wore her frizzy black hair in a braid. Renate relished the chance to deconstruct her rival's demoded outfit, from the unembellished puffy blouse, to the thick wool skirt, to the clunky shoes. The dour-looking girl interested her more than Benjamin. As expected, the boy had broken down. After all that pompous talk about the freedom of faith, thought and love, he had settled for one of his tribe. Renate could not judge him for it too harshly, as she had essentially done the same.

The Messer family house on the east end of St. George Avenue became her new unofficial residence. *I'm living in sin with my lawyer*, she kept saying during fits of silent hysteria. She was sharing her bed with a man who had heralded the end of her childhood, her role being closer to that of a nurse than of a mistress. In spite of the elegant décor and luxury appliances that were only available in the most upscale hotels, Renate could not get comfortable in that house. She felt the malevolent presence of the ghosts from Sebastian's past, namely his wicked Baltic stepmother. Zivile's favorite place was the bathroom containing a nickel plated brass shower. Renate could not allow herself to bask in the warm water for too long, as she could feel invisible hands tampering with the temperature controls.

Between lovemaking sessions Sebastian behaved like a sullen, affection-deprived child who needed constant reassurance. Renate found herself missing the old Sebastian, prickly and condescending. His acrid free-flowing arrogance was replaced by something infinitely worse—existential angst. He talked, mostly about himself. His egocentrism did not go anywhere. That part of the old Sebastian remained intact.

The only thing worse than listening to him talk was listening to him brood in silence.

"What are you thinking?" she asked him one night as they were getting ready for bed.

"I'm thinking my life has been a joke. I spent my best years chasing the two-headed eagle, trying to win favor with Russians. What did my efforts amount to?"

"What brought this on?"

"Today I got a letter from my uncle Henrik in Brandenburg. He was just appointed principle at a lyceum. He invited me to teach political science."

"As a token courtesy?"

"Why are you so hasty to dismiss it?"

"Because people say things they don't mean all the time. It's like a random acquaintance saying, 'You're always welcome in my home.'"

"Uncle Henrik isn't one for meaningless pleasantries. He even quoted a salary. Basically I could go there tomorrow and start right after the Christmas break. Yes, I'm a little overqualified for the position, but I cannot say that my law diploma has been bringing me much joy lately—or income, for that matter."

"I doubt that the teaching job will be more joyful or lucrative. You hate children."

"Not *all* children, just the stupid and unruly ones. Clever and well-behaved children I can tolerate. Uncle Henrik is very selective about whom he admits."

Wrapped in a velvet bathrobe, Renate dipped her hand into a bowl of dried blackcurrants. "Why are you consulting me on this matter? You don't need my approval. We don't owe each other any explanations."

"We... we don't?"

"For God's sake, we aren't in love or anything."

We're not in love. There, she said it, with that exquisite nonchalance that for a moment knocked the breath out of Sebastian. And he had seen her cynical side! She timed those comments perfectly, while they were cooling off in each other's arms after a climax. Actually, that acquired callousness was a part of her appeal.

"We're just miffed at the world," she continued, "as we have every right to be. The alternative would be throwing some home-made kerosene bombs at other people's homes."

"Like our Lithuanian friends do?"

"Look, just because I don't love you, it doesn't mean I don't wish you well. Maybe this job in Brandenburg is exactly what you need. I won't beg you to stay or take me with you. One less thing for you to worry about."

Sebastian yanked the bowl with currants out of her hands. "Are you waiting for an official invitation? The truth is I wouldn't mind if you joined me. Uncle Henrik would find you a teaching job. Art history, perhaps?"

"How would you present me to him?"

"As my wife, naturally." He proceeded to untie the belt of her bathrobe. "Uncle Henrik doesn't need to know the truth. He won't ask for a copy of the marriage license. We can work at the same school, live in the same house, sleep in the same bed, all while continuing not to be in love. Just like a real married couple!"

"Aren't you forgetting something?" She nodded to a fading stretchmark on her lower abdomen. "I'm someone's mother."

Her sudden reference to her estranged son left Sebastian irritated. Over the course of their affair she had not mentioned Dominik more than once or twice, which led Sebastian to believe that she was not all that heartbroken over the separation. Why did the brat suddenly become relevant?

"Now it's my turn to speak candidly," he said, wrestling her flat against the mattress and pinning her hands above her head. "Drop this farce of maternal guilt. You don't miss your son one bit. If you truly wanted to reclaim him, the harpies of Raven's Bog wouldn't have been an obstacle. A determined mother would walk through a wall of fire."

Renate opened her mouth, preparing to say something in self-defense, but Sebastian silenced her with a possessive kiss, much like the one he had given her by the river in front of the Golden Goose tavern. She had already found out that he was not the world's gentlest lover. He did not hesitate to put nails and teeth to use. His technique had been cultivated by his first serious mistress who apparently liked a rougher touch. Since the very beginning of their affair, Renate's neck had been covered in bruises and bite marks at various stages of healing which she had to cover with scarves. Not that she minded the element of pain. It added new colors to the erotic palette. The immense Second Reich era bed was where they came to release their hostility against the thoroughly corrupt and unfair universe. The feather mattress soaked in their rage along with their body fluids.

Renate was growing used to Sebastian's mood swings. She knew he could leap from self-pity to violence in a matter of seconds. Those bursts did not last long, but he could do a lot of damage in that span of time. Half-naked and on her back, she was clearly at a disadvantage.

"If ten years from now your maternal instinct awakens, I'll be eager to oblige," he said, plunging into Renate's subtly resisting body. With the first thrust, her head banged into the wooden headboard. "We'll have glorious offspring! I'm making you a very advantageous offer, security and liberty in one, with the option of continuing your bloodline. You'd be an idiot to decline it. Just like you, I'm not driven by love. It's something greater—national solidarity, a concept, which I hope isn't entirely foreign to you. When I look at you, I see a German woman of fine breeding, hurled into disgrace through her father's lunacy."

Renate stirred underneath him. She could taste the salty blood in her mouth from the burst capillaries. "Leave my dead father out of this."

"Unfortunately, I cannot." Soaring arousal did not interfere with his ability to articulate. He made his points clearly even between the thrusts. "Everything that's happened is a result of his moronic deathbed decision. I've no idea why he hadn't considered me for the role of your husband. I thought I'd earned his trust through impeccable service. Where did I fall short? At least with me, you would've wanted for nothing. I would've made damn sure you got all the comforts you deserved. I would've invested your money wisely. Imagine the life you and I could've had! You see the damage your father had caused, what he'd robbed us of?"

Renate's self-preservation instinct howled from beneath the sheets. She had a bad feeling that this time she would end up with more severe injuries than just a few scratches and bruises. That night Sebastian was angrier than usual. Another shove against the headboard, and Renate would end up with a concussion. She needed to find a way to reroute his rage. Killing a mistress in bed would not look good on his curriculum vitae.

"All right, I surrender," she cried. "I fibbed."

That grabbed Sebastian's attention. For a second he stopped moving and just hovered over her, sweat dripping from his chin. "What did you fib about?"

"About not loving you."

CHAPTER 37

Into the Void

Raven's Bog—December, 1885

After caring for his younger sister for ten years, Benedict Korczak was ready to dump the burden of responsibility on someone else. In late autumn of 1875 a typhoid epidemic had ravaged their village, wiping out most of the Korczak family, sparing only the two oldest children, who were sixteen and twelve at the time.

Surviving on a modest bequest, Benedict managed to finish his iconography apprenticeship. Large commissions were few and far in between. He was yet to be invited to work on any of the major cathedrals. There was no shortage of artists in the cities, men who had received their training in Italy and France. Benedict could not possibly compete with them. He did not expect his short wings to take him to the same heights as eagles.

By his early twenties he had carved a niche for himself as a provincial iconographer and restorer, traveling from village to village, with Emilia attached to his hip. He gave her menial tasks, just to keep her from asking him every five minutes if she could help, but she was by no means instrumental to his work. He could mix his own paints and clean his own brushes. The surfeit of questions and offers of assistance broke his concentration. Over the course of their travels Emilia had gotten a few erroneous ideas in her head: that she was a serious ecclesiastic artist, or at least an apprentice to one, and that eventually she would be able to serve God in the same capacity as her brother.

In reality, Emilia was nothing but a nuisance. She had developed early, in all the wrong places. Her brain never caught up with her hips and her bosom. There was nothing lascivious or deliberately provocative about her behavior. She simply had never been schooled in the art of sexual politics. Her blouses always fitted her a little too tightly, but only because she had nobody to help her adjust her wardrobe. The girl continued wearing the same articles of clothing she had worn before her mother's death. Her ripe breasts were always on the verge of spilling out of her tiny ruffled blouses. She wore her hair down in messy waves, adorning it with a bow on top. That hairstyle was straight out of *Alice in Wonderland.* Benedict had read the first anonymous Russian translation of Lewis Carroll's absurd masterpiece. That was the kind of loony world his sister lived in. In her own mind Emilia was an ethereal creature working towards a higher purpose. Obviously, men saw her differently. Some were halfway decent, some questionable and some downright scoundrels. She engaged in conversation with all. It was Benedict's job to see that she did not get violated.

Finally, a marriage proposal came from a medical student named Janek Zielinski. Benedict was ecstatic. At last, someone was willing to take his sister off his hands. His jubilation was short-lived: Emilia declined. She would not say why, no matter how sternly he pressed her. She kept shaking her head, the gauzy bow swaying. Benedict's moment of liberation was postponed indefinitely.

"You're twenty-two," he said. "How much longer will you tag along with me?"

"Until the right man comes along."

"The Zielinski boy isn't good enough for you?"

"Oh, he's good. I just don't love him."

"What do you know about love, dreamy cow?"

After three days of silent war, Benedict finally got the answer to his question when he saw his sister in the company of Tadek Dombrowski, a walking disaster of a man. The two were standing underneath an apple tree on a heap of dried leaves and half-rotten frostbitten apples, holding hands and whispering. Benedict had a funny feeling they were not discussing the color scheme for the rosette window. It was a well-documented fact that voluptuous brunettes were Dombrowski's weakness. Emilia looked just like his first wife, the one he had fucked into an early grave, pardon my Polish. Who could resist glossy raven locks slathered over a pair of perky tits? Certainly not Tadek Dombrowski. Conveniently, his second wife was out of the picture. He needed someone to get him through the cold winter, and a plump stupid girl made for an excellent bed warmer.

Benedict spent the next few minutes cursing under his breath and kicking the barn wall pretending it was Tadek's groin. Having released some of the fume, he emerged from behind the corner and barked at his sister, "Time to go home!"

Emilia gaze remained glued to Dombrowski's face. "What's the rush, Benek?"

"I said it's time to go!"

"Won't you stay for dinner, Master Korczak?" Thaddeus proposed genially, in deliberate contrast to Benedict's abruptness. "I already asked Agatha to set two extra plates."

"Don't bother, Dombrowski. My sister and I will eat at home."

Thaddeus released Emilia's hand reluctantly. "Next time, perhaps?"

Benedicts' stomach turned as he watched his sister stroke Dombrowski's cheek before walking away. "There won't be a next time," he said. "I got a big commission in the city. I cannot spend any more time on your chapel, Dombrowski. Find someone else to finish the job."

He grabbed Emilia and dragged her away into the twilight.

***

"I don't know why I must repeat this," Benedict said when they were sitting in the buggy, "but in my line of work, having a spotless reputation is non-negotiable. I cannot afford the luxury of a scandal."

"What makes you think there'll be a scandal, Benek?" she asked innocently.

"Damn straight, there won't be one. You're not setting your foot here again. My sister won't become a barnyard joke. I won't have the field hands at Raven's Bog wink and grin at one of the Korczaks. We're done with that man and his ludicrous designs."

"Are you talking about Tadek Dombrowski?"

"No, I'm talking about Czar Alexander!" Benedict spat over the side of the buggy and whipped the horses. "It's no secret that Dombrowski is a failure as a landlord. I volunteer my services, and how does he repay me? By compromising my sister. He's already driven one wife into the ground. The second wife was smart, she got away. So now he's molesting the neighborhood women!"

"You're being needlessly harsh, Benek. He's not a

malicious man."

"Not malicious, just a little forgetful. It must've slipped his mind that he's still married."

"Not much longer." Emilia turned her shoulders out, causing the top button to come undone. "His wife's been gone since the summer. Abandonment is grounds for divorce. The deserted spouse will be free to remarry. The family law has provisions for situation such as this. The wronged party deserves a chance at happiness."

"Is this... what Dombrowski promised you?"

"It's something I've looked into on my own accord."

Benedict nearly dropped the reins. He'd underestimated his slow-moving sister. In matters concerning her selfish interests, she showed impressive resourcefulness. Of course, that explained why she rejected Janek Zielinski's proposal. She had already started weaving a love nest with Dombrowski!

"Tadek is the man I've been waiting for my whole life," Emilia continued. "I don't mind waiting a few more months, or even a year if need be. His servants adore me. They already treat me as his wife. He let me hold his child."

"Is there anything else of his you've held?" Now Benedict was frightened in earnest. "What has he done to you?"

"Nothing I didn't want him to do to me."

Benedict stopped the carriage in the middle of a dark road, threw his sister on the ground and gave her a few lashes with a horse whip. Emilia took the abuse without a sound, even though her cheeks turned crimson. Her docility only fueled Benedict's anger. The meek cow was suffering for what she believed to be love. He threw the whip aside and started kicking her. Ten years of struggles and deprivations, ten years of sharing his hard-earned bread with that pouting parasite, and she repays him by wrecking his reputation!

Who would hire him now that his only sister was a certified slut?

"Tomorrow," he said, jerking her head up by the hair, "you're going to go back the Zielinskis', apologize to Janek, plead temporary insanity if you must, and tell him you accept his offer, if it's still on the table. If you continue to resist, your married lover will be next. I won't be as gentle with Dombrowski as I was with you."

***

That evening Thaddeus did not have much of an appetite. He sat down at the dinner table only as a courtesy to Agatha who had gone out of her way with the expectation that the Korczaks would be joining them. All he could think about was vodka. He craved the spirit more than ever and could not wait to be alone with his bottle.

The moment he stepped outside, December frost gripped him. In the hour he had spent indoors the temperature had dropped dramatically.

He had his theory on why Benedict stormed out the way he did. There was no commission in the city. Perhaps he got into a squabble with the architect or just got tired of working without pay. Ah, it was only a matter of time before the architect quit too. Who wants to do charity in such brutal temperatures with so little daylight? Thaddeus would have to find a way to finish building the chapel in time for Christmas as a gift to his people and a symbol of new beginnings.

Now, Emilia's wellbeing concerned him. He could not shake off the eerie suspicion that she was frightened and in pain. What if their wobbly buggy had tipped over in the dark? Ripples of frozen mud had made the roads treacherous. Tomorrow morning he would go to the Korczaks' and make sure that Emilia was safe. Seeing her from afar would suffice.

Remorse was gnawing at him. He had not intended for their affair to unravel so rapidly. He cursed his impatience. Emilia had not put up any resistance. It just happened. He could not remember how the Korczak girl ended up in his arms. Thaddeus simply did not have the willpower to decline her unskilled, impetuous caresses. And yet, he was still another woman's husband, and now an adulterer. The stigma he could live with. The guilt from ruining a virgin was a heavier burden to shoulder. There was no easy way of making an honest woman out of Emilia. First he would need to locate Renate, face her and propose a painless way of ending their marriage on terms that would be acceptable to her. What if Renate tried to lay claims on Dominik? She had not seen the boy since the summer, but Thaddeus feared that she would not relinquish parental rights without a fight. And how would he tackle the issue of his religion? The law on the territory of the Russian Empire was written to reflect the dogmas of the Orthodox Church, which allowed divorce. As a Catholic, he would need to seek an annulment, and he had no idea how to start the process or how long it would take. Would he be allowed to remarry in a Catholic church? What a mess he had caused.

In a strange way, the guilt made Thaddeus feel closer to Antanas. They both were sinners, a murderer and an adulterer. He remembered the blacksmith's words, *It's so easy. Yer don't know what yer capable of 'til yer try it.* Antanas was right. One transgression inevitably led to another. By covering up his half-brother's crime, Thaddeus had become an accomplice. That was why they needed to finish building the chapel.

Holding a flickering lantern in one hand, he walked over to the construction site. The outline of the building looked more formidable in the dark. When finished, it would be twenty meters high. The plain white cross crowning the vaulted roof would be visible from afar. Thaddeus placed the handle of the lantern in his teeth and started climbing the scaffolding. It had drizzled in the afternoon, and by nightfall the wooden planks and the metal bars were glazed in ice. The slick leather gloves were not helping him gain traction.

A solitary raven, the namesake guardian of the estate, was perched on the edge of the eave facing the east side. The arrival of a human intruder did not disturb the bird. It held its position, twisting its head with the regal nonchalance of a general.

Having reached the top tier of the scaffolding, Thaddeus sat down on a wooden plank and looked at the village sprawled underneath. The night was stunningly clear. He found himself caught between two black plains of lights, with stars above him and the glowing windows of the huts below. To stay warm, he drank from his vodka bottle, until the glowing dots started blurring together.

When all his senses started kicking their shoes off and forming a drunken line dance, he spied from the corner of his eye what looked like a cloaked figure of a woman floating down the path towards the cemetery. Black hair was skimming the white triangle of her face. It was impossible to make out her features from such a distance, but she had an air of infinite melancholy about her. Delicate bare hands were folded on her chest, as if restraining a lament.

Wavering, Thaddeus rose to his feet, his heart thrashing beneath the deerskin coat.

Jolanta! My Jolanta...

His foot slipped on the icy plank. The same instant the raven let out a militant cry and took off from its post, darting into the void.

CHAPTER 38

The End of the Eclipse

Vilnius—December, 1885

Sebastian came home in the middle of the day to find Renate in the throes of packing. Towels, bedding, tablecloths and garments were scattered all over the bedroom. Instead of the customary kiss she gave him a feverish glare.

"What's all this?" he asked. "Are you putting together a charitable donation?"

Renate wiped her sweaty hands against the skirt of her dress. "We need to talk."

"Perfect timing. There's something I need to tell you as well." He held up an envelope. "The stars are aligning in everyone's favor."

"Go ahead, I'm listening."

"No, you go first."

She circumvented the trunk and stood before Sebastian. "We cannot continue like this."

"Agreed."

"I cannot take it anymore, the ambiguity of our arrangement. This house has an oppressive effect on me. I keep hearing voices, footsteps. So I've decided—"

"Go on." He seemed impatient for her to finish her speech so he could jump to his.

Renate rose on her tiptoes and clicked her heels like a soldier before a general. "I'd like to go to Brandenburg with you. But first I want to obtain a proper divorce. Surely, with your connections, you can make it happen quickly."

Sebastian grimaced. Clearly, that was not the reply he was waiting for.

"Hold off telling your husband anything. My plans have changed. I'm not going to Brandenburg. I'm going to St. Petersburg instead." His angular face beamed with a boyish smile. "A most marvelous thing happened to me. I just received a letter from a certain lady."

"Lydia?"

"No, someone I knew before Lydia, someone I've loved since my university days. She wasn't free at the time, but now she is. Here, read it yourself."

He held the envelope to his lips for a few seconds before passing it to Renate. She opened it with limp fingers and peered into the Russian text.

Dearest Sebastian,

After eight years of silence, I'm finally writing to you. My husband Peter experienced something of an epiphany and became infected with Tolstoy's ideas. He said he was tired of this life full of artifice and deceit, so he resigned from his position at the University and filed for divorce. He called our marriage a joke, and jokes are only amusing the first time around. Apparently, there's a peasant girl who stole his heart and whom he intends to marry as soon as the divorce is final. They already have a country house picked out outside Kolomna. Peter was good enough to leave me the apartment and much of his savings—he has no need for such "filth" anymore. He is taking his eighteen-year old son from the first marriage. Remember, his first wife died? Poor Anastasia must be flipping in her grave to see her boy yanked out of a prestigious military academy. My seven-year old, Constantine, is staying with me. The poor thing is bewildered. Peter had always been cold towards him, but being deserted isn't something any child is prepared for. He keeps asking me if it's his fault, if he'd done something to make Papa angry. Can you imagine what it does to a mother's heart? Constantine's greatest fear is that now that our ties to the University have been severed, he'll never realize his dream of becoming a lawyer. What a tragedy that would be. He's ambitious and articulate beyond his years, with an affinity for all things German. With Peter gone, he has nobody to play courtroom with. It was the only thing they ever did together, reenact famous trials. Who'll be the paternal figure in his life? If you still have any affection left for me, please come.

Fondly,
Elizabeth Suhanov

Enclosed was a picture of a boy with a stiff Prussian jaw and pinched nostrils. It was not hard to figure out why Elizabeth's husband had been so cold towards the child.

"Do what you must," Renate whispered, returning the letter to Sebastian.

Even though it sounded like Renate had released him from the need for any further explanation, Sebastian felt like he had to continue justifying himself.

"Do understand, Elizabeth and I had a pact that overrides every other promise I ever made. I do despicable things when I'm apart from her. I've been a miserable ogre for the past eight years. You were one of my unintended victims. Well, it all stops right now. The ogre is dead. The eclipse that had lasted for eight years is over. I'll atone for the wrongdoings of my past, starting with you, my poor friend."

Renate believed him. The transformation was undeniable. She had never seen Sebastian smile so broadly, so uninhibitedly.

"I'll do what's in my power to help you get the much-deserved fresh start," he continued with renewed enthusiasm. "If you still want to divorce Thaddeus, I'll contact a colleague who specializes in family law. You can go to Brandenburg on your own and work for my uncle. I'll write a most glowing character reference. I have a single cousin named Gunther. A tremendous fellow! Twenty-four years old, plays piano, looks like me only shorter and blond."

"Splendid... Another arranged marriage, another blond man."

"It doesn't have to be Gunther. If you've had your share of the Messer men, it's understandable. You'll be far from your past and fancy free." Sebastian took the liberty of placing his hand on her shoulder. "What's the matter with you?"

"Something dreadfully undesirable is happening to me." She pointed to her stomach. "Inside me, to be exact. I was going to tell you."

Sebastian backed away with a wince. "That certainly complicates things. Your husband will be delighted! He always wanted a large brood, didn't he? Don't give me this killer look. It helps to have a backup scheme."

"You know damn well the child isn't his! I haven't been with him since the summer."

"Well, it certainly isn't mine. Unlike Thaddeus, I've always been careful."

"Just like you were with your last married mistress?"

"I was young and selfish then," Sebastian retorted defensively. "With you I was meticulously careful. You told me how much you hated being pregnant. I'd never saddle you with another brat. Surely cannot speak for the rest of your bedmates! Besides me and Thaddeus there's also the Asher boy. Let's not forget about him."

"Actually, now is a perfect time to forget about him," Renate said lowly.

In the past week she had done some investigation and learned that the entire Asher clan had disbanded. Benjamin had gotten engaged to one of the Kaufmann daughters and moved into the loft above the jewelry shop. Leah had married her perfume dealer and moved to Riga. Esther had scooped up Jacob and fled to America. Daniel was the only one left behind. To the former patriarch, it was a matter of pride. He would not be smoked out of his territory.

Seeing Renate so distressed, Sebastian felt pangs of remorse. There he was, basking in his own bliss, while his fellow countrywoman was struggling to calculate who had fathered her last baby.

"We'll think of something." He planted a warm wet kiss on her forehead. "I imagine we have a little bit of time. Look, if you don't want the brat, I know a doctor..."

"Hell, no," she moaned. "I don't need a murder on my conscience."

"Who said anything about murder? Let me finish. I know a doctor who'd be happy to take the brat off your hands and raise it as his own. His wife is barren; they already have three adopted children. I'll help you cover your tracks. We'll do it in a discrete and civilized manner. I won't abandon you."

CHAPTER 39

Provisional Government

Raven's Bog—December, 1885

On the third day after the master's burial, the servants started sinking their fingers into his possessions. A few went into his bedroom and pulled out the drawers. If Thaddeus possessed any valuables, they would be easily accessible. In light of his unconditional trust, it would never occur to him to hide anything. To the servants' chagrin, so far the most valuable item they found was a box of letters from his first wife. There were a few loose cuff links and lapel pins left over from Thaddeus' father.

The looting party was interrupted by Antanas. He barged in with a freshly sharpened axe and threatened to start chopping off fingers. The icy shine on the blade as well as the expression on his asymmetrical face left no room for doubt that he had every intention of carrying out his threat, so the marauders scurried away like a pack of mice.

That night Antanas assumed the seat at the head of the table as a self-appointed patriarch and led the rest of the household in a prayer.

"Our life must go on," he concluded, his eyes full of dark

fire. "I'm in charge of the land now, from the tools to the livestock. I'm of the same blood as the late master, so yer can call me Master Dombrowski. If the new leadership isn't to yer likin'—yer welcome to leave. Though yer will be asked to turn yer pockets inside out."

The servants sat through his inaugural speech in silence. They knew damn well that Antanas was not the new lord of the manor. After Master Dombrowski's death the property fell into the hands of his estranged widow, who had not been heard from in six months but who could turn up at any moment. Nothing would stop her from kicking them off the land and selling it. Still, it would be unwise to argue with Antanas in his present state. Playing along and keeping up the pretense would buy them some time. Who wanted to end up homeless with the winter approaching?

"Yer've outdone yerself, Agatha," Antanas declared after dinner, mimicking Thaddeus' tone. "The only food missin' was bird's milk."

***

Young Arturas spent the entire night shivering and tossing, unable to get warm even under three layers of lambskin. The same horrid images flashed before his eyes every time he closed them. It was him who had found Thaddeus at the foot of the unfinished chapel with blood frozen in his hair and ice crystals in his open eyes. He remembered running back to the village, screaming his lungs out. He remembered digging the grave, sawing the wood for the coffin and wrapping the master's body in a linen cloth. There were other people around trying to help him, though he felt utterly alone. Worst of all, he sensed that the tragedies plaguing Raven's Bog were far from over. There would be more suffering and bloodshed. Antanas frightened him. The blacksmith never parted with an axe, even at night. He carried it around at all times, like a royal staff.

At dawn Arturas put on his padded coat and went into the stables. He had not shed a single tear at the graveside of his master, but as soon as he found himself in the company of his beloved horses, he lost all composure. His arms wrapped around Gita's neck, he wept. The young mare was pregnant, and Arturas feared he would never see the foal. Since Antanas had declared himself in charge of the farm animals, he would eventually start selling them, and Gita was the most valuable horse.

Klaudia Baginski, his summertime sweetheart, stood by his side, rubbing his shoulder with her frostbitten fingers.

"My father spoke to Master Rozpondek, who promised to take you in to mind the stables. We'll see each other every day. Doesn't that make you happy?"

The boy wiped the snot off his nose and nodded. "Uh-huh... I'll say."

"Father says if everything goes well, he'll bless us to wed." Having made sure that his face was dry, Klaudia graced him with a deep grown-up kiss just like the one she had given him in the woods on the day Dominik was born. "By springtime, everything will be forgotten."

Before resuming his chores, Arturas took Gita for a walk outside. God only knew how much time he had with her. Klaudia gave her grieving betrothed some space. She did not insist on accompanying him on the walk. Before plunging into his new life at the Rozpondek estate, he needed to disengage from his old life.

Having spotted a couple of fresh eggs in the chicken nests along the wall, Klaudia picked up a basket and started collecting them before the shells cracked from the cold. Anything to help Bronia, with whom she had gotten friendly over the past few months. In preparation for her wedding,

Klaudia wanted to know everything about pleasing a man, and Bronia seemed like someone who knew a thing or two on the subject.

A gloved hand rested on Klaudia's shoulder. The girl turned with a shudder to see the gaunt face of Master Dombrowski's second wife. She was wearing a tailored grey suit with a long fitted jacket and a bustled skirt, a top hat with a fishnet veil and a jeweled collar. The redness of her eyes was noticeable even through the veil.

"Be quiet." Renate pressed a velvet-clad finger to Klaudia's lips. "I come unarmed. I won't tell anyone you were stealing eggs. It'll be our little secret."

Klaudia swatted the gloved hand off her mouth. "You don't belong here."

"I know that, my pet. I'd like a word with my husband."

The gardener's daughter trembled and backed away. "Your husband... is dead!"

"Not of a broken heart, I assume."

The flippancy of the remark knocked the air out of Klaudia's lungs. The girl spent the next few seconds gasping. "Master Dombrowski," she managed at last, "died a martyr's death, while building a church for his people."

"*Mein Gott*... I told Thaddeus it was a bad idea. I knew someone would get hurt." She rubbed the opal medallion on her necklace. "Anyway, I'd like to see my son."

"Dominik doesn't need you."

"He doesn't know me."

"And he never will."

"I've made my peace with it. I hope his surrogate mother has concocted a believable story to tell him. One day he'll ask questions. Don't worry, my pet. I haven't come here to steal the boy from this rural paradise. I'm having another child. I just want to say goodbye to Dominik."

"That's all?"

"I've no plans to sell this place, if that's what you're asking. It's not worth the trouble of putting it on the market. Tell your friends they can rot in this pit. I'm going to Brandenburg."

"Then go!" Klaudia tossed her hands up.

"Not before seeing my son."

"What do you want from me?"

"Nothing extravagant. I just need you to fetch the baby and bring him to me, so I can have a few moments alone with him."

"You must be daft to think I'd do something like that!"

Renate sealed Klaudia's lips with her fingers. "Hush. I told you to be quiet. You want the whole village to come running? One day, God willing, you'll be a mother too. And the first time one of your children falls ill, you'll remember this day and what you denied me."

There was no sport in terrorizing Klaudia. It did not take too much effort to reduce the peasant girl to tears. She was already shaking and blinking. Without further ado, Renate pulled one earring out and stuck it into Klaudia's scarf. "It's high grade garnet. Will that convince you? Bring me the child, and I'll give you the other earring, and the necklace to boot. That's a lot of jewelry for a small favor."

Klaudia slipped the earring into her pocket. "Damn you."

"Glad we have an understanding. I'll be waiting."

Left alone, Renate surveyed the place where she and Thaddeus had spent their first night. The strange, surreal summer of 1884... The news of Thaddeus' death did not shock her. For the past few days she had sensed that he was in a different place, hopefully with Jolanta and their four children. Two lovers later, she could not be angry at her clueless, gullible husband. She had her eyes set on

Brandenburg and the teaching job. Sebastian had kept his word. Before reuniting with his St. Petersburg love, he had written to his Uncle Henrik praising Renate's knowledge of art history. The only loose end was Renate's pregnancy that would soon become noticeable. She and Sebastian had not yet decided on how to explain the child's paternity. Thaddeus' death actually played in Renate's favor. Now she could claim in good conscience that she was a penniless widow, forced to earn her own livelihood. By falling off the scaffolding at the right time, Thaddeus had done her an enormous favor. Now she would be spared the hassle of obtaining a divorce. She could have the new baby in peace and under the Dombrowski family name. Then she could start looking for her next romantic escapade as a free woman in a city teeming with young bankers, lawyers, doctors and insurance brokers. The possibilities were infinite! For the first time in eighteen months, things were looking up for Renate. Still, she wanted to see Dominik before bidding goodbye to the Russian Empire, even if it was a frivolous whim on her part. The child would probably scream like he did the last time she tried to hold him.

Klaudia was surely taking her time. Perhaps, she was looking for something warm to wrap the baby in.

With a sigh, Renate glanced at her pocket watch. It was quarter past nine. She had a charter carriage waiting for her a few hundred meters down the road. If she was not back by nine-thirty, the coachman would leave without her, as he had other passengers to pick up on the way to the city.

Suddenly, she heard noises outside the stable. Footsteps. Whispers. Metal clanging. The door swung open, and Renate saw the familiar gang: Antanas bearing an axe, a few field hands armed with scythes, Agatha with a butcher's knife and Bronia with scissors.

Klaudia stepped forward, pointing her finger at Renate. "The witch has come here to take the child."

CHAPTER 40

All the Tarts in the World

Vilnius—January, 1886

The news of Theodor Nekrasov's hasty marriage sent a ripple of resentment mixed with relief through the ranks of single girls. At least now the rivalry was over. With the coveted bachelor out of the equation, the scorned girlfriends could settle into some semblance of a truce, which eventually turned to solidarity. They took comfort in badmouthing Theo's bride. The loose cut of her wedding dress alone provided plenty of gossip material. As far as everyone knew, she was a failed artist of German stock who suffered from some skin disease. Pregnancy only exacerbated that condition. The red blotches on her face showed even through the veil. She was rumored to have spent time in prison—or a lunatic asylum. God only knew what Theo saw in her. She must've cast a spell on him. On the other hand, he deserved to suffer for abandoning his faithful working class harem.

The ceremony took place at St. Anne's Church, a tiny Gothic masterpiece from the early 1500s with an elaborate façade and a detached belfry that was built three centuries later but in the identical style.

After a purely nominal honeymoon in the randomly picked city of Trakai, the newlyweds moved into a new flat on the bottom floor of what once was a historical mansion. The couple living upstairs had a son who took tuba lessons, so the whole building was vibrating between five and seven every night.

Having pulled some strings, Theo was able to get Aurelia a part-time assignment at the city hall on the condition that she would keep her herself inconspicuous and anonymous. The accounting supervisor did not want the rest of his workers to get the idea that it was a new tradition for them to recruit their pregnant wives to earn a few extra rubles. If women were indeed as sovereign and capable as certain manifestos claimed them to be, they should form their own guilds instead of stealing jobs from their men.

One morning in mid-January Aurelia received a surprise visit from her brother. Theodor had already left for work. She answered the door wearing her husband's bathrobe over her nightgown. Lounging in bed until ten o'clock was becoming a pernicious habit, one that Aurelia intended to kick. Being Theo's wife, she was still expected to come to the city hall every day, even though he was not draconian about the schedule.

Aurelia had not seen her brother since their spat at Asher's Atelier the previous summer. Her wrist still ached on occasion, especially when it rained, but she harbored no grudge against Sebastian, dismissing the incident as just another case of sibling horseplay gone awry. It was a pity he had not come to the wedding. Perhaps, he was embarrassed to look Theo in the eye after their grapple on the deck of the steamboat. Perhaps, he had nothing to brag about. So when Sebastian showed up at her doorstep decked out in tweed and cashmere, a wedding band on his finger, Aurelia gathered that St. Petersburg was treating him well.

"I'm working in admissions at the University," he shared. "Professor Suhanov basically handed his wife over to me, along with the job and the apartment. He said I always was his favorite student, and he couldn't think of a better successor. Indeed, Suhanov is a transformed man. He has such an air of wisdom and forgiveness about him."

"But you haven't reached that level of enlightenment yet?"

"Not yet. For now, I'm enjoying my obscenely lavish life in the northern capital."

"Then what are you doing here?"

"I came here to collect a few things, to clear out my study. I'm putting the family house up for rent. Not sure I'm ready to sell it yet. If you and Theo know anyone looking for lodging—"

Aurelia puffed a sneer. "If all his colleagues poured their salaries into one pot, maybe they'd be able to rent a single room."

"But I'm offering a fantastic deal. I want to fill the house with respectable, industrious people who'd take good care of it in my absence."

Sebastian's plunge into philanthropy reminded Aurelia of a passage from Dickens' *Christmas Carol*. He was "as merry as a schoolboy, as giddy as a drunken man". Still, the idea of being indebted to Sebastian did not sit well with her.

"You should advertise and charge the market price." She glanced down at her loosely draped belly. "By the way, in case you haven't noticed yet, you're going to be an uncle."

"About that..."

"What?"

"Forget it." He wiggled his fingers squeamishly. "I really should keep my mouth shut. What's done is done."

354

"Ah, to hell with diplomacy! We haven't seen each other for a year and a half, dear brother. I've missed your acrimonies."

Sebastian flexed his shoulders, feigning hesitation. "This could be my residual pessimism talking. I hope my fears are unfounded, and you aren't in for a world of disappointment. I know what happened last summer. You're in a peculiar position—a ruined woman of noble birth."

"Damaged goods from a reputable manufacturer," Aurelia confirmed cheerfully.

Sebastian picked up a miniature globe from the bookshelf and spun it a few times. "Let's be candid. As far as lineage goes, you're a few tiers above Theo's usual pickings. No doubt, it flatters him. Right now he must feel like a knight who rescued a blue-blooded girl from a scandal. Once the novelty of chivalry wears off, he'll start pining for his old ways. It's only a matter of time before Theo reverts to being a marzipan-gobbling philanderer."

Aurelia pulled a loose thread out of her sleeve. "That's the least of my worries. I don't expect fidelity past the honeymoon. And as much as I enjoy Theo's svelte form, I won't grieve it. Let him have all the tarts in the world."

"I'm curious to see what will happen after you give birth. How long will Theo's patience last, listening to the screams of a brat who isn't his by blood? That will be the ultimate test of Nekrasov's chivalry. For now, the child isn't real to him. It's just a nameless entity inside your belly. It's easy for an infatuated fool to say 'I'll love it as my own!' while it's not causing him any inconvenience. As long as his sleep is uninterrupted, and his carnal appetites are satisfied, why shouldn't he be gracious and accepting? But will he continue loving that squirming lump of flesh after it keeps him up for a few nights?"

355

Aurelia rubbed her hands. "Luckily, I know an excellent folk recipe: vodka and herbs. It'll keep the baby quiet, so the parents can do their business in peace."

"Fine, turn it into a joke." Sebastian slammed the globe back on the shelf. "I speak from personal experience. I remember how your mother treated me. I also know how Professor Suhanov treated Constantine. There's a lot of mental damage to be undone. The poor lad is yet to fully accept me as his real father. He still pines for the man who raised him for the first seven years of his life, however cold Suhanov was. On some days Constantine clings to my leg. On other days he pretends I don't exist. One time he kicked me in the shin and told me he hated me. The next day I cancelled all lectures because he begged me to stay and play courtroom with him. Not that I'm complaining. It's my punishment for fathering a child with a married woman."

"Theo is nothing like your professor. And I never deceived him. He knew all along where this child came from, and it didn't deter him. We'll have more children."

"That's what worries me. Once Theo tastes of real fatherhood your by-blow will be pushed aside. I just don't want you to be surprised if that happens."

Having finished his speech, Sebastian grabbed his hat and made a dash towards the door. His sister's voice arrested him. "Do you even care what happened to *her*?"

"I've no idea... to whom you're referring," he fibbed with a stutter.

***

Before going to the city hall that afternoon, Aurelia stopped by the gendarmerie to see an old friend from her days at the Lukiškės prison. Officer Rudenski was conveniently on break when she arrived.

"Do you have the report from Raven's Bog?" Aurelia

asked.

"Maybe," he replied elusively, still miffed at her for running off with the accounting clerk. "It's just not for your eyes, Madame Nekrasov."

"Then paraphrase."

Rudenski tormented her with suspense for a few more seconds. Aurelia kicked him in the shins a few times. He marveled at how much pain her tiny feet could inflict even through the leather of his military boots. "Bravo, Madame Nekrasov. You'd make a fine interrogator."

Aurelia seized his thumb and twisted it. "I come from a line of witch hunters. Speak."

"Alarms went off before the end of the year. Once again, the taxes hadn't been paid. Dombrowski had a history of falling behind and incurring penalties. When the adjuster arrived on site, his jaw dropped. The peasants were roaming the estate, eating and sleeping in the main house, drinking beer from the master's cellar, using the bathhouse."

"The landlord didn't mind?" Aurelia asked, releasing his hand.

"He's been dead for months. Fell off the slippery scaffolding and cracked his head. The servants had buried him next to his first wife."

"What will happen to the property?"

"It'll be sequestered, most likely. It's not worth much, all sand and swamp."

"And where will the peasants go?"

"Couldn't care less, to be truthful. It won't be easy for them to get used to another employer. Dombrowski had spoilt them rotten. Then again, their fate hasn't been my primary concern, Madame. We've our hands full investigating the disappearance of Dombrowski's wife. A few of us will head out to Raven's Bog first thing tomorrow morning."

Aurelia latched onto his arm. "Take me with you."

"In your condition?"

"I can be one of the lads for a day. Your colleagues don't need to know."

"And how did you intend to pull this off, dare I ask?" He eyed her belly. It was noticeable but not enormous. With some creative use of fabric, it could be concealed.

"Leave it to me. I'm the queen of illusion."

There was something vaguely Shakespearean about her statement, something that echoed *Twelfth Night*. Rudenski thought of how much trouble he would get into for their prank if they got caught, yet the prospect of spending an entire day with Aurelia while flaunting his courage and resourcefulness was much too tempting. That office beaver she was married to could not compete with a dashing enforcer of justice.

"Fine, meet me here at five-thirty in the morning," he said at last. "There'll be four of us. Don't be late. And for Heaven's sake, don't wear high heels."

CHAPTER 41

What's On a Dead Man's Mind

Vilnius Town Hall, Castle Street

Situated at the end of Castle Street, Vilnius Town Hall had undergone several transformations. It had started in the early 1400s as a Gothic building and had since been reconstructed many times. The most recent design, dating back to the end of the eighteenth century, was credited to Laurynas Gucevičius, a Polish-Lithuanian architect who had spent his youth touring Western European countries and cultivating his own take on the neo-classical style. That man's life story was an account of a remarkable rise from obscurity to glory. Born a peasant's son near Kupiškis in northeast Lithuania, he had gone on to become a professor of architecture and topography at the Artillery and Engineering Corps' School of Vilnius. A staunch opponent of Russian Imperial influences, Gucevičius had led a contingent of local civil guard during the Vilnius Uprising in 1794. His involvement in the revolt had cost him his position at the academy, though he had returned there three years later in 1797 as head of the newly founded architecture department. He had continued doing his work under the new regime for the glory of the old country. Like the Gate of Dawn, the Vilnius Town Hall embodied the spirit of Baltic pride.

Even a confirmed philistine like Theodor Nekrasov understood the historical and political significance of the building. Conscious of the unglamorous nature of his job, he drew inspiration from the walls of the magnificent edifice. He wondered if those things mattered to Aurelia, since she at some point had been so fascinated by her maternal ancestry. Or was her Baltic fever over? Had she found a new obsession for herself?

Heavy-hearted, Theo resisted the urge to keep checking his pocket watch. Aurelia was running late again, for the second time that week. Was it a sign that she had already started tiring of his company?

At half-past two in the afternoon, Her Majesty finally made her entrance.

"You were expected by noon," he said without lifting his eyes from the fiscal report. "I was beginning to worry."

"It took me a bit longer to get out of bed this morning. I was feeling faint."

"Then you should see Dr. Klein."

"Oh, I don't think it would be necessary. I'm much better now."

"Then you weren't so ill after all." Theodor slammed one folder shut and put it on top of a growing pile of accounts. "Clearly, you had enough strength to put on your dress, curl your hair and powder your nose."

Aurelia hung up her coat and leaned over to give him a peck on the temple. "Don't get so agitated, darling."

Theodor shut his eyes for a few seconds, hoping to blink away a bourgeoning headache. "What... did I tell you? We've been through this before. You cannot do this."

"Do what?"

"This... What you just did." He clenched his hands into loose fists in front of his face. "Touching me, calling me pet names. Not that I don't savor those fleeting tokens from you, but this is precisely the sort of familiarity my supervisor frowns upon. We'll both get dismissed."

"There's a perfectly logical explanation for my tardiness. I just cannot get into it now."

What Theo found most enchanting about his young wife was that she always had a perfectly logical explanation for everything.

"I realize you aren't accustomed to a rigid schedule," he said, twirling a fountain pen to calm his nerves. "It pains me to encumber a free Bohemian spirit with paperwork. I know you'd rather be slithering through the alleys with a magnifying glass in your hand instead of dragging your feet through the hallways lined with cardboard boxes."

"I happen to like the smell of wet cardboard and ink."

Theodor spun in his swivel chair. "Your deceased father is probably tossing in his grave."

"How do you know what's on a dead man's mind? He could be laughing this very moment."

As far as Theodor remembered, a sense of humor had never been Adolph Messer's distinguishing trait. The man would have dismissed a cook on the spot for serving his soup the wrong temperature.

"In his eyes I'd just have been an overreaching parasite. I stole a purebred mare and harnessed her to plough the fields."

"Pedigrees are worthless. You can't spread them over toast."

"You and I know that, but some people think differently. Some would say that I ought to feel ashamed that my wife has to work, yet I'm not. My mother had always worked alongside my father in their little flower shop. Perhaps it's not the life Adolph Messer had envisioned for his daughter, but it's the best I can offer. I assume you like our new flat and want to continue living there."

"Why, of course. I especially enjoy the nightly tuba concerts."

"Then it'll take some effort on your part. I suppose such things aren't common where you come from. Women from your circle exert themselves solely for pleasure. The moment pleasure wanes, all exertion stops. There's no consequence to idleness. Alas, I'm not from that circle. I never promised you unlimited leisure. Forgive me for not being a magnate."

Theo's tone was neither apologetic nor accusative.

"Forgive me for not being a shop girl." Aurelia unlocked the filing cabinet and started tackling the pile of receipts. "Sebastian says that in the next twenty years they'll start awarding law degrees to women."

"And if you want to live to see that glorious era, try not to break your neck or die of starvation. That would help."

"He also says that women will start wearing trousers and cropping their hair short."

"You don't need to wait another twenty years for that. I won't stop you."

₵ℍₐₚₜₑℝ 42

Imperial Reconnaissance

When Rudenski saw Aurelia the next morning, he stifled a gasp of admiration. The crafty girl had exceeded his expectations by transforming herself into a shapeless, sexless roly-poly figure. She had braided and coiled her hair up beneath a Russian trooper hat with ear flaps tying under the chin. Her face was drowning in the fluffy rabbit fur, with just the freckled tip of the nose exposed. The contours of her body disappeared under the padded overcoat.

Rudenski introduced her to various colleagues as his nephew Nicholas, who was contemplating a career in law enforcement. "The lad still hasn't regained his voice after a cold, but he's well enough to accompany us. He won't be a nuisance, I promise."

Satisfied with the explanation, the men took turns shaking Aurelia's hand. She hummed greetings through the knit scarf covering her mouth and promptly hid in the back of the enclosed van drawn by two horses. The van looked like any other cargo vehicle with one tiny window on each wall. There was no imperial imagery of any sort.

With everyone onboard, Rudenski lit his pipe and laid out the action plan to his men. "We leave the van at a crossroad half a kilometer away from the estate and walk the rest of the way through the woods. We enter the house through the back door. Based on the adjuster's report, there aren't many people left at Raven's Bog, just the blacksmith with his family and a few farm hands. It's hard to predict how much resistance we'll encounter, but hold onto your revolvers just in case. Those Balts won't hesitate to put their scythes to use."

Knowing that Aurelia was listening, Rudenski made sure to give his voice a dramatic, authoritative ring. From his vantage point he could not see her face, but he sensed she was watching him and soaking in the foreboding ambience of the dawn.

Aurelia's back and hipbones had been aching for the past few days, and sitting on a cold wooden bench was not helping. Still, she resisted the urge to fidget lest she should attract attention from Rudenski's comrades. She could not compromise the man who had already put his title and his badge in peril for the sake of indulging her curiosity.

***

Raven's Bog

When Bronia saw six gendarmes standing in the kitchen, her immediate reaction was to offer them some caramelized milk from the oven and some potato griddle cakes. Rudenski was glad he had eaten a full breakfast that morning, so he was not swayed by the aroma and could stay focused on the investigation. The place certainly did not smell, or look, like a crime scene. A little girl was playing with a longhaired cat on the floor. Two infants were sleeping side by side in a large wicker basket. A middle-aged woman was spinning wool by the window.

Aurelia stayed in the dark drafty vestibule, kneeling on a pile of rabbit skins. Her face pressed to the crack in the wooden wall, she could hear and see what was going on inside.

"Where are the rest of the workers?" Rudenski began.

"Everywhere," Bronia sighed wistfully. "After Master Dombrowski's death, they started leavin'. Some found work at the Zielinskis' estate. Others headed over to the city."

"And who's this boy?" Rudenski pointed at the dark-haired infant.

"Oh, that's Dominik, the young master. He's been in my care since he was born."

"And his natural mother?"

"Lady Renate? She doesn't live here anymore, I'm afraid."

For a peasant girl, Bronia possessed an impressive amount of self-control and good social graces. She knew better than to avert her eyes while questioned by the gendarmes, so she looked straight at her interrogator, though not too steadfastly. Her comely face and clear voice contributed to the image of a wholesome provincial ingénue. Still, Rudenski was not easily deceived.

"Then where *does* your lady live?"

"Who knows?" Bronia shrugged. "She's been gone since last summer. She could be stayin' with one of her beaus in the city. She never liked this place anyway."

"So she got up and left, just like that, huh?" Rudenski snapped his fingers. "Leaving her son behind?"

"She wasn't too fond of him either."

"Not nearly as fond as you are of your children, I imagine?"

Rudenski nodded at his two armed companions. One of them scooped up Magda from the ground, and the other one yanked Edgaras out the basket.

"I can tell you're a devoted mother," the gendarme continued, staring at the petrified milkmaid. "You'd hate to be parted from your children, wouldn't you? Start talking."

It was Agatha's turn to step in.

"Ah, leave my daughter alone," she said, pulling the kerchief off her head. "I'll tell yer everythin'."

"So Granny has a voice!" Rudenski shouted. "Praise, Jesus! Tell us, Granny, where is Lady Renate?"

"All over the place." Agatha made a broad sweeping gesture. "In the bog, in the woods, in the potato field, in the old well that's run dry. Have no worries, officer. We gave Her Ladyship a burial fit for a witch."

A witch... Rudenski reminded himself that these people were mentally and spiritually stuck in the fifteenth century.

"Yer city folk think us pagans, but we're good Christians," Agatha spoke ardently. "We know an unclean spirit when it enters our midst. Her Ladyship was a witch, not awfully potent but damned stubborn. Those are the worst kind. She couldn't wipe all of us out in one strike, so she slowly bled us."

Rudenski glanced behind at his men. "Someone should be recording this."

An elderly gendarme pulled out a notebook and a pen and started scribbling. Emboldened by Rudenski's undivided attention, Agatha assumed a more imposing attitude. Never before had she had so many uniformed men express such interest in her.

"Good thing yer writin' this down," she continued. "Let the world know of the sufferin' we've endured in the past year and a half. She was brought by some sly German in the middle of the night. He looked like a demon in his black suit, those shiny shoes like hooves. No doubt there was a pair of horns hidin' beneath that hat, and a tail coiled inside those trousers. The way he pranced out of his buggy? Yer would think hell-mouth yawned and coughed him up. The moment Lady Renate arrived, the cattle started fallin' ill. Three healthy milkmaids miscarried, all buxom girls. Yer should've seen how heart-sick the master was, such bitterness shroudin' him. When he decided to build a chapel, the witch wasn't too pleased, smoke pourin' out of her ears. She's the one who caused him to fall from the roof. She wanted him dead, so she could take over the farm and turn it into grounds for satanic rites. That's right, she promised her firstborn to Lucifer. But we wouldn't give up Master Dominik. He's nothin' like his mother. His soul was sanctified by his father's goodness. Right before Christmas she came to claim him. What were we to do, officer? When yer dispose of a witch, yer need to keep the pieces 'part, or else they'll find each other and grow back together. Oh, and there was a bulge in her belly. The witch was with child, conceived by her Jew lover, no doubt. So we cut it out, wrapped it in a cloth and buried under the apple tree."

The hag did not sound contrite or fearful, her tone steady and casual, with a few boastful notes here and there. In her mind, she had done God's work. Rudenski did not detect any obvious hatred. Getting rid of Lady Renate was as trivial as pulling a ragweed.

"The prosecutor will want to hear this." He straightened his uniform and then looked at the two peasant women. "You're coming with us."

Silently, mother and daughter put on their bulky coats and wrapped kerchiefs around their heads.

CHAPTER 43

Imperial Justice

Walking a few meters behind the captives, Rudenski elbowed Aurelia. "Now you see what we get paid for."

She brushed the rabbit fur away from her hot forehead. "You mean nothing like this ever happens in Russian settlements?"

"Surely it does. Peasants are the same everywhere. That's what happens when people who were meant to be subjugated are given freedom."

The captives were seated on the bench across from the gendarmes, who made no effort to intimidate or humiliate them. The men behaved as if they were guarding inanimate objects. Bronia was allowed to reunite with her two natural children. Three-year old Magda showed no sign of terror. The prospect of going for a ride in the company of uniformed gentlemen excited her. Sucking on her thumb, she studied the shiny buttons on their light-blue tunics. Little Edgaras started grunting and tugging at the collar of his mother's coat, looking for the breast. Dominik was planted into Aurelia's lap.

"Make yourself useful," Rudenski said. "The Dombrowski boy one must be kept separate. He's precious evidence."

Of the three children, Dominik was dressed the lightest. Having nothing on except for a long buttoned-down shirt and knit leggings, he started shivering. Aurelia unwound the scarf covering the lower part of her face and wrapped it around the baby.

"Your nephew hasn't begun shaving yet," a younger gendarme remarked, marveling at Aurelia's delicate chin and smooth neck. "No stubble, no Adam's apple. How old is he?"

"Thirteen. Rudenski men are late bloomers, but then they turn into hairy ogres overnight. Give him a few years. Nicholas is determined to join the army."

"He'll have to slim down first. He bit a little round in the middle. A few weeks of army diet will fix that problem. Bread, water and raw cabbage. He'll be lean like a birch rod."

"Enough already," Rudenski snapped, unnerved by such excessive attention to Aurelia. "Leave my nephew alone. He's only here to observe."

Still, the junior comrade would not be silenced easily. "If this lad wants to succeed in the army, he better get used to being poked and ridiculed. Before they allow you to arrest murderous peasants, you'll have to fight in a few wars for the Czar. Just try not to have your limbs blown off. On the battlefield they won't give you a fancy witch's burial. They'll just dump your body parts into one pit."

The young gendarme's remark solicited a wave of approbating laughter from his comrades. A bit of comic relief was most welcome. Even with their mission partially accomplished, they were facing a long ride back to Vilnius in the company of two repugnant peasant women and three children.

When the van started moving, Bronia wiped a tear. "We left the stove on. The chicken stew will burn and stink up the kitchen. The lads will have nothing for supper."

Agatha dug her claws into her daughter's hand. "No tears. We won't be seein' our kitchen for some time."

Bronia continued reeling and wailing lowly with her mouth closed, clutching her son to her breast. Her wailing was interrupted by a sudden snapping sound, as if a large pebble hit the wall of the van at a high speed. The narrow window was blown to pieces. A second later Rudenski slapped himself on the neck, as if stung by a bee, blood trickling through his fingers.

A juicy Russian profanity fell from his lips. He had hoped they would not have to use their weapons that day. Of course, no arrest is complete without an ambush. He could really use a few extra men. In fact, he had asked for more, but his superior commander would not give him more than five. In the expert opinion of the latter, six armed men was more than enough to subdue a gang of rowdy peasants.

The next shot brought down one of the horses. Now it was the driver's turn to curse. The van tilted and came to a halt.

Bronia stirred on the bench, her countenance jubilant. She recognized the sound of her husband's rifle. After Thaddeus' death, Antanas had repaired it. "No fear," she whispered to her children. "Papa won't let 'em take us away."

Everyone heard her pledge but did not react to it. The gendarmes were trained not to fall for such provocations from the captives.

Rudenski moved his hand, exposing the oozing gash on his neck. "How does it look, Panaev?" he asked a younger comrade.

"Like hell, sir."

"If I drop half-way, Dubrov is in charge. And after him—Mikulin. Understand?"

"Yes, sir."

Panaev crouched by the shattered window, his revolver ready. A lull descended upon the scene of the melee. The driver was in the most precarious position, being fully exposed and vulnerable to a bullet from any angle.

Bronia started crooning a mournful Lithuanian lullaby, holding her children close and swaying them. Her voice had a hypnotic effect on the gendarmes' whose nerves were stretched taut. Panaev's eyes started getting glassy from the reeling folk melody.

Aurelia felt it was her time to intervene, even at the expense of her disguise. "This isn't a lullaby," she said to Rudenski in Russian. "The milkmaid is summoning her husband. She's telling him how many men are in the van, where everyone is seated."

Panaev snapped out of his trance. "Why, Commander, what a high-pitched voice your nephew has. He's a polyglot too."

Aurelia shifted her gaze to the young gendarme. "If I were you, I'd lower my head. You're about to have your brains blown out." Feeling hot all of a sudden, she untied the ear flops and pulled the rabbit hat off, causing her messy braids to tumble down.

Panaev's square jaw dropped slowly. "What... the hell?"

All eyes turned to the bleeding commander. Rudenski responded with a lopsided shrug and a don't-ask-me glare. "They won't shoot at the van," he said, his head tilting more to the side. "We've got the children."

"Oh, they'll shoot, all right," Aurelia objected with breathtaking familiarity. "I know their lot. They aren't thinking that far ahead. I think you should preempt them and open fire. It's up to you, Michael."

Michael. The men nearly fell off the bench. From the chanting milkmaid to the cross-dressing redhead dispensing strategic advice, this was arguably the most bizarre excursion they had ever taken. Who in the name of the Czar did this highhanded wench think she was? They would not have expected such whimsical pranks from Rudenski, who was famous for his orthodox tactics.

A third bullet entered the van through the window, shattering one of the wooden floorboards and kicking up a fountain of splinters. Aurelia shifted Dominik in her lap. "Told you! Looks like you'll be using your guns, whenever your commander is ready to give an order."

Rudenski blinked, raised his index finger and held that pose for a few seconds, his breathing increasingly labored. Engaging in forest warfare was a daunting task. His men were better armed, but they were at a disadvantage compared to the peasants, who knew every shrub, every tree. The light-blue uniforms complete with red stripes on the caps made them all the more conspicuous to the enemy. Truthfully, Rudenski had no idea what the hell he was doing. His wound was not deep, but the bullet had hit an artery. He had a hard time thinking straight, let alone articulating, with blood trickling out of his mouth. Still, his men were waiting for instructions. Staying inside the wooden box was not an option.

"Panaev and Dubrov, you come outside with me," he said finally. "Mikulin, you stay in the van and guard the peasant women. Aurelia, take the Dombrowski boy as far from here as you can. Holitsyn will give you cover. If you hear gunshots, don't turn around. Just keep on walking. Colonel Olszewski lives about two kilometers down the road. It's a red house with a crane well. You cannot miss it."

Aurelia rose to her feet. At the last minute Rudenski pulled out a Denisov model revolver and dropped it into the roomy pocket of her overcoat. "Just in case. There should be four rounds left, so use them judiciously. You... *do* know how to use it, right?"

"I'll figure it out. I've seen it in the last production of *Eugene Onegin*."

"There you go." He blessed her with a jerky nod. "God speed."

She unlatched the side door and stepped out into the bourgeoning Baltic blizzard. The cloudy sky was coughing up first flurries. Instead of carrying the Dombrowski orphan in her arms, she threw him on her back, securing him with a scarf for convenience as well as personal safety. If Dominik truly presented any value to the peasants, they would not risk killing him by shooting at her from behind.

Humming a German marching tune, Aurelia started trekking towards the safe house as fast as she could with one child in her belly and one on her back. Luckily, Dominik was light and flaccid. It was only the warmth of his breath on Aurelia's neck that signaled to her that the boy was still alive. As far as she knew, Holitsyn was right behind her at a distance of about ten meters, judging from the crunching of the snow beneath his boots. The mid-winter storm was picking up. Flakes were falling from the sky like goose feathers out of a slashed pillow.

Through the whistling of the wind Aurelia heard a low beastly growl. The creature before her had long muscular legs, a thick neck adorned with a lush silvery ruff, a pair of golden eyes and a set of impressive fangs. It had all the attributes of a wolfdog, the stuff of Lithuanian folk tales. Her late mother had joked about some lecherous nobleman taking the shape of a wolfdog to beguile maidens. This mongrel appeared to be more domestic than wild. A full-blooded wolf would shy away from anything on two legs. This one had clearly been trained to obey a human master and attack on a cue. Locking her eyes with the creature, Aurelia continued humming, with screams and gunshots behind her. She remembered Rudenski's orders to keep walking, despite the premonition that she had lost Holitsyn somewhere along the way. Her hand slipped into the pocket, feeling for the revolver. She only had a nebulous idea of how side arms functioned.

Suddenly, a flying metallic object split her left eyebrow, spraying blood all over the snow. Reeling from the blow, she looked down and saw what looked like a crooked old horseshoe. Within seconds, her left eye swelled up, blurring her vision. Barely keeping balance, she spun around and saw the attacker—a peasant boy a few years younger than her. His wind-blasted face expressed belligerence and terror in equal measure. In all likelihood, he was unarmed. The horseshoe had been his most potent weapon.

"So you think you're David from the fucking Old Testament?" Aurelia said in Lithuanian. "You need to practice your throw. What will your beastly ringleader say?"

At the sound of his native language the terror on the boy's face intensified. He lunged at Aurelia, locking his hands around her exposed throat. Dominic fell out of the makeshift harness into a snowdrift. Paying no heed to the whimpering infant, the youth tipped his red-haired adversary onto her back. With one knee pushing into her chest and another into her belly, he proceeded to choke her.

It did not take long for Aurelia to accept that she was at a disadvantage. The odds of her winning this wrestling match and making it out of the woods alive were slim. The blow to the head had left her disoriented and weakened. Despite being younger, the village goon was stronger than she was. Those hands had tossed logs and restrained horses. Clearly, he had no qualms about killing a pregnant woman, Renate's death being a case in point. Aurelia had no desire to share the fate of her former schoolmate. That would be such a pathetic, embarrassing way to go. She felt the wolfdog's teeth sinking into her calf. The stupid mutt, trained for low-brow mercenary work!

Suddenly, Aurelia stopped resisting and went flaccid. The stable boy's hands remained at her throat, though their grip loosened slightly. He continued sitting on top of her, wheezing. Perhaps he had not expected the victory to come so soon. The wheezing quickly turned to convulsive sobbing.

Aurelia had no idea what she was doing, and she had exactly two seconds to do it. Unnoticeably to the boy, she slipped her hand into the pocket of her coat. Without pulling the gun out, she angled the barrel towards her adversary and held down the trigger.

***

Colonel Olszewski's house

Sixty-year old Gregory Olszewski surmised that a peaceful retirement in the countryside was not in the cards for him. He had several homes in various corners of the Empire, yet his favorite retreat was a quaint cottage in the Dainava region. It was there that he chose to spend the winter of 1886, far from the vanity fairs of Vilnius and Warsaw, where he was still expected to show up in full regalia and retell the stories from his past campaigns to the new generation of soldiers. No matter how many times he told himself that he was done with military, clearly the military was not done with him.

The excitement started about two o'clock in the afternoon, when he heard gunshots coming from the woods a few kilometers away. His hearing was sharp enough to discern a volley generated by a simple hunting rifle from that generated by a real army weapon. It was no huge surprise to him when half an hour later a handful of gendarmes showed up at his door asking for permission to use his premise.

"We've got some dead, some wounded and some prisoners," Panaev reported. "We need a place to... take an inventory?"

The old colonel smiled genially. "Go right ahead. Just make sure you clean up the blood. Basia just scrubbed the floors this morning."

Olszewski was always up for a good casualty-counting party. He had not enjoyed one since the Crimean War over thirty years ago. After telling his housemaid to brew another pot of tea, he lent Panaev a horse from his stable to help pull the van filled with corpses. They counted seven males, their ages ranging from twenty to forty. Dubrov, a stellar marksman, displayed the body of Antanas with the same pride a hunter would flaunt a carcass of a prize buck. "My handiwork," he boasted, thumbing himself in the chest. "It took three bullets to bring him down, but I did it. I swear his chest is made of steel."

Sipping his tea, the colonel looked at the asymmetrical features of the dead man and hummed pensively. "Hey, that's Dombrowski's blacksmith. You don't forget a crooked visage like that. I'll be damned. There was always something odd about Raven's Bog. It'll need to be exorcised before being put on the market."

Aurelia was sitting in a rocking chair in the corner, her bandaged head thrown back and fingers slowly undoing her braids. For the past hour she had been suffering from spasms in her lower back. Perhaps, she had pulled a muscle during her wrestling match with the stable boy. The spasms kept getting deeper and more intense. Against the colonel's instruction to stay put, she got up from the chair in hopes that movement would help the pain. The gash on her forehead started bleeding again.

She went into the tool shed where the prisoners were held. Arturas was crouching in the corner, his feet shackled, his baggy pants stained with blood from the shallow flesh wound in his right thigh. When Aurelia pulled the trigger, she was not aiming for any particular body part. She certainly was not making a conscious effort to spare his life. It just happened that at the last moment Arturas shifted his position. The bullet that would have otherwise lodged in his lower back ended up grazing his quadriceps. She could tell that he was as embarrassed by the lightness of the wound as she was by her lousy marksmanship.

"Why are you crying, little cretin?" she asked him. "Are those tears of fear or remorse?"

"Of joy," the boy sniffed. "The brute is dead."

"What brute?"

"Antanas." The boy rolled up the sleeve and showed a letter "D" branded on his forearm. "He dragged me into the smithy, tied me up and... He said if I were to leave, he'd kill me and Klaudia, the girl I was s'posed to wed. If I whispered a word of what we'd done to Her Ladyship... 'Twas his idea to get the wolfdog. Milo, the old mutt, died on the master's grave. Antanas got that yellow-eyed beast from a travelin' breeder. He fancied himself a duke."

Aurelia had heard enough. She patted the boy on his greasy head and walked over to Rudenski, who was sitting on a wooden box with his neck bandaged, smoking Colonel Olszewski's tobacco. Each time he exhaled a puff of smoke, a drop of blood would come out of his left nostril. His right foot was twitching, tapping the floor lightly, as if he heard some folk reel inside his head. His overcoat was undone and

THE GATE OF DAWN

his chest partly exposed, sweat pooling in the clavicles. Aurelia took a minute to toy with the Orthodox cross twirling on a plain thread.

"Sorry I lost your revolver," she said.

"Don't worry about it. Side arms are more for show than anything."

Aurelia glanced behind. "There's ungodly bawling coming out of the van."

"That's the milkmaid."

"Someone should tell her that her children are all right."

"What's the point? She'll never see them again anyway. She and her toothless mother are done for."

"What do you think they'll get?"

"Life in a labor camp, most likely. They're both sturdy, so the Empire will get a good ten years out of them."

"Is there any chance of having their sentence softened? They did cooperate by testifying."

Rudenski shook his head. "Please, don't..."

"Don't do what?" She immobilized his sweaty face between her hands. "Worry my bleeding little head over the fates of these two peasant women? Did it occur to you that they're victims of that yellow-haired goblin? They were cajoled into playing along."

"I don't believe they were cajoled. Antanas was more of a puppet than a puppeteer. The idea to hack the Dombrowski widow to pieces didn't come from him. Men are only as brutal as their women lead them to be. Anyway, that's my philosophy. The judge may see this matter in a different light. My job is to pull the trigger."

"How convenient."

"Hey, you wanted to see how things were done in our line of work. You have enough material for your novel."

Aurelia's hands slipped off his face. Her gaze suddenly

moved down to the puddle forming around her on the floor. "Look, my boots are wet. Is it all from the melted snow?"

She winced and, without making a sound, dropped at his feet.

Rudenski snapped his fingers, summoning his lightly wounded comrade. "Holitsyn, take Madame Nekrasov back to the city. She needs a doctor."

CHAPTER 44

Imperial Elegy

Vilnius, Theo's apartment

She is resting now.

Many a man had heard those trivial words of consolation after his wife had lost a child. Dr. Klein could not bring himself to recite that routine statement to Theodor. Tossing and bouncing on the mattress, Aurelia was babbling up a storm, addressing the bedposts as if they were people. Her intonations covered a broad spectrum, from somber to jubilant, from pleading to vindictive, always theatrical.

All right, where's that beastly thing? That freak, that slimy red monster that popped out of my belly, where is it? I know it's still in the house somewhere. I can still smell it. When is the undertaker coming? The sooner you get that deformed creature out of here, the better. I know what I saw. Ugly Petras from the folk tale. That's what I want on his tombstone. Ugly Petras.

"Is it all right that she keeps thrashing like that?" Theo asked the doctor.

"It'll be some time before things are all right again. It was no ordinary stillbirth. Your wife has lived through a violent assault. It's hard to tell how much of it she remembers. We won't know until the fever subsides."

"Shouldn't you give her some sedatives?"

"It wouldn't be wise to sedate her. She has a generous gash above her eyebrow. It's better to keep her awake and observe her behavior. If she starts showing signs of lethargy, then we have a graver problem on our hands."

Theodor stood in front of a window, secretly thankful for the blizzard that kept the doctor trapped inside their house. He was not ready to be left alone with his delirious wife.

"She keeps calling out for someone named Michael," Dr. Klein added. "Any idea who that person might be? A relative, perhaps?"

"The only male relative she has is her half-brother Sebastian, and she wouldn't be calling him to her bedside. Michael is the gendarme who took her to Raven's Bog."

"The one with a hole in his neck?"

"Yep," Theo puckered with an air of exasperation. "Aurelia is prone to impetuous acts. She cannot stay in one place for more than two minutes. She starts fidgeting and growling like a cat trapped in a sack. I've been thinking... Perhaps, it's better to let the cat out, before someone gets scratched badly, you know?"

He looked at the doctor, seeking approbation.

"Contemplating a divorce, eh?" the old man asked casually. "I don't blame you. I wouldn't be thrilled either if Frau Klein was running around with gendarmes behind my back."

"I don't know what I was thinking when I proposed to her. My brain was still cloudy from the bout of pneumonia. Clearly, she's not made for marriage."

"Some women aren't. The natural mechanism in them is defective, and any attempts to fix it have been unsuccessful so far. There's no shame in walking away from a broken toy. It'll never work the way you want to work, no matter how many times you take it apart and reassemble it. And, since there's no child in the picture, and probably won't be, given the extent of the damage to her body..." Dr. Klein flicked his sinewy hand. "Ah, I shouldn't be telling you what to do."

"No, I welcome your advice. My parents aren't alive. They would've smacked some sense into me."

In violation of his customary austerity, Dr. Klein hugged the frazzled young man. "If you were to venture down that route, I'd recommend giving it some time, if only for the sake of propriety. If you divorce your wife too soon after the stillbirth, it'll make you look callous and potentially undermine your chances of attracting a respectable young woman in the future."

Theodor squinted, his filial meekness turning to hostility. "You think I give a damn about propriety?"

"There's something else to consider. In a few months Aurelia will turn eighteen and be eligible to claim her share of the inheritance."

"Great!" Theo threw his hands up to the ceiling in mock jubilation. "She can fund her own excursions and pay for her own funeral."

"So you don't consider yourself entitled to a fraction of her fortune, after all the inconvenience you've endured?"

"Bah! I'll probably spend it on opium. Won't even bother with alcohol. Skip straight to the hard stuff."

Dr. Klein backed away from Theo. "I really should be on my way, before the blizzard gets too severe. If anyone under the roof needs a sedative, it's you, Master Nekrasov."

***

Smoking became Theo's preferred vice, and the owner of

the tobacco shop his new best friend. Within days of picking up the habit his beautiful clothes were reeking. The acrid substance changed the chemistry of his body and soul. He continued to lose weight. He stopped shaving. Every morning a gaunt scruffy face looked back at him in the mirror. Theo suddenly found himself longing for Sebastian's company, but then he remembered that his old friend was busy living his Russo-Teutonic fairy tale. Sebastian had spent eight years apart from the woman he loved and who reciprocated. It was a clean and sweet pain from an open wound that continued bleeding but never got infected. Theo's pain was of a different quality, black and rancid.

Ugly Petras... Alas, it was not a product of Aurelia's postpartum fever. Theo saw the same thing she did—a fleshy gargoyle. Dr. Klein did not make any comments in regards to the child's appearance. In fact, he acted like it was any other stillbirth. Before leaving that night, however, he reiterated his cryptic message about certain women not being made for monogamy and procreation. Did that mean that Aurelia's body would continue spouting monsters? And how could Theo ever think of himself as an honorable Christian man after having such thoughts? A few months earlier he had made a flippant and cavalier promise to love another man's child. It had been his expectation all along that said child would look like any other. The alternative had not even crossed his mind. Now with Aurelia's son out of the equation he could not help feeling relieved. And what if the child had lived, in the form he'd been born in? Then Theo would be saddled with a deranged adulterous wife and a misshapen child. How would he present the hapless creature to the world? He would have to take it out in broad daylight at some point. And people would actually think he had fathered it, he, Theodor Nekrasov, the jovial bon vivant, whose children were supposed to resemble playful cream-fed kittens. Dear God, how his jilted girlfriends would gloat! At least, Theo did not need to worry about that. Ah, whom was he trying to deceive? He was but a selfish, faint-hearted coward, quick to make promises and just as quick to rescind.

There was one small thing he had done to atone for his cowardice: ensure a dignified burial for Aurelia's son at a Lutheran cemetery. Visiting the grave before work became his morning ritual. He would stand and smoke in front of the granite plaque that read: Peter, son of Theodor Nekrasov, January 15, 1886.

One morning in early February he spotted a gendarme standing outside the cemetery gate. His neck was wrapped in a thick knit scarf, his head tilting slightly, which gave him a scrutinizing air.

"Michael Rudenski," the man introduced himself.

"Glad to see you're recovering from your injury."

"I've been unforgivably lax about following doctor's orders. The bullet hit a muscle, leaving a nerve paralyzed. I may never be able to hold my head straight again. From now on, I'll have to look at the world at a fifteen-degree angle. Still, I should count myself lucky. Another centimeter and I'd be dead."

"Clearly, God wanted you to put in a few more decades of service."

"True. When my sick leave is over, they'll deploy me to the Caucasus. I hear the scenery is breathtaking, and the natives are ferocious."

"Is that your punishment?"

"A mandatory promotion, more like it." Officers of Rudenski's caliber did not get decommissioned easily. "I'll be in charge of an entire garrison. My superiors don't think that Baltic climate agrees with me. Foggy weather leads to foggy judgment." His intact shoulder rose and fell slowly, like a wounded bird's wing. "Aurelia wanted to know how arrests were conducted. She said it was for some detective novel she was writing. How could I stand in the way of a future masterpiece?"

Struggling to maintain eye contact with Rudenski, Theo felt his own head tilt. "Well, it never hurts to convince a girl that you give a damn about her artistic ambitions before taking her to bed. You don't want to come across as some lusty single-minded brute. Yes, I speak from experience. I'd used that trick in my wild days. *Mea culpa.*"

"Master Nekrasov, is this an invitation to a duel?"

Theo sniffed spitefully. "I don't duel with cripples. Besides, dueling is rather passé. Since you're here, let's pretend for a moment like we're civilized, progressive men, shall we?"

"I'll give it a try."

"To be completely transparent, I've no financial means of supporting an incapacitated wife." Theodor sounded like a general of a defeated army negotiating the conditions of surrender. "She's not getting better in my care. I must be doing something wrong. Or I'm the wrong man for her altogether. She keeps asking for you. Those are the only coherent things that come out of her mouth. If you wish to whisk her off to the Caucasus, I won't protest. I'll settle the legal matters. Her brother is a lawyer, and he owes me a favor."

"Tempted as I am to take advantage of your selfless offer, I fear that Aurelia's anarchistic disposition may present a certain problem. What if she tries to poison my men's meals or their minds? Alas, I'm in no position to take her off your hands. I would, however, like to offer monetary support. That's why I came. And before you decline my offer and tell me that you don't accept handouts—"

"I wasn't about to decline it. Every ruble would help."

"Splendid." Rudenski exhaled. "That means all scores between us are settled? I can leave for the Caucasus with a reasonably clear conscience?"

"Don't ask me. I've no idea what's on your conscience. I've got enough sins of my own."

"One last thing. The Dombrowski boy. He's at an orphanage with the two other children we salvaged. The place is drafty and moldy there. The other two are of peasant blood, as common and sturdy as ragweed, but Dominik is fragile. He'll perish if he stays there. His nose has been running since he got there. His upper lip is raw and crusty."

"Why are you telling me this, Officer? I can barely keep my own nose dry."

"Just hear me out. I'm trying to locate Renate's relatives in Brandenburg. With any luck, one of them will adopt the boy. The search itself can take months. Until then... It would be grand to put him up in a temporary home. So I thought... Are you listening?"

"Yes." Theodor did not like where the conversation was heading. The officer was buttering him up for something awfully burdensome, something Theo knew he would not have the heart to refuse.

"I thought of you and Aurelia. She's still your wife, at least for the foreseeable future."

"Why, we're the golden couple of the Empire! You really think this is a good idea to drop someone else's child in Aurelia's lap?"

"It might cheer her up."

"My wife is cheerful enough already, chirping from sunrise to sunset like a sparrow. I wouldn't trust her with a child if she was the last woman in Vilnius. It's a question of safety. How do you know she won't bash his brains out? I have a better idea. Why don't you take Aurelia and the kid? Trust me it's the lesser of two evils. As an accountant, I understand numbers. We're both fond of Aurelia, but she clearly prefers you. Right now all three of us are miserable. If I release Aurelia to you, that number will be reduced to one."

***

Before going to the city hall Theo stopped by the bakery and ordered a dozen macaroons, two buttered rolls, a cinnamon croissant and a soft pretzel with cheese filling.

He heard a breathy exclamation from behind the glass case. "Master Nekrasov? I didn't recognize you with the beard."

The ruddy-cheeked blonde in a snow-white ruffled apron looked vaguely familiar. Theo had taken her to a dance hall a few times. She could quadrille like nobody's business, and her lips were as hot and swift as her feet.

"Good morning, Frederika."

"It's Francesca."

"It's lovely to see you, Francesca."

"Where have you been all this time?"

"Here and there."

"We missed you, Master Nekrasov." She insisted on addressing him formally, but the flirtation manner in which she purred the "r" in his surname sent shivers through Theo's emaciated body. "See that table by the window where you'd always have your coffee?"

"My opera box!"

"I'm tempted to tie a ribbon around it. Every time I see someone else sitting there, it makes me sad."

"Don't be sad, Frederika. I mean Francesca. It's going to be a good year."

"Indeed, it will! My parents are hosting a pastry chef from Prague, who's coming for a demonstration. We need a discerning customer's opinion. Would you like to come and sample his dishes?"

"I'd like that very much."

EPILOGUE

The Wheels of the Locomotive

Fotanka Street, St. Petersburg—February, 1905

God save the Czar! What Czar? Oh wait... We no longer have a czar! Those words were on everyone's lips following the massacre of unarmed demonstrators by the Imperial Guard. The sentiment cut across all social circles. Thousands of jaws, bearded and clean-shaven, dropped in utter shock. The conflict itself was not exactly unexpected. Workers had been rumbling for quite some time. There had been countless other strikes in the months prior, the most famous being the one at Putilov Ironworks in December of 1904. By early 1905 the city was without electricity or press. It was only a matter of time before things got hot and violent. Still, nobody had expected a bloodbath of such proportions. Holy Mother of God... Nicholas II had shown his true face.

Before dawn on Sunday, January 9th, workers and their families had started gathering in the industrial districts of the city. They proceeded to march toward the Winter Palace under the leadership of Father Gregory Gapon, carrying icons and singing patriotic hymns. The protestors, for the most part, were simple apolitical men and women, innocent of any revolutionary ideas. They were faithful to the dogmas of Orthodoxy and the autocracy of the Czar, whom they perceived as a benevolent father figure. Their intention was to present a petition asking for more humane working conditions. They had no clue that Nicholas II was not even in the city. On their way to the palace square, they were met with volleys from the Imperial Guard. Nobody could give an exact number of casualties. Some sources claimed there were fewer than one hundred deaths, while others inflated the figure to four thousand.

Upon learning about the magnitude of the tragedy, Nicholas II stated that he was "pained and saddened". That comment fell like a spark into a bottle of kerosene. Even though the orders to shoot had not come directly from the Czar, the blame came down on him. Journalists in other parts of Europe were pointing accusatory fingers at the two-headed eagle.

***

On a frigid night in early February, a lanky dark-haired youth wearing the Imperial Military Academy uniform entered the headquarters on Fontanka Street requesting a transfer to Vilnius. It did not escape his attention that the portrait of the Czar had been moved from the waiting room into the administrative office. The on-duty recruiter, red-eyed and giddy with fatigue, was trying to keep himself awake by sipping tea the color of tar.

"Last name?" the recruiter inquired, stifling a yawn.

"Dombrowski."

"First?"

"Dominik."

"Patronymic?"

"Fadeevich," the young man replied after a second of deliberation. Did he get that right? That was how Son-of-Thaddeus would transcribe into Russian.

"A Polack, eh?"

"On my father's side. My mother was German."

"Even better." The recruiter slapped the desktop. "A Fritz mother! As they say, the best things in Russia are German. The Empire welcomes you with open arms, Private Dombrowski."

"That's what the Empire needs—another soldier."

"Hey, at this rate we're grateful for every able-bodied man who can shoot. We really got our rear kicked by Japan."

"To be honest, I'd rather be in Japan fighting a real enemy than gunning down unarmed civilians on Russian soil."

Dominik exhaled that phrase with some effort. His phrase was not considered blasphemous in light of recent events. Still, it was an act of epic disloyalty to the person who had raised him, Michael Rudenski.

For his service in the Caucasus, the former gendarme had been admitted into the ranks of the elite Preobrazhensky Guards. On January 9th, his detachment was positioned opposite the Alexander Gardens where much of the bloodshed took place. Since that fateful day the young man had been avoiding his guardian at all costs.

Rudenski and his wife had never formally adopted Dominik. The original agreement was that they would foster him until one of his distant blood relatives would turn up. Attorney Messer had made some initial inquiries in Brandenburg, but his efforts had not amounted to anything, so eventually he lost interest and switched his attentions to more pleasant activities, like his job at the University and his expanding family. In addition to their love child Constantine, Sebastian and Elizabeth produced three daughters. The parents made it their mission to cultivate the new stock of Russo-German alpha-females that would hopefully pull the increasingly sluggish Empire into the twentieth century. Leni was a brilliant mathematician and physicist. Kitty, a heavenly mezzo-soprano, was studying opera. Baby Lily, the most stubborn and argumentative of the three, had the makings of a future lawyer—it was only a matter of time before the universities would start giving out legal diplomas to female students; the snippy little bitch was the apple of her father's eye. Sebastian became so engrossed in the budding careers of his daughters that all other pet projects were pushed aside. Besides, there was no pressing need to pull Dominik out of the foster home. He seemed reasonably stable in the care of the Rudenski spouses. Though they never complained about him being much of a burden, they were prepared to give him back at any moment. Throughout his childhood he had referred to them as Sir and Madame.

When Dominik was old enough to question his relationship to those around him, Aurelia explained to him that his real mother was murdered by a bunch of peasants and chopped into pieces. There was no designated grave, since the body parts were scattered all over the estate. But, if he was curious, he could definitely visit Raven's Bog, or whatever it was called by the new owner. In fact, she would come with him for moral support. It would be a welcome break from her editorial job at *Niva*.

"If you have a problem with shooting at people, you shouldn't be in the military," the recruiter told Dominik. "Maybe you should become a monk instead. Now that Father Gapon has left Russia, we'll need another charismatic leader for the underprivileged."

"Maybe I'll do just that," the young man muttered before collecting his papers. His travel pass read in Cyrillic: Домбровский, Доминик Фадеевич.

***

Fontanka Street, St. Petersburg

Dominik had six hours before the train to Vilnius, so he used that time to visit Aurelia's older brother who insisted on being called Uncle Bastian. The purpose of the visit was to say goodbye and find out how Constantine was recovering from the gunshot wound incurred during the demonstration. Sebastian's firstborn was an ardent proletariat sympathizer and spent much of his time educating the workers about their rights. On that fateful Sunday he had taken his advocacy one step further and actually joined the ranks of the protestors dressed as one of them. Now his right arm was paralyzed from the elbow down.

Sebastian and his wife embraced Dominik and even offered him some of their good cognac and butter biscuits. The patient himself, pumped up with morphine, stayed behind closed doors. Every now and then a muffled groan would escape from his bedroom.

"I've always respected the Emperor as an entity," Sebastian said. "But Nicholas II is a joke! Will you argue that the past decade has been a disaster? Look at the Japanese campaign alone. *Mein Gott!* He has that perfect combination of callousness and lack of common sense. I don't blame anyone who rebels against him. Now, my son is a man of principle. It's hard for him to contain his rage in the face of injustice and mismanagement. I would've done the same if I didn't have a family to support."

Elizabeth was standing behind her husband, kneading his upper back and nodding through his speech.

"Don't take it as a direct attack on your foster father," she said to Dominik. "I'm trying not to be too judgmental of him. Sometimes family members end up on the opposite sides of the barricade. Knowing Michael Rudenski, I don't think he enjoyed firing at those people. After all, he was merely following orders."

Dominik shook his head. "That's the thing. He wasn't following orders—he was giving them. Then Madame Aurelia came out with her camera and took photographs for posterity. She wanted to capture the massacre. I just..." He blinked and held his breath for a few seconds. "I just cannot stay in this city, in that family. I'll do something dreadful."

Elizabeth reached out across the table and brushed a crumb off the corner of his mouth. "We love you like a...." *Not like a son, of course. That would be an exaggeration.* "Like a nephew." She glanced at her husband, asking for permission to share a risqué tidbit from family history. "You know that your dear Uncle Bastian had an affair with your mother, right? He even contemplated running away with her, but ultimately he chose me, because... well, we had a pact. But he never, ever stopped caring about your wellbeing. Isn't that so, my love?"

"Lizzie is right," Sebastian confirmed. "If you're inclined to court one of our daughters, you have our permission. You're not related to us by blood, so it wouldn't be considered incest. We'd love to keep you in the family."

Dominik wondered what kind of sedatives the Messers were on to talk so nonchalantly about such intimate matters.

"It's very generous of you, but I've already made arrangements to transfer to Vilnius."

"You think it's quieter in the northwest? There're labor strikes all over the Empire. Hate to disappoint you, there's no safe haven. This strike epidemic is spreading like cholera."

"I'm not fleeing from hostilities, Uncle Bastian. And I sympathize with the protestors. They're the wheels of the locomotive, and wheels need to be greased. I'm just trying to put some distance between myself and my foster parents."

"If you're going to Vilnius, I want you to look up an old friend of mine." Sebastian pulled out his fountain pen and scribbled an address on a piece of paper. "You should have no problem finding him. Last I heard he owned half of Castle

Street."

Right before Dominik was ready to leave, Constantine crawled out of his bedroom, wearing a roomy Turkish bathrobe over his pajamas. He gave his mother a kiss, took a sip from his father's cognac bottle, and walked the guest to the door.

"I heard what Mama said to you," he slurred, squeezing Dominik's shoulder. "About courting my sisters? She was just being polite. Don't get any ideas. If you as much as come near them, I'll shoot you dead, you imperialist scum. Understood?"

They looked each other in the eye, laughed and shook hands.

***

Castle Street, Vilnius

When Dominik got off the train in Vilnius, he realized that the revolution stirring in St. Petersburg had not reached the Northwestern provinces yet. Thankfully, the city had electricity, and businesses were running as usual. If anything, the workers appeared to be more conscientious and courteous. Within the first two minutes at the railroad station he was approached by half a dozen vendors offering him meat pies and tobacco. Despite being famished, Dominik declined the pies. He had heard that the meat was not always fresh and did not always come from acceptable sources like pigs and cows. According to rumors, the vendors were not above adding a bit of ground cat and dog. He did, however, buy a few hand-rolled cigarettes. Smoking was a safe solution for dulling hunger. He had learned it from Madame Aurelia. His most heart-warming childhood memory was of her blowing acrid clouds into his face. One day he broke down and asked her if he could take a puff, so she indulged him. That started his oral fixation.

There was no shortage of cabriolets outside the station, yet Dominik decided to walk, in paralyzing cold, dragging a suitcase filled with books and winter clothes. When he reached the residential block on Castle Street, he had to check the address twice. The posh three-story edifice with a spacious balcony decorated with fir wreaths looked more like a historical hotel than a private home. Was he even in the right place? Perhaps, Uncle Bastian had made a mistake? As prosperous as the Messers and the Rudenskis were considered, their St. Petersburg apartments were dwarfed by the quarters of Uncle Bastian's friend.

Judging from the multitude of colored lights in the windows and the sounds of a Viennese waltz, there was a party going on. Hopefully, the residents would not be too cross with the intruder. Dominik dropped his suitcase on the porch and rang the bell.

A drowsy young woman answered the door. She had a plain round face and thin light-brown hair in a loose braid. Looking into her dusty-blue eyes with minimal lashes, Dominik felt very vague, very distant memories resurfacing from his subconscious. He had seen those features before.

"I'm here for Master Nekrasov," he said, tipping his hat.

The girl surveyed the visitor, then turned her head and shouted over her shoulder. "Papa, there's some cadet at the door!" She returned her attention to Dominik. "Sorry, he can't hear a thing with this damned music on. Come inside. By the way, my name is Magdalena."

"Lieutenant Dombrowski."

"Another Dombrowski, huh?" A rolling chuckle escaped from her ample bosom unconstrained by a corset. "How uncanny. So am I. At least by blood. Whatever that means nowadays... I'm a Nekrasov now by adoption. There's no other name I'd rather wear. Papa Theo lets me eat all the sweets I want *and* he urged me to study medicine in Warsaw. I just came back for the winter break. Papa insists that I stay put for another week or so, with everything that's happening."

Dominik had no trouble believing that his hostess was a medical student. She was more than sloppy—she was deliberately unglamorous. Following her down the hall, he noticed that she was walking with a slight limp. He did not pick up any traces of pain or discomfort. It appeared that she had walked like that her whole life.

The enormous flat smelled of freshly baked cranberry buns and was swarming with children, their ages ranging from toddler to adolescent. They were busy smudging chalk over the walls, pulling hair out of the senile terrier and rubbing crushed biscuits into the carpet.

A portly gentleman in his mid-forties rose from his cushioned throne by the fireplace and enveloped Dominik in his cashmere hug.

"Lieutenant Dombrowski! Thank God you didn't get shot by the Bolsheviks on your way here."

"Uncle Bastian wasn't joking when he said you lived in a palace."

"I like to think of it as a giant circus tent. As you can tell, we don't do much whip-cracking here."

Dominik could not take his eyes off the plate with smoked sausage. Having not eaten in twenty-four hours, he gulped back saliva. He was too proud and well-mannered to invite himself to the table.

"Do you... do by chance have a glass of water?"

The tremor in his knees did no escape Theo's attention.

"Water? Not in this house. Only beer from our personal brewery."

"You... you have a brewery?"

Theo shrugged in comic self-deprecation. "It's just a little hobby I took up. I didn't expect it to amount to much, but before long orders were rolling in. Everyone wanted a case of my artisan brew. I tell them the magic ingredient is my ignorance. I'm trying to enjoy my quaint little businesses before the socialists take them away. Please, sit and eat. I assume you didn't fall for those meat pies at the train station?"

"I was warned," Dominik replied, sticking a fork into the cold sausage.

"Good. You'd be writhing in agony and foaming at the mouth by now."

Theo looked away to avoid making the ravenous guest self-conscious. Dominik spent the next few minutes assaulting the cold sausage with the ferocity of a soldier storming a fortress.

"Are all these children yours?" he asked when the last slice of smoked meat settled in his stomach.

"Now they all are! The twin boys are mine by blood. The older girls came with my wife Veronica: one by each prior husband. The rest are adopted."

"So this is your second marriage?"

"Third," Theo bragged. "After divorcing Aurelia, I took up randomly with this girl Francesca, or Frania, as everyone called her. Her parents owned a chain of bakeries. We had no children. For some reason Frania couldn't carry past three months. So one day we just said 'to hell with it' and paid a visit to an orphanage. There was a girl with a mangled foot and her younger brother. Alas, our happiness was short-lived. During that trip to the orphanage Frania picked up influenza and died of complications, leaving me very sad and wealthy. A few weeks later I met Veronica, who was twice widowed and equally wealthy though not as sad. So we decided it made sense to pour our wealth into the same pot, throw the sadness out the window, and start afresh. Now look at us! Funny how the cards fall."

"Funny indeed."

A burly blond youth around Dominik's age walked into the dining-room carrying a stack of medical notebooks.

"This is my brother Edgaras," Magda said. "He's preparing for his entrance exam. Excuse his body odor. He hasn't bathed in days."

Edgaras dropped the books on the table, surveyed the face of his long-lost Dombrowski cousin and then cut straight to the chase. "So your mother got hacked into pieces by our parents?"

Magda kicked her brother in the shin. "You're so bloody rude!"

"Oh, and you're the queen of subtlety? Slicing corpses all day long..." He looked at Dominik. "We're a bunch of circus freaks. Papa Theo is right. God, it must feel so strange for you to be in our company."

"A little... I think what's happening in St. Petersburg is ten times stranger."

Dominik's ability to maintain a global perspective moved Edgaras. "Well, cousin, if it's any consolation," he said, reclining against the back of the chair, "our mother paid dearly for her misdeeds. On the way to Siberia, she tried jumping off the train while it was moving. She broke most of her bones, silly thing. She died in a ravine of hypothermia." Edgaras gave his eyes a comically spooky expression. "While she was half-conscious, wolves came and started gnawing at her flesh."

That statement earned him another kick from his sister. "Shut up! How do you even come up with such rubbish?"

"Mama Bronia came to me in my dream."

"Like hell! You don't remember Mama Bronia." Magda grabbed a notebook and whacked her brother on the head, which only intensified his amusement. "You were barely one when it all happened. You don't even remember Mama Frania. You shouldn't be making up stories about the dead."

"Don't underestimate the abilities of the human subconscious." With an animated face like his and a talent for imitating voices, Arturas would have made a fine actor. "If you discipline your mind, you can even see your past lives. You can peel away the layers to reveal the core of your essence."

Magda took a break from beating up her brother and cast an apologetic glance at Dominik. "Are you listening to this? A future anesthesiologist talking! Scary, isn't it? This is what happens when you experiment with ether and chloroform. You start hallucinating."

Edgaras cast off the mask of giddiness and assumed a more formal posture. "Jokes aside, getting killed was the best thing our natural parents ever did for us."

His sister nodded in agreement. "If they were still alive, we'd be rotting away on that boggy farm."

"Not even! We would've gotten evicted by now. I heard the place really went to hell. It sat on the market for ages. Nobody wanted to buy a property where the landlady was hacked up by the servants."

"People are such skittish prudes." Magda rolled her eyes. "No sense of humor. No sense of mystery."

"Last I heard it was bought by some writer with a penchant for horror. Hey sis, you should pay a visit and show him your mangled foot."

"That should provide enough material to write an entire series. *Tales from Raven's Bog.*"

Edgaras threw a crumpled napkin at his sister and laughed. The siblings could joke about their family history, because they did not remember most of it. The past had very little to do with their present, which was filled with privilege and promise, even in light of the recent upheavals. Listening to their ludic bickering, Dominik felt the invisible vice around his skull loosen a bit. The sudden rush of oxygen to his brain made his eyes tear up.

"Hey, cousin, what's your faith?" Edgaras asked out of the blue.

"I... I'm not quite sure. Who gives a damn?"

"I have a perfect place for you: The Church of Who Gives a Damn, also known as Our Lady of the Gate of Dawn. You're still a Christian, right? More or less? Just, please, don't be a sulky nihilist."Edgaras rattled the back of the chair on which Dominik was sitting. "Get up, cousin. They have a visiting priest from Grodno saying a late night mass."

Dominik had just spent several hours walking in freezing darkness, and the idea of going back outside did not thrill him. Still, he did not want to antagonize Edgaras so early in their acquaintance. Something told him they would be spending quite a bit of time in each other's company.

"Fine, take me to the holy place," Dominik said as he buttoned his uniform.

Arms linked, the three Dombrowski grandchildren walked down Castle Street that looked crusted in sugar.

"This is arguably the safest spot on the continent," Edgaras said as they passed through the Gate of Dawn. "The chapel will outlast the Russian Empire."

THE END

ABOUT THE AUTHOR

Marina Julia Neary

Marina Julia Neary is an award-winning, internationally acclaimed expert on military and social disasters, from the Charge of the Light Brigade, to the Irish Famine, to the Easter Rising in Dublin, to the nuclear explosion in Chernobyl some thirty miles away from her home town.

Notable achievements include a trilogy of the Anglo-Irish conflict—*Brendan Malone, Martyrs & Traitors*, and *Never Be at Peace*. She continues to explore the topic of ethnic tension in her autobiographical satire *Saved by the Bang: a Nuclear Comedy*. Her latest novel, *The Gate of Dawn*, is set in 19th century Lithuania, the land of her paternal ancestors. The gruesome events described in the novel took place in her ancestral estate on the border of Lithuania and what is now northwestern Belarus.

IF YOU ENJOYED THIS BOOK
Please write a review.
This is important to the author and helps to get the word out to others
Visit

PENMORE PRESS

www.penmorepress.com

All Penmore Press books are available directly through our website, amazon.com, Barnes and Noble and Nook, Sony Reader, Apple iTunes, Kobo books and via leading bookshops across the United States, Canada, the UK, Australia and Europe.

SAVED BY THE BANG

BY

MARINA J. NEARY

Welcome to 1980s Belarus, where Polish denim is the currency, "kike" is a pedestrian endearment, and a second-trimester abortion can be procured for a box of chocolates. Antonia Olenski, a catty half-Jewish professor at the Gomel Music Academy, wavers between her flamboyant composer husband, Joseph, and a chivalrous tenor, Nicholas. The Chernobyl disaster breaks up the love triangle, forcing Antonia into evacuation with her annoying eight-year-old daughter, Maryana.

After a summer of cruising through Crimean sanatoriums and provoking wounded Afghan veterans, Antonia starts pining for the intrigues and scandals of the Academy. When the queen of cats finally returns home, she finds that new artistic, ethnic, and sexual rivalries have emerged in the afterglow of nuclear fallout. How far will Antonia go to reclaim her throne?

PENMORE PRESS
www.penmorepress.com

A Gathering of Vultures

Donald Michael Platt

Murder, mutilation, and carrion.... in paradise?

"There shall the vultures also be gathered, every one with her mate." - ISAIAH 34:15

Professional ballroom dancers Terri and Rick Hamilton aspire to be world champions. Unfortunately, Terri's recurring back and health problems place that goal well out of reach. They travel to Terri's birthplace, Florianópolis, on the scenic island of Santa Catarina off the coast of Brazil to vacation and visit their best friends and mentors.

Along the picturesque beaches, dead penguins and eviscerated bodies wash up on the shores of paradise, and Antarctic blasts play counterpoint to the tropical storms that rock the island. The scenic wonder is home not only to urubús, a unique sub-species of the black vulture, but also to a clique of mysterious women who offer Terri perfect health and the promise of fame—at a terrible price.

PENMORE PRESS
www.penmorepress.com

The Chosen Man

by

J. G Harlond

From the bulb of a rare flower bloom ambition and scandal

Rome, 1635: As Flanders braces for another long year of war, a Spanish count presents the Vatican with a means of disrupting the Dutch rebels' booming economy. His plan is brilliant. They just need the right man to implement it.

They choose Ludovico da Portovenere, a charismatic spice and silk merchant. Intrigued by the Vatican's proposal—and hungry for profit—Ludo sets off for Amsterdam to sow greed and venture capitalism for a disastrous harvest, hampered by a timid English priest sent from Rome, accompanied by a quick-witted young admirer he will use as a spy, and bothered by the memory of the beautiful young lady he refused to take with him.

Set in a world of international politics and domestic intrigue, *The Chosen Man* spins an engrossing tale about the Dutch financial scandal known as tulip mania—and how decisions made in high places can have terrible repercussions on innocent lives.

PENMORE PRESS
www.penmorepress.com

Penmore Press

Challenging, Intriguing, Adventurous, Historical and Imaginative

www.penmorepress.com